# Praise for at Mount Forest Island

"A ghost haunts the woods... Supernatural meddling with satisfying, well-paced action... A solid series addition."  —*Kirkus Reviews*

"Camalliere's work spans several genres: historical fiction, paranormal suspense, and a healthy dose of women's lit.... The prologue grabs the reader's attention [and] the book delivers an action-packed finale."
—Windy City Reviews

"Takes a mystery and runs with it through generations of family entanglements, the lasting impact of life choices, and the consequences of love.... Highly recommended for both mystery and historical fiction readers searching for something different."  —Midwest Book Review

"Twists and turns as well as a paranormal aspect... The characters are interesting and unique. The locations...are based in fact which makes the story even more interesting."  —Books, Cooks, Looks

"A most unique approach to a mystery... Will totally appeal to every fan of Cora as the mystery solver.... If you are a fan of mysteries involving the Mob in Illinois dating back to Capone's time, this book could be for you."  —N. N. Light's Book Heaven

"Stands out from its genre!... Thrilling, captivating, and addictive from beginning to end... Fast-paced, action-adventure that should not be missed!"  —Red Headed Book Lover

"This is the kind of book you can enjoy when an author takes their time in putting together historically accurate detail, weaving it carefully into the story so you feel like you are 'there' in the plot.... Into the Chicago Underworld of Mobs and old grudges where ghosts linger in dark places... I learned a lot about this city through [Camalliere's] skill."
—L.B. Johnson, author, *Small Town Roads*

# What Readers are Saying

"With a mystery story that spans generations, pristine character development, and in-depth detective work this book never slows down."

"Love her books! Always look forward to the next one. So much history about the area crafted into the story."

"Her pedigree as a top-notch historian of the fascinating world of southwest Chicago shines through every page, ancient ravines and waterways, haunted roads… Perfectly captures the magic of these storied places."

"I especially enjoyed learning about the locations and the history and mysteries buried there."

"Five-star rating based on wonderfully well-drawn characters, their relationships and development…There is depth and authenticity to these people that had me rooting for them."

"Excels at weaving personal lives with bigger-picture historical and political entanglements…. A fine story evolves that combines historical mystery elements with psychological insights."

"Wonderfully conceived and beautifully written… A historical mystery that spans generations… A cadre of exceptionally well-drawn characters… Splendid and satisfying mystery with the many parts tied up nicely and the characters having been challenged to grow. A dab of paranormal seamlessly adds an additional dreamy dimension."

"I particularly like the group effort gathering and digging out facts and then piecing them together for a most interesting solution."

"Group investigation, family drama, organized crime, and the supernatural, her story is varied but balanced and guaranteed to garner a diverse readership."

# The Mystery at Mount Forest Island

# The Mystery at Mount Forest Island

*Pat Camalliere*

~~~

Books by Pat Camalliere

*The Mystery at Mount Forest Island*
*The Mystery at Black Partridge Woods*
*The Mystery at Sag Bridge*

~~~

*The Mystery at Mount Forest Island* © Copyright 2020, Pat Camalliere

All rights reserved. No part of this book may be used or reproduced in any manner whatsoever without written permission from the publisher, except in the case of brief quotations in critical articles and reviews.

This book is a work of fiction. Names, characters, places, and incidents either are products of the author's imagination or are used fictitiously. Any resemblance to actual events or locales or persons, living or dead, is entirely coincidental.

First Edition   ISBN 13: 978-1-937484-72-9

AMIKA PRESS   466 Central AVE #23 Northfield IL 60093   847 920 8084
info@amikapress.com   Available for purchase on amikapress.com

Edited by Jay Amberg and Ann Wambach. Cover photography by Sondem and Chris Schauflinger, Shutterstock, and Ilker, FreeImages. Designed and typeset by Sarah Koz. Body in Janson Text, designed by Miklós Tótfalusi Kis in the 1690s, revived for Mergenthaler Linotype by Chauncey H. Griffith in 1937, digitized by Adrian Frutiger in 1985. Titles in Dwiggins Uncial, designed by William Addison Dwiggins in 1935, digitized by Richard Kegler in 2001. Thanks to Nathan Matteson.

~~~

This novel explores the value of friendship and is dedicated to the friends who inspired me to write it.

To Dave and Sandy, who lived there; they shared their story.

To Forever Friends Dorothy, Betty and Joann; they shared their lives with me.

To my best friend and husband, Chris; we share it all.

# Prologue
## Autumn 1928

Al never lost sight of the fact that I was the older brother, and I, in turn, never forgot that he was the one in charge. We were the Capone brothers, and family loyalty came above all else. Al was the force. Without him none of us would be doing what we were doing and well off because of it. Practical matters were left to me—I took care of the details.

As I drove out to meet Al at his favorite hangout, the Palos Golf Club in the forest preserves off 107th Street, I wondered what problems he would put on my plate today. Problems were the nature of our business, and mood changes were Al's nature.

Distracted, I cut the corner too sharp and barely missed smashing into the knee-high stone walls that lined the entry road to the golf course. The drive climbed gradually through woods that covered the bluff of the Sag Valley, passing a gravel road that intersected it on the right. Nearly blinded by afternoon sunlight flickering through branches, I knew I was driving too fast. Keyed up by irritation and jitters, neither my body nor my car would stop racing.

I figured Al wanted to talk about Jimmy Emery. I liked the guy. He had always been dependable, but lately he was starting to pay too much attention to his damn horses and the business could suffer. Al would want me to get him back on track. No pun intended.

I was in no mood to deal with another problem. The whole damn morning and part of the afternoon was a waste. Just after the boys started work at daybreak, the main conveyor went down and we had to hold up the line for three hours. To put the downtime to use, I told the crew to load three trucks and take the product to the barn.

The barn, not far from our bottling establishment, had been a lucky find. The owner said it was built around the time of the Black Hawk War to let early settlers gather if Indians attacked, and later it became a stop on the Underground Railroad. With thick stone walls and windows only thin rifle slits, the dim interior kept the place the right temperature for storage. The farmer had his own needs and so required a little persuasion. I pointed out to him that there is always something a man values more than the use of his barn. He saw the truth in what I said, and we made a friendly deal. He stayed out of our way, and he kept his mouth shut.

But this morning we found that the night pickup failed to empty the barn, and no space was left. There was no possibility of leaving product where it could be seen, of course, so the only alternative was to bring it back to the factory. Nothing got done.

The trees thinned as I approached the top of the hill and arrived at the clubhouse. As I exited the car, a breeze rustled the leaves in the ravines nearby. Some fall color already showed, patches of bright gold and red, but only young trees lined the fairways.

I tried to relax, but my body refused, as if there was some reason to rush. I leaned against the car and let the breeze cool my face. It occurred to me the wind might have affected Al's score. I shook my head. He always thought he was a better golfer than his score indicated. It wouldn't be good if the both of us started off in a bad mood.

The peace was disturbed by the crack of wood striking ball, followed by a loud yell. I couldn't tell if the yell was celebration or disgust. Golf was Al's passion, not mine. I remembered what golfers said about this hilly course: it was a great place for those with one leg shorter than the other.

The breeze switched direction, bringing a penetrating chill. It seemed to predict changes to come, not only weather, but also changes to challenge our way of life from other directions, in and outside the business. I released a long breath and headed toward the clubhouse. This might be one of the last nice days of the year. I would try to enjoy it.

"Hi, Ralph!" the cashier greeted me as I entered. Her face lit up and she waved me over to the counter. "Al and his friends are on the patio upstairs—is little Ralphie with you?"

I smiled back, noting once again her comfortable, homey appearance. Not Al's type, too old and too plump, but a real sweet lady. "No, Norma, Ralphie is home with *Grandmacita* Theresa in the city." Norma looked disappointed. "Why?" I asked.

"Joe made those cookies your son likes. So when Al got here I grabbed some to hold for Ralphie, in case you came."

"Can you wrap them up? I'll tell him you sent them. He'll be happy."

"Sure, Ralph. Just stop back on the way out. Be sure to bring your little guy around soon, will ya?"

Most people had a rough go of things these days, and yet there were people like Norma who went out of their way with little kindnesses. Smiling, I climbed the stairs to the rooftop patios.

At the top of the stairs I was greeted by raucous laughter and Al's loud voice, which always got high-pitched when he was onstage. "So who the fuck cares about the score? It's a beautiful day and a beautiful place to be, right boys?"

I turned toward the commotion, and there was Al, holding court at a round table under one of the covered patios. The three men with him each wore his own idea of fashionable golf wear. One wore spats over his shoes, an argyle sweater-vest, and plaid knickers—an outfit that took balls. Half-full tumblers and empty plates covered the table. The staff here knew to turn a blind eye to whatever was in the glasses, which of course came out of the trunk of a car owned by of one of Al's buddies.

Timmy, Al's caddy, wasn't there. He had either left or was waiting for a ride. The kid must have the patience of a saint, because Al was a terrible golfer who often threw tantrums or expected Timmy to help him cheat. That was the sort of power game Al played. But Al and the kid hit it off. Maybe Al didn't want to break in a new kid, who wouldn't know what was expected.

Catching sight of me, Al waved a hand. "Ralph! Over here!" He turned to his guests. "Here's my big brother now. I want you guys to look at the hair on that head—I'm sure he robbed it from me, got my share somehow. Yeah, sure, we both got the receding on the foreheads, but look at how thick and curly the rest of his head is. *Chepreca!* A shame! If I could only figure out how to get it offa his *gabbadost'* and onto my own hard head, watch out, bada bing!" The men laughed harder than Al's comment warranted.

"I got you beat in the height department, too, if you notice," I said, with a grin. "But no matter how I try, I'll never match your belly." Only family could get away with saying things like that. Al let out a whoop. He loved his family—everyone knew that.

"Ralph, let's step away from here. These guys don't wanna hear more family stuff like that," he said, chuckling. He stood up and grabbed my arm. We walked toward the edge of the roof above the first tee and gazed out over three ravines that met here. A short distance to the south, Saganashkee Slough sparkled in the sun. I breathed the fresh, clean air.

"Don't you love this place, Ralph?" Al asked. *"Ma che bell'!* It's beautiful, remote, no one bothers us. We talk business, they got good food, we have fun, play some golf. You got it good out here, away from the action—places to golf, to swim, those toboggan slides come winter. How come you got it made and I got stuck with the *jamokes?"*

"Somebody's got to bottle the merchandise and handle distribution. You know we had to move some of the operation away from the action. You're doing what you're good at and I'm doing what I'm good at. There's trade-offs."

"Yeah, I'm near Ma, that's a good thing." He fell quiet, crossed his arms, rested them on his belly, and stared toward Saganashkee Slough glistening to the south.

"So what's up, Al?"

"Let's go for a walk. Don't want these *stunads* to get any ideas. Too many ears to hear what we're talking about."

"Sure."

As we moved past the table, Al said to his buddies, "This won't take long. Family business, *capisci?"*

Al and I left the clubhouse and wandered through the grounds.

"Down the block from the house, Ralph, that Irish family? The old man's bad off, gonna kick soon. Wife and six kids—the Irish, no?" He winked. "Anyway, they got nothin', gonna get thrown out on the street. Fix it for 'em, okay?"

"They got nothing to do with us, Al," I pointed out.

"They're needy, Ralph. That's all we gotta know. Take care of it."

"Okay, Al, okay."

Out of earshot, Al launched into a familiar rant. "Maybe it's time to get out," he said. "I'm sick a the crap. I get the blame for every crime that happens in this country. I'm only givin' people what they want. We don't point a gun and force someone into a gambling house or to take a drink. Yesterday I got a letter from some woman way the hell in England. She wanted me to go there and kill someone was giving her grief. Said she'd make it worth my while."

We circled the clubhouse, moved away from the open roof with its patios and occupied tables. "Not to mention the parasites in our own crew, always looking for some favor, always in some trouble, always the hand out," I said.

Al waved his arms as he talked, engaging his whole body. "I got enough money—there's plenty a money for all a them, but still they try to cut into my territory. They think I'm gonna just let them get away with it? It's my business. I don't need to be doin' business with crazy people."

We stopped at the top of a ravine and looked out over the Sag Valley. I dug the toe of my Italian-leather wingtip deep into the dry leaves and let out a long breath. "Who's the troublemakers, Al?"

"Those *scocciament'*, those pain-in-the-ass Heights boys," Al began. "I'm the guy sets the rules and protects their territory in exchange for a percentage of the action. Emery runs the Heights, cooking product in the basements and running all them restaurants and fancy houses. Now these guys wanna do things their own way. They don't know enough about the business, what works, what we gotta do to keep it that way. We gotta do what we gotta do. That *patz'*, that crazy Emery, all he thinks about these days is the ponies. Says prohibition won't be around forever, we gotta position ourselves."

"Does he have a point?" I asked.

He brushed aside my question with a wave. "Even if he's right, the ponies is only part a the gamblin' picture, not the whole fuckin' thing. We got the clubs, the slots, the books, the loans, even legit businesses. You know all this. Instead of takin' control he's keepin' his own string a horses, breedin' his own stock, sees himself with some fuckin' Kentucky Derby winner or somethin'. Wants to buy some horse ranch, five to six miles southeast of where we at now. *Murudda!* The man's got no brain. Point is, he's already ignorin' what's got to be done today. Next he'll be runnin' down to the Florida tracks, and his outfit won't be keeping the business goin' when he's away. The whole Heights operation's goin' in the toilet if he doesn't get his head on straight. I can't believe him—I'm godfather to his girl for Chrissake! That makes him family and how do I ignore that? And now he wants to do his own thing? *Maron'!* What the fuck am I supposed to do?"

"He had a good idea about the roofs, Al," I said. When the law realized making alcohol produced enough heat to melt snow off roofs, they flew small planes over suspect areas after snowstorms to find roofs with no snow for houses to bust. Emery sent his men out to paint the roofs of his places white.

"Yeah, so one good thing he does. But how about the big picture? So here's the thing, Ralph. How's it gonna go we get in a war over this? Our interests, specifically your interests, are right in the middle a his fuckin' territory. You know he's controllin' everything south of 95th Street, everything from Indiana to Joliet. You're right in the middle a that. All fine and good he listens to me and that's how it's set up, but these guys get too big for themselves, they don't listen all the time. I don't want you caught by surprise. *'Uarda la ciunca!* You're gonna get hurt. You gotta keep your ear to the ground, ya hear me?"

I looked around. A cloud moved in front of the sun casting the lovely ravine into shadow and turning the colors to shades of gray. The day didn't seem so nice anymore. As I feared, the family business had a way of creating its own mood.

Valerie traveled this road frequently and knew she was moving into an area of open fields with nothing to shelter the car from the wind and rain. Instead of the increased battering she expected, the rain abruptly slackened and revealed unbelievably on the road ahead…

"No! It can't be!" She screamed and rammed her foot frantically on the brake pedal.

It was over in an instant—the car went into a spin, there was a loud thud, and incredibly the driver's side window just exploded, glass flying, the car struck nose down, dizziness….

Then excruciating pain, loss of consciousness, and she saw no more.

—Pat Camalliere, *The Mystery at Sag Bridge*

# Part I

# Chapter 1
## March 2015

People who knew Valerie Pawlik might have said she was a loner, but she had never felt as lonely as she did now.

Seated in an armchair, leather or perhaps a high-quality synthetic she supposed, she ran her fingers over the soft surface. If she remembered correctly, it was bright turquoise or maybe soft orange or gray, the Lemont Public Library's color scheme. Sunlight from a nearby window warmed her. Surrounding sounds seemed loud to her now: a page being flipped, a scratching pencil, a clearing throat. Someone walked nearby, probably looking over the selections on the fiction shelves behind her. An overweight adult woman, she speculated, from the heavy breathing and spaced footsteps. The woman had probably stared at Corky when she passed by, not expecting to see a dog here. Valerie placed a hand on the sleek fur and then rested her arm in her lap.

Alone and lonely were not the same thing: she knew that now!

She couldn't go home—it was Sally's home really—before she thought through what Father McGrath had proposed. She had to make a decision. Better to be alone in a public place than in that stifling atmosphere. So she had the Dial-a-Ride driver take her to the library, despite the fact he would not be available later. She patted the pocket that contained her cell phone. After she made her decision, she'd call a cab.

She had the basics down now: how to dress, feed herself, and move confidently with her guide dog or a cane. Father McGrath was helping her prepare for the rest of her life. She couldn't leach off Sally and Grace forever, didn't want to, even if she had felt welcome there. She was too independent—well, her personality was independent, even if her situation wasn't. But above all she had to consider Molly.

Father McGrath suggested she get help from Cora of all people! Cora, who had ordered Valerie out of her home and told her not to return. The argument that followed provoked Valerie to seek revenge, and then there was the accident. How could she go to Cora now with her hand out, especially about such a private matter?

Father's words played over and over: "None of this is going to be easy. Think of it as practice for a *life* that won't be easy. Cora has the skills and experience you need to solve the mysteries that threaten your future. She's also a caring and forgiving sort. Settle the argument; rekindle your friendship."

"But we were never friends," Valerie had said. "We were oil and water from the start."

He had replied, "That doesn't change the advice. You were the antagonist in the relationship, remember? That's another thing you need to deal with. Cora's the right person, and I advise you to have at it."

Father McGrath was her only friend at the moment. She had always thought friends unnecessary, but he had pointed out more than once that her situation was different now. With the absence of dependable family, she needed friends. He wouldn't always be there.

Thinking about it now, her hands shook and she gripped her knees in panic. Corky stood and put her head in Valerie's lap, nudging, sensing her mistress's distress.

Valerie stroked the silky head and gradually calmed.

Where was the proud, confident person she used to be? She must reawaken that person. She had to—her future depended on it. She'd try Cora and if that didn't work, well, then she had to try something else.

She reached for her phone. She'd give Father permission to call Cora and explain. Would Cora even agree to talk to her? She'd soon find out.

She could do this! What else *could* she do?

~~~

Billy Nokoy didn't try to fool himself. He was what he was, and in the opinion of most people he was a loser, like his father.

Billy grew up spending long hours alone at home, waiting up to help his single-parent father to bed after lengthy days of janitorial work followed by nights at the local watering hole. Often his father, who dearly loved his son, came home sad and ashamed, sobbing because he could not be a better parent and his son deserved so much more than he was able to give. Billy often feared his life would be the same as his father's.

No, Billy had to confront his problems and build a better life.

Today he sat at one of the library's public computers, sliding the mouse aimlessly on the mouse pad, following the cursor with his eyes on the screen, oblivious to everything around him. He had come to the library to research paranormal phenomena, but he couldn't settle his thoughts.

What the hell had he done? What could he do about it now?

His friend Nick had said, "I had a crazy notion you ended the matter by releasing a bolt of lightning at him."

"What do you mean?" Billy had asked.

Nick explained that everyone present told a different story. Nick's version was that Billy sent a visible bolt of energy that pinned the man to a tree.

"Of course that couldn't have happened," Nick said, laughing. "There was lightning and a storm."

Billy had gone still, realizing Nick's story was similar to what he remembered himself. Having someone confirm his impression made it more believable. He hadn't been able to shake the wild idea.

His powers of reasoning would never measure up to those of his childhood friends Nick and Dawn, brilliant scientists at nearby Argonne Laboratories. During their school days, his friends got top grades effortlessly while he studied endlessly. He wasn't stupid; his mind just worked slower. Nick and Dawn tried to coach him, but he wanted to succeed on his own. His track record had been abysmal.

While his friends had been accepted into the biological science program at Washington University, Billy had been rejected by the seven schools he applied to. He tried to remain cheerful as Nick and Dawn left the reservation to start their important lives, while he stayed behind in Dowagiac, Michigan, to attend junior college and work as a dealer at the casino. He planned to treat his friends to an evening out, but it didn't turn out the way he expected. After two months of training, he found himself assigned to the five-dollar tables, where the tips were paltry and the hours few.

One evening he got assigned to one of the twenty-dollar-minimum blackjack tables. He hoped to finally prove himself. At last. A chance to turn things around.

He dealt a card to a large man with a shaved head, bulging forearms, and a surly expression. The card put the player over twenty-one. "Hey, asshole," the man said, "you dealing off the bottom of the deck?"

Billy blinked. Unsure how to handle angry losers, he was hurt that someone would accuse him of cheating. He didn't know what to say.

"No," he said, glancing around for help that didn't materialize.

The player took advantage of Billy's obvious discomfort.

"They teach you that in dealer school?" he went on. "Hit me—no, you'd just want the card back, you Indian giver." And later, "My momma always told me never to trust an Indian." Similar insults continued until Billy's dinner break.

When Billy returned to the table, the bully was gone, probably asked to leave by the more experienced dealer who covered while Billy was off the floor. In the player's place was a white-faced man who was sweating profusely. After losing hand after hand, all his chips gone, the man looked around desperately as if there were somewhere else to go, someone who would bail him out. He turned to Billy, trembling. "Can you loan me fifty dollars?" the man said. "Please, I'm good for it."

Billy had seen men like this before, men who lost everything—frightened, desperate men. Men who couldn't stop when they were losing, and if their luck turned they couldn't stop because they were winning. Compassion overcame him…but for the last time. When his shift was over he handed in his license and left. His dream of impressing his friends evaporated.

That had been years ago. He sighed now and clicked his mouse. As he waited for Google to launch, he caught motion with his peripheral vision and glanced away from the screen. An attractive woman wearing dark glasses was leaving the library, accompanied by a golden retriever. He realized the woman was blind and was impressed by how confidently she moved through the library.

She walked past a tall, muscular-looking man who stood viewing the "new books" racks. The man turned to watch her leave; then he glanced around before going quickly out the door without any checkouts. He looked older than Billy's first impression of him.

Billy returned to his thoughts. If only he could get the right break. But he was the guy who never got the breaks, never got the job, never got the girl. His latest venture, the one that had brought him to Lemont, had proved it once again, ending in catastrophe like everything else he touched.

If only he could succeed at something…anything.

An elderly woman at the computer next to Billy waved to the reference librarian. "What's wrong with this thing? Is it something I'm doing? The screen keeps going black."

The librarian leaned over her and clicked for a while, then shook her head. "I guess you'll have to move to another computer. I'll get our tech guy to look at it," she said.

"The same thing happened at the other one," the woman said, pointing to the end of the table.

"Yes, that is odd," the librarian said, rubbing her mouth with a forefinger.

It seemed he wasn't the only loser in here today. Some people just weren't meant for computers.

Billy returned to his thoughts. His only real friends in Lemont were Nick and Dawn, although Cora and Cisco had been kind. Before he brought the matter up with Nick again, he wanted to be sure it wasn't overactive imagination. His friends knew he was prone to wild ideas and bizarre explanations.

But he had to know: What if what Nick said was true, if he had suddenly developed an unexplainable power? Was it an answer or an obstacle? Could he control it or shut it off? Could it give him a chance at a life that didn't leave him feeling inferior? Or was it another stroke of bad luck that would set him back further?

Who might help him? His coworkers at OfficeMax or casual friends at bars? No. He imagined what they would think if he broached the subject —that he was a crazy Indian, probably.

Cora, though. She had been there when it happened. She could tell him what she saw that day and give him an opinion. She had hinted once about having a supernatural experience, so she might take him seriously.

He logged out, pushed himself up from his chair, and reached for his hoodie. Yes, he would get Cora's advice.

~~~

Cora Tozzi felt the weight of guilt. If it weren't for her, Valerie wouldn't be blind.

She peered out the window near her front door, standing to the side so she wouldn't be seen. She gave a nervous laugh. How silly. Valerie wouldn't see her waiting.

She wandered back into her kitchen; straightened the tablecloth that was already straight; checked for the fourth time that the coffeepot was ready to switch on; wiped the countertops she had wiped minutes before; and fingered cups, plates, and silverware stacked ready for use. Valerie wouldn't see the newspapers, magazines, and mail on the sideboard, but Cora hoped the kitchen smelled clean. She sniffed. Waiting coffee grounds overpowered any other scents.

She wished she could just pick up a book, curl up in a comfortable chair, and drift asleep instead of meeting Valerie. Lately things she would have happily looked forward to seemed burdensome.

Cisco kept urging her to unload some things on her plate, but that would mean giving something up, and what was she willing to part with? Back in her college days she had worked two part-time jobs and had taken twenty-four credit hours her senior year…so she wouldn't miss anything. She got it done, didn't she? She was proud of her accomplishment, but she'd never want to live that year over.

"You're not twenty years old anymore," Cisco said. True, but in her mind…she wasn't ready to make any changes.

Today—was she accepting responsibility for someone else again? When Father McGrath called her yesterday he talked her into it, and she *did* feel she owed Valerie. This time she wouldn't get involved, just make peace and give Valerie some encouragement. She promised.

Memories replayed in her mind—the women around her table, Frannie in tears, Cora telling Valerie, "You're not welcome here anymore," Valerie's furious face.

Then the news from a neighbor: Valerie's car ran into a ditch.

She hadn't seen Valerie since the accident.

She hung a towel on the handle of the oven and returned to her vigil at the front door. A sudden breeze swayed the branches of the pear tree in the center of her front lawn and blew stalks from last season from the nearby cornfield across her driveway. Cisco would be none too happy about the mess—he would worry about the grass getting off to a good start.

Cora saw the field through the eyes of a historian, one of the last vestiges of farmland from which her quiet subdivision had been carved. Massive farm equipment would soon arrive, turning the clock back 175 years when Lemont was mainly fields of crops, like the fifteen-acre patch a hundred yards from her home. The sun moved behind a cloud as if catching Cora's mood. A shiver ran down her back, and for no apparent reason she had a sense of foreboding.

She transferred her weight from one leg to the other. She wanted to be positive, but one of the reasons for this meeting was to confront and resolve old differences. She glanced over her shoulder, despite the fact she was alone in the house, and rehearsed a few greetings in her mind.

"Hi Valerie! How are you?" No, too cheery. And if Valerie was well, she wouldn't need Cora—wouldn't be coming at all.

"Valerie! It's so good to see you again." An obvious lie. And would Valerie think she was insensitive if she used the word "see"?

"What can I do for you today?" Not a greeting at all, too uncaring and too businesslike.

Cora wanted to help Valerie, of course, but she didn't understand why Father McGrath insisted she was the right person. What good could she possibly do? "Let her tell you," he'd said.

Valerie probably hated Cora and she would have every right. Did she believe their argument had anything to do with the accident…what?… two years ago? The rumor was that Valerie said a wolf caused the car to veer off the road, but no one believed her story. Did she still think that? Cora could shed light on what happened, but Father McGrath had cautioned her not to discuss it too soon—it could create more hard feelings and set Valerie's recovery back.

What would Valerie do if she figured out Cora's part in her blindness?

Despite their anger with each other at the time, she'd been stunned when she heard Valerie had lost her sight. Their argument seemed so petty now. Would Valerie sense her true feelings? Valerie had been rude and difficult, but she was never a fool.

Cora didn't know how to act around blind people! She avoided people with disabilities. She wasn't proud of that, didn't *want* to be like that. She remembered how important dignity would be to Valerie.

She was going to botch things up; she just knew it. She couldn't think straight when she had the fidgets. She was overthinking, creating imaginary outcomes.

Why hadn't she insisted that Father McGrath be present today or even Cisco—people who knew the whole story? Should she have refused to meet Valerie at all? Maybe she should call Father now to see if he could join them. She took a step back from the window and reached into her pocket for her cell phone.

It was too late. A tan minivan came up the street, pulled into the circular drive, then backed out, turned, and parked so the passenger door was near her front stoop. The driver, an energetic, elderly man wearing a navy-blue jacket with a Chicago Bears logo and matching baseball cap, got out, circled the van, and opened the passenger door. A golden retriever jumped out and waited.

A guide dog! She hadn't thought about that. The dog would have to come in the house. Cora used to own dogs, but a *strange* dog had never been in her house. Would it sniff around, lift its leg, or leave hair all over? Service dogs were supposed to be well mannered, but there was a service dog that came to the library and it gagged and left puddles of vomit on the rug. She squeezed her eyes shut, ashamed of her uncharitable thoughts.

She backed away from the window, pulled back her shoulders, took in a deep breath, and opened the door. Stepping onto the front stoop, she called, trying to inject a welcoming tone to her voice, "Hello, Valerie. Is there anything I can do to help?"

A hand grasped the edge of the van roof and Valerie slowly emerged, got her balance, and straightened. She looked much the same as the last time Cora saw her, except for the dark glasses she wore. Valerie's cheeks and the sides of her mouth quivered, like when one tries to smile but fails.

*I wonder if she's as nervous as I am.*

"Hi, Cora. If I could hold your arm…?"

Valerie had always been fashion conscious and was dressed impeccably today, her trim body in well-fitting jeans, a solid top, and multicolored fitted jacket. The color combination was imaginative and perfect. Did a friend or relative select her outfit each morning? Her dark hair was short now, in a pixie cut that suited her, every hair in place, and her lips were carefully colored. Cora pulled her hand through her own hair, white, thin, and stubborn, and she felt a moment of envy. Valerie probably never had a bad hair day and had never struggled with an extra thirty pounds.

Valerie grabbed the strap attached to the dog's harness. Cora stepped from the stoop onto the driveway and moved next to her, nodding to the driver, who stood aside watchfully. Valerie, moving confidently, reached out and placed her free hand just above Cora's elbow. Cora moved toward the stoop and Valerie followed.

"There's a step up here, and then a few steps to the doorway," Cora said.

"I remember that," Valerie said, her voice soft and polite.

Damn! She'd probably insulted her already.

# Chapter 2

Valerie had been a self-centered, demanding, rude person, in Cora's opinion. Why should she be any different now?

Cora set a mug of black tea on the place mat in front of Valerie. She hoped Valerie caught her hint that the oak table in her eat-in kitchen needed protection from spills. Cora had made coffee, but Valerie preferred tea. She offered coffee cake, still warm. Valerie said she never ate sweets, which hadn't been true at their book club discussions. Cora started to pet the dog. "She's a working dog. She can't do her job if you distract her," Valerie said. At least the dog was well mannered.

It was like trying to get one of her grandsons interested in gardening or history, while the only things they cared about were computer games and food. Valerie's responses to Cora's awkward "safe" questions had been polite but verging on curt.

She shook her head. Cisco had warned her against getting involved in people's problems. The visit had just begun and she already wished it was over. But they were both captives—Valerie couldn't leave until the Dial-a-Ride driver returned. They'd have to make the best of the situation.

The old Valerie would have looked smugly superior and made snide or derogatory comments. Today Valerie was reserved but fidgety. She sat stiffly with her chin in the air and jumped when the refrigerator kicked on. She wrapped her arms across her chest and rubbed them as if she were chilly, but when Cora asked if she wanted a sweater Valerie said she wasn't cold. The visit must be very important to her—so important she went to great lengths to seek the help of a person she probably despised.

"Father McGrath said you're living with your brother here in Lemont," Cora tried again, hoping Valerie would embellish on that fact.

"Yes."

"It must be a relief to have someone who cares about you to fall back on." *Oops! Was this a mistake?*

"You could say that." Valerie's right hand clenched into a fist.

Cora went to the sink, picked up a dishcloth, and dabbed at a nonexistent spot on the table, trying to think of what to say next. The dog, lying on the floor next to Valerie, jerked her head up and Cora jumped, having forgotten…Corky, was it?

Maybe she should have served wine….

"How's Molly?" she said at last, sitting down again. "How old is she now?"

"She's eleven. She's with her father." Valerie put a fist over her mouth and sat facing the window, as if looking into the sun through her dark lenses. Perhaps she felt the warmth. After a moment, she added, "Sally and Grace don't feel they can deal with both me and a preteen."

So—there *was* something behind the short answer about her brother. Before the accident, Molly was the only thing Valerie enthused about, but her ex-husband had been seeking custody of their daughter and planning to bring her to California, Cora remembered. He must have done that. Odd, Valerie didn't seem to want to talk about Molly. Sally and Grace?

"Oh," Cora said. "Sorry…what's your brother's name?"

"Salvatore, Sal Junior. Sally, we call him."

She watched Valerie jiggle a leg, readjust her seat, and tap her fingers on the table. Her responses, though, were self-assured. She realized Valerie was feigning confidence so Cora would know how competently she was dealing with her blindness. Ironic—why would Valerie want to impress her? But wasn't *she* trying to impress Valerie, to make her believe hard feelings had been forgotten?

Perhaps they both felt guilty, each believing they did something awful to the other.

Cora glanced at the time. The driver wasn't due for an hour.

Cora fidgeted too, looking at her hands on the tabletop and playing with her fingernails. She could stare right into Valerie's face instead, and Valerie would never know. Feeling rude, she watched Valerie anyway. Valerie faced the tabletop and started playing with her fingernails. Cora couldn't stifle a snicker.

"Did I do something funny?" Valerie asked, lifting her head.

"You're playing with your fingernails."

"That's funny? Why?"

"Because I was doing the same thing when I looked up and found you doing it."

After a moment Valerie chuckled.

Encouraged, Cora added, "And because we're both trying to impress each other and doing a piss-poor job of it."

The chuckle turned to a laugh and before they knew it both women were laughing heartily.

Cora wiped moisture from her eyes and Valerie fumbled in her purse for a tissue to blot tears from behind her glasses.

"Okay, this is getting weird, we're mirroring each other again," Cora said, and they dissolved once more.

In the process of wiping her eyes, Valerie knocked her glasses off. They bounced off the table and landed on the floor. The dog promptly sat on them and growled, which prevented Cora from picking them up.

"How do I get this beast to let loose of your glasses?" Cora asked in mock frustration. The animal turned its attention from one woman to the other, seeming confused by the guffaws her mistress was emitting. Valerie probably didn't laugh very often.

Cora saw that Valerie's eye sockets were filled with prostheses, the irises the same color as the startling blue-green that had once made heads turn. The absence of life in the globes was shocking. Valerie sensed the reaction with embarrassment, pushing Corky away and feeling around until she found her glasses. "Damn eyes, water more than they ever did when they were useful," she muttered as the laughter died and she slipped her glasses back on.

Valerie reached over and removed Corky's harness. "So she can relax," she said. Corky looked around as if she wanted to investigate, then gave a loud sigh, circled, and curled up under the table.

"Why were you trying to impress me?" Valerie asked. "I'm the one who should be making up to you after I tried to make you lose your election. I was cocky and insufferable."

"I didn't know if you were still mad at me for kicking you out of the book club. And I didn't want you to realize how uncomfortable I felt around you. I've never been comfortable around people with disabilities." She didn't mention the part she had played in Valerie's accident.

"I didn't want you to know my doubts. But what is it about blindness that makes you uncomfortable?" she said. Her smile faded, but Valerie had never smiled much. She slouched in her chair, her hands resting comfortably on the table, appearing to relax at last.

"I don't know." Cora thought for a while. "I guess I don't want to offend you by doing or saying the wrong thing. I'm so clueless I don't even know what the wrong thing is and ashamed I never took the time to find out."

"Lots of people do that. It doesn't take me long to pick up that vibe."

"Maybe, but *I* don't want to do that. And I'm also afraid that people with disabilities will be pushy. You weren't easy to be around before you were blind. I didn't want us to get confrontational again."

Valerie gave a half smile. "Well, now at least I admit I was rude. I'm trying—we'll see how that goes."

"And I'm not sure how I can help you. Cisco thinks I'm over-involved already, and I do have a husband to keep happy."

"I have no answer to that." Valerie seemed to shrink. "Maybe coming here was a mistake."

"No, no—you're here. Let's talk it out, today at least." She paused. "It must be important."

Valerie propped her feet against a table leg, crossed her ankles, and faced forward, chewing on a thumbnail. It took a while for her to speak.

Finally she said, "Father McGrath helped me do a lot of soul-searching, Cora. Mastering living skills as a blind person is only step one—I have a lot of life left and what am I going to do with it? What I want is—to support myself and get Molly back."

"Won't that be hard?"

Valerie waved her arm in frustration. "Of course it will! Everything since my accident has been hard—you can't know. I lost more than my sight. I lost my job, the respect of people I knew, my home, my daughter —everything!"

Her arm dropped back to the tabletop. "It's like you take eggs and flour and sugar, put them in a bowl, and stir. They become dough, something new, and they can never be eggs and flour and sugar again. I can't have *my* life back, but I want *a* life. I've got the physical stuff down, but nothing's wrong with my brain and there's no reason I can't be productive."

"Will your brother and sister-in-law take in Molly? Didn't you say that was a problem?"

She frowned. "I don't want to be dependent on Sally forever, Cora. You probably picked up that we don't get along so well, but we're trying. I want my *own* life, my own place to live, with Molly, without limitations. But it scares me."

Cora was moved but didn't say anything. She couldn't see how Valerie could do what she wanted. She could be in for disappointment.

Valerie sighed. "I refuse to give up, to let others take care of me. But, still, people like me, blind people, have to have friends. There are things we need help with—like rides or handling emergencies. Real friends won't make a deal out of it—won't make you feel dependent." She paused, cleared her throat, and went on. "I'm sure it won't be a surprise to you that I don't have many friends. Your book club? That was it pretty much. I'm not the kind of person others warm up to. There are reasons…we'll get into that."

Cora coughed and took a sip of coffee. "You want me to help you make friends?"

"Not exactly. I need a friend to start. I need to know I can do it, that I can trust someone and I can *be* trustworthy, not just an f-ing know-it-all." She smirked. "I was an idiot, Cora. A brainy idiot, but still an idiot. I may have been a great administrative nurse, but I was a loser in the relationships department—in my marriage, socially, at work. I thought it didn't matter if people liked me; 'smart' took the place of everything else and everyone else. I was so damn smart I was stupid!"

Cora didn't see much value in commenting.

"I guess you could say it was a come-to-Jesus moment, realizing I had to depend on people. Father suggested I improve my social skills, and I suppose he's right. I'm the one with the problem, the one who needs an attitude adjustment. It's like inventing a new me." One side of her mouth turned up wryly.

"So Father McGrath thinks you and I should be friends? I'm your practice assignment? If we can patch things up you have a chance to succeed?"

"Well…Father did suggest I could afford to screw up with you, but I'd better learn how to get along with people before I reach a point of no return with Sally." The women snickered.

Valerie went on, "And there are other problems."

"Like?"

She sighed. "It wasn't feeling superior to others that made me insufferable."

Cora was beginning to see a different side of Valerie, one she might even get to like. "I've been accused of acting superior myself," she said with a chuckle.

"When we discussed my life before the accident, Father thought I needed…well, someone who had the skills to investigate my past. There were…issues. Family issues, secrets, mysteries…"

She paused. Cora gave her time to think. This sounded interesting.

"I had a miserable childhood. I lost my mother when I was thirteen and then the only person who cared about me not long after. I thought I could never get close to anyone again. Then I married Tom and that didn't work out any better. I never knew who I could trust. I relied on being strong, relied on myself, but in the process I let myself in for a world of hurt and loneliness."

Cora looked away, forgetting once again that Valerie couldn't read her face. If Valerie was looking for trusting relationships, how was she going to feel when she found out Cora was hiding information about her blindness. Damn it. But Father had told Cora not to bring it up too soon…

"I never knew," Cora said. "But why would you want to resurrect that? Lots of people have lousy childhoods. Please don't tell me you're looking for closure—I'm not a big proponent of that." Cora stood up, tapped the teapot to be sure it was still hot, and warmed Valerie's tea. Corky looked up expectantly—probably hoping Cora was bringing food.

"Then maybe you're not the right guy after all," Valerie said, her face drooping.

Cora realized she didn't want to let her down.

Valerie took a sip of the hot tea, reached over to put her hand on the dog's head, and then felt around for her purse on the other side of her chair. She didn't pick up the bag though; she just sat as if staring into space.

Cora rested her chin on her hands and backtracked. "I'm not saying I won't help you—it's just a personal belief. I've always felt people should accept the past for what it is, past, and do what it takes to go on. Awakening old hurts and rehashing guesses doesn't seem to me a productive part of the equation. Closure comes from accepting the situation you're in and deciding how to go forward."

There was no response, so she went on. "But I *do* like digging into the past, finding answers to things others have overlooked. I bet Father told you I wouldn't be able to turn that down, right?"

Valerie leaned over the table. As Cora had done, she propped her elbows on the tabletop and rested her chin on her hands, but couldn't know they faced each other in identical positions. "He thought I should be proud of facing the physical aspects of my recovery so successfully. But we weren't sure I had enough left to confront the rest of my life—he used the 'depression' word."

"Making a new life, starting alone and from an unfamiliar place—a paradigm shift, isn't that what they call it? Why does he think looking into your past will make a difference?"

Valerie laughed. "I hear doubt in your voice, Cora. I took some convincing too. But he's a psychologist, and I don't seem to be doing so well on my own, so I thought I'd try his advice. He says it will strengthen my feelings of achievement and acceptance."

"You'll need to tell me more then." Oh, no. What did she just say? Did she just invite Valerie back into her life and agree to dig into her past? Cisco wasn't going to like this….

The thought faded as she watched Valerie's face grow serious and her hands flutter and then move to the tabletop, as if she were going to stand. Corky watched alertly, but then Valerie settled back in her chair.

"If I were home, I'd get up, pace around my kitchen, and throw my arms around, like my Italian family does."

Cora chuckled. "Cisco throws his hands around when he talks too. Remember, you used to pick on him about that?"

Acknowledging Cora's comment with a smile, Valerie lifted her chin.

"I'm asking you to help me find my mother and get her back, so I can get my daughter back."

"Oh!" was all Cora could manage. Wow. So this was about Molly after all.

"My mother abandoned us when we were young. One day she was there, and then I never saw her again."

"You lived with your father? Like Molly does?"

"Ouch," Valerie winced.

"Sorry, Valerie. I didn't mean anything by that, just the similarity popped into my head."

"It's not the same. My father wasn't home much. We had to live with my grandmother and my aunt and uncles."

"You were thirteen, you said? Were you close to your mother?"

"No, not close at all. She was nice to everyone except me. I grew up like Cinderella, fetching and carrying, doing chores, taking care of Papá, Paula, Sally. When Mamma said jump, I jumped, but she always found fault with what I did."

Perhaps Valerie's compulsion to appear better than others traced back to such treatment.

Valerie paused and then added, "She called Paula 'Pumpkin' and Sally 'Amore,' or 'Pudge.' Me she called Valerie. I thought no one cared about me." Her voice quivered, and she reached for her purse and pulled out another tissue.

Something Valerie said struck Cora as familiar. She struggled to remember but then gave up.

This wasn't the first time a friend confided in Cora about a life that resembled a soap opera. She wasn't sure she wanted to get involved again, but then she had the experience, so if not her, who? She let out a slow breath. Here we go again!

"Don't knock those glasses off again," Cora said. "Maybe you should just leave them off if this is going to get worse."

Valerie giggled, blotted her eyes, and put her glasses back on.

"You didn't get along, but it still upset you when she left. Why?" Cora asked.

"My uncle Angelo said Mamma really loved me, maybe best of all, but there were things I didn't know. Maybe he was trying to make me feel better, I don't know. Mamma and I never got a chance to work it out before she left."

Valerie rubbed the tissue behind her glasses again and sipped her tea, which by now was cold. She was probably stalling, or perhaps she had said more than she intended. Confiding the reasons behind her lifelong bitterness must be tremendously difficult. Cora's respect for Valerie increased. The more she unburdened her soul the worse Cora felt about holding back.

"Maybe Angelo knows something he hasn't told you. Where is he now?"

"He's dead." Valerie's voice shook, the pain clear on her face.

Tears of compassion filled Cora's eyes. No wonder Valerie was so embittered. "So that's why you're afraid to form close relationships? First your mother, then your father, your uncle, Tom…"

Valerie nodded, not ready to speak yet.

"What happened to Angelo?" Cora asked in a soft voice.

She cleared her throat and swallowed. "He was a Chicago policeman. They said he was shot in the back by a sniper with a high-powered rifle from a high-rise in the housing projects. That night he was going to take me for dinner and a gondola ride at the Villa Venice, just the two of us."

Cora remembered the Villa Venice, a popular Mob-owned restaurant that once featured performers like Frank Sinatra. It was gone now, destroyed, probably not long after Valerie's uncle was killed. She thought Valerie's story sounded overly dramatic and wondered how much of it was true, but then she felt guilty.

Valerie banged a fist on the table. "It's not fair! After how hard I've worked. Now I need a personality transplant. And it's not only my eyesight I've lost, but also my daughter and my independence. I don't know how to change. You have friends, Cora—tell me what to do!"

Cora's eyes stung again. This poor woman. It was like history repeating itself, Valerie losing her mother at a tender age, then her own daughter in the same situation. Valerie must be afraid Molly will turn out as miserable as she is. How could Cora refuse to help?

She reached over and laid her hand on Valerie's arm. "What you didn't say, Valerie, is that despite my bossy, irritating, Cora-knows-best attitude, I manage to have some friends."

Valerie offered a little close-mouthed smile and sniffled.

"The worst is over, Valerie. It won't be easy, but we'll find a way. Every word you've told me today shows me you're a survivor. What does Father think will help the most?"

Determination returned to Valerie's face. "I have to know the truth, Cora. Why my mother left us, where she went, where she is now, what she's been doing. And I don't believe that sniper story. Something was going on before Uncle Angelo died, I just don't know what. Something had him really upset and it wasn't the job, something personal. I have to know who killed him, why he died."

The doorbell rang. Valerie jumped and Corky woke and leapt to her feet, hair raised. Cora stood, put an arm around Valerie's shoulder, and gave her a one-arm hug before going to the door.

# Chapter 3

"Billy?" Cora said. "Uh…it's good to see you, of course, but I'm a little surprised."

Standing on Cora's doorstep, Billy blinked and then stared at his feet. Strands of straight, shoulder-length, dark hair blew across his face in the breeze. His evasive and unsmiling mannerisms, combined with sharp cheekbones and a pea-sized dusting of hair that grew in a dimple in his chin, made him appear shifty.

Cora knew his quiet demeanor was due to awkwardness and painful shyness, yet she was reluctant to invite him into her house. Not only was she uncomfortable due to his sudden arrival, but he also couldn't have come at a worse time.

Billy was a childhood friend of Nick and Dawn, a young Potawatomi couple Cora knew. Cora had met the three Native Americans when they were co-writing a book. She didn't know Billy well but had no reason to fear or dislike him.

She glanced toward the kitchen as she waited for Billy to explain why he had come. She had to get back to Valerie. What was the time? How soon would the driver return? She and Valerie were at a crucial point—or were they? Perhaps they had both had as much as they could handle for the day and might benefit from thinking things over or letting their subconscious minds tell them what to do next. Cora was a firm believer in what she called "incubation."

"I'm sorry to drop by. I didn't have your number and I had to do something before I lost the guts…" He trailed off, looking up with an embarrassed grin.

"Something? Like *what* something?" Cora prompted.

He stared at his feet again. Cora glanced down to see what was so interesting and saw only muddy hiking boots. "Uh…I need some information and I thought of you. You could have some answers I need." He wiped his hands against the legs of his jeans.

"Well, of course I'll help you, if I can, but this isn't the best time. I have company, you see…"

"I'll come back." He started to turn away.

Cora sensed this was very important and if he left now he would not, in fact, come back.

"No, wait," she said, reaching out to touch his arm. "It doesn't make sense for you to come back if it turns out to just be something I can't help you with. What's this about?"

"Last fall, on that island? Something unusual happened. I need to know what you saw." He started to back away toward the dark-blue truck parked in her driveway.

A slight man, he seemed small, lost, and a little frightened. She found herself feeling sorry for him. According to Nick, Billy hadn't made friends since moving to Lemont. Like her guest in the other room, he seemed to be a loner.

She heaved a sigh of resignation and said, "Well, of course—it's not simple, is it? Come on in then. We can try to sort this out at least."

She tried to put his dirty boots out of her mind and waved him in. "Come to the kitchen and meet Valerie Pawlik."

~~~

"What do you want me to say, Cora? Haven't we been through this before, more times than we can count?" Cisco Tozzi said later that evening.

He got up from his recliner, picked up his coffee cup from a tray table, and tramped into the kitchen. His footsteps, heavy for a mid-height, slight man, rattled the nearby cabinets. When they had lived on the second floor of a two-flat building he walked softly so as not to disturb their tenants. Cora bit her tongue, wondering, not for the first time, when he had lost that habit.

She put her feet up, leaned into the corner of their dark-brown leather sofa, and worked a jigsaw puzzle on her iPhone while she waited for

Cisco to resume the conversation in a more reasonable frame of mind. His objection to her plans to help Valerie and Billy was no surprise, but she knew he wasn't really angry. Despite his posturing, he just needed to have his say. He placed his cup in the microwave, set the time, and waited for the beep.

"It's not a matter of managing your time better," he called from the kitchen. "It's too much on your plate. When are you going to learn when the plate's full you have to take something off it, not just pile more on top until the whole mess lands on the floor?"

She didn't reply.

He reentered the room and settled back in his chair. "You're always scolding *me* for being a soft touch. What makes you think you can do anything for these people? You don't know Billy all that well, and you could barely stand Valerie years ago when she was in your book club. Jesus, you even kicked her out, which started the whole thing to begin with."

"You think you're telling me anything I don't know?"

"You attract strays, Cora, like cats hanging around the back door when a restaurant throws out leftovers. Why do people keep coming to you, and why do you always give in?"

"I'm a sympathetic ear, I guess. And I'm not judgmental. Father McGrath asked me to help Valerie."

"You're not judgmental?" he snorted. "Not publicly, maybe. So you talked to her, like you promised him. You're done."

"She needs a friend."

"And that has to be you? Why? Don't forget what happened the last time you two tried to be friends. What part of that didn't you understand? And what am I supposed to do while you're chasing mysteries again, hang around like a third wheel? You know I'm not good with this compassionate support stuff."

Despite his disclaimer, Cisco's support was indispensable to Cora. It was a part of his nature he didn't realize. She ignored his complaint and turned off the iPhone. "Valerie's motivated now. She needs friends and doesn't have any. I'll be a challenge."

He barked a short laugh. "In more ways than one. Think she knows what she's in for?"

"Actually, she's met the challenge already. I found myself liking her today, in fact. But that's not the real issue—I told you what she said about her childhood. I can help her find out what happened to her mother and uncle. She'll need access to research tools we have at the historical society —genealogy and newspaper records—she'll need the presence of a sighted person. That's why Father sent her to me, despite our history. He, of all people, understands."

"Have you talked to Father McGrath since you spoke with Valerie?"

"I wanted to talk to you first."

"Huh—well now you're making sense. When are you going to do that?"

"I'll be seeing him Saturday at St. James. I'll pull him aside."

"I still don't understand why he's putting the two of you together. He knows firsthand what it was like to be on the receiving end of that wolf's wrath. Does Valerie know it attacked her because of what she did to you? I wouldn't think he'd want that connection made."

Cora shook her head. "I don't know what she thinks. By the time we figured out how to talk to each other and she explained what she wanted, Billy was here, and then her driver arrived. We barely had time to pick our next meeting date. The wolf is guesswork anyway, and the danger is over."

He went to the kitchen table and began gathering newspapers and junk mail. "Tomorrow's trash day," he mumbled. He got some paper bags from the garage and stuffed them with a week's worth of old newspapers he'd accumulated in a corner behind a chair. With his back to her, he asked, "Why do you have to talk to Billy too? Can't he talk to Nick and Dawn? He's their friend—we hardly know him."

"Are you through with that pile on the end table?" Cora watched him sort through the stack. She'd never understand why he sorted things into multiple piles throughout the house instead of a single place, but it wasn't important enough to quibble over. Then, she might have to change some of her own habits, like leaving notepads and books everywhere.

She swung around and reached for her shoes, remembering when she first became acquainted with Billy. Their friends said he was acting strange and might be behind an attempt to sabotage the book they were writing. After they discovered the real villain, Billy had been injured. They rarely saw him afterward. Why *did* she want to put herself out for him?

"I don't know. Maybe he doesn't want his friends to know he's upset. He said he had questions only I could answer about the day he was injured.

I can at least hear him out. After Valerie left he started rambling about Isle a la Cache. I just couldn't get my head around another needy person today, so I made an excuse and told him he'd have to come back."

Cisco chuckled as he finished putting papers in the bag. "I can't see Valerie and Billy hitting it off—such different personalities. How did that go?"

"Awkward, as you'd expect, especially at first because Valerie's dog growled at him. Billy said he was used to that. Way back in history white people's dogs didn't seem to take to Indians." She chuckled. "But Valerie seemed really interested in Billy's Potawatomi heritage and asked him questions. The look on Billy's face, it was kind of funny, actually. She's still stunning, you know. She's got to be at least twenty years older than he is, but he looked smitten."

"But not Valerie, surely. Does she know he's under thirty?"

"Probably not. Billy's not the brightest guy. He reminds me of Floyd, your former golf buddy. Short, thin, same quiet, simple sort of guy. The classic example of you-know-you're-a-hillbilly-when. Real nice, harmless, means well, but shit's always happening to him."

Cora tended to feel superior to people with limited education, but Floyd had been an exception. Just moments ago she had said she wasn't judgmental. Oh, well. She was softening as she grew older, less demanding, extending to others the patience her own growing list of shortcomings required.

Cisco smiled. "I miss Floyd," he said. "I suppose Billy is like him. The only clue Billy gave you was that he wanted to compare his experience at Isle a la Cache with yours? That's what he said?"

"That's it."

"That shouldn't take long."

"No. Before I forget to tell you, the bulb over the kitchen sink went out when Billy came in. You'll need to change it."

"I just changed it...shouldn't have gone out...." Cisco walked over to the sink and flipped the wall switch. The light came on. He shrugged his shoulders. "It's working now."

"That's strange—it flickered and died yesterday. And I hit the switch too, but it didn't come on."

"I'm not going to waste time fixing something that's not broke."

"I wouldn't expect you to."

She joined him in the kitchen, poured some coffee for herself, and placed it in the microwave.

With her back to Cisco she said, "You know how cold and haughty Valerie can be, well, at the front door when she was leaving, she squeezed my arm and told me how relieved she felt after talking to me."

She turned and looked Cisco in the eye. "Knowing Valerie, can you understand how much it took for her to do that? I think she's afraid. She needs me, and maybe Billy does too. I want to help them. It makes me feel useful, Cisco. If I can, if that's what they want, shouldn't I do that? How can I turn them down?"

He shook his head. "That's what I get for marrying a good woman." He stepped forward and pulled her into a hug. "You're feeling guilty for what happened to them, aren't you?"

"I suppose I am. They wouldn't have been hurt if they hadn't gotten involved with me."

He rubbed her back and sighed. "Make me a deal, okay?" he said, his mouth buried in her hair.

"Yes?"

"We're taking the family to Ireland this summer. We can't miss that."

"No, we can't. I don't see a problem—it's three months away."

"You think you have things under control, but it never turns out that way. So go ahead, meet them, but wrap it up as soon as you can."

He planted a kiss on her forehead and released her.

"If Valerie and I are to be friends it won't end there," she said.

"True, but our other friends aren't time-consuming, so Valerie doesn't have to be either."

"Deal."

"And need I say, once again, leave me out of it."

# Chapter 4

Saturday afternoon, Cora drove through the elaborate wrought iron gates that greeted visitors to historic St. James at Sag Bridge Church. An expert on local history, she pictured the place as it might have appeared thirteen thousand years ago, an island in glacial Lake Chicago, a larger body of water than the present Lake Michigan. Today almost all of Mount Forest Island was an immense forest preserve, including St. James, buried in the woods at its western tip. Usually Cora felt an aura of a distant time and place here, touched by a surreal stillness, but right now her thoughts were on her planned conversation with Father McGrath.

She drove past Saginaw Hall, the parish center, up the hill along the cemetery, through an arch that announced the founding of the church in 1833, and into the parking lot.

Today's program wouldn't start for an hour, but the lot was already half full with the cars of actors and church members. Father Mike O'Connor, St. James's pastor, was known for his creative programs.

Today's reenactors, including Father Mike himself, would be reading in costume from the letters of John Adams and Thomas Jefferson, highlighting the conflict between the two men as they struggled with their personal beliefs and with each other. Cora would assist with sales and food, and Father McGrath would be the moderator.

She found Father Mike in the main hall of the parish center, dressed in a brown coat, black waistcoat, tan breeches, and long white stockings. Oblivious to the chaos around him, he spotted Cora near the doorway, beamed, and waved. "Cora! Good to see you!"

She gave him a quick hug. "Is Father McGrath here yet?"

"There's time, there's time. Could you set up downstairs? I left the books near the fireplace. Gerry put up a table for you. Should I send Father down when he arrives?"

"Yes, please," Cora said, knowing it wouldn't likely happen. She had to catch Father McGrath before the program; she couldn't count on him to stick around when it was over.

She collected an armload of books and descended the stairway to the lower hall. Parishioners were busy in the kitchen preparing hot dogs, hamburgers, sausages, salads, and desserts. Near the bottom of the stairs stood an empty table for Cora to display the books Father Mike wanted her to sell. Buyers would have to pass her on their way to get food. She unfolded two chairs in an adjacent empty room where she and Father McGrath could talk privately and then arranged her display. On her last trip upstairs she saw Father McGrath at the doorway.

Father McGrath, a small, slender man, wore a toupee that Cora thought made him look like an Afghan hound with a comb-over, but he wore it proudly, neither embarrassed nor apologetic. She once accused him of having bought the hairpiece on clearance. He denied that, but he quipped that he had a friend who was a taxidermist. He and Cora had met at a community event, hit it off, and remained friends. A trained psychologist for the archdiocese, he lived at an in-town parish that provided him with space for counseling, and he also said Mass to fill in. He gave lively, entertaining sermons; was active in the community; and his appointment schedule was full.

"Downstairs, quickly, before you can't get away," she said, heading toward the stairs. He winked and followed.

They escaped to the room Cora had prepared and closed the door. "I can't guarantee no one will come in, but they won't stay if they see us in private discussion," she said.

"Just the two of us? I'm a priest, remember—got a reputation to keep," he said, looking doubtfully at the flimsy folding chair. There was a knock on the door before he got a chance to sit.

"Jefferson wants to change one of his lines. He wants your opinion," the visitor said.

"Perhaps Father Mike can answer his question?" Father McGrath said. As soon as the door closed, there was another knock.

"Would you like a bottle of water by the podium?" the visitor asked.

"Sure. I'll get a friend to change it into wine—it's cheaper that way," Father said.

After the visitor departed, Father suggested they go for a walk instead. Cora readily agreed, grabbing her sweater as they slipped out the back door.

~~~

They walked up the hill without speaking at first, Father striding easily and Cora laboring a bit on the steep grade. They passed the grotto of Our Lady of the Forest and then the rectory and went through another gate and into the graveyard that surrounded the old church.

Cora often lectured visitors about the place, but Father McGrath knew its history well: how Indians valued this hill for its unobstructed view in three directions and down two valleys and how Father Marquette stopped there in 1673, said Mass, and pointed out that a canal here would connect the Great Lakes and the Mississippi River. That canal was finally opened in 1848 and was responsible for the growth of Chicago.

As they took the sunlit path through the cemetery toward the church, Father asked, "So how did you and Valerie get along?" His voice was low and gravelly, breaking over the last word, coming out high-pitched and strange with an almost echoing effect.

Cora was well accustomed to her friend's voice and relieved that his popularity as a speaker remained unchanged after the injury that caused the speech abnormality. They had shared life-changing experiences, and she would do almost anything for him. Now, how was she going to break it to him that, after two sleepless nights, she was having second thoughts about being able to help Valerie?

However she said, "Amazingly well. But to cut to the chase, I feel guilty about not telling her what I know about her accident. The two of you must have talked about it. What does she think happened?"

"Not really. Our sessions were focused on preparing her to reenter the working world." He kicked a twig off the blacktopped path. "Physically, she's coped fantastically, but she's not mentally ready for independent living. It's not going to be easy for a blind nurse to find a job."

They passed the church doors and continued around the building, where the ground dropped steeply toward the Sag Valley and the Saganashkee Slough. The hillside was covered by some of the oldest graves. Cora liked to wander here, reading the names and dates on the stones and imagining the lives of these people in the difficult, early days of Sag Bridge and Lemont.

She stopped to catch Father's gaze. She wasn't going to let him avoid her question.

"What does she think the facts of her attack are?"

He glanced away and headed toward the rear of the church. "She has a vivid image of a snarling wolf standing in the road before the accident. She accepts what the doctors said, that it was probably a delusion brought on by her head injury. She thinks she blacked out and doesn't remember tearing at her eyes in panic to get shards of glass out."

"You didn't tell her the wolf attacked you too, did you?"

He shook his head. "She didn't know me before she came to see me, didn't know my voice had changed or that the collar hides the scars. I didn't see any point in telling her—she's fragile right now. I didn't want to give her something else to worry about."

She stepped in front of him and faced him with her hands on her hips. "This puts me in a predicament, Father. Explain to me how can I be the trustworthy friend she's looking for without telling her I suspect the wolf attacked her for the same reason it attacked you—because it was protecting me."

"You have to gain her trust before you can help her," he said. "You're right. She'll need to know about the wolf, but it's too soon. If you told her now, it could drive her away before you two develop the friendship she needs. Prove yourself in other ways, by being understanding, supportive, accepting—and by helping her solve some mysteries in her life. You're good at that."

Gain her trust? While she was hiding such vital information?

"You said she was 'fragile.' Why did you use that term?" she asked.

"Since she became blind, she's only been around people who are invested in helping her. But, what happens when she's out among others who don't care, who see her as a problem and ignore or reject her? It's going to happen. She has to learn how that feels and how to cope with it, especially since she had poor social skills to begin with."

He scratched the top of his head, displacing his hairpiece slightly. "Social situations are challenging to any person who deals with sudden blindness. Some people get sad or depressed. Her situation with her family adds another complication. Normally family and friends would be there, but she has neither, really."

He threw his arms out, and Cora caught an expression of…frustration? Desperation? She was struck by how deeply this man wanted to help Valerie.

"She's learned how to function in a life of darkness but not yet how to *live* in it. She's always been a loner, but now being alone frightens her. Yet, she's resistant to the idea of dependency."

They walked on in silence, taking the path down the hill toward the east end where headstones burrowed into the woods. She was beginning to understand her potential importance to Valerie.

She reached out and put her hand on Father's arm to stop him. "I'm still trying to understand how uncovering her past is going to help her," she said. "So far I only know that her mother left her and the uncle who took her mother's place was killed."

"I could say there are restrictions about what I can legally disclose, but of course you need to understand if you're going to help her and that's not really the issue here. I think it's better if she tells you about her past in her own way and time and better if you hear it directly from her."

They walked on and stopped at a stone mausoleum. He touched the warm stone. Cora had the feeling he wasn't really seeing it, just using it as an excuse to think over his next words.

"She may be finished with the past, but the past isn't finished with her," he said. "People who suffer abandonment feel all they have is themselves. It hampers their lives. Something unjust has happened, and it leads to rage and setting impossible, uncompromising personal standards. They are often unaware that they harbor intense anger and self-loathing. Some learn to deal with it, but for Valerie it's complicated by sudden blindness and the mysteries of her past."

Cora finally understood. It was no wonder Valarie was afraid to form close personal attachments since the people she loved had failed her.

They strolled on and reached the far end of the graveyard; beyond that was wild brush.

Cora stopped and held up her hand. "Did you hear that?"

"What?"

She felt a tingling at the back of her neck and rubbed it, peering nervously into the thick foliage. It was unusually chilly here. "Like someone whistling a tune. Probably just a bird," she chuckled.

Father turned back, walking faster now. She hurried to keep up.

He spoke as if he needed to remind himself. "To get through living-skills training, which is challenging, she convinced herself life would be back to normal once she had that down. She's smart, so her head knew the reality, but in her heart it was a different matter. When she finished, it hit her like a ton of bricks. Her life as she knew it would never be normal again. A letdown was inevitable. I'm trying to help her make a new life, not return her to the same one."

The empathy Cora felt when she and Valerie talked hit her anew and tears stung her eyes. "So that's why you sent her to me, as a controlled experiment, and you're cautioning me to go easy on her, which I would do anyway, by the way."

They were now near the parking lot, the section of the cemetery Cora knew was designated for the graves of paupers and people who had died violently. She squeezed her eyes shut, remembering the emotional encounter she had had with a ghost here two years ago. But that was over.

He cleared his throat and turned to face her. "Valerie needs to build up her confidence. She needs positive reinforcement in ways that have nothing to do with her blindness but instead prove she still has value. Even one person who recognizes the good in her or acts on her behalf will go a long way. But she has a better chance at success if she comes to terms with the things that made her bitter to begin with. Traumas like hers don't go away by ignoring them. They lurk in the background, and they fester..."

He waved a forefinger. "How can she face something until she knows what really happened? If she finds her mother and confronts her, it could heal her scars and give her the confidence she needs to succeed in her new life." He grinned. "You see her differently now, don't you? You two are bonding, aren't you?"

Cora eyes met his and nodded. It was true.

He stopped and gazed toward the church, its white steeple glinting in the sunlight, and he pointed to the cross at its top. "Look."

Following the direction of his finger, Cora saw two turkey vultures, one perched on each arm of the cross. They watched the vultures leave their perch and swoop in circles around the graveyard before flying toward the woods.

"The Vikings used to think vultures were a sign of rebirth," Father said.

Cora's scalp tingled. *An omen?*

# Chapter 5

Billy stood at the water's edge, gazing south across the Saganash-kee Slough, legs apart, hands clasped behind his back. A gentle breeze wafted off the shallow lake, lifting his dark, shoulder-length hair. It was early—early in the season, early in the day. His truck was the only vehicle in the lot. No fishermen were along the shore, although usually a few arrived at the crack of dawn. Hell, the place even attracted ice fishermen. But the ice was gone now, the tents stored for the year. Absence of distractions might help clear his head he hoped.

What was happening to him? Imagination? Coincidence? Nothing at all? Was he going mad?

The tribal elders would say spirits were involved.

He had replayed the disturbing scene again and again in his mind and did so one more time now, desperate for a clue.

On Isle a la Cache last fall, a man Billy trusted struck him down and grabbed Billy's friend Dawn. He tried to rescue Dawn but couldn't get up. Frustrated and furious, Billy was possessed by extraordinary energy —as if electricity built in his body and flew from him toward Dawn's captor. The man was thrown backward, hurled against a tree, and impaled by a tremendous force. Billy lost consciousness then.

When he woke, Cora was sitting at his side, holding his hand, and talking softly. Later, after his recovery, Billy had only flashes of memory and a disturbing, impossible idea that something within him had created the energy that struck his attacker.

Then, walking in the historic section of Lemont one night, a streetlight went out when he passed under it and then blinked on again when he was a distance away. He would have said it was a coincidence, except the same thing happened over and over and in other places.

He stopped wearing his watch because it quit running soon after he put it on. When he put in a new battery, the watch stopped minutes later. He bought another watch and it stopped too.

Then, at times of intense emotion or in certain locations, such as when he walked in the woods or near the quarries, the sensation of tremendous energy building within him recurred.

It was frightening.

He had to pull himself together and take steps to improve his future. Could he control this energy or shut it off? Was this a curse or a gift? An opportunity or another stroke of bad luck?

Cora had been there when it happened. She might shed light on the problem. But she didn't have time for him when he stopped to see her.

The sun appeared now, defining the ridge of the bluff on the other side of the slough, spreading red, gold, and orange across the still surface. Billy closed his eyes, trying to tune to nature, imagining rhythmic chants and inner calm. But his thoughts disturbed the peace he came here for. He shivered, zipped up his black sweatshirt, and retrieved his black baseball cap from his truck. Billy spent many hours roaming the forests around Lemont. Perhaps a stroll through the woods would free his mind.

He crossed the deserted, two-lane 107th Street and headed west on its shoulder, where he had seen a path leading up the bluff on the north side of the Sag Valley. A chain prevented cars from entering. The path must have been a service road once, since bicycle and walking trails that filled these woods were narrower.

He climbed the trail west through woods dense with brush. Despite the leafless branches this early in the year, it was not long before 107th Street and the view of the valley was obscured. Most of the trees had slender trunks, the woods not old growth but more recent in origin. The trail was hard-packed, studded with weeds and rocks. In places, granite pavers were exposed and limestone flags lined both sides.

This wouldn't have been a service road. Too fancy, too expensive. It must have been an entrance to impress visitors.

His boots made almost no noise as, true to his heritage, Billy walked softly by habit. Soon a narrow trail branched off to the right. Both trails continued uphill, one northwest and the narrow one northeast. He decided to follow the main limb, where he knew St. James at Sag Bridge Church was secluded in this part of the forest.

As he ambled, his thoughts turned to Cora's friend Valerie. Surprised to recognize the same blind woman he had noticed at the library two days ago, he was once again impressed by her dark beauty and her confidence despite her blindness. Here she was preparing to reenter the professional job market, while he, strong and able-bodied, worked as a part-time clerk at an office-supply store. What was wrong with him?

Valerie had asked a lot of questions. He enjoyed talking to her and lost his self-consciousness. When people asked about his Indian heritage, it was usually because they saw him as an oddity. Valerie seemed different—interested in him as a person. Maybe he would get a chance to know her better, but why would she want to know him? They had nothing in common and he wondered how old she was.

"On your left!" came the warning. He glanced behind him in time to avoid two young men on mountain bikes. Both men were fit, their progress uphill effortless. They wore identical red-and-yellow helmets, and both wore gloves, biking shoes, short sleeve jerseys, and biker shorts, even this early in the year. He shook his head wondering how much their gear cost and surprised he hadn't heard them coming. He raised a hand in greeting, which both men returned as they passed.

As he approached the top of the hill he caught a glimpse of a large building ahead through the trees. Had he come upon a maintenance facility of some sort near Archer Avenue? Or had he reached St. James? He thought the church was some distance away. What else would be out here?

When the trees cleared he found himself looking over a grassland. Beyond it a crumbling, generous-sized parking lot surrounded a large, gray concrete building with a red-tile roof. A balcony extended across the open second floor, covered by three roofed sections, one in the center and one at each end.

What the hell? Why hadn't he heard about this place? His personal problems temporarily replaced by curiosity, he crossed the grassland and parking area to explore.

The building was not only deserted but abandoned. Bigger than a restaurant, it might have been a country club. In the forest preserves?

He stepped inside the building through a central entrance that appeared sound but minus what once must have had grand doors and windows. He had a visual image of walls covered with fancy mirrors and fixtures, elaborate sconces and furnishings in the Art Deco style. The image was so real that he got the distinct feeling he had seen the building before.

Elaborate staircases on each side of the large central room soared to the ceiling. To the right and left were arches that disappeared into gloom—perhaps banquet rooms. Billy went into the room on his left, dim and distinctly creepy. Scarce light penetrated the clerestory window frames, revealing dirt, dried leaves and branches, nests, animal droppings, shards of glass and mirrors, and other assorted debris.

Why hadn't this place been demolished? Long-neglected, disintegrating, it must present a liability. What if a child, roaming the trails and woods, fell from the roof? Or what if crumbing walls landed on someone?

He climbed the stairway, testing his weight with each step. Partway up he heard a rustling noise below. Uneasy, he looked over the railing but couldn't see what caused the sound.

On the upper floor, he stepped onto a balcony. Tall scrub and slender trees blocked what he thought was once a view of the Sag Valley and slough. To the west and north, across a ravine, rose another hill. This explained why the building was hidden from roads and more popular trails. Open patios stretched between three roofed sections. Again a strong image, like a memory, formed in Billy's mind, a space filled with tables and lounge chairs; busy waiters; patrons wandering about, gazing over railings at the scenery and laughing and talking with friends as they enjoyed meals and drinks. Trancelike, he wandered from end to end, searching for clues to what this place had been. He found, among some crumbled, terra-cotta roof tiles, a small black, plastic film container and a round metal knob with numbers etched into it.

No one used film anymore. The knob could be anything. And why hadn't someone picked the items up long ago?

He exited the building and stood looking across a network of ravines that converged nearby. Bright beams of sunlight slanted through the brush and glinted on a piece of metal. Billy dug it out with the toe of his boot and picked it up. Lead-gray with rusted and glittery spots, the L-shaped object was four inches by an inch thick on one side and three inches by a half inch on the other and resembled a duck's head. Billy put it in his pocket along with the film canister and metal knob.

He heard a faint whistle carried by the breeze—a fragment of a melody, somewhat familiar but he couldn't identify it. When the sound stopped abruptly, he thought he saw motion at the top of the hill, but when he focused on the spot nothing was there. Probably the bikers he'd seen earlier. But if so, wouldn't the colorful helmets have been visible? It could be anyone of course. The isolation of the place struck him. He looked around, the tips of his ears tingling.

Curiosity satisfied, he headed back the way he had come. When he reached the point where the path divided, he paused, wondering whether to call it a day or see where the other path led. *What the hell*, he thought again. He might as well check it out while he was here—he had nothing better to do.

The path was narrow with puddles and dried weeds. It had probably been dirt or gravel. Once again, he glimpsed buildings through the trees before the trail widened and he arrived at a farm he guessed was from the early 1900s. The farmhouse looked like those scattered across the countryside, a dark red, two-story frame building with enclosed porches on either end. A large cottonwood tree threw shade over the house. On the north side of the trail was a large gray pole barn of more recent, although not modern, construction. He'd seen barns like this used as storage facilities, some converted to shops or businesses. Beyond the house was a smaller building with rotting wood and a roof that had fallen in.

The farm seemed lived-in. A black vintage car was in the yard, an expensive-looking sedan in great condition that dated back to the forties, maybe earlier. He walked around it, noting Cadillac and V-12 emblems, a 1954 Illinois license plate, and a chrome hood ornament—a graceful woman in Art Nouveau style.

Three horses, sleek and well groomed, were in a paddock set in a ground depression on the far side of the barn. They lifted their heads to watch him. A cat trotted over and rubbed against his legs. Billy hesitated. Was he trespassing? He thought the property was owned by the forest preserves. There were no warning signs, and no one seemed to be about. He headed toward the barn rather than the house, wondering how the car, or anything else, got up here.

At the paddock fence, the curious horses ambled over to check him out. He liked horses and horses liked him. He held out a hand for them to approve before reaching out to stroke a silky neck. One of the horses nudged his shoulder affectionately. In the lazy quiet, he heard again a faint melodic whistle. It grew in volume; he recognized the tune and filled in the words: *Weep no more, my lady. Oh weep no more today!*

Billy looked up to see a man on horseback riding over a hill north of the house. The rider, a handsome man of average height with broad shoulders, appeared to be in his fifties, but he radiated energy like a much younger man. He was bareheaded with thick, dark curls, slicked in place with a greasy substance. He wore crisp black pants, a fancy leather belt, and a white button-down, long-sleeved shirt, the sleeves rolled up to his elbows, the shirt tucked neatly under his belt. Black riding boots seemed to be the only accommodation to being on horseback, and he wore no outerwear despite the season. He was unsmiling, but showed no surprise to find Billy petting his horses. He rode up and slid off a sleek English saddle.

That was strange. Most riders on these bridle trails used Western saddles.

The horse drew Billy's attention. It was a huge animal, a dark-brown mare with white wrappings on her front legs, the sort of thing one saw at racetracks, not on pleasure horses. Sleek, with powerful chest and hindquarters, she danced and pulled against the reins her rider held.

"*Calma, bambina,*" the man said, stroking the horse's neck and soothing it with shushing sounds. He turned to Billy. "Isn't she lovely," he asked, reaching up and rubbing her muzzle.

"A beauty," Billy agreed, wondering why the man didn't question what he was doing there.

"She win the Derby, just you watch, no matter what they say," the man said with a mild, unrecognizable accent, shoulder against the horse's flank, still stroking it fondly.

"Um...okay." Assuming the man referred to the Kentucky Derby, Billy knew the race was for three-year-old horses. *For the old Kentucky home, far away*—the melody repeated in his mind. He wondered why a Derby contender, horses that normally never left tracks or stables, would be ridden on bridle trails.

"Dolly Val, *tesoro*, my pride and joy." The man started to lead her toward the barn but turned to stare into Billy's eyes.

As if making a statement, the mare lifted her tail and deposited a pile on the grass.

"Ha!" the horseman barked. "She leave us some road apples, never mind no road in sight!" He laughed. "So, you wandered over from the old clubhouse?" he went on.

*How did he know that?*

"So that's what it is. I wondered," Billy said.

"Been shut down ten years now, maybe more, ever since they build that laboratory right next to it," he said.

"That laboratory?" Billy looked blank.

"'Course, that's closed now, too." He eyed Billy suspiciously. "You didn't pick nothing up while you were on the golf course, did you?"

Ah...so it was a golf course clubhouse. But surely it had been closed much longer than ten years.

"Um...," Billy said again, "I did, actually." He reached into his pocket and pulled out the film canister, the knob, and the metal object and held them out.

The man looked them over but narrowed his eyes and didn't handle the objects. After deliberating, he said, "Someone took pictures, snooping around again—they find nothing. The knob—maybe from those ham radio *buttagots*. And that metal looks like it's from a golf club, probably a Sabbath stick, but I never seen one like that."

For no apparent reason, the man's eyes hardened as he sneered, "Be careful who you trust. You could lose what you love." The man's eyes took on an intense golden sheen that was suddenly frightening.

*What was that about?* Billy looked away. Something was off here. Was the man a horseman or a farmer or did he have a screw loose?

Whoever he was, he gave Dolly Val a final pat and started to lead her toward the barn. "You'll excuse if I tend to business before the little lady here gets impatient. She's a *gavone*, eats everything in sight," he laughed, his good humor returned.

Billy wondered again why the man didn't kick him off his property. Watching his step for the "road apples," before he left, Billy couldn't find the pile. How could he have imagined that?

As the horseman neared the barn door, he called over his shoulder, "I'd stay away from that golf course, I was you. *'Uarda la ciunca!*"

# Part II

# Chapter 6
## 1954

Florida seemed pretty good to me lately. My age was catching up to me. Why not let Mickey have the problems? Let him deal with the Chicago boys, their stake in the ranch, the truth about Dolly Val.

Al never gave me the credit I deserved, never thought I knew how to handle the job. Yeah, sure, he was boss a the Chicago Outfit, of which we was all a part. Ya can't say he screwed that up. Al was the best, forget about the East Coast bunch.

I pulled the Caddy up to the chained entrance and left the engine running while I got out and used the key Ted gave me to open the lock on the chain across the abandoned driveway.

I followed the stones that lined the drive and the trail of crushed weeds Ted's car left. Right away trees blocked the sight of 107th Street and the valley. I spotted a red cloth tied to a branch where Ted marked the turn for me and continued creeping along his faint track. My thoughts returned to Al and how I ended up at this place.

"Vincenzo," Al would say. In private, he used my Italian name, Vincenzo Ammirati. "Vincenzo, I can't let any a the boys run wild, even you. There's got to be control here, and I'm the guy that makes the rules. No matter how good a friends we are, I can't let the boys see you going your own way. It's bad for business."

I had to remind him that our Heights boys were the guys that muddied the waters on Valentine's Day. We was the guys that planned the hits and arranged the muscle. The Feds could never prove a thing. It hadn't a been for us—well, we saved the Outfit's *culi'*.

Al's long gone now, these past ten years or more. After the tax guys got him he was never the same, even when they let him out a the joint. People said his head was screwed up, but I got to admire how he set things up. Chicago's operation's still strong today, still buying favors, still staying ahead a the Feds. But one thing Al never understood was the Heights operation was different from Chicago.

Once Prohibition ended the Syndicate changed. Nitti knew what he was doing, but he never had power like Capone. The bootlegging wasn't profitable no more, but we already had our people in place, handling the gambling joints and the prostitution.

Our Heights boys were the guys what controlled all the places that was inconvenient for Nitti's gang, a huge territory, and we never held back his cut a the take—he got every penny coming to him. Let Chicago take care a the street money, the payoffs, the unions, and those "legit" businesses. The Heights did what we do best: joints, "hotels," and bookies.

We got our own politicians and officials on the payroll. From the Strip to across the state line everything's running like clockwork. We're expanding in all directions, plenty a business just waiting. We don't need interference. All Chicago's gotta do is stay outta our way and collect the money we send them. Even wagering is different out here—we're not big into the fights or the ballgames. It's horses that brings in the moolah.

That's where the profit's at—the tracks. You own the horses, you control the races. You control the bookies in the stands, you control the take and your ten percenters cash the winning tickets. With my ranch and a few bucks in the right palms to look the other way, it's like taking candy from a baby.

Dolly Val—my favorite lady, my goldmine—that mare could run fast or run slow, whatever it took for the best payoff. We had to withdraw her after the complaints were filed, but she's still in our stable and useful in other ways.

Until the track officials decided to enforce the rules—which brings me out here today, where the wind turns around and comes back.

Through the trees ahead I saw a barn and then the red farmhouse. This location was hidden, I had to admit. I went past a big cottonwood tree and parked in the yard, away from the tree so as to protect the Caddy's wax job. I went into the house and used the john. Ted wasn't in the house, so I went to find him, whistling a tune in the peaceful sunlight.

Ted was a godsend in more ways than one. Not only did he manage the Tinley farm, but also when things started heading south he came up with the solution.

I found him in the barn. That's what I paid him for of course. He was sponging down Dolly Val in her stall, sudsy water running down his bare skinny arms. "Hey, Jimmy," he said. "How ya doin'?"

"Can't complain, Ted," I said.

"Be careful a your fancy clothes out here."

I glanced at my creased black pants and imported tassel loafers. What the hell—I had a closet full a them.

He put down the sponge and picked up the mare's hind foot, examining it closely.

"Is there a problem there?" The last thing I needed was for Dolly Val to go lame. I took off my suit coat, draped it over a nail, rolled up my sleeves, and went into her stall. I rubbed her dark brown flank and then scratched along her halter straps. Frustrated at her ties, she tossed her head, then closed her eyes, rested her head on my shoulder, and nudged.

"I don't think so," he said. "Took her out on the trails this morning. Gotta be sure she didn't pick up no stones."

"Yeah," I said. "Be sure."

"Give me a minute, Jimmy," he said.

I wrinkled my nose, detecting a medicinal odor. "Ya got liniment in there?" I asked.

"Of course." He sounded offended. "Take a highbred animal like this from her element," he said, stroking her back, "she needs some calming down. She likes the fussing and the liniment does more than soothe muscles and sores—gets her comfortable and relaxed. Isn't that right, sweetheart?"

I stepped out, leaned against the door, and watched over its top. Ted ran a sweat scraper across a few remaining wet spots, wiped her hindquarters and legs, and wrapped her front legs with white bandages. Then he grabbed his grooming tools and left the stall, fastening the door behind him.

"It's nice today, Ted," I said. "Let's talk outside."

We went to the paddock and leaned our arms against the fence. Three a our foals, two colts and a filly, came over to investigate. Few animals are more curious than horses, although it takes some doin' to work the skittishness outta them. I patted the neck of a young bay colt.

"What's happening at the farm, Ted? I'm not sure if I should go by there or not."

"No reason you shouldn't. They're not looking to pick you up, just be sure none a your horses show up at the tracks anymore."

I sighed. "Dreams all busted and gone to hell. Fuck 'em."

Ted grinned. "And the horse they rode in on, right?"

We laughed.

"If people didn't know about you before the investigation, they do now," Ted said. "The 'Mystery Man of the Outfit.' Before this is over, it's a dead cinch you'll be banned from the tracks."

"I guess I overdid the fixes or had too many books in the stands. It's been working since the thirties—how was I to know the regulators were gonna start taking this sort a thing serious?"

"What are the boys in Chicago saying? Can they protect you?" Ted asked.

"Nah, they're pissed too. Think I went too far, giving them grief. They're happy letting me be the fall guy. It takes the pressure off a them."

"How about those new Organized Crime and Racketeering agents? They worried about that?"

"They don't take that serious neither. No money behind it, bunch a clowns runnin' it. Hoover's not been after us for years."

We fell silent, but something else was bothering me. I had to be careful how I asked, but I wanted Ted's opinion.

"What do you think Mickey's take is on all a this, Ted? He's been makin' himself scarce."

"You think he's the one talked to the officials, Jimmy?" He sounded shocked by the idea.

"Nah—why would he do that? It'd be his loss. No, I meant him and me, in light a all this heat. He's young and ambitious—what's he think about takin' orders from an old man?"

"He's never been much interested in this end a the business, far as I know. I'm the wrong guy to ask. I know nothing about the rest a your business, only the horses."

"He knows who to respect here, right?"

"Far as I know, Jimmy. I never heard him disrespect you in any way. I'm sure it's nothing against you, personal. He's just got that short-man's syndrome. That or he's covering for that kid brother a his what's always screwing up."

I let out a deep breath and took a long look around. Ted said the place was a farm to start out, a caretaker's house when the golf course was open, and it was abandoned after they built the secret laboratory. The forest preserves still owned it and kept the utilities running. Ted greased some palms to get us to watch the place for them. The isolation played right into our hands.

"Not much point in keeping the ranch now, is there?" I said at last.

"Lucky we snuck the best stock out before the Feds confiscated the stable."

I looked into the distance, catching a glimmer of light reflecting off the marsh in the valley. "Thank God we got Dolly Val out in time. At least we saved her and the foals."

Ted glanced away before he said, "Yes, we saved your horse, Jimmy." He sounded irritated, but what did I care what people thought about my passion for my prize mare?

"You're sure it's safe here?" I asked.

"We've been over this. No one comes here, Jimmy. The old church is fenced, the road is chained, and the public stays by Maple Lake and the bridle trails. No one comes over the hill to the farm; no one can get here from the road unless they climb a bluff on foot through god-awful brush. Who would do that? Who's gonna come? Even if they do, what do they find? A farm and a few horses, looks like private property, who cares? Our friends at the FPD sure ain't gonna say nothing, they're no *chiacchioron'*—they'd get in trouble for letting us use the place."

"The bosses like this place too. Already making plans for the clubhouse and barn to hide stuff, a need for that turns up. Place for private meetings too, you know how to get in. Now we're out here, opens up other opportunities," I said.

I looked at the big tree in the yard. I remembered Al saying he wished he could retire, but he never really got out. I was sick a the business too and just wanted to spend time with my horses for whatever years I had left.

I shook my head and heaved a long breath. "So now we got the best stock out here, what's the plan for the ranch?" I asked, without looking at Ted.

"Gimme the go-ahead, Jimmy, I'll sell the place for you. Should get a nice profit. You won't be needing it no more."

I'd have to figure out how to split the profits and keep everyone happy. They didn't have to know all the details. The beginning of the end…but Ted was right.

"Sell it, Ted."

## Chapter 7
### Late Summer 1958

Barbaro dug his toes into the rim of the tire and grasped the rope hanging from a branch of the big old cottonwood tree that shaded our farmyard. He never sat on the tire like a normal kid. He dumped himself lots of times, but he never learned. The tire swerved, but that wasn't enough. He had to throw his body around to make it wobble more.

"Pull up your suspender strap and roll up your jeans," I said. I expected him to ignore his older sister, and he did.

I shook my head and concentrated on the fishing reel I was trying to untangle. Uncle Teddy had promised to show me where he fished if I was ready before dawn, so I had to get it done. On our own, us kids didn't get many bites. I'd been waiting all summer to find out Uncle Teddy's secrets. Summer was almost over.

Barbaro must have read my mind. "I'm glad Uncle Teddy moved into the chicken coop, Jemma. Now Mamma and Papá sleep downstairs. I only have to share with Angelo and Nello."

I laughed. "I hope you didn't say that to anyone. They'd get the wrong idea. It's not a chicken coop. It's a chicken *house*, and there's been no chickens in it for years and years. Uncle Teddy makes more than toys for you in his workshop. He fixed the place up real nice so he and Auntie can sleep there and give us more room in the house. In fact, I wish I could sleep there—it's cool at night, unlike under our hot roof."

We were cramped in our little farmhouse with Uncle Teddy and Aunt Chickie living with us, and that was most of the time. When it got cold again they'd have to move back into the big house, which was a *small* house. We'd all have to sleep in the two large upstairs rooms again, Mamma and Papá and all five of us kids. Angelo and Nello especially hated sleeping in the kids' room, now the twins finished high school and considered themselves grown men.

Mamma always grumbled about too many mouths to feed and too little money despite all the strong, healthy men in our house. Papá had his own business. He was away for long hours and looked worried lately. The twins helped Papá sometimes, but more often they were off with friends.

Uncle Teddy, Papá's brother, was what Angelo called a free spirit. We couldn't depend on him, but he was a lot of fun to be around, and I guess we owed him because he found the farm for us to live when Papá couldn't make the rent payments. Aunt Chickie didn't help unless Mamma got upset and laid down the law, which never lasted long. So it fell on me to help Mamma.

"Aunt Chickie lives in a chicken coop," Barbaro sang over and over until I wanted to belt him.

Sitting on a log under the big cottonwood tree, well away from Barbaro's swing, I unwound some line from the reel until I couldn't get past a knotted mess. I pulled up loops, hoping to find one that would free the tangle. It took a lot of concentration. I worked carefully, hoping to finish before the mosquitoes found us.

Barbaro smashed the tire against the side of the tree, startling me, and not just me but a robin who flew off with an angry cry.

"Where's Papá?" Barbaro asked, apparently unfazed by the thud that made me drop the knot and lose my place.

Bobby, as everyone except Mamma and Papá called my kid brother, was even more annoying than most nine year olds. I know I wasn't such a pest when I was his age four years ago. I growled at him and picked up the mass of loops in my lap again. "Today's Friday, isn't it," I answered.

"Yeah, so?"

"Well then, you know where Papá is, Bobby. Every Friday he heads to Polka Dot's. We won't see him tonight, and you wouldn't want to if you did. He won't be fit for talking to." I sighed, frustrated that the knot wouldn't loosen.

"Oh. Yeah. Friday." He rearranged his toes, trying to straighten the arc of the swing, and slipped, catching himself just in time. "Well, where's Nello then? He's not home either."

"You know the answer to that too."

"I do?"

"Of course you do. Where do you think Nello gets the money to take some fancy girl out on Saturday night? He goes out to Polka Dot's, hides in a corner until Papá falls asleep across the bar, sneaks a few bills out of his pocket, and comes home bragging. Nello will be along once his pocket's full enough. Shouldn't be long after dark."

Bobby dropped off the tire, ignored the dust on his butt, grabbed the tire with both hands, and threw it as hard as he could, trying to make it go higher each time. I knew what would happen next: he would become distracted and the tire would crash into him, knocking him off his feet, and with luck he'd only go screaming into the house with minor scrapes and bruises. "Mamma said don't do that," I said.

He ignored me. "Nello sure likes his girls," he said. "Patsy, Patsy, Pudding Pie. But there'll be a new one by and by," he singsonged. "Hey, that's a good song isn't it? Don't I make up good songs? Hey! Look at this!" He bent over the grass to pick up a huge black beetle. The tire on its return hit him in the temple and he went sprawling.

He jumped up right away. "It doesn't hurt," he said, but he was sniffling, his eyes shiny, and he rubbed a goose egg on the side of his forehead.

He was okay, just the wind knocked out of him. "Bobby, you do the same thing over and over and it always gets you. When are you going to learn? Go to the house so Mamma can put some ice on that."

He ignored me. The beetle was still in his hand by some miracle, and he came over to show me. "This is going to be fun. Watch," he said. Holding the beetle upside down, legs squirming in the air, he plucked off one of the legs. "Beetles don't jump when you do that. You can just keep pulling another leg off until they're all gone."

"Ick! Something's wrong with you, Bobby. I can hardly wait until you grow up," I said. I set down the still-tangled reel, left him standing there with the legless beetle, and headed for the barn. Maybe I'd have better luck with the reel after I finished my chores.

Chores! I had more than my share: housework, vegetable garden, and sometimes stable work too. The twins were off doing whatever boys did after finishing high school. No one ever told me what was so important they couldn't help at home. That's just the way it was in Italian families. It wouldn't be so bad if I got any thanks for my efforts, but my work was never good enough to please Mamma.

Our barn was not like the tall red ones on many old farms. Ours was big and low and open with stalls on one end, a hard-packed dirt floor, metal walls, and a metal roof. Uncle Teddy said it was built to store equipment when the golf course was open, with a few stalls on the end for forest rangers' horses. Now all that was in it was Baby and a rusty old car the twins were fixing up.

Uncle Teddy usually took care of Baby. She was here when we moved to the farm. He said she was once a racehorse and had belonged to a friend who died a couple of years ago. There was no one to care for her anymore, so we did. I didn't care where she came from—I was crazy about her.

I let Uncle Teddy think he conned me, but there was little I loved to do more than take care of Baby. If I told him I wanted to do it anyway, I'd lose my bargaining power. Today we made a trade: he'd take me to his best fishing place tomorrow if I did the stable chores all weekend.

Inside the barn it was a little cooler but really stuffy, and Baby's head hung over her stall door. She usually threw her head up and nickered at me when I came in, but today she just drooped with her eyes shut. She needed air and exercise.

I lifted the light halter from a hook on the wall, entered her stall, rubbed her forelock, and slipped on the halter. I led her outside to the paddock and turned her loose. Instead of trotting around the fence like she usually did, she drifted over to the shade.

I returned to the barn for the wheelbarrow, behind stacked bales of straw and hay. The dim, empty area seemed enormous and spooky. I shouldn't be afraid of an empty space, but it reminded me of the blind end of the Gully, where snakes and maybe worse things rustled but couldn't be seen. Anything could be hiding in the shadows.

I peered into the gloom. My ears tingled as I listened for the whistled melody I sometimes heard. Today there was only silence.

I took the wheelbarrow into Baby's stall. When I had it filled with old bedding, I pushed it across the paddock to the manure pile. Our paddock was big with a few trees. Uncle Teddy said at one time there were more horses here. Some were very expensive and needed shade trees to protect them.

I dumped the wheelbarrow and then picked up a can beside the pile. The warm compost was alive with squirming worms. Holding my nose, I dug some for tomorrow's fishing and then went back in the barn to lay fresh bedding, fill the water trough, and put out Baby's feed.

With summer almost over, I wanted to sneak away, ride the trails on Baby, climb a tree, or lay under one on an old blanket in the woods with one of the romance books I had recently discovered…or a favorite horse story. Escape chores!

But Mamma didn't want me to go off alone anymore. She wanted one of the twins to go with me, and they were never around or willing to do that. Mamma used to let me go off by myself when we first moved here, but she read something in the paper and now said the woods were dangerous.

I wish she hadn't told me that. I'd never been scared to walk or ride alone—I loved the woods. But I did get jumpy near the old clubhouse and in the barn. Those places were fine in the daytime, but after dark they felt kind of creepy.

And then, sometimes in my bed at night with the windows open, I would wake up and hear voices, whistling, or metal clanking, or I would see lights through the trees.

Papá said it was bugs hitting the screen, but he looked at Mamma and she turned her back. They must have another secret, like why I shouldn't ride in the woods alone and where Uncle Teddy found his fish. Well, if they wanted to keep secrets, I figured it was okay for me to have secrets, too. I didn't always obey Mamma about the woods.

Now I circled behind the stacks of hay and straw bales. Something whizzed past my ear and I cried out, but it was only a barn swallow. I should have been used to them by now. "Damn birds," I mumbled. Then I heard rustling from behind the hay and that *was* alarming.

I peered into the dim barn, then back at the bales. My imagination was getting to me. A mouse or one of those pesky chipmunks. But…

I heard what sounded like hushed breathing. A lump formed in my throat. Too frightened to call out, I stared and listened. Something leaped out from the pile toward me and shouted, "Boo!"

"My God, Bobby!" I said, my heart pumping hard and fast. "Did you have to do that?"

He laughed, stomping his feet and dancing in a circle, but when his laughter died he got serious. "Did you ever see anything out here, Jemma?"

"What do you mean, see anything? Here in the barn?"

"I don't know. Not just in the barn, but in the yard or in the trees. Just imagine something maybe. Something big and ugly, with sharp claws and yellow eyes that glow at you from the dark. Something like that?"

"No, silly. Did you?" I didn't want to frighten him, but he looked scared already so I let him talk.

"Out of the corner of my eye, maybe. From behind the straw where I just was."

"Well you were just there, and there was nothing back there."

"Not now, but it comes after dark."

"What does it look like? What you just said?"

"I didn't see no face—I don't think it had one."

"How could it not have a face?"

"I swear, Jemma! No face! Just a big raggy hole where a face should be. It doesn't roar or talk, just whistles."

"Oh shush! You're too big to be seeing monsters anymore."

"Maybe I'm not so big, Jemma. I swear it almost got me one time."

"You've seen it more than once?"

"I don't come here after dark anymore. Mamma says not to."

I giggled and tried to distract him. "'Fraidy cat!"

"Am not!"

"Are too!"

That went on for a while and Bobby seemed to forget his fear. I didn't tell him about my experiences. He was frightened enough.

I wondered if my family was involved in something they wanted to hide. Or if someone else was out here? Was it dangerous? How could I find out? Mamma, Papá, and the twins refused to tell me anything.

Maybe Uncle Teddy would tell me tomorrow.

As Barbaro and I walked across the yard toward the house, in the growing dimness of dusk, I told him, "You come get me right away, Bobby, you ever see anything like that again. We'll look together."

## Chapter 8

Late last night the phone ringing woke me up. I heard Papá shuffle out of his bedroom downstairs and into the hallway to answer it. Lucia just grumbled and turned over, but I got out of bed and hid at the top of the stairs to listen.

Papá didn't say much, only, "Hold the line, I'll get Teodoro." Then he hurried into his bedroom and when he passed the bottom of the stairs half a minute later he had his pants and shoes on and he ran out.

Soon Papá came back with Uncle Teddy. He listened to whoever was on the phone, but I heard him say, "raid," and "how many slots?", and "how many trucks, Mickey?", and "okay, right away; have them wait on the road." Then he rushed out.

I went to the window that looked over the farmyard. I saw Uncle Teddy run up our lane, and I heard Papá come upstairs to wake up the twins. "Quietly!" he said, and then they all followed Uncle Teddy.

Three sets of lights showed through the trees from 107th Street. They didn't move at first, but then they climbed the hill. About halfway here they turned toward the old, deserted clubhouse and I saw red taillights. Heavy engines roared in the crisp night air, and after the engines shut down I heard other sounds, rattling and banging and now and then shouts of: "Watch out!" "Not there!" "The last one!" "Move up!"

It wasn't the first time this happened. And, it meant Uncle Teddy wouldn't be back until nearly daylight. Then the trucks would pay us another midnight visit a few days later, and the whole business would happen in reverse.

I wasn't allowed to ask questions. It had something to do with why we lived here and how Uncle Teddy got money, even though he was always home and we didn't see him do any work...unless you count selling his fish.

But last night busted up my hopes, and I knew our fishing trip was ruined. This morning I was in a mood and more determined than ever to find out what my family was keeping from me.

I wasn't happy. Uncle Teddy was supposed to rescue me from Mamma before she gave me work to do. I wished I got along better with Mamma, but I was sick of her criticizing me. She was always busy, never time to talk to me, only to give me work to do and to tell me I did everything wrong. I had precious few moments to do things I wanted to do, since on top of chores I had to keep an eye on Lucia and Bobby.

Papá was away working, and the twins only showed up to eat, sleep, and get their clothes washed, which I got stuck ironing. Angelo had his head in a book all the time, studying to be a policeman. He was short, thin, and didn't talk much, not what you'd expect for a cop, let alone a Chicago cop, so I wondered if the police would take him. Aniello, we called him Nello, only thought about building muscles and impressing girls.

Lucia was three years older than me but couldn't be left to do things by herself. People called her "slow." She sat with the little kids at school and the teacher put her in the back of the room to color most of the time. I loved Lucia maybe better than anyone, but she wasn't much help.

Bobby, he was a kid and spoiled to boot.

So that left me. It was no wonder I tried to run off to the woods when I could with Baby, a blanket, and a book.

When Uncle Teddy finally walked into our kitchen this morning, I was sitting at the big wooden table in the middle of the room. I had left my fishing gear in front of the porch door where he had to stumble on it. I was wearing rolled-up jeans, an old blouse, and my floppy sun hat tied under my chin. I pointed at the clock on the kitchen wall. It was after 11 A.M.

He didn't say anything. He poured coffee from the percolator Mamma always left on the stove, found a pastry in the breadbox, and pretended not to see me. I exaggerated a sad, pleading look to make him feel guilty—and kept my eyes on him until he gave in.

He ate his pastry over the washboard sink, brushed crumbs off his hands, came over to the table, flicked the brim of my hat, and said, "I guess you still want to go fishing."

Mamma was resting, not there to tell me no, and so we went, not according to the original plan, but better than not at all. Maybe he felt guilty. I figured I might be able to coax some secrets out of him.

We walked down to 107th Street, crossed the road, went around the west end of the slough and along the earthen dam to the far side. There was no road there and few fishermen wanted to drag their equipment so far. We had the place to ourselves. Uncle Teddy stopped where some tree branches hung out over the water. We baited our hooks and threw out our lines.

"Not too far, sweetheart," Uncle Teddy cautioned. "There's a deep spot a few feet out. Fish gather there because it's cooler."

I thought it must have been where they removed some dirt when they built the dam.

We relaxed in the shade on the soft grass. Uncle Teddy usually came home with enough fish to feed not only our family but to sell to neighbors for beer money. However, fish liked to sleep in the middle of the day, so we could be wasting our time. But, I knew his secret place now, and I could always come here again. I hoped to learn more secrets and I had my questions ready.

"How come we get to live out here? The kids at school live in neighborhoods or on farms, not out in the woods."

He grinned. "Because we're special. You got to know somebody to get to live at a place like this—you got to have friends in the right places. You like it here, no?"

The birds were singing in the trees. I heard a cardinal, and then a big glob of bird poop fell right on my hand.

I wrinkled my nose and wiped my hand in the grass, then on my jeans. "I was going to say I *love* it here, until that bird let loose," I said. Uncle Teddy roared with laughter.

It felt good to hear him laugh and know I was the cause of it. Maybe there was something I could do right after all, no matter what Mamma thought about me. Plus, now I had him laughing, it might loosen his tongue.

"There are so many places to go," I said. "We have Baby, and we hunt and fish, take a rowboat out on Maple Lake, sneak into the Gully across the canal. It's the best place in the world. We don't own it though, we're only staying here, right?"

"Right. The forest preserves own it. But don't tell nobody about going in the canyon or hunting—the rangers make an exception for us." He pulled a handkerchief from his pocket, wet it in the water, and handed it to me to finish cleaning my hand.

"I wish we could own it and stay here forever. But why does the forest preserves have the farm and clubhouse? It's all closed down."

"Yes, and that's why we live here. Someone has to keep an eye on the place."

"How did that get to be us?"

He narrowed his eyes. "You got a lot of questions today." He reeled up a little line. I finished with his handkerchief, frowned, and looked around for a place to put it. I finally decided on the fish bucket and dropped it in using two fingers.

"I used to run a stable for a man who raised racehorses," he said. "He kept them here a while, until he died, a year or more before we moved here."

"So then we got to move here after he died? What happened to all the horses?"

"Only a few were left. I sold them and gave the money to his family."

"Is that where Baby came from?"

"You're pretty smart. Yes, Jimmy was nuts about that horse, and I just couldn't let her go."

"She *is* special, I think." I played with my pole for a while and then said, "Was that his family making all that noise last night? I got up and there were trucks by the clubhouse."

He looked away, which made me think he was fudging the truth, like Barbaro does when he's hiding something. "Just some friends, getting together."

"Why do they come in the middle of the night? Are they Papá's friends or yours?"

"Drop it, Jemma." He leaned forward and stared into my eyes. "Just some friends. We're keeping something for them for a few days. You stay away from there until I tell you. Promise?"

Even without his tough words, I knew unexplained comings and goings were forbidden subjects, so I opened another one. "I promise. But why are that golf course and the big clubhouse closed down? Why don't they still use those?"

"Back during the war, they built a big research laboratory right next to it. It was top secret. They were learning how to split the atom, which led to bombs they made out west. You learned about World War II and the atomic bomb in school yet?"

"A little bit. But why did they close the golf course?"

"The lab was a secret, I told you. They didn't want people walking around, looking over the fence, seeing all them guards, and asking what's going on."

*Secrets again, even before we came out here. This place grew secrets like weeds.*

"Did you ever see anything scary out here? Barbaro's been seeing monsters, he says."

His head jerked up, and his eyes stayed on mine. "Bobby? What kind of monsters?"

"Something with glowing eyes and no face, he says."

"That's crazy," he said. He laughed but looked away again. I was sure there was more he wasn't saying.

"Well, I never saw nothing like that, but I did see other stuff," I said, showing off a little.

"What other stuff?"

"Like lights in the forest during the night. Like sounds… Someone rustling around, horses nickering, leather creaking. Someone whistling a tune. Like a crowd cheering or a loud party. The sounds are real faint, but that's what it sounds like, a crowd or a party."

He looked a little upset, almost angry. "Lights play tricks, or someone could be out there with a flashlight. And you're probably hearing Baby from the barn and the wind through the trees or something going by on 107th Street. You know how sound travels at night."

I shook my head. "I don't think so."

My bobber jerked suddenly and disappeared under the water, the line grew tight, and my pole bent. At last! Uncle Teddy told me everything to do until the fish was landed, as if I needed instruction and had never caught a fish before. But we grinned at each other.

"Nice catch and good work," he said, holding up what looked like a three-pound bass before putting it in the bucket. Not record size, but pretty good for Saganashkee Slough.

We settled down again and I recast my line. "Why doesn't Mamma want us to go out into the forests anymore? When we first moved here it was okay."

He was quiet a long time, convincing me he knew the answer but was trying to figure out what he should tell me. We had plenty of time so I just waited him out.

"At first she didn't know how close we was to where they found those dead girls," he said at last. "She didn't tell you 'cause she thought you were too young to know about that. She just don't want you to go out there, since they found those girls, and those three boys before that in other forest preserves. She's afraid you'll run into some bad man out there."

It was my turn to think things over. Mamma didn't want me to leave the farmyard and didn't even want me alone with Uncle Teddy, but we snuck out today anyway. I would be in for it when I got home.

"A girl at school, she said girls have to worry about rape. What's rape?"

He looked at me long and hard. His eyes were kind of funny-like. His tongue worked at the corner of his mouth.

Finally he said, "There are men, sick men. They touch girls in private places. It makes them excited and then they hurt the girls."

He put his hand on my leg.

I looked at his hand. "Is that what happened to the girls that got killed? But what about those boys? It happens to boys too?"

He took his hand away and shook his head.

"I really don't think your Mamma wants me to talk to you about this. Old-country women like your Mamma just want to do what it takes to keep it from happening, they don't like to talk about it."

"I'm not a baby, Uncle Teddy—I'm going to high school in a few weeks. I know about sex and babies. I just didn't know about the rape part."

His face looked red even though we weren't in the sun, and his eyes still looked strange before he turned his head.

"We know you're not a baby. In fact, we're sick of people saying how mature you are for your age. You'd think you were twenty the way people talk." His voice sounded rough. "We have to remind ourselves sometimes you *are* still a child. We worry about you because that sort of thing, seeming older when you're not, can get you in trouble.

"We should be getting home."

I didn't think he really wanted to leave yet; he just wanted to stop my questions. I could see from the set of his jaw and the way he looked out on the water. Sharing secrets was over.

But I wasn't a child anymore. I longed to feel like the older girls in the teen romance books I read. I lay back on the grass so Uncle Teddy wouldn't see my hot face as I remembered reading and resting on an old blanket in my secret clearing on a hot sunny day with dragonflies buzzing by and touching myself through my clothes in hot, throbbing places. I had my own secrets.

I knew what Uncle Teddy meant about people mistaking me for older, and I knew what it felt like to fall in love and to be loved too.

# Chapter 9

"*Maron'!* Get out of here!" I yelled, slapping wildly at the insects that whined around me. I usually worked in the garden in the afternoon, but this Sunday I wanted to finish my chores before Mass so I could disappear after.

By now, the spinach was done and there were only side heads of broccoli. A few stunted cucumbers and zucchini trailed on the ground, but the rest of our large garden behind the house was still growing.

I moved through the neat rows and filled colanders with Italian plum tomatoes and green and banana peppers. I lugged them to the kitchen table. I returned for the more time-consuming, thick pods of borlotti and cannellini beans and I snipped the tops off the traditional herbs with scissors—oregano, Italian basil, parsley, and rosemary—before they turned to flowers. Later I'd tie them into bundles to hang on the porch to dry. The onions and garlic would stay in the ground for now.

The twins helped Papá dig and plant the garden, and then they never went near it again. Papá kept it weeded and watered, but it was up to me to pick the vegetables. That took at least an hour every day.

Lucia washed everything for Mamma to can. She slowly shelled the beans and cleaned each vegetable carefully and thoroughly. The happiness on her face told us how much she wanted to be useful.

The truth was, I really didn't mind the garden work, although I told Mamma I hated it. The garden was peaceful and left me time to think.

While I picked the tedious beans, I thought about what Uncle Teddy told me yesterday.

While I was washing up in the kitchen after we got home, Uncle Teddy pulled Papá aside. They glanced at me and then whispered. All I could hear was, "When will they pick up...?" and then, "...something else out there..." They both looked worried, and then Papá's voice got a little louder and he said, "That useless kid brother never showed up...," before Uncle Teddy shushed him.

I pretended I couldn't hear them. They thought it had nothing to do with me, but I wasn't naive. Italian families, especially Sicilian families like ours, sometimes did jobs for mobsters. Doing "favors," it was called. To turn down a relative or a friend who asked for a "favor" could be dangerous. But we didn't talk about it.

So I was faking it yesterday when I pretended I didn't have a clue what was going on. I suspected what I saw during the night might not be legal. But who were they doing favors for, and what were they doing?

Papá had given that midnight phone call to Uncle Teddy. People said Uncle Teddy was a freeloader, but he was getting money somewhere, maybe through friends. I was willing to bet the man who used to raise horses here was a mobster, and Uncle Teddy was in charge of the nighttime favors.

Papá's business made deliveries for grocery stores and beverage companies, and he had trucks. Trucks came to the clubhouse during the night. Were they Papá's? What about Angelo and Nello? I could believe Nello was involved in something illegal, but Angelo? Angelo wanted to be a policeman. That didn't fit. But both twins went out that night.

The papers and television said mobsters were violent and killed people. But no one was nicer than Uncle Teddy, except maybe Angelo. You know what Uncle Teddy does when he has money? He collects little metal cars, Matchbox cars, and shows them to us. That's only one of the things that makes kids like him. I couldn't believe he'd be violent, ever.

Then I remembered the strange look on his face when he was talking about what bad men do to young girls and boys. I'm not stupid. I can tell when people are hiding something. But I refused to think about that.

I couldn't make sense of what he told me yesterday. I'd have to keep my eyes and ears open like I'd been doing.

I piled up the full colanders and headed to the kitchen.

~~~

The whole family was ready for Mass, but Angelo had to find Barbaro, who was hiding, playing a prank to make us late. Barbaro always had to be dragged to church, whining the whole way. We didn't get to St. James at Sag Bridge until the ushers were ringing the church bells, so I had to skip my usual walk through the cemetery.

I liked to read the gravestones and make up a life and family based on nothing but names and dates, especially the oldest stones with blurred carvings at the graves of children. Sometimes I ended up running into the church when the parishioners were already singing.

This morning, Barbaro played with the hat clip on the back of the pew. When he let go of it, it made a metallic snap and people sitting nearby jumped. Papá swatted the side of Barbaro's head and he threw himself back on the bench and pouted.

I love St. James Church and I love God, but the Latin responses of the Mass, our priest's boring sermon, the mumbling, the heat, and the sitting so long lulled me. My mind drifted. I suppose I wasn't much more respectful than Barbaro today, since my thoughts weren't proper for church.

What bothered me was that some things about Baby didn't make sense. If all the other horses were sold, why did Uncle Teddy keep Baby? If she was the best, wouldn't he have gotten the most money for her and sold her too? And why did they keep a racehorse in the middle of the forest? I had been reading horse stories since I was eight years old. I knew racehorses needed exercise and tracks to run on. There was nothing like that out here.

When we first moved to the farm I couldn't believe I had my very own horse. Well, she wasn't mine exactly, but I could ride her whenever I wanted. I had read *The Black Stallion* over and over until the pages started falling out. I could almost feel what it was like to jump on the bare back of the Black and let him run himself out on the island, all alone.

I rode Baby instead and got that warm and tingly feeling that would take over my brain until I couldn't think of anything else or stop the thinking. Even sitting here in church now I got that pressing feeling between my legs.

This summer I started reading books older girls read. Angelo brought me to the library every two weeks and I filled my bag with teen romance books by Rosamond DuJardin and Janet Lambert. Then I discovered *Jane Eyre* and *Gone with the Wind*. Books filled all my time that wasn't spent doing chores. None of my school friends lived nearby, so my only friends during the summer were books, and I'm afraid they turned me into a dreamer.

When my chores were done, I'd ride Baby to my favorite grassy place, hidden in a ring of woods. I'd let Baby graze, and I'd lay in the shade of a tree on an old blanket and read and read.

On rainy days, I'd go to a corner of our enclosed front porch, where Papá has a portable record player and a record collection. I'd close my eyes and dream, casting myself in favorite scenes from books as the music played: the stirring hoofbeats of the *William Tell Overture*, the playful melodies from *Peter and the Wolf*, the dramatic *1812 Overture*, the romantic *New World Symphony*, and sometimes tragic arias from Papá's operas with Mario Lanza and the Great Caruso.

Books and music *were* my best friends, until Petey...

And that brought me to my own secret that I had pushed out of my mind while trying to solve family secrets.

One afternoon, soon after school let out for the summer, Baby and I were in my special place. I looked up from my book and there he was, a big, tall, muscular man, watching me from the edge of the trees. At first I was scared and jumped up. But then he grinned—he had the best grin— and I recognized him from school and relaxed. He had always treated me nice, although I *did* wonder what he was doing in the woods. Soon the question didn't matter.

He walked over, sat on my blanket, and pulled up his knees. "What are you reading?" he asked, patting the blanket beside him.

I was embarrassed to tell him at first, but I sat back down across from him. Petey has a way of entertaining the answers out of me. It wasn't long until we were talking and laughing. Sitting with him, my heart beat faster, and I'm sure my face was red, but the longer we talked the easier it got.

When he put his hand on my knee, oh! I shivered and stammered and could hardly think of anything to say. I'm sure he noticed but he pretended not to. He just talked on and on and I didn't have to say a word.

He was so...well, beautiful. His thick, curly, dark hair falling over his forehead, his dreamy dark eyes, the ghost of a beard. He made the twins seem like boys still. His voice was soft, and he looked in my eyes like he was interested in what I thought and did, and he made me laugh. His face gave the impression he was hiding something amusing.

"We shouldn't tell anyone about this," he said before he left. "People might get the wrong idea because I'm so much older than you."

He asked when I could get away again and I told him.

If I'm late, he's never angry, only happy to see me. He gave me a copy of *Wuthering Heights* once, because I told him I wanted to read it. One day he brought his guitar and did an impersonation of Elvis. I clapped and laughed. He was so good.

"You should do that on stage," I told him. I was surprised when he told me he did just that. He was joking, of course, since he worked at my school.

"Now that you've graduated, I won't see you at school every day," he said recently. "Are you looking forward to high school?"

"I was," I said. "I'm ready to make new friends and learn new subjects. There's only two girls and one boy my age at our one-room school. But now I'm afraid I won't get to see you."

"Don't worry. Leave that up to me. Just be sure your parents don't find out. Your father might try to stop us."

It's a good thing I trusted him not to go too far because I didn't trust myself. He liked to touch me, but never where he shouldn't, just put an arm on my shoulder or held my hand. His hands were big and rough, but his touch was gentle. It made me feel weak and I couldn't think straight.

He did kiss me on the lips ever so softly the last time we met. I can still feel it if I close my eyes. He touched my cheek afterward and said I was beautiful.

I never thought I was beautiful. I have a horse face or a sort of man-like look and too much hair. But people say I have a great figure, and, as Uncle Teddy said, I'm mature for my age. The only thing I know I'm good at is making people laugh, so I made Petey laugh too.

I shouldn't have been thinking about Petey in church, but once his face was in my mind I couldn't stop. I kept seeing the way his tongue licks slowly around his half-smiling lips and my face got warm.

Nello poked me. It was time to get in line for Communion.

# Chapter 10

I was upset with Lucia.

I had an Italian glass barrette, a beautiful thing with tiny yellow, pink, and purple flowers in a glass band. Papá's brother bought it for me in Italy. I kept it on the dresser by my hand mirror, but it wasn't there now.

I searched everywhere, until I noticed Lucia. She usually made herself sleepy at bedtime by clutching Nana, a stuffed dog from her favorite movie, *Peter Pan*, while looking at picture books or magazines. Last night she was sitting on the edge of the bed, staring at the floor, and peeking at me out of the corner of her eye.

*Guilty*, I thought.

"Lucia," I said. "Do you know where my barrette is?"

"No," she said, in a tiny voice, head down, hiding her face. Lucia didn't lie very often, but a muscle in her jaw twitched, a dead giveaway.

"Let me see your box," I demanded.

"No," she said again. She lifted her head and met my eyes defiantly.

I grabbed her arm and pulled her from the bed. "Get your box or I'll get it myself."

She sniffled, then in slow motion she got on her knees, fished under the bed, and dragged out a small wooden box with a rounded top and metal bands like a pirate chest.

Her collection of treasures seemed useless to me: rocks, bits of snakeskin, pictures cut from magazines, Little Golden Books *Perky Little Puppy*. She did have a beautiful pale-blue, crystal rosary, also a gift from Papá's brother. She often took it out and held it, rubbing her fingers over the beads and mumbling.

And there was my barrette. I snatched it out, gave Lucia a dirty look, and left her box lying open on the floor for her to put away. I took a handkerchief from my dresser, wrapped my barrette in it, and put it in my top drawer.

Still on her knees, Lucia touched some of the items in her box and smiled. She closed the box carefully, fastened its latch, and pushed it back under the bed. She looked at me hopefully, but I frowned, so she climbed onto the mattress, clutched Nana, and rolled onto her side to face the wall, as far from my place in the bed as she could get.

When Papá and Mamma moved to the downstairs bedroom, the boys moved into their old room, and Lucia and I had a big room to ourselves. Now, when Barbaro wet the bed, the twins had to take care of it and we didn't have to smell his pee all night. But Lucia and I had only one large bed to share.

The bed sat lengthwise against the only interior wall, so Lucia could roll against the wall and not fall out of bed. The mattress was old and lumpy and sagged in the middle. We often slid into each other during the night. On a hot night, we poked each other. On chilly nights we pretended to be annoyed but huddled for warmth.

We were in for a poking night, regardless of the temperature.

After Lucia fell asleep, I felt guilty about how I treated her. She was the first to notice and comfort one of us if we were upset. She never cried, just looked at us with big sad eyes. Like a six-year-old child, not her sixteen years, she meant no harm. She was just attracted to my barrette. I was willing to bet she wanted to keep it safe.

I was expected to watch her when I was home, and I loved her like the sweet, innocent child she seemed to be. I defended her when people called her a retard. Because she didn't go shopping with us, I would always buy a surprise for her. Sometimes we would just goof off and she made us laugh with her silly dances. But then other times she'd get careless and neglect her personal hygiene or move my things, and I'd be angry with her. I hoped she knew I didn't mean it.

Before long she rolled against me in her sleep, and I let her stay there.

I didn't much like touching, but I wasn't mad anymore. I was glad she was my sister and I let her be.

Later I had a dream, one of those nonsense dreams about exploring a house with rooms that made no sense and with dirt floors and walls of rough stone. I woke up when Lucia threw out her arm and hit me on the side of my head.

"Ouch!" I yelled.

Bright rays of moonlight flowed through our windows. Lucia was on her back, her eyes wide open, staring at the ceiling with her face and her body as still as death. Her chest rose and fell silently. Her lips were parted and her jaw sagged a little. She didn't blink, not once.

I sat up, called her name, and shook her, but she didn't look at me or say anything. I should have gotten Papá and Mamma, but I hesitated. Lucia had had fits before, but she wasn't biting her tongue; in fact, her face was relaxed. She seemed happy and smiled a little.

The skin around her throat tightened, and a deep voice, a man's voice, came out. "*Calma, bambina,*" she said, the eerie-sounding words echoing in our big quiet room.

Then in her soft, normal, serious voice she said, "I will, I promise."

After a pause, the man's voice came again. "It's Mickey! '*Uarda la ciunca!*"

And again in her normal voice, "I'll be very careful. She won't get hurt."

Lucia's face relaxed, her eyes closed, she rolled onto her side and curled against me, peacefully asleep.

After holding her for a moment, I turned over to think. What was she talking about, and what had happened?

Frightened, I didn't know what to do. If she had had a seizure, she seemed fine now. I recognized the Italian words she said, but they were not words we used. They seemed to be a warning.

Should I wake Mamma or Papá? It was over now, and they would only find Lucia sleeping. Lucia probably wouldn't remember anything. They wouldn't believe me, or they would think Lucia was talking in her sleep. Wasn't that what had happened?

I rolled over again and hugged her tightly, rubbing my cheek against hers. My precious sister. Who would guard her if not me? She remained sleeping.

A vaguely familiar, whistled melody pierced the quiet night, followed by rustling leaves.

I slipped out of bed and went to the bedroom window. I searched every inch of the yard with my eyes. Nothing moved and the wind was still. Then, from the direction of the old clubhouse, I saw lights flicker through the trees. A glowing orb floated near the edge of the woods at the far side of the front yard. It was smaller than the moon and didn't throw any light past itself.

With the orb came other faint sounds, like the distant pounding of hooves, muted music, a crowd of excited people. Closer sounds…then whispers, indistinct. Then again faraway, the crack of metal striking something; a sharp cry; and a single, deep voice, but no clear words.

My heart pounding, I pulled my gaze from the glowing orb, searching for an explanation. Where the bluff dropped steeply toward 107th Street and Saganashkee Slough, a stocky man sat on a dark horse. The white shirt he wore and the white bandages wrapping the horse's front legs made them easy to see in the moonlight. Both man and horse were motionless. Before my eyes they faded to nothing, as did the strange light and sounds—the last sound to be heard was the same whistled melody that first caught my attention.

Then all was silent again. And only the moon cast its glow over the now-empty farmyard.

I stayed at the window for about an hour, shivering, unable to sleep, my mind replaying the incident, but nothing else happened.

I should have been terrified, but I wasn't. Oh, the light and sounds were frightening enough, but the strange voice that came from Lucia, the man on the horse, left an impression of someone watching over us, someone protecting us from some unknown danger. Could I trust that feeling, or was it part of the illusion to make me relax and allow evil in? One of the boys at school once said young children were "susceptible to possession," when we were talking at recess about ghosts and devils. Lucia was like a young child; was that what happened to her?

I could no longer pretend what was happening on our farm could be explained only by activities my family was involved in. The man on the horse was not Uncle Teddy, no one was moving about our house, and I was sure everyone was asleep.

I was a lonely girl, but never more lonely than during that hour. Who could I turn to? Who might believe me? I didn't know what to do. At last I decided that in the morning I would tell Angelo what happened and let him decide.

What if Angelo didn't believe me? What should I do?

No one else in my family would do anything. I had no close friends except Petey. I wanted to tell him. He would believe me, but it could be days before I saw him again. And what could he do? If he came here to our farm, Papá might guess about us and stop me from meeting him.

The sky turned cloudy and the moon disappeared, taking its light with it. I went back to bed and curled myself around Lucia. The contact comforted me for a while. Then Lucia rolled away, and I got cold.

I turned my back to Lucia, wrapped my arms around my chest, and pretended it was Petey, not Lucia, who slept next to me. After much tossing and turning, I fell asleep at last just as the darkness was starting to fade.

~ ~ ~

Angelo had been in a hurry when he came down to the kitchen for coffee, but I whispered to him, "Meet me in the barn—it's important." I ran out there to wait.

"What is it?" Angelo said, entering the barn while buttoning his shirt. "I'm meeting friends at the quarries. They're out there already. I have to find my swimsuit and pick up Tony—and I'm late."

I wondered how he and his friends arranged to be off on a workday, unless they all grew up spoiled like boys in other Italian families, who years later expected their wives to spoil them too.

Baby rested her head on my shoulder and I stroked her as I told him about Lucia and what I saw and heard from the window. Angelo just shook his head. "My little dreamer, *patatina*," he said, as he patted my cheek. "If you got your head out of those romance books now and then you wouldn't imagine so much."

I pulled away from his hand. I took teasing from Angelo, but I'd take a swing at anyone else who called me "little potato." It was better than what he called Barbaro, though—*polpetto*, or "meatball."

"I wasn't dreaming," I insisted. "I got up and sat at the window. I was wide-awake. And I never saw Lucia like that before."

"You were dreaming when you woke up, half awake and half asleep. Lucia was the tail end of your dream; you know how they hang on before you're fully awake? Then you heard some ordinary noise and got up to go to the window and started to fall asleep again as you sat there. You imagined or dreamed again in that half-asleep state. Dreams sometimes feel so real you don't know if they happened or you imagined them."

I shook my head violently. "I didn't *imagine* anything, Angelo. I saw and heard what I saw and heard!"

"Then it must have been the ham radio guys out there on the clubhouse roof again." Just like everyone I'd been talking to the last few days, Angelo avoided looking in my eyes too.

"I know well enough what ham radios sound like, Angelo. It wasn't that. Besides, they always come on Friday and Saturday nights, never on Sunday, and not so late."

"Well, then call me if it happens again so I can see. I got to go."

He left me standing there, feeling from his rushing out that he knew something he didn't want to tell me. It was the same old thing. I was being kept out of the picture and not being taken seriously.

But Angelo was a grown man now, or at least almost. He didn't think what I saw was important. I was the kid here. I was supposed to be thinking about starting high school and my boyfriend, not about taking care of my family. I had to trust someone.

Maybe Angelo was right. Maybe I was seeing and hearing things that weren't really there but just in my dreams or imagination…

But even if the stuff in the farmyard was imagination, I was worried about Lucia.

I turned to Baby and rubbed my cheek against her face. I pulled away, looked into her gentle eyes, and scratched her forelock. "And who are you, *bambina?*" I said.

# Chapter 11

It was harder to see Petey once high school started. Some days were chilly, but mostly the fall had been warm and dry, even hot some days, and on those days it was hard to be in school when I'd rather be with Petey.

Petey came up with the idea, and I bribed Barbaro by promising to give him my two-headed snake. It wasn't much loss, as Ranger O'Malley had taken the ugly thing to check it out, and who knew if I'd ever get it back. But Barbaro didn't know that.

It worked this way: usually our grade school teacher picked up me and Barbaro at the bottom of our lane and took us to the one-room school, where I got on the high school bus. When the teacher came, Barbaro told her I was sick, and I hid in the woods and waited. Petey was conveniently "sick" from work and met me. It would soon get too cold to meet in the woods, but I trusted Petey would come up with another plan.

One day Petey had asked me to help him hide something.

"It's very important that no one find it and that it's protected from wet, heat, and freezing," he said, handing me a small, black plastic container.

I started to take the lid off but he grabbed it back. "Don't open it!" He hesitated before saying, "The film isn't developed and it'll be ruined if light hits it."

"Why are we hiding it?" I asked.

"Just do it, Jemma," he said.

I thought I knew why he involved me. He liked to think I was under his thumb and wanted me to prove it. He'd tested me like this before. So I went along.

At first I thought about taking it to the quarries, where the older kids swam in summer, but I couldn't think where to hide it there.

So instead I thought the Gully would be perfect. It was private, fenced, and you couldn't see the canyon until you got right up to it. So we went there, found a hole in the canyon wall, put the container inside, and wedged stones in front of it. Then we marked the spot by stacking some large rocks below.

That had been weeks ago, and today I was so angry with Petey. He had let me down and all I could think about was getting even, doing something just as bad to him. That film we hid was so important, he'd be in big trouble if he lost it. So I decided I would move it and not tell him where it was until he was nice to me again.

It was almost two miles to the Gully. I had counted on riding Baby, but when I got to the barn Uncle Teddy was there. He said I couldn't ride her that day and not to ask any questions. I pouted but it did no good, so I was in for a long walk. It took almost two hours to get the canister. Then, watching for snakes, I scattered the rocks we had left as a marker.

Now I would re-hide the container at the clubhouse.

The clubhouse was less than a quarter mile from our farm. Barbaro, Lucia, and I often played on the roof, throwing stones across the three ravines that met in front of the building. Every summer ham radio operators came, to tune in all over the world from the highest hill around. Either Papá or Angelo brought me and Barbaro to watch.

By the time I got to the clubhouse today it was almost hot. As usual, no one was there. I was a little nervous. What with Lucia's spell and Barbaro telling me about seeing glowing eyes, I was spooked about going inside that empty clubhouse. I didn't want to see things that weren't really there, although my head told me I should be more afraid of things that *were* there.

I gathered some stones, and went up the stairs. Although I stayed in open areas, I found myself jumping at nonsense: something at the corner of my eye, a chipmunk running across the floor, imagined voices or unexpected sounds. It was creepy, but I tried to ignore it. The place had always been safe. Why should today be any different?

On the roof, I walked along the patios and threw stones at the ravines.

I wished Barbaro saw the rock that hit the tree across the ravine, because he wouldn't believe me.

When the stones were gone, I went to a corner, pried a loose brick from the outer wall with a stick, slid the container into the hole, and put the brick back. From a distance no one would ever know the wall had been tampered with.

A bit braver after the rock throwing and completion of my mission, I left the clubhouse and crossed a ravine, following a path on the other side into the woods. Mamma told us never to go there, so that must be where the laboratory used to be. It wasn't there anymore, having moved across the river to the north side of the Des Plaines Valley, where Papá said they were creating the first nuclear submarine, to be named the *Nautilus*.

I had wanted to check out the old lab before the summer was over. Well, summer was over, I hadn't done it, and I was halfway there. Our teacher told us the world's first nuclear reactor had been built there, but we weren't told what was left after the buildings were torn down.

Sweat rolled down my back and temples as I looked for signs of the old lab. The woods were a little cooler, but the grasses had been so dry that Papá had set his alarm to wake him up every two hours so he could walk to the top of the hill and look for fires at night. We were the only people around except for the ranger at Maple Lake, and watching for fires was part of the agreement we made with the forest preserve.

As I walked, something didn't feel right. Like at the clubhouse, I jumped at every little creature and every branch that creaked in the breeze. I kept thinking someone was following me, but when I turned around I saw nothing.

Then I saw something glistening ahead through the trees and I froze, my heart pounding, remembering the glowing eyes that scared Barbaro. Then I realized the flickering was light hitting water. I went on to a small pond and walked around it. On the far side was a grassy area with piles of rubble behind a metal fence. I didn't have the guts to climb the fence, but I walked around it and didn't see anything interesting.

When I passed the pond again, I realized I was near where I had found the two-headed snake.

The Gully was supposed to be full of snakes, but I never saw snakes there. I found the two-headed snake in July when I took Barbaro, riding double on Baby, to the ranger's cabin at Maple Lake and left him there to play with the ranger's son.

As I was riding home, Baby shied and I almost fell off. After I calmed her I went to see what made her jump. It looked at first like three black wires flailing around a sapling stump. It was a black garter snake; only this one had two heads, each at the front end of eight inches of body, with a tail about twice as long. I figured that each head had found a separate way around the sapling stump, and the creature was stuck there trying to free itself. I had to have it of course, and I ran back to Baby and got a rag from the saddlebag, dropped the rag over the snake, tied it closed, and slid it into the saddlebag.

I showed it to the ranger when I rode back for Bobby, and he was amazed. "I wonder if it's something in the water," he said. I laughed. People always joked and blamed the water. I never thought of Argonne at the time.

Today I stopped at the edge of the pond. I looked in the water for snakes or any other sign of life. At first there was nothing, and I wondered why I didn't see minnows or water walkers in the shallows. Then I saw something shimmer, and I looked more closely.

There were tiny creatures floating around, unlike anything I'd seen, and I'd done a lot of fishing in these ponds and lakes. Each one was about an inch across, shaped like a tiny beret, see-through except for little white bags hanging beneath and clear threads streaming below. There were hundreds of them. I walked around the pond. Wherever these creatures were there was no other life, but where they were absent tiny fish and water insects swam around.

I looked around for something to put them in. I found an old rusty can, probably left behind by a fisherman I thought, until I looked closer.

About twenty feet from the edge of the pond were the remains of a campfire. Next to this was a half sheet of plywood partially covering a hole in the ground.

I peeked into the hole. It was as deep as I am tall and inside was a pot, fry pan, bowl and cup, a flashlight, a sheet of plastic, a blanket, and a backpack.

I gasped and jumped away. Someone was living in this hole in the ground! I was really spooked now and looked around quickly, but no one was about.

I hurried to the pond, pulled the can through the water to capture as many of the little beings as I could, and rushed away until the woods were well behind me.

This strange day was not over yet.

I stopped back at the clubhouse on the way home. It was crazy to think my hiding place might have been found so soon, but I had to check. Hidden behind the patio wall on the roof, I heard voices nearby.

At the end of the clubhouse was a shed near one of the ravines. Angelo said when the golf course was open a man sat inside and told golfers when they could start to play. The roof of the shed was gone now, and only three partial walls were still standing.

Angry men's voices came from there, but the men were hidden in the ruins of the building. I was going to sneak away before they saw me, when I thought I recognized one of the voices. It sounded like Angelo—or was it Nello? It was hard to tell the twins apart, even face-to-face. At a distance it was impossible.

I crouched down behind the patio wall.

"I don't care what Emery wanted!" I heard. "He's dead!" That voice was not familiar.

"You've got balls, I'll say that!" said the Angelo-Nello voice.

"What about the Valentine's Day guns?"

"Ted said Jimmy put them out here before he went to Florida. Nobody's looked for them in years. Who cares anymore? Even if they're found, there's no one left to prosecute."

"I'll tell them that, but they won't buy it. There's too much at stake, and you'll do what I say, not what Ted says," the unfamiliar voice said.

"So where is it?"

"It's taken care of. You don't need to know any more."

"And who gets the blame if word gets out? We'd be better off if that horse was nowhere to be found."

One of the men laughed. "Blame it on Petey. Now that he got picked up on that Peeping Tom charge, he's the perfect patsy. As far as the horse goes, if it comes to that, I'll get rid of it."

At those last words, out of a clear sky, came a tremendous roar and flash of light, like a thunderclap and a bolt of lightning. I peeked over the wall in time to see the dry grass at the foot of the shed burst into flame. Two men emerged from the smoke, but I couldn't see who they were. They ran off toward 107th Street and out of sight.

I wiped tears with my arm to clear my eyes. I couldn't think straight, but I had to. These men, maybe one of my brothers, were going to blame Petey for something, and it couldn't be good. Petey a Peeping Tom? Everything I loved was being threatened, and if my moving the canister was found out, I'd be in the thick of it myself. What had I done?

I wasn't thinking about revenge anymore, just about trying to save all of us. Should I take the film out and put it back? It was too late to go back to the Gully today. I'd never get there and back before dark, and I didn't want to be caught with it. No, I'd leave it where it was until I talked to Petey or I came up with a plan.

I stood up. The clearing blazed with flame and smoke, sparks rising into the air caught by wind from the west. The fire would be out of control unless I turned in an alarm and got help immediately—but then people would know I'd been out here spying.

I raced toward home. I'd come up with some story. But there would be no one to talk to today. As long as I could stay on my feet, I'd be pounding the ground with the flappers we kept ready in the barn for just such an emergency, as would every able-bodied man, woman, and child we could get to help.

We had to keep the blaze from racing into the woods and igniting the dry leaves and fallen trees that covered the bluff.

We had to stop the fire before flames reached and reignited the peat bog to the east, which was just put out last winter after burning for seven years. The wind was blowing in that direction.

# Part III

# Chapter 12
## March 2015

Seated in a blue Adirondack chair on the paver patio in her backyard, Cora adjusted her wide-brimmed hat and navy-blue, zippered jacket to be sure no skin was exposed to the late-afternoon sun. The day was comfortable enough, but she had already had four skin cancers.

Billy, in the chair next to her, played with the zipper of his maroon hoodie and opened and closed his mouth a number of times. His eyes darted away every time he caught Cora's stare. In the uncomfortable silence, she doubted if he would ever get out what he came for. Was his hesitation shyness or was he afraid? Afraid to talk to her? Or...some other reason?

She had promised to answer his questions, but she wouldn't fill in the conversation gaps. She'd wait him out or he'd leave. She leaned back, crossed her arms, and surveyed the yard. The cornelian cherry tree would have to be pruned severely and the white pine trimmed up. And the Luisa weeping crabapple had become a monster. She sighed. She'd never gotten a handle on how to shape weeping trees.

"That day on the island," Billy said, interrupting her thoughts, "I woke up on the ground and you were sitting by me."

Cora jerked back to attention. *Finally!*

"Yes," she said. "A storm was raging and everything was chaotic. We didn't know how badly you were hurt, so I kept you awake and talking until the ambulance came."

He blinked rapidly. "Thank you."

He paused, passing his hand over his head, then, "Did I...do anything before I blacked out or after I woke up?" He looked away into the bare branches of the nearby maple tree moving gently in the soft breeze and murmured, "Anything unusual?"

She knit her brows. Her memory of the day was sharp, but the events themselves unclear.

"Because of the storm and confusion, when I got there I didn't know that was you on the ground. I just saw Cisco bending over something. After we called 911, I stayed with you. Why do you ask?"

He fussed with his hands, shuffled his feet, glanced at her, and then stared at the tree again. "Nick said…he said he saw…something that looked like lightning come from me. Then he laughed, like the idea was crazy. Said everybody had a strong imagination that day."

Ah…so that was his concern. All of them had credited Nick's version of the events to excitement, illusion, and the horrific lightning that blinded them.

"We all remembered things differently. None of us are sure what really happened."

"That's what Nick said. You didn't see what he saw?" Billy finally met Cora's eyes.

Surprised by the searching intensity in his eyes, she pressed her lips together and shook her head. "No. I didn't."

"Okay then." He stood up but made no move to leave.

Cora lowered her chin and squinted at him. "That's it? That's what you wanted?"

He lowered his gaze and nodded.

She shook her head. Her curiosity would never let it go at that.

"Billy, you wanted to see me. It couldn't have been easy to come here, and you made a big deal out of it. There must be more. You sit right back down. I made time for you, and you're not about to leave without telling me more."

He took his chair again and slumped like a chastised, obedient child, head hanging. Nick had once described Billy as a lost dog, and she couldn't help but feel the description fit. Resigned to pulling the story out of him, she opened her mouth to prompt him, but he glanced at her, looked away, and started to stammer.

"It's…hard to explain. I don't know myself, only…since I moved to

Lemont, something is different. Something about *me* is different. Something inside me...I don't understand what's going on." He searched her face again, perhaps hoping to find encouragement there.

He raised his chin. "I *feel* things. Powerful things. It's scary."

"Like adrenalin rushes? Or hot flashes? I understand men get those too, but you're too young for that." She smiled but was careful not to laugh. Clearly Billy saw this as a serious matter.

He shook his head emphatically. "That's not it." He raised his right arm, pointed at his wrist, then glanced at her.

"Let me show you. First my cell phone started acting up. I couldn't depend on it so I got this watch. Here—look." He leaned over and showed her the watch face.

For a moment she didn't notice anything and then suddenly, "Oh my God! The second hand—it's moving—it's running *backward*, counter-clockwise! I've never seen that!"

He shot her a lopsided grin and sat back down. "Hang around me, you'll see a lot of that sort of thing. I walk into a bar, the TV stops. The staff at the library avoid me because their computers don't work right when I'm there. I walk down a street at night and the streetlight goes out...then back on after I go by. I feel a pressure building up inside me, waiting to explode. I have no control over it."

Cora recalled the kitchen light that went out when Billy visited. She bit a thumbnail and moved her head slowly from side to side, feeling a surge of apprehension.

Not again! She had thought the supernatural business was done with!

But what Billy was describing was nothing like her previous experiences at St. James. Her voice was calm when she asked, "You think it has something to do with what Nick saw? Did you tell him that?"

"I haven't told anybody, only you, just now. I thought I was going nuts."

Why did people think she had the answers to their problems? How many people had come to her with their secrets? She had lost count. Cisco was right: she drew them like a magnet.

While she struggled with whether or not to get involved, Billy went on, his thoughts gushing like air out of a punctured balloon.

"Maybe it's my Potawatomi heritage, passed down from my ancestors—spirits, the Wendigo, Trickster. But this doesn't happen back home, only here. Something around Lemont brings these episodes on, especially in the woods. Later I wonder if I only dreamed it. Then yesterday… I know where I was, but something wasn't right. I can't get it out of my head."

"Where? Back on the island?"

"No, in the woods across from Saganashkee Slough, off 107th Street."

"What happened?"

He told her about walking the trails and finding an abandoned building where he picked up some intriguing remnants, and a farm where he met a man on horseback. The man had spoken with an accent and used some foreign words, and he insisted his horse was going to win the Kentucky Derby. "The situation, what he said… seemed screwy."

The area was near St. James, where Cora had met the ghost, and also near the buried nuclear waste. A golf course had been in those woods too, a long time ago, she knew. But she knew nothing about a farm. Could buildings still be there, buried in the wilderness off the trails? What was it about these woods?

She realized she was already trying to figure out how to tackle Billy's problem. Cisco wasn't going to like this.

Billy looked at her hopefully. "Would you go there with me? Maybe, Cisco too? I'll show you."

# Chapter 13

The following morning, Cora watched Valerie find her way to the kitchen table with only Corky's help. A coffee cake sat unwrapped on the countertop. Cora wanted a mid-morning snack, even if Valerie didn't.

Sitting stiff-backed, Valerie accepted a piece of cake with a sheepish grin. Apparently she ate sweets after all.

"Big or small?" Cora asked.

"Big," Valerie said.

Cora pushed thoughts of Billy out of her mind to concentrate on Valerie. After talking to Father McGrath at St. James, she now had to pinpoint what Valerie wanted her to do and write down the details.

Cora admitted to being a control freak, but she thought looking at all sides of issues balanced things out. Her frequent questions weren't objections, but rather invitations to consider the numerous spiderwebs her own mind traveled. Valerie was a control freak too. She formed strong opinions quickly, but assuming her decisions were hasty would be wrong. There was a potential for butting heads.

Clearing a space on the table, Cora knocked her notepad to the floor. Valerie startled, an expression of alarm on her face. "What was that?"

"I just dropped my notepad," Cora said, wondering why Valerie was jumpy. Did she have doubts about what they were doing? Did she sense Cora was withholding information from her?

"Oh. Then you're preparing to make lists?" Valerie said with a lopsided grin.

Cora chuckled. Her friends joked about her ever-present notepads and list-making. She didn't care—these tools were what got the job done.

"Guilty."

"I'd be disappointed if you weren't," Valerie said. "Tells me you've decided to help."

But would Valerie let Cora approach matters her own way? She could get results faster if she asked questions in an order logical to her, then summed up the critical points, and outlined an action plan. However, with two strong personalities at the table…

Valerie said, "How about if we start by answering whatever questions you have there, Cora? Then you can tell me your ideas about what we should do next."

Yes! This new Valerie was growing on her.

Cora pushed her empty plate away and picked up her Cross mechanical pencil. Her writing materials were crucial to her thought process. She preferred thin-ruled legal pads and had been known to search half an hour for her mislaid Cross pencil instead of using a substitute.

"So, we have two problems: to locate your mother and find out why she left, and to either verify or disprove how your Uncle Angelo was killed. Is that right?"

Unexpectedly, Valerie's face whitened and froze. Her hands shook. She opened her mouth and then closed it.

"What's wrong?" Cora said.

Valerie took a deep breath and exhaled. "It just dawned on me that we may really find Mamma. It's been so long. Maybe I won't like what we find. Maybe we'll make things worse. Maybe this isn't a good idea."

She clenched her hands into fists and then made herself busy by removing Corky's harness so the dog could relax.

Second thoughts? It must be hard for such a reserved person to reveal intimate facts and feelings. Valerie had broken down the first time they talked. How embarrassing that must have been for her, and how difficult to admit her fears and doubts now.

"Once the secrets are out, you'll never be able to go back. You won't be able to make guesses for her or excuses for yourself. Are you sure you want to do this?"

Valerie leaned forward. "When I met with Father McGrath, I kept saying over and over, 'It's okay, it's okay.' He said I did that because it *wasn't* okay."

She raised her chin. "I *have* to do it, Cora. Not knowing is keeping my life on hold."

Cora picked up her pencil again. "Okay then. Let's start with your family. Introduce me to them and tell me what your life was like."

Valerie spoke in a soft, unemotional voice, choosing her words carefully. "We grew up in an old section of Oak Lawn, in a new, but small, three-bedroom ranch house in a poorer part of town. My sister, Paula, is a year younger than me, and there are less than three years between me and my brother. My father was born in Sicily and met my mother there, and they came to the States."

That was a coincidence. Cora had grown up in Oak Lawn too. "So your mother was born in Sicily?" she said.

"No, Mamma's parents immigrated to Chicago in the late 1930s and she was born here. She was visiting Sicily when she met my father. They lived there until I was born and then came to the States. Paula and Sally were born here."

"Was your family close?"

"Not really. My grandparents lived on the next block, but we didn't see them much. I don't think Mamma got along with them very well, and Papá was more interested in his buddies than the family. Mamma's brothers visited, but they were busy with their own lives. We went to family gatherings, picnics, and fishing trips, like when the smelt were running. There were aunts, uncles, cousins, but I don't remember them all anymore."

"Let me catch up," Cora said, rapidly jotting notes while Valerie picked at her coffee cake.

"Is there more tea, Cora? The cake is wonderful. Did you get it in town? I'll have to tell Grace."

Cora freshened Valerie's tea and sat back down. Corky looked at Cora with interest and sneaked in her direction. Cora glanced at the Oriental rug under the table, wondering how much dog hair was on it. Cisco, who did the vacuuming, would have something to say.

With Corky's head on her knee, Cora rubbed behind the dog's ears with her left hand and picked up her pencil with the right.

"So then one day your mother walked out. Did anything lead up to that? Were your parents getting along?"

"We had moved to Chicago by then. The West Side was a better neighborhood in those days, and Mamma and Papá opened a business, a storefront upholstery shop. I was pretty young, eight, when we moved. We lived in three crowded rooms above the store, and us kids stayed with Mamma's cousin Luisa during the week. I had to get used to a new school, make friends, and take care of Paula and Sally since Mamma was so busy. I was angry because I had a lot of responsibilities and wanted to go back to Oak Lawn and my friends. Kids don't think much about whether their parents are getting along or how their business is doing."

Valerie reached her hand down to feel for Corky. "You little sneak," she said, discovering the dog wasn't there. "I caught you wandering off. You know that's not allowed." Her voice sounded fond, not irritated.

Cora filled in the loops of words on her notepad, distracted by her own thoughts. Where did the money for the business come from? A poor immigrant father, probably wouldn't have had much equity in their house. Cisco's Italian relatives often helped each other with loans. The situation seemed familiar to Cora. She had had a friend whose situation was like Valerie's mother's.

"Can you tell me about the day your mother left, Valerie?"

"One day Luisa pulled me aside when we got home from school. She looked sad, so I knew it wasn't something good. She said Papá called her and that Mamma had closed up the store, packed her things, and left a note saying she was going away and he shouldn't try to find her. I was in eighth grade then."

"No reason given?"

"Not according to Papá. We had no reason to doubt what he said—not as kids, anyway. Now I'm not so sure."

"Did you hear from her at all after she left?"

"We got cards on our birthdays, Christmas, sometimes presents, but she never called or let us know where she was, why she left, what she was doing. The cards stopped a long time ago."

"Did you keep anything? Where were the postmarks from?"

She shook her head. "I was angry, and I never saw the envelopes."

Corky, bored now that Cora was paying more attention to the notepad than to her, nudged Cora's leg a few times. When Cora ignored her she went back to Valerie's side, placed her head on Valerie's foot, and fell asleep.

"You said you didn't think your mother cared for you, but you still felt awful after she left."

"I did. At first I was really angry and then I was busy trying to help Papá, Paula, and Sally. I was only thirteen. I was buried in responsibility and didn't let myself think too much about Mamma because it hurt."

Valerie shifted in her chair uneasily. "I didn't know how to help them, and Papá just left everything to me. He treated us okay, but he wasn't around much even when Mamma was there. And after she left…let's just say it was worse. He'd put on a happy face for us, but before long we got on his nerves. He'd go out and leave us alone. Then he went to jail and we went to live with Nonna."

"To jail?"

"It wasn't a big deal, only a few weeks. Something to do with his business. But when he got out he didn't come back for us, just left us with Nonna. He visited often at first but then less and less." She sighed, took off her glasses, and rubbed her face before putting them back on. Valerie must feel comfortable with her now.

"How did Paula and Sally take it?"

"That's one of the reasons Sally and I don't get along. He thinks I should just forget her. He said he and Paula got over it, and I should too. So he says. But I think he won't admit his feelings, and Paula was never right after Mamma left."

Valerie frowned. "Living with Nonna wasn't much of an improvement. She had a small, old, two-story frame house and we had to sleep in the living room. Nonna was old country, rough, and didn't speak much English. Nonno was dead by then, and Mamma's kid brother was getting into trouble and hanging out with a bad element. Mamma's sister had Down syndrome. The twins came around, but boys weren't expected to do housework. Nonna had her hands full and the last thing she needed was three more kids to care for and three more mouths to feed. She was always yelling."

"Out of the frying pan?" Cora was reminded again of her friend from high school days, who had three children and an Italian husband who spoke little English, like Valerie's father. She had spent a lot of time in her friend's house but hadn't known the rest of the family well. Valerie's family seemed much the same.

"It would have been awful if not for Uncle Angelo. He's the only one that talked to me like *me*, you know what I mean? He was interested in what I did, spent time with me. He was *kind*. For the first time I felt like someone cared."

"And then he was killed. A policeman, you said, shot in the back from a high-rise by a sniper with a high-powered rifle. But you don't believe that. Why not?" Cora tapped her pencil softly on her notepad, then set it down, and leaned forward watching Valerie's face.

"He was so proud of what he was doing. The police force had instituted 'Walk and Talk,' or something like that, to improve relationships between people living in housing projects and the police, especially at Cabrini-Green, where he was killed. The idea was to make policemen a friendly presence in the projects. He'd been out there for the better part of a year, walking the courtyards between the high-rises and the streets, hanging out, making friends, listening to people's troubles, and trying to help. It was a dangerous job, but he loved it and said the residents trusted him."

Valerie tightened one side of her mouth and shook her head. "Lots of people in the projects knew and liked Angelo. The man they convicted of killing him was someone he had told me about. Angelo was especially close to him. He would have asked Angelo for help, not shot him."

Cora considered. What Valerie said made sense but would anyone have believed a teenage girl? "You said something else was going on?"

"Angelo was acting strange for about a month before he was shot. He wasn't eating or sleeping, and he was pacing a lot. I kept asking him what was wrong, but he always said nothing. He insisted we keep the drapes closed. He peeked out the window before he left the house and looked around his car before he got in it. At home he grabbed the phone before anyone else could, then went behind the door and talked in whispers. It wasn't hard to tell something was wrong. When I asked, he told me the police were checking up on him. He was supposed to live in Chicago to be on the force, and they thought he was spending too much time in Oak Lawn. But I thought he didn't want me to know the real reason."

Cora examined her notes. "Anything else unusual you can think of?"

"About Mamma or about Angelo?"

"Anything at all."

Valerie considered. "Mamma used to talk about a place they lived when she was a kid, a farm in the forest preserves near 107th Street. They helped the rangers watch for forest fires and vandals and took care of the property. Mamma and her brothers and sister all grew up there. She had a horse and she told stories about a secret laboratory, a deserted clubhouse, and strange sights and sounds. This was in the 1950s, I think. I was never out there, but I felt like I knew the place from Mamma's stories. It sounded creepy, which was pretty attractive to an unhappy kid."

Cora's eyes went wide and her pen stopped. This had to be the same place Billy had described: a farm in the woods near an old clubhouse and 107th Street! So Valerie's mother had lived there in the fifties or sixties. Amazing! The farm couldn't still be there after all this time, could it? She would have heard about or seen it by now, although she hadn't been to that particular spot.

Apparently picking up Cora's reaction, Valerie said, "What?"

Thinking quickly, Cora decided not to complicate matters for the moment. "Nothing," she said. "Just someone else mentioned a place like that to me recently." She returned to her notes, underlined a few, and put stars by others. She turned to a fresh page and drew columns.

"Valerie, do you mind if I ask Frannie to help us? She's got a real knack for online research. Lately she's been trying to track down a family member on genealogy sites. She'll know how to locate your mother faster than I will. I think she would be a real help, and she loves to do this sort of thing."

Valerie frowned. "Frannie? I guess you've forgiven me but has she?"

Cora chewed on a thumbnail as she considered Valerie's question. Valerie's insensitive remarks to Frannie had started the chain of events that led to Valerie's injury. She couldn't be sure Frannie had forgiven Valerie, but Cora thought she could bring her friend around.

"She's pretty outspoken, but she's quick to accept an apology if it's sincere."

Valerie kept shaking her head. "I don't know, Cora. I was really mean to her. Why would she want to help me?"

"She and I have been through a lot together. Apologize. Bribe her with an interesting project, and she'll come around. I'll talk to her."

Valerie appeared doubtful but nodded. "If you think that's best."

"So let me make a list of people to talk to and get some dates. You're living with Sally here in Lemont now, but the rest of your family…?"

Valerie was shaking her head. "There's just me, Sally, and Paula. I think Paula lives in Phoenix—that's where she was last we knew. She's pretty much a flake, and I don't even know if I could find her. Sally's not much help either. Oh, he's a nice enough guy but not a self-starter and makes things easy on himself, if you know what I mean."

"You mean he's lazy, weak, and selfish?" Cora asked.

Valerie laughed. "That's a bit strong, but not totally inaccurate." Her face reddened. "I haven't told Sally what we're doing, Cora. He wouldn't approve and things are dicey enough already."

Cora rubbed her forehead. She put a question mark by his name. "Okay. You called your sister a flake. Why is that?"

Valerie heaved a sign. "She was a moody, angry teenager, and she never grew out of it. She could hardly wait to grow up and move away. All I know is she's somewhere in Arizona."

"What about your father?"

"Died of a heart attack, 1986. And Nonna and Nonno have been dead for years."

This wouldn't be easy. Cora started to outline the steps of a plan. She wrote names at the top of three columns: Cora, Valerie, Frannie. She and Frannie could search old newspaper articles, review national and local events before and after pertinent dates, and look for clues. They could talk to Sally if Valerie would allow it and to Valerie's remaining aunts and uncles. And try to find Paula. Pull up her father's obituary. Look for information to establish why he'd been in jail.

"So let me get some names and dates. I'll give Frannie a call and get her on board. We'll brainstorm and I'll get back to you. Your mother's brothers and sister?"

"The twins were the oldest, Angelo and Nello." She snickered. "Nonna said she gave her children special names. Angelo meant angel, and Nello, that's Aniello, meant little lamb. Aunt Lucia, the one with Down syndrome, was Lucia, 'light.' And Barbaro, 'strong and happy,' was the baby.

Nello fell off the face of the earth, but Barbaro is around somewhere and you might find him. Lucia died too, long ago."

"What year did your mother leave?"

"In 1974."

Cora fired off questions and filled in dates without looking up. "And the last time you heard from her?"

"About ten years later."

"About 1984... Okay. And Angelo was killed when?"

"In 1975."

A cop killed at the projects. There must have been a lot about that in the papers. Frannie could start there. She jotted a note to read the stories to Valerie to see if anything jumped out at her.

"Your mother didn't come home for Angelo's funeral? Or your father's?"

"No. She sent flowers." Valerie dropped her head and rubbed the back of her neck.

"What was Angelo's full name?"

"Angelo Nicholas Vitale." The name sounded familiar, but it was a common surname.

"Oh, duh! And your mother's name?"

"Jemma," she said. "Jemma DiMaso."

Cora's hand froze in mid word. Her free hand came up and covered her mouth. Oh my God! She wouldn't have far to look for answers to some of Valerie's questions. She only had to search her own memory. How many secrets was she going to have to keep from Valerie?

# Chapter 14

"If you don't think I'm trying hard enough, why don't you try spending a day in my shoes," Valerie yelled.

"That's not it," Sally said. "We're just asking about alternatives. You haven't even started to look for work, let alone for another place to live. We realize it's going to take time, but we want to know you're moving in that direction. Is there anywhere else you can stay?"

"Where might that be, my dear brother? Some halfway house for the disabled?"

"Well…"

Sally and Grace were probably looking back and forth, egging each other on, and the image made Valerie furious. They probably thought a home for the disabled was where she belonged. Whether or not they were doing what she presumed, she felt humiliated.

"Fine," she said. "Since I'm such a burden on my only remaining family, God knows I wouldn't want to put you out any longer. You need all four of these bedrooms just for the two of you."

She pushed herself up from the kitchen table and did her best to stomp toward her room, but she felt ridiculous, slowed by the need to check for obstacles and feel for the end of the stair railing. She wanted her words to stick with them and to not make a fool of herself by tripping over something or bumping into a wall. Corky followed her quietly.

Reaching her room, she slammed the door, catching Corky. The dog let out a yelp. Valerie dropped to the floor and hugged her. "Poor baby, I'm so sorry. Your mistress can't do anything right." Tears flowed down

Valerie's cheeks falling on the soft fur. "Thank God for you, baby. We're in this together, aren't we?"

Valerie got up, locked her door, and flopped into the cozy chair between her bed and a small table that held her computer, squeezed under a window in her crowded room. There she could listen to outdoor sounds, hear activity on the street, and warm herself on sunny days. But the night was cool now and the window was closed.

She sat, chest heaving, trying to control her heart and breath rate. She'd be damned if she'd start sobbing. Yet again, she was being betrayed by the very people who were supposed to love her.

What was so awful about her? Why was she so unlovable?

After talking to Cora she had felt renewed confidence. Sharing goals, ideas, and laughing—when was the last time that happened? But when she returned home and replayed their conversation in her mind, she remembered an awkward moment when she had the distinct impression Cora was hiding something. Her mood changed to dread. "Oh, no, not again."

She had called Father McGrath, but instead of reassuring her he suggested they discuss the matter at their next session...whatever that meant.

Her morale was back to ankle high. Her ambitions were foolish. It was too hard: she was trapped and had too many strikes against her.

What was she going to do? Even if Sally and Grace let her stay, they wouldn't let Molly move in. If she went into housing for the disabled, there would be no place for eleven-year-old Molly either. How would she pay for housing? Tom would never allow Molly to live with her without a suitable home, and she couldn't argue with her ex-husband about that.

Her dreams were crashing down around her.

She had been seriously jarred when Cora pointed out that Molly's situation was similar to what her own had been—an absent mother and a father who meant well and went through the motions. She hadn't put the situations together before, but she did now.

Cora hit the nail on the head. She needed to lavish the love on Molly she herself had never had, so Molly would not wind up an unhappy, angry, and bitter person like her, like her mother, and like her mother's mother.

For the first time she wondered if she and Jemma had taken the same path for the same reasons, creating a false front to hide feelings of inferiority brought about by an uncaring mother. Did Jemma strike out at Valerie because she learned that behavior from her own mother? Was this family doomed to pass the trait to all their female progeny?

There was a knock at the door.

"Valerie?" Sally called softly.

"Go away, Sally."

"Please, Valerie. This is hard. Let me in and let's talk calmly."

"Impossible. I'm *not* calm. I won't be calm for a long time, if ever."

"Valerie? Please?"

She brushed at her face. It was dry.

"You know how to unlock the door from the outside. Do it."

She heard him fiddle with the lock, step into the room, click on the light at the end of her long dresser, close the door, and sit on the bed. She caught the sharp scent of his perspiration. He cleared his throat a few times, sniffed, but said nothing.

"Well, you're here. What?"

"I'm between a rock and a hard place here, Valerie. It's not like we want to send you away, but Grace is used to just the two of us, and she likes it that way. She doesn't feel comfortable in her own house, like she has to entertain all the time, be careful what she says, and not disturb you with loud music or television. She's reluctant to invite her friends over. And there's dog hair to clean up. Put yourself in her position, Valerie. Would you want a semipermanent houseguest?"

Valerie worked her mouth.

"My friend Cora took in her mother. Lots of people take care of family when they are in need."

"It's been two years already, Valerie. Maybe if she had some idea how much longer you'll be here, it would help."

"Help Grace, or help you?"

He let out a long breath. "Okay, it's not just Grace. We just want our home back to ourselves. We don't have any children by choice, and we want our own lives. I guess we're selfish, but is that so awful? You know we'll help you find a place, get resettled—we're not heartless. Please understand."

"The sad thing is, I do understand." Her voice broke. "I just want so bad for it not to be true."

Sally stood up, went to her, and pulled her head against his chest. He bent and kissed the top of her head. "I wish it wasn't."

She stiffened but then relaxed against him. Her voice was muted as she spoke into his body. "I'm making real progress now, Sally. Real progress. I can't tell you today, but give me a month to figure things out. In a month I'll come up with a reasonable move-out date. Just a little more time, okay?"

She felt him nod. He eased away and left the room, clicking off the light and closing the door behind him. If he locked the door she didn't hear that. Corky came over, settled by Valerie's feet, and sighed deeply. Valerie reached over the chair arm to stroke the dog's back.

She had made Sally a promise, but could she keep it? If she didn't act right away, she'd have to give up dreams of independence and hope she and her daughter could reunite after Molly grew up.

Was it reasonable to depend on Cora to work miracles? Cora would have to set personal matters aside. Was Cora trustworthy? What about Frannie? Would Frannie forgive and lend a hand?

Valerie had learned to use a program that changed the text on her computer screen to voice, but did that compare to Frannie's nimble fingers? Could Cora and Frannie get answers she'd been unable to find in a lifetime in just a month? And would that allow enough time to find and retrain for a job she could do as a blind person? Sally had only asked for a plan, but, even so, it seemed impossible.

She felt so alone!

A car door slammed on the street, followed by a murmur of conversation. The voices triggered another soft, shy voice. That friend of Cora's, Billy, it was his voice in her head. Cora had described Billy as a lost soul. She wondered now what he looked like and how old he was. For some reason, she found herself hoping she'd get a chance to know him better.

Forget it! She had more immediate concerns. What if they found Jemma? Did she think Jemma would step in and take care of her and Molly after all this time? How old was Jemma now? She did a quick calculation. In her seventies, not too old to help…

Maybe she should just forget all this. Did Molly even want to live with her? Maybe she loved California, where the sun was always shining and the lifestyle was focused on play. Molly was a young adult now, with all the baggage that came with that. Was she menstruating yet? Valerie was ashamed to realize she didn't know.

She put her face in her hands and rubbed it. Her stomach ached and acid rose to her throat.

She started toward her small bathroom to find the bottle of antacid but was interrupted by a buzzing coming from the little table next to her chair. Her cell phone. Probably a "crap call." No one ever called her. But, it might be Cora… She accepted the call.

"Valerie?" The voice was slightly familiar, but she couldn't identify it immediately.

"Yes?"

"It's Aster."

Aster? Aster Blossom Pawlik, Tom's new wife—there couldn't be another Aster calling her. The California girl, the flower child that was now Molly's primary caregiver. Whatever—who was she to judge? As far as she could tell, Aster was a pleasant enough person who was trying to be good to Molly, even if Valerie's impression was that she was rather flighty, with her long, straight hair, tattoos, and snug T-shirts.

"Did something happen to Molly?" Her chest tightened and her heart pounded.

"No, no, Valerie. Molly's fine. I asked her not to call you, to wait until we knew more before…," Aster's voice cracked, came to a stop, and she started to sob. "It's Tom, Valerie."

"Tom…?" Her stomach clenched.

The anguished voice rambled on. "He's had a stroke. The doctors said it's bad. He's going to live, but he won't be able to take care of himself for a long time, if ever. I don't know what I'm going to do. He's going to rehab in a few days, but the insurance only covers ninety days and then I have to bring him home and find some way to take care of him. And with neither of us working I don't know where the money's going to come from and…"

Aster broke down. As Valerie waited for Aster to regain control, the immensity of the situation began to sink in.

When the sobbing dwindled to a series of heavy breaths, Valerie said, "That's awful, Aster. I'm so sorry. When did it happen? Does he understand what's going on? Can he communicate?"

"Yesterday morning. He's awake now and responding a little. The nurses say he understands, but his speech is so garbled we don't really know. He can't use his right arm or leg. We got him to the hospital early. That's good they told me, but it's too soon to know how much improvement to expect."

"He recognizes you, right?"

"I think so, but the doctors aren't real encouraging." Her voice rose to a squeak and she forced out, "He looks in my eyes, so pleading, like he's asking for help, and then just that fast, he gets angry. I can't stand it—I have to look away. I feel like I'm failing him. I'm such a coward."

As the shock wore off, Valerie's nursing skills returned. About thirty-six hours post stroke, awake and somewhat responsive, that was good. The brain would swell for a while after the insult, before any real improvement was expected, but the signs were good for recovery. How much recovery, it was too soon to know. The doctors were being cautious, as they should be.

"Aster, don't feel guilty. I know you want to reassure him if you can, but he's not likely to remember this. Just stay with him, touch him, talk to him. That will help stimulate his brain and speed recovery. You can do that, even if you can't look in his eyes, can't you?"

She heard sniffling and a weak, "Yeah."

"Thanks for calling me, Aster. Please give him my best."

"I will, but there's something else, Valerie." She paused, and Valerie's heart started pounding. It wouldn't be something good.

"I can't take care of Tom and Molly too. I know Tom would agree. Molly should be with you now. When he finishes rehab, after the ninety days, we have to send Molly to you, Valerie. She's with Mommy and Daddy now, but they're not all that healthy either. We can't take care of her anymore. It will need to be you and your family."

# Chapter 15

Cora hesitated on the doorstep, surprised to see beads of sweat on Valerie's forehead and her hair plastered around her face. She wore a damp gray sweatshirt, sweatpants, and running shoes. She wasn't wearing the dark glasses she usually wore in public.

"Sorry," Valerie said, out of breath. "I was working off some jitters on the treadmill."

It hadn't occurred to Cora to wonder how a woman so obviously fit as Valerie stayed that way. Running the neighborhood or on a track would be a challenge unless she had a partner.

She followed Valerie into the living room. "Why don't you sit on the sofa while I change out of these sweaty clothes," Valerie suggested. She turned and climbed the staircase behind her, disappearing down an upstairs hallway. Corky appeared from another room. She sniffed at Cora and then padded up the stairs in search of her mistress.

The room was painfully neat. A single large painting, a winter forest scene in neutral tones of brown and beige, hung over a gray-tweed sofa that sat on a bare, glossy hardwood floor. The living room opened into another room filled with dining furniture and a large china cabinet, its shelves containing not china but boxes and figurines.

Cora took advantage of the break to rehearse what she had to tell Valerie based on the previous night's telephone conversations, beginning with Father McGrath.

"I see your dilemma," Father had said. "Valerie doesn't know why she was injured and now she doesn't know you knew her mother. Yet you and I know it all. When she finds out she'll be angry we kept this from her, even though it was for her own good."

"Exactly."

"Valerie called me too. She suspects you're hiding something." He sighed. "You were right all along; you need to tell her the whole story right away. Seems you're better for her than I've been."

Cora had then placed a call to her friend Frannie, who took a little convincing but finally agreed to help investigate Jemma's and Angelo's past on the internet. Cora got the impression Frannie felt some responsibility for Valerie's accident too, and she played that card.

Next Cora called an older friend, Linda, to see if she could fill in some blanks about Jemma. "I have no clue why Jemma left Chicago," Linda had told her. "If I remember right, she moved to Goodyear, Arizona, near Phoenix, I think, with Kathleen. We only saw her one time afterward, when she visited at my house, remember—around 1980?"

Cora thought it unlikely Jemma was still in Goodyear. Cora would have to track down Jemma some other way.

Now that Cora's memories from more than forty years were coming back, she remembered that Jemma had talked to her about living on the farm, and, in fact, St. James had once been Jemma's church. Which then brought Billy's recent experience there into the picture.

Then this morning Cora and Cisco had been doing some spring yard cleanup. When the cell phone in Cora's pocket rang, she was holding down a pile of branches with one foot while Cisco tied them. She struggled to fish the phone out of her jacket.

"Hello?" She listened. "A stroke? Oh my God, how awful. Are you okay? No, you're not okay, what a stupid question. Are you home alone? I'll be there within an hour."

"What happened?" Cisco asked when she ended the call, as he scooped a pile of dry leaves and stalks into a paper bag.

Filling him in on Valerie's desperate situation, she was struck by another complication. "Oh my God!" Her hands flew to her face.

"What?"

"I have to tell her what I know about her accident and that I knew her mother. What's that going to do to her?"

"You can't put it off?"

"And what? It'll only be worse when I tell her later. She's already suspicious. Maybe if…" She looked off into the distance.

"You're not thinking of bringing Valerie and Molly here?" he said.

She blinked. "I didn't think that far."

"You'd better think that far before you go running off. It could come up."

"You're right. If I offer a temporary arrangement, we know it might not end up temporary. So maybe I'll just say I'll help her figure something out and leave the door open."

Cora had felt guilty then and felt no less so now. Foremost in her mind as she waited for Valerie to return was a need to unburden herself. But when Valerie entered the room the petite woman seemed even smaller, and the hand she placed to her cheek shook. Her voice seemed hesitant but got stronger as she described the previous evening. Cora listened in silence while Valerie told her everything.

"I thought Molly should live with Tom while I learned how to live in a world of darkness," she said after she finished. "I was consumed with my own problems and didn't think about the effect on Molly. Much as I wanted her childhood to be different from mine, it seems I'm no better than my mother was."

"You didn't have a choice, Valerie," Cora said.

"She's eleven years old, Cora. Do you remember what happens when a girl is eleven? I didn't. I had to refresh my memory on a nursing website."

Cora wondered how she managed to read it.

"This year she could grow three inches. Her breasts will develop, pubic and underarm hair too. She'll be embarrassed by acne. Hormones will confuse her. She may start menstruating."

Valerie pointed and gestured as she ranted, dramatizing each point, much like Cisco did. She mustn't realize she had the same habit she used to criticize him for.

"Do you remember what middle school was like, Cora? More responsibility, less direction, and lots of peer pressure. She'll obsess about her appearance, possessions, and social activities. She'll want to make her own decisions but doubt her choices. She'll need her mother!"

She propped an elbow on the arm of her chair and dropped her chin into her palm. Cora wondered if Valerie was thinking about how her own mother had failed her. How difficult it must be for a woman who had always been cool and aloof to reveal such intimate feelings. She must miss Molly terribly.

"I've got to be better than a father who needs constant care, a pleasant-but-ditzy stepmother with too much to do, and elderly grandparents consumed with their own health issues." She took a deep breath. "I don't expect you to have answers."

"No," said Cora. "You expect me to listen."

"Before now I could never talk about such private matters," Valerie said.

She must be a mind reader. Would she feel the same after Cora confessed all she knew?

"Do you want to know what I think?" Cora asked.

"Please."

"I think we have to quit wasting time, find your mother, and see what happened to your uncle. Even if we're unsuccessful, we have to get that out of the way and find you a job and a place to live."

Cora stood up. Corky, who had seemed to be asleep, picked up her head. "Is it okay if I walk around here? Helps me think."

"Sure."

Cora crossed her arms and wandered around the room. When she got to the china cabinet she saw it was filled with Barbie dolls. God! Valerie, of all people, living in a house full of Barbie dolls? If that indicated what sort of people she was living with, it was no wonder she felt out of place. Cora had to help find a way to get her out.

"You said Molly will be coming in three months. We have some time. I say give it a try. Surely Sally will be okay with three months if he sees things moving in the right direction. When Molly gets here the two of you can look at places together. I'll help. What do you think?"

Valerie pressed her lips together and ran a hand through her hair. "I still haven't told Sally what we're doing."

Cora stopped wandering and blinked.

"He'd think I was stalling, avoiding his wishes. He wouldn't understand why I'm wasting time trying to find Mamma."

"What does he think you're doing?"

"Working with the Lighthouse to find job and housing opportunities."

So Valerie wasn't opposed to hiding some truths herself. It seemed Valerie had been no better than Cora.

"We have a lot to do in a short time," Valerie said, frowning. She rubbed her forehead with the fingers of both hands as Cora reseated herself. When she raised her head her expression was both doubtful and hopeful. "Cora, you said 'we.' Like Father McGrath said, you don't give up."

Cora snorted. "Huh! What would be the point? Giving up doesn't get you anywhere, unless it was a mistake in the first place. We didn't make a mistake, did we?"

"No…" Valerie still seemed lost in thought.

"You have a team now, you and me and Frannie. Maybe Cisco, but he doesn't know it yet." She winked, a meaningless gesture, but she didn't want to poke Valerie with an elbow.

"So Frannie agreed? Did you have to talk her into it?"

"Not really. I was going to call you today to see when we can get started."

A corner of Valerie's mouth turned up. "How about tomorrow?"

"Sure. But I have to tell you something first."

Valerie's face lost color. "I suspected you weren't telling me something. I wasn't wrong, was I?"

Cora leaned toward Valerie. "I wanted to tell you right away. But… I knew your mother."

"What?" Valerie stiffened. Corky jumped up, danced, and then put her head on Valerie's knee.

"When I was in high school and for a few years after. I used to hang out in Jemma's house in Oak Lawn."

"How long did you know?" Her voice was cool. Cora couldn't read her expression.

"Not until you told me her name. I had to talk to Father McGrath before telling you, but I was going to tell you, no matter what."

"So tell me now."

"I had just started my senior year of high school. Your family moved next door to Linda, my best friend. She and Jemma became friends. Then Linda invited me and we started going to Jemma's after school instead of going home. I went there just about every day during my senior year."

"I must have been born by then."

"You were. You were about two. Pumpkin—I never knew her as Paula—was about six months old, and Jemma was pregnant again. After your brother was born, we called him Pudge."

Valerie caught her breath at the nicknames. She turned away from Cora, toward the window. Her voice quivered.

"What was she like, my mother?"

"I never knew anyone with such energy and love of life. She was always laughing and hugging people, her good humor infectious. She saw only the happy side of everything and everyone. I didn't think she was anything like the woman you described—that could be why it took me so long to make the connection." She paused. "It was so long ago...fifty years? I never even knew you lived in Oak Lawn."

Valerie turned back with a doubtful expression. "How long did you know her?"

"Only a couple of years—after that I only saw her a time or two. I was busy at college, made new friends."

Suddenly Valerie looked exhausted. She said, "I don't think I can talk about this anymore today. I need to let these new developments sink in."

"I understand, and...I'm sorry Valerie. But there's one more thing. It's important."

She groaned. "Go on...if you must."

Valerie turned toward the living room window again, as if to gain strength from the warm sun streaming through it. "It's something else I'm not going to like, right?"

"I'm really sorry I didn't tell you right away." She cleared her throat. "It's about your accident. Everyone thought your story about seeing a wolf on the road was in your head, but maybe you did see a wolf—not a real wolf, but a ghost. I saw the animal too, three times—in the woods, when it attacked Father McGrath, and again last fall. That's why his voice is so strange."

Valerie stiffened, frowned, then shivered, still facing the window.

Cora explained the secret she, Frannie, Cisco, and Father McGrath kept—what they came to believe about the ghost of a young woman consumed with a desire to protect Cora, who took revenge after Valerie tried to ruin Cora's reputation, using the spirit of a wolf for the deed.

Valerie listened in silence. After Cora finished she said, "So you think this…*spirit* of a wolf…attacked me as payback for what I did to you? But why did the wolf attack Father McGrath?"

"He was trying to stop the spirit from haunting me. She didn't like that."

"And he didn't want you to tell me?"

"He thought you had enough to deal with, and the knowledge might be more harmful than helpful."

Valerie finally turned away from the window, her voice chilly. "That's a pretty weird story, Cora. Do you really expect me to believe it?"

"Don't look at me like I'm nuts. I don't care if you believe me or not. What's important is that I'm honest with you and that you trust me. We can't work together if you don't."

"Why *did* you tell me? For my sake or for yours?"

"I don't know. I only know I was born cursed with the truth gene, and I can't act any other way."

Valerie dropped her head, probably weighing her need for Cora against Cora's deceit and a ridiculous story about a wolf and a ghost. She probably thought Cora was off her rocker and was doubting her decision to involve Cora in her problems. Or perhaps she was just angry, thinking Cora, like everyone else in her life, was letting her down.

Yet Valerie couldn't investigate alone. She'd fail without Cora.

"*If* what you say is true, you didn't make the accident happen. You couldn't stop it," Valerie finally said.

Valerie picked at a thread in the seam of her chair. "I guess you believe what you've told me, but I don't believe in ghosts, Cora. What bothers me is that you or Father McGrath didn't tell me."

"What good would it have done? You were recovering; Father and I didn't want the world knowing what happened to us. No one would have believed us, just like you don't believe now. How would knowing have changed anything?"

She thought a while longer and then sighed. "I guess it doesn't change anything, Cora—not really. But I have to think this over."

"Do you trust me now?"

"I don't know."

She finally turned toward Cora. "Didn't we agree I don't have a lot of friends to pick from?"

After a moment the women both giggled.

"We *do* always find something to laugh about, Cora. I feel…not so alone. Does anyone else know this story?"

"Only Frannie, Cisco, and Father McGrath—and a policeman, but he doesn't believe in ghosts either and isn't about to say anything."

"I won't either." She paused again. "I have to live with this a while, Cora."

"There's one more thing," Cora said.

Valerie was shaking her head. "More…oh, God, no!"

"About what we do next. You remember Billy?"

Valerie rubbed the side of her neck. "Billy? The Potawatomi man I met at your house?"

"Yes, that Billy," Cora said.

Was that a blush Cora detected on Valerie's cheeks? No, that couldn't be. Although, Valerie and Billy were the two loneliest people she knew…

"Billy said he found an abandoned golf clubhouse, a farmhouse, and a farmer on horseback out in the forest preserves. I think it's the same place you said Jemma grew up."

"Whoa! That's weird," Valerie said.

## Chapter 16
### September 1963

"Where're we going?" I asked Linda Kuchar, my best friend. "You're heading toward your house."

"It's a surprise, Cora!" she cackled. Linda cackled a lot, one of the reasons I liked her.

I didn't smile, though. I hated surprises. I liked to stay in control, and Linda knew that. We'd been close since sixth grade.

Linda was cute and perky. She had shiny brown, flipped-up hair. That day she wore a plaid skirt with a kick pleat in the front and a short-sleeved, baby-blue sweater with a white lace, detachable collar. Our senior year of high school had just started.

I had lost twenty-five pounds since starting high school, but I hadn't managed the tricks of stylish hairdo, makeup, and dress, like our more popular classmates. Linda and I were the same size, but if we switched clothes she'd still look perky and I'd still look dumpy. I know—we'd tried.

My arms loaded with heavy books, I struggled not to drop them as I hurried after Linda. She had a single book. She sailed easily through assignments, got away with missing some, and still got As.

We were both honor roll students. I was just as smart as Linda, but I obsessed over directions, read every word at least twice, and always, always did my best. That took longer. I was raised by parents influenced by the Great Depression. I was careful, thrifty, respectful, and obedient.

I wished I could be like Linda: carefree, creative, joking. I wasn't much fun.

It should have been the other way around. I lived on the better side of town. The houses in Linda's neighborhood were small and old—wooden one- and two-story homes, some with outhouses, and a few resembling shanties. Some homes were nice; others were untended and shabby with sagging porches, chipped paint, and overgrown, weedy lawns. Some held a dozen children. When the owners moved out, these houses were often torn down and replaced by new brick homes with attached garages.

Linda's house was little more than a shack, with no running water or bathroom. A large tree shaded the lot; the untrimmed grass was thin, needing only an occasional pass with a push mower. Her kitchen was heated by a potbellied wood stove. The only workspace was an old-fashioned sink and drain board on tall legs. A large wooden table and four chairs sat in the center of a linoleum floor, the pattern worn off in spots. Full, gallon jugs of water were piled beneath the sink, filled at a neighbor's. The house had electricity, but not central heat or plumbing.

Linda, her older brother, younger sister, two-year-old baby brother, and mother lived there. In a room next to the kitchen was a sofa that unfolded into a bed. It was always open, and a television was always on. A living room during the day, at night Linda and her sister slept there. Two small, unheated bedrooms completed the house, each only large enough to squeeze in a dresser and single bed. In a cold storage room, a toilet sat on an unfinished rough board floor; the toilet wasn't attached to plumbing and was emptied when necessary. I didn't use their "bathroom."

But the house was clean and Linda's clothes were neatly pressed. She never seemed to think she was disadvantaged—or if she did, she never mentioned it. Linda's cheerful mother seemed more interested in drinking beer from a quart bottle and joining our fun than acting like a mom, but friends were welcome anytime.

Linda wasn't my poor friend, just my friend, and fun to be with. Fun was important. Otherwise, high school could be frightening.

I lived a half mile away in a newly furnished, modern, three-bedroom ranch, in a subdivision of similar homes with well-kept lawns. I had my own bedroom. My father had a regular job, came home for dinner, and belonged to the Knights of Columbus. We went to Mass every Sunday, my mother was a housewife, and my kid brother was a pest. We lived by rules in our neighborhood; our mothers saw to that.

So why was Linda always laughing, and why was I cautious and dull? I felt like something was missing.

That summer before senior year we spent little time together because we both had summer jobs. I didn't have a clue what Linda wanted to show me that day. As we approached her house, I stopped short.

"Where did that come from?" I said. Next to Linda's house was a new brick ranch home.

Linda laughed. "That's my surprise!"

"A house. You dragged me half a mile to show me there's a new house next to yours, instead of the empty lot? Why couldn't you just tell me?"

"No, no," she laughed again. "It's not the house. It's who lives in it! Come on!"

She grabbed my arm knocking some books to the ground, scooped them up, and threw them back on my pile any which way. I trailed after her.

We climbed a short flight of concrete steps to a small porch. The front door was wide-open. Linda didn't knock but pulled the screen door open and walked into the living room as if it were her own. "We're here!" she shouted. I winced.

A woman-girl, not much older than me, strode into the room, heavy footsteps rattling the floor and tinkling unseen glassware, face beaming, arms thrown wide.

"You must be Cora," she said, her voice deep and somewhat intimidating. She threw her arms around me, pulled me over her pregnant belly, and rocked me one way and then the other with an enthusiasm that almost knocked me off my feet. My books tumbled to the floor; I wondered if they would survive the afternoon.

"Pick those up and throw them on a chair," she ordered Linda.

The room was in disarray, the furniture of the hand-me-down variety: a mismatch of blond wood, plush upholstery in ugly shades of green and gold, and a rattan bar that stood in a corner behind two bar stools. My grandmother collected things from her alley she insisted were still good and passed them out to her family. Perhaps this woman's family used the same designer. My schoolbooks joined an accumulation of blankets, clothing, and toys on the sofa, its cushions out of place.

She relaxed her embrace and held me at arm's length, turning me from side to side to examine me closely. "She'll do," she said at last. I must have passed some sort of test. I'm sure I looked more than a little embarrassed. I had no idea how to react to this welcome, let alone to the person giving it.

As she studied me, I made some observations about her. Average height but taller than Linda and me, who were both short. Thick, straight, dark-brown hair pulled into a messy ponytail. No makeup on her strong, somewhat masculine face. Large jaw, large nose, thick lips, prominent thick eyebrows. Warm brown eyes glinting with humor. Not a pretty face, but full of energy and intelligence. Pregnant. Big pregnant.

She released me. "She'll do," she said again, nodding at Linda. "But I thought you said she was fun. She looks freaked out."

"You just blew her mind, Jemma. Give her a minute. She'll be cool."

Before any more could be said, we were interrupted by a loud, angry wail. "Be right back," Jemma said, and she rushed to the rear of the house. She probably never did anything slowly.

She returned with a chubby baby in her arms, who she was rocking and cooing, *"Zitto,* Pumpkin. *Silenzio, calma, mia* Pumpkin. *Zitto, zitto."*

This was my first exposure to Italian.

Another wail came from what I presumed was the kitchen.

"Every time, first one, and then the other. Go see what Valerie wants, Linda."

Linda crooked her finger and I followed her into a long kitchen. A chrome and Formica table sat under a picture window at the front end. I suppressed a shudder at the turquoise-and-white-checked tabletop and turquoise vinyl chairs. This style was the rage, but in my opinion it was ugly. Between the table and the work area was a playpen with a little girl gripping its top; she was red-faced and screaming at a pile of stuffed animals and toys on the floor. Not a single toy remained in the playpen.

"I think she just wants her toys," I said. Although I knew nothing about babies, I thought the girl seemed kind of big for a playpen. She was on her feet jumping and demanding, "Toys!" I thought she might be over two years old.

"She'll just throw them out again." Linda picked up a well-worn, stuffed pony. The little girl squealed and reached for the pony. We put all the toys back in the playpen, and we were immediately forgotten.

We returned to the living room. Jemma sat in a chair with her chest entirely exposed, Pumpkin firmly attached and enthusiastically working away at Jemma's right breast. Embarrassed, I looked around, anywhere but at Jemma. On a table next to the sofa was a stack of books: Daphne du Maurier's *The Glass Blowers*, John Fowles's *The Collector*, Morris West's *The Shoes of the Fisherman*, and Victor Lasky's *J.F.K.: The Man and the Myth*. A framed black-and-white photo hung at an angle near the front door: a farmyard with a teenage girl and a younger boy sitting on a large horse. The girl resembled Jemma.

"Sit, sit," said Jemma, waving at the cluttered sofa. "What went on at school today, Cora?"

I pushed aside discarded clothes that filled the couch. "Um…we talked about *The Last of the Mohicans* in English…," I began, trying to avoid staring at Jemma's breasts.

"No, no, borrr-ing! What was *fun?*" Jemma interrupted.

I drew a blank.

"We skinned a cat in biology," Linda said.

"All right! That's more like it! Did the skin just pull off or did you have to slice it away?" Jemma turned to me again and waited for my opinion.

"Kind of both—we had to tease the skin bit by bit from the muscle while we pulled at it. There's this stuff called fascia that holds the skin on so you can't just pull it off," I said.

"In study hall, Mr. Hughes kept scratching his balls, and the whole class cracked up," Linda said. "He went ape shit, but when we quit laughing he started scratching again and it set us off again. What a skag! He had no clue what we were laughing at."

Jemma nodded toward me and said, "I bet Miss Innocent here was all red in the face. Do you think she got off on what he was doing?"

I felt my face get hot again. This went on for a while, until it dawned on me that they weren't picking on me, they were waiting for me to join them. I was more than a little square.

It wasn't long before Pumpkin, full and happy, fell asleep. Jemma checked on Valerie, holding Pumpkin in one arm against her still-naked chest. "She's sleeping too," she said. "Far out." She didn't lower her voice. Loud noises didn't seem to bother the sleeping children.

Jemma left the room to put Pumpkin back in her crib. When she returned she had a sly look on her face.

"Your friend is too uptight," she said, winking at Linda. "She needs a jump."

"Right on!" Linda said, bouncing with excitement.

Jemma grabbed my arm and pulled me up from the sofa. "Come on!" she said, dragging me toward the back of the house where I assumed the bedrooms were. She was strong and I didn't want to seem rude.

I threw a look of panic at Linda. "No, wait—"

"Come on, come on, you'll like it," Jemma said.

"Don't worry," Linda said, holding her sides, laughing, probably at the look on my face. "She's right...you'll like it."

Surely what I was thinking wouldn't really happen! Linda wouldn't... But Linda seemed entirely taken with her new friend. Who knew what they were into? Well, then, I'd have to fight Jemma off when it got to that point. I had no polite solution.

Jemma pulled me into a bedroom, closed the door, released my arm, and then leaped onto the bed. She rolled off the opposite side giggling and came back to stand next to me. "Go ahead, jump!" she ordered.

I realized what she wanted me to do then. With less enthusiasm, I sat on the side of the bed, rolled across it, and when I stood up on the other side Jemma cackled, grabbed my arm, and pulled me back into the living room, where she announced, "Okay, we had a jump. Doesn't she look better already?"

"Right on!" said Linda.

I couldn't help but giggle. I didn't really understand what was going on, and I wasn't used to this kind of abandon. I guessed "jumping" was something they did when things got dull to recapture the outrageous, and the misleading term "jump" was the whole point of the charade.

Before we left, Jemma said she was making lasagna on Saturday and invited me to learn how to cook Italian. She wouldn't take no for an answer, and truthfully, despite some pretense at reluctance, I wanted to be there.

That was how it was at Jemma's house. Hilarity in the moment—crude and silly, yet good-natured. Freedom that was new to me. Jemma had a knack for pulling out personal thoughts, for releasing what I held tight. Although I was uncomfortable and a bit scared, I was mesmerized. Jemma wasn't for everyone, but she filled a need in me, and, as we grew closer, I sensed I filled a need in her too.

I became a Jemma groupie.

# Chapter 17

"Why can't you come straight home from school? Where are you going?" my mother wanted to know.

How could I explain Jemma to my mother? I couldn't explain her to myself, and I certainly couldn't let on how we entertained ourselves.

I told my mother Linda and I went to Jemma's house to do homework. My mother wasn't crazy about Linda. Mom thought she was silly and loud, but she learned to accept her. I didn't tell her what Linda's home and family were like either, afraid she'd forbid me to go there.

The homework part was true—we *did* do homework, and Jemma joined us.

Jemma hadn't finished high school, and she was curious about what we were doing and studying.

"Cora writes the best slam books," Linda said. "A question in one she passed around study hall today was about crushes on movie stars. Most girls said Paul Newman, Richard Burton, Cary Grant, Gregory Peck, or Sean Connery. Some didn't read the question right and put down Bobby Darin, Ricky Nelson, or Elvis. But Georgina Scott put down Dick Van Dyke!"

Linda cackled. "Can you imagine? Dick Van Dyke? I mean he's funny and all. But sexy? God! Get real. We went ape shit, and Georgina flipped out. Mr. Olson came to see what was going on but I grabbed the book and sat on it."

Jemma listened to our homework questions and surprised us by how much she knew. She thumbed through our books and asked us to explain things, often with Pumpkin at her breast and Valerie toddling around the kitchen. If teaching was the best way to learn, teaching Jemma could explain why our grades kept going up despite all our clowning around.

We learned from Jemma too. Some Italian, especially swear words. Italian customs, stories about colorful relatives, about life in Sicily. Best of all we learned how to cook Italian food. Jemma made us do the work. She directed. Cooking at Jemma's house was as much fun as anything.

"Heat the pot first, *then* add the oil." It was olive oil, of course, from a quart bottle next to the stove, and the gravy pot was huge—bigger than any in our kitchen.

"Don't be so stingy with the oil, cover the bottom…that's better."

In went three and a half pounds of ground beef, a pound and a half of ground pork, and two chopped onions.

"Keep breaking it up. Be patient. It takes a while. Use the wooden spoon, the long one. Keep breaking up the meat until it's all crumbles."

Linda would throw her elbows out as she stirred, swaying from one foot to the other and singing, "Hello Muddah, hello Fadduh!"

I'd laugh and call out, "Here I am at…Camp Granada!"

Jemma would drop her voice, which was raspy anyway, to its lowest registers and sing, "Walk like a man, talk like a man…"

And we'd all chorus, "Walk like a man my son-uh-uh-uhn!"

When the meat and onions were brown, we added crushed garlic and cans of tomato puree and tomato paste, and then we doubled the volume with water so it would cook down slowly. Then parsley, basil and oregano, salt and pepper.

"Just a pinch of baking soda, not too much or it will be flat—that's too big! Okay, see how it foams up, takes some of the acid away? And a pinch of sugar, maybe half a teaspoon, you don't want it to taste sweet and it doesn't take much to ruin it. Let me taste it now. A little more salt—that's right. You taste it, so you'll know next time."

It cooked for hours. She told us tomato sauce, or gravy, was an object of pride in Italian homes. Some thought a two-hour gravy was fine, others swore by six hours. Jemma thought four was right.

"Cook it slow, no bubbling, just let it cook down. Stir every twenty minutes or so, for two minutes. You can skim some of the fat off, but leave a little for taste. See that dark line on the sides of the pot? Work that back into the gravy when you stir. The flavor gathers there; if you don't stir it in, you leave all the flavor in the pot instead of the gravy. No, no! Don't take the spoon out! Leave it in there—it adds taste too. When you see meat poking above the liquid, you know you cooked enough water out."

Sometimes she made meatballs and added neck bones for richer gravy. Or sometimes braciole, which was a lot of work: pounding beef, frying bacon, and combining it with grated Romano cheese and seasonings, then rolling, tying, browning, and bubbling in the gravy. But meat gravy, which we used to make lasagna, was my favorite.

Like many Italian families, Jemma grew her ingredients in a large vegetable garden that took up half of her backyard. She canned tomato sauce and green peppers and dried herbs for use year round.

"Maybe that Jemma's not so bad, after all," my mother said, when I made Jemma's lasagna recipe for a party.

Another friend of Linda's, Kathleen Sweeney, joined us now and then. Kathleen was even more of a square than me. And, I wasn't the butt of jokes when she was there.

We were Kathleen's only friends. She lived a block over from Jemma, in one of the old, two-story wooden houses, and was the oldest child in a large Irish family. She was average everything: average height, average weight, average school grades. She had dark, frizzy, greasy-looking hair; she walked with a slouch, and her clothing was outdated and worn. Kids made fun of her at school and called her scuzzy because of her looks and habits, like jerking her head and playing with her zits. She was used to being made fun of, so we picked on her too, at least Linda and I did.

Her mother made her do housework and watch the younger kids. She was afraid of her mother but never told us why. When she could, she escaped to Jemma's house.

Linda, who had gone to Jemma's Labor Day family picnic, filled me in about Jemma's family.

"Her parents seemed kind of cold. They spoke Italian to the older relatives and ignored everyone else. Jemma was the life of the party, always hugging everyone, joking, and mouthing off, like she does with us. Her mother gave her dirty looks."

Jemma's older sister, Lucia, had Down syndrome.

"Lucia mostly watched all day. She laughed when something amused her, but not always appropriately. She stared at Jemma with big puppy eyes. Jemma treated her nice and let her hold Pumpkin. You should have seen the look on her face—like Jemma just gave her a million dollars."

Jemma had three brothers. Angelo and Aniello—called Nello—were twins. Angelo lived in Chicago with his wife, who was pregnant with their first child. He had recently been accepted by the Chicago Police Department and would start training soon. No one knew exactly what Nello did besides act the big shot. He lived with his parents in Oak Lawn but spent most of his time with friends and relatives in the western suburbs.

"Whatever he does, it must pay good," Linda said. "He drove up in a light-blue Studebaker Gran Turismo, and I heard he's a big spender with the ladies."

Barbaro, Jemma's kid brother, was a junior in high school. Jemma worried about him dropping out and about his friends.

"He's been arrested for underage drinking, driving without a license, shoplifting—basically being in the wrong place at the wrong time. Nello always gets him out. He's just like Nello when it comes to girls. Claims he had sex when he was eleven. Can you believe that?" Linda said.

"Barbaro?" I said. "I've never heard that name."

"The younger relatives call him Bobby. From what I could see, he's got a screw loose. And he's a bullshitter."

One afternoon, Jemma told us about Nonna, her grandmother, who had died a number of years ago. Old country as Jemma's mother and father were, Nonna was even more colorful.

"She wore a long black skirt but no underwear. She would take us kids places on the bus. Once when we were waiting at the bus stop, she had to pee. She pointed to the sky and told us, 'Look, look, a plane.' Then she spread her legs apart and let loose while we searched for a plane that wasn't there. Didn't even get her shoes wet," Jemma said in apparent admiration.

Nonna had been religious to the point of eccentricity. Nello had been hit in the head and despite the doctors' dire predictions miraculously recovered. "Nonna took credit. She said he got better because she made a a deal with God for Nello's life. She brought me with her to church to make good on her promise. 'You and God are my witnesses,' Nonna told me. 'I promised to keep His altar railing polished, where people kneel in His presence, if He would save Nello's life.' She dragged me to the end of the railing, knelt, and started licking the railing. It was disgusting! I can't imagine God liked that sort of bargain, but damned if I could stop her," Jemma said.

It was clear from the way Jemma talked about her that she had loved Nonna very much. I was fascinated by the pictures Jemma was painting of the old world.

Meanwhile, I was becoming increasingly involved with school activities.

In advanced biology class one Friday, I was shocked when Jimmy LaPlante, out on hall pass, ran into our lab, yelling, "The president's been shot!"

Mrs. Orr turned on a radio. The news was very bad. Many people wouldn't find out until they came home and turned on their televisions. Who doesn't like to be the first to tell important news? My father was home alone. I asked to make a phone call and was given a pass. There was a public phone booth in the front school hall. I sat down, pulled the door closed, and put a dime in the slot.

"Have you heard the news?" I said, when my father answered.

"What news?"

"It's the president. He's been shot!"

"Shot! Is he okay?"

"No…he's…he's dead." That's when the full impact hit. I couldn't speak over a lump in my throat. Tears poured down my cheeks and I sobbed. I heard my father crying on the other end of the line.

School was canceled on Monday so we could all watch the funeral on television. Jemma, Linda, and I watched at Jemma's house. It was hard for us to say what we felt, since we weren't used to sharing sad things, only fun things.

We saw the president's three-year-old son, John-John, salute his father, and we believed he did it spontaneously, not because he was told to. We saw the riderless horse and heard the newscaster explain it was a tribute to a fallen soldier, and we believed Black Jack was Jackie Kennedy's horse, even though it was said later that wasn't true.

I think Jemma cried the hardest. She cried silently, tears streaming freely down her cheeks. She just let them run and drip from her chin. When I opened my mouth to say something, she waved at me to be quiet.

I remembered seeing *J.F.K.: The Man and the Myth* in her living room the day we met. If she had read the book, she mustn't have believed the unkind things written about Kennedy and his family.

Linda didn't shed any tears, but I saw her chin quiver and her teeth clench tight. For once she had nothing witty to say.

We didn't visit Jemma during the week following the funeral. We would be tempted to laugh if we were together, and we weren't ready to laugh yet.

## Chapter 18

Jemma's husband, Sal, had a killer smile. He was gorgeous—average height, stocky, with thick curly hair. But the way he stared at me made me uncomfortable. Maybe men from Sicily acted like he did, but I had a feeling that behind his smile he was thinking things I didn't want to know.

We were at Jemma's kitchen table doing homework when we heard the back door open and someone entered the utility room. Jemma jumped up, turned on the faucet, and started piling dishes in the sink. Sal walked into the room and said something in Italian. He sounded bossy, a bit angry. Jemma dried her hands. She moved toward us and gestured at me. She seemed uncharacteristically meek and a little nervous.

"This is Cora," she said. "The one I've been telling you about."

I stood up, smiled, and approached him. He looked me up and down and then gave me a hug that felt too clingy. He let me go, winked, and said, *"Bel culo."* As he left the room, behind Jemma's back, he turned and gave me another wink. Then he opened his mouth, stuck his tongue out, wiggled it rapidly from side to side, and laughed.

I asked Jemma what *"bel culo"* meant.

"Nice ass," she said. She laughed, but it sounded forced. I had never seen her look embarrassed before, but she did then. Linda saw the thing Sal did with his tongue and laughed too.

I didn't have a nice ass. It was flat, which is only a little better than fat, and Sal hadn't seen my backside. I assumed the comment was one he used a lot.

Every time I saw Sal after that I pictured the wiggling tongue. He rarely spoke to me, but he'd catch my eye and make gestures now and then. I didn't know what the gestures meant and suspected I wouldn't like it if I did. I didn't want to admit to my friends that I was naive, so I didn't ask. I was square, remember.

I also thought he was disrespectful to Jemma. But, I couldn't picture the two of them together. Something felt wrong. I was sad for Jemma.

During the Christmas holidays, Linda and I helped Jemma get ready for Christmas Eve. We made an edible tree, stacking crispy sweet balls of fried dough on a large round platter and then pouring honey over the top. This was the only baking we did, because Jemma said relatives would bring cannoli and cream-filled *zeppoli* bought on Taylor Street in Chicago.

When spring came, Jemma made asparagus. My mother had tried unsuccessfully to get me to eat asparagus. Jemma cut it on a slant into one-inch pieces and fried the pieces in a large pan with a half-stick of butter, and when the stalks were bright green with a little brown she added a dozen scrambled eggs.

I rolled my eyes when I tasted Jemma's asparagus. "Outta sight! Where has this been all my life?"

One day Jemma met us at the door and asked if we would excuse her for a few days since she didn't feel well. One side of her face looked red and a little puffy, and she was holding one arm with the other while she struggled with the door. She was smiling as always, but I didn't think she was telling the truth.

I began to wonder if Jemma's life was as terrific as she led us to believe. What came to mind were gangsters.

The Mob entered my mind because Jemma avoided talking about the Mob, which made me suspect her family had some sort of connection. When her brothers Nello or Bobby got in trouble, they got out of it easily. Also, sometimes friends or relatives came by dressed—well, they dressed like how I thought mobsters would dress—in tight black shirts and pointy shoes, and they drove expensive-looking, big black cars. They were good-natured and friendly to us, and then they would take Sal outside and leave after talking to him.

I had asked Jemma about these guys. I said, "I met a girl from Kentucky. When I told her I was from Chicago she was horrified. She thought everyone from Chicago was a gangster and asked if I knew Al Capone. I was surprised. Do you know anyone in the Mob?"

Jemma had laughed but looked uncomfortable. "Most Sicilians know someone in the Mob, but we don't talk about it. Men have their business. Women look the other way."

"Your family too? Really?"

"It's rumor, Cora. Only rumor. Italians got that reputation. Sometimes things aren't what they seem. Don't worry about it." She had laughed it off.

I couldn't help but wonder if some such aspect of Italian life had something to do with Jemma's bruised face and arm.

I didn't say anymore. It was exciting to a point. I was interested, but I only wanted to talk about it, not experience it.

In the fall I started my freshman year at St. Xavier College, determined to get off to a good start. I didn't have much time for old friends, but Linda talked me into going to Jemma's family picnic one Sunday in late September.

"You have to meet Jemma's cousin Carlo," Linda said. She had been talking about Carlo for over a month and was clearly obsessed.

The spring family picnic had been held at Sagawau Canyon. The place had once been a YWCA camp, but now the forest preserves owned it. Most of the time it was closed and entrance was not allowed, except for occasional educational programs. Somebody in Jemma's family knew someone who got a permit for the picnic. We had explored the rustic, rundown cabins and splashed through the creek at the base of the canyon.

The fall picnic, though, was held at a public grove, McClaughrey Springs, a small place with only a dozen picnic tables. A pretty little creek, studded with rocks to jump across, ran beyond the tables, and on its far side was a great sand hill. The hill ran about a hundred feet high, with woods on either side. We climbed the almost perpendicular hill, two steps up followed by one sliding back down, taking twenty exhausting minutes to climb it, using both hands and feet to reach the summit and then racing down with giant leaps, shoulders thrown back for balance, trying to stop before landing in the creek.

When I couldn't take any more sand, I helped cook. Jemma's aunts had gathered something she called "gardune" from the roadside, a weed with blue flowers.

"You've never had gardune? You're in for a treat," Jemma said.

We removed leaves and spines from the stalks, peeled them, cut them into one-inch pieces, and soaked them in cold water and lemon. I was leery of eating anything that grew along the road, but Jemma said I'd love it and she'd never been wrong. We boiled and then fried the stalks—in butter, of course—and then added eggs like we'd done in the spring with asparagus.

The result was sort of mushy and stringy, but it tasted nothing short of wonderful. Jemma said it tasted like artichokes, but I hadn't eaten them either.

"You have to try artichokes the Italian way," she said. "They look like big green pine cones, and you stuff bread crumbs flavored with herbs and garlic at the base of each leaf, then steam them until they're tender. You pull the leaves off, dip them in melted butter, and pull off the soft part with your teeth. It's great."

"Sounds like a lot of work for a mouthful," I said.

After we ate, Linda wandered off with Carlo. I heard her peals of laughter from a distance. Carlo impressed me as a smooth operator who was fun to be with, but he was too old and acted like he owned her. Something about him seemed dangerous to me. Linda was crazy about him.

Jemma and I strolled up the creek, while a couple of aunts watched over the napping Valerie and Pumpkin and the new baby, Pudge. It had seemed that Jemma was pregnant a ridiculously long time before her son was born, but perhaps she seemed so large when I met her because she kept her belly after giving birth to Pumpkin. Even now, she waddled as she walked.

We came to a pretty clearing and sat on a fallen log, enjoying the peace and quiet, away from our customary chaos.

"You and your brothers and sister speak English very well for having been born in Italy," I commented.

"That's because we weren't. Mamma and Papá came here in the 1930s. We were born in Argo-Summit."

I was surprised. The family seemed foreign. I had thought they were all immigrants.

"You grew up in Oak Lawn?"

"Part of the time. We moved around. We lived on a farm near here for a few years, before I went to Sicily." She waved her arm to indicate the surrounding woods. "That's why the forest preserves are so familiar to us. We even had to fight forest fires."

"Wow—that must have been scary."

"We were careful. Usually only what's on the ground burns. We had to stand with our backs to the wind and beat the ground with long paddles we called 'flappers.'"

"So how did you meet Sal? How long has he been here?"

"I met Sal in Sicily. I was visiting family. I went to school in Sicily for a while, just a few months, and then I met Sal and married him. We stayed there at first—Valerie was born there—but then Sal wanted to come to the States. He said there were more opportunities here than in Sicily."

"For work you mean? What kind of work does he do?"

She stared at the gurgling creek, glinting blue where the sun hit it. She crossed her arms and rubbed them. "Oh, different things. He has family and friends in construction. They give him jobs. Sometimes he loads or drives trucks; sometimes he works with carpenters or masons, whatever they need done. His family and my family, they take care of him. Sal and I are cousins, you know."

I didn't know, and I was shocked. "Cousins! How can you be married? Isn't that incest or something? And weren't you awfully young? What were you, fifteen?"

She laughed. "Not that close, more a cousin of a cousin kind of thing. Marriages like ours are pretty common in Sicily."

I was only a little relieved. "Why did you go to Sicily? Did your brothers go too?"

"No, just me. Mamma had her hands full and wanted to get rid of me for a while." She laughed, but I got the feeling this wasn't really a joke.

"Your mother and your father, too, they're nice and stuff, but…I may be wrong…it seems like you avoid them." I had heard them snapping at Jemma and didn't think they were nice at all.

"I guess I got a bit difficult around eighth grade. We fought a lot. Rather than argue with me, my mother thought I'd learn how to behave from relatives back in her hometown. We didn't realize I'd be gone so long, almost three years."

That didn't seem a very good reason, but I only knew their culture through Jemma. So instead of pressing I said, "Or that you'd come home with a husband and two kids. That's very romantic. Quite the love story."

"You could say that." She didn't look at me.

I remembered the day she met us at the door holding her arm.

"Is everything okay?" I asked.

She smiled weakly. "Italian men have a little different way of looking at things, different from American men. But yes, everything is fine." I thought she seemed sad.

"It's just…" She didn't finish her thought, but gazed into the trees, her attention caught by a birdcall.

"I wonder what kind of bird is making that sound. I can't find it. Can you?"

I didn't want to be distracted. I suspected I was about to learn something important about my friend.

"No," I said. "It's just what?"

She chewed on a thumbnail and then sighed. "It's not the life I thought I'd have. I thought I'd put my brain to more use than being a housewife. I don't know, I thought I'd have time for things I loved, things I miss."

"What things?"

"Oh…nothing important." She looked at me with a grin that seemed more sad than happy. "I told you we used to live on a farm. I had a horse, Baby. I was a dreamer as a kid. I rode Baby out on the trails alone, and I read a lot of horse and romance books. I wanted a romance, like in the books, but the end of the story…" She paused, put a forefinger to her lips, gazed away with a dreamy look, and then smiled and turned back to me.

"I suppose that involved marriage and kids, so you could say I have my happy ending. Sal's quite the good-looking guy, and he treats me okay. The kids are great."

We sat for a while without talking. I didn't get her point—couldn't put my finger on what Jemma thought was missing. There must be more to the story.

"Before I went to Sicily, I had a crush on a guy. He was older than me and worked at my school. I suppose I thought I'd end up with him. But then I went to Sicily and everything changed."

"What happened to him?"

She looked away from me and said in a quiet voice, "I have no idea. I never saw him again." When she turned back, her eyes glinted with their customary humor. "Did I tell you our farm was haunted?"

"No! Really?"

"Well, I thought so. I used to hear strange sounds in the night, and I saw this man on horseback now and then."

She told me stories about a haunted golf course, buried nuclear waste, strange animals she found, and her sister talking in weird voices in her sleep. "Like a different person, a man speaking Italian in a deep voice, about horses and danger and warnings."

Perhaps she was dramatizing to make a good story, but she had seemed uneasy when we talked about spooky stuff on other occasions.

"Does stuff like this still happen to you?" I asked.

"Not since I left the farm."

When we were walking back, I asked, "What happened to your horse?"

"Baby? Baby was killed. While I was in Sicily. The family was getting ready to move from the farm—she got away and ran out on the road. A truck hit her and they had to destroy her. I'm glad I wasn't there when it happened—that I didn't have to see it."

My friend had abandoned her dreams and left a boyfriend behind to start a life with Sal. Did she regret that decision? She'd had three children with him, and she seemed happy. But after this serious conversation, the only one I ever had with Jemma, I suspected her usually cheerful demeanor was an act. Was the laughter we shared a way to escape her problems?

I theorized that Jemma faced difficulties by living in the now. She said you made your own happiness. If you acted happy, you were happy. No matter what happened or how you felt about it, you had to get up, dress up, show up, and make the most of life. I try to follow her example to this day.

But *that* day, walking beside the creek, I saw sadness in Jemma's face. I didn't realize it at the time, but she knew we were already moving in separate directions.

Jemma had become so much a part of my life, it was hard to believe we would drift apart after only a little more than three years. By the time I was in my third year of college, Linda, Jemma, and I had taken paths that did not include each other.

# Chapter 19
## April 1967

The greatest disaster to strike Oak Lawn, Illinois, happened while I was preparing for final exams and writing my senior thesis. Cisco and I were making plans for our wedding. It couldn't have been a worse time—but when is a good time for a disaster?

St. Xavier College was a fifteen-minute commute from Oak Lawn, but my senior year I moved into a dorm to be more immersed in my studies. I was taking twenty-one credit hours besides auditing a four-hour bacteriology course I thought I needed.

Alone in my room late on the afternoon of Friday, April 21, a gust of wind hit the window. I looked outside. The sky was dark, the air an unnatural greenish color, the wind bending the few young trees behind the dorm, and the little lake nearby murky and rippled.

Two hours earlier I had walked from class to the dorm. It was a beautiful, sunny spring day, the temperature in the 70s. Now classmates were banging on doors, yelling for everyone to get to the basement. Tornado warnings had been issued on the radio. There were no sirens in those days.

Violent storms and tornado warnings occurred every spring. Storms blew things around and looked scary, but that's about all. Comprehensive exams were next week, my thesis was unfinished, and my adviser had me preparing slides for oral presentation. I didn't know how to make slides. So, like many other students that day, I kept on working and checked the window now and then. The sky went from green to black. I turned on my ceiling light. The wind howled and the windows rattled as sheets of rain struck like a waterfall. But the storm was soon over.

I was marking the labels of some slides when Gloria Hughes threw my door open.

"On the radio!" she said, red-faced and breathless. "A tornado!"

"Really? Where?"

"Oak Lawn."

My home and my parents and my kid brother Jack were four miles away in Oak Lawn. On the radio, the newscaster's voice was excited. A tornado had touched down in Oak Lawn—confirmed, few details yet, but much damage was expected.

I waited in line at the phone down the hall. When it was my turn, I got only a busy signal. About nine in the evening, a classmate came for me.

"It's your mother—on the phone."

The first thing my mother said was, "We're all okay."

Relieved, I said, "That's good. I couldn't get through to you."

"I thought you'd be worried." Her voice sounded strained.

"These things get exaggerated on the news, but I'm glad you called."

There was a long silence. Mom was always blunt when she was upset. "Cora, do you know what happened?"

"A tornado hit somewhere, but I don't know much more."

"Cora, it's bad. It's a nightmare. The National Guard is here. No one can go in or out."

My scalp prickled. Should I call Cisco to come get me? Would the guards let us in?

"But you're all fine?" I asked, even though she'd already told me. "How about the house?"

"Jack and I are fine. The house is fine. But your dad was in the school gym when it struck. He was at the corner that was last to collapse, but he escaped. The gym is gone."

Oh my God! The gym collapsed around my dad! But he escaped…

"I was working at Jewel. It came through the parking lot but missed the store. The front windows blew out. All of us had moved to the back and no one in the store got hurt. But the bus station across the street is gone too." Her voice broke. She took a shaky breath before adding, "I can't recognize anything. Just piles of wood, bricks, and metal…people are dead."

I didn't know what to say, couldn't think straight. Our house was a block from the high school, two blocks from the bus station. "Our house? Jack?" I asked yet again.

"Like nothing happened—a few small branches off the trees. Jack said all he saw was dark—and he could see and hear the wind, of course."

"That's what happened here, too."

"If it had been fifty feet in either direction...," I heard her catch her breath again on a sob, "either your dad or I...would have been a direct hit."

"Oh, Mom," was all I could say.

"Your father—I have to get back to him. He got blown down, hit with pieces of glass and metal. He's very emotional. He ran to the house as soon as it was over. He saw Jack was okay and then came to find me. He had to go through the tornado area—the destruction, the bodies.... By the time he got to me he was sobbing, saying, 'I thought I lost you, I thought I lost you.' Your dad needs me now. I have to pick glass out of his face and hands, help him calm down."

The next morning the National Guard let Cisco and me through the barricade when I showed them my driver's license and address. As Mom had said, our house was untouched. So was the area immediately around the barricade and the streets we had taken to approach the house.

After seeing for ourselves that all was well at home, we walked near the touchdown. Nothing was recognizable. We were too upset to want to see more, and we left.

Then we went to check on friends. I realized with a shock I hadn't seen my Oak Lawn friends for a year.

Jemma's house was gone, only rubble and foundation to mark the place of so many cheerful memories. Linda's old house, right next door, still stood in all its former squalor.

~~~

Late in the fall that followed the tornado, Linda called me to get together. She suggested a Saturday afternoon. We'd pick up Jemma and go to a restaurant, Italian of course.

Linda now lived in a two-room, basement apartment in an old bungalow on the West Side of Chicago. She started laughing as soon as she opened the door. "How did you know how I'm wearing my hair now?" she said, as I entered.

People sometimes mistook Linda and me for sisters. We were the same size and coloring, with shoulder-length, mousy-brown, difficult-to-manage hair. The style those days was shoulder length, teased high on top, the ends flipped up in a sassy curl that resembled a sausage. Looking at Linda was like looking in a mirror.

Besides identical hairdos, we both wore pink twinset sweaters, but the duplication stopped there. I wore a light gray, stitched-pleat skirt and Linda a black skirt with a kick pleat. Black flats had replaced the neatly folded-down white, bobby socks and penny loafers we wore in high school.

I'd never been to that part of the city near Cicero and Madison Streets and the Lake Street el that Linda rode each day to her job at the Prudential Building in downtown Chicago.

"I'm sharing the apartment with Kathleen, but she's working today—doing inventory. She'll join us when she gets off," Linda said.

"Kathleen?" I said, surprised. "How did that happen? I thought you didn't care for her."

"She's okay. She's like a mama. She tells me what to do and then does it herself when I don't do it soon enough to suit her."

"That's another way of saying she's bossy?"

"Right on."

"And you like that?"

She shrugged her shoulders. "There are advantages. She's company. She puts up with me. That's not so easy."

"We used to say she had cooties."

Linda giggled. "I forgot that. She doesn't. In fact she's a clean freak."

We left Linda's place and walked south on Cicero Avenue to where Jemma lived. She and Sal hadn't been able to afford to rebuild the house in Oak Lawn after the tornado, Linda told me. They all landed in the same Italian neighborhood.

"How's Carlo?" I asked. "You two still hot and heavy?"

She wrinkled her nose. "For the moment. He's got a wife, you know."

I didn't know. "What? Doesn't the whole family know you two are a thing?"

"Yeah, well, Chickie, his wife, isn't too happy, but she puts a good face on it, for the kids."

"But what about you? What's in it for you?"

"You met Carlo. He treats me like a princess. But that's a problem too." She watched my eyes. "He's pretty possessive. I'm afraid to break it off."

"You mean he might hurt you?"

She watched her feet for a few steps. "I don't know, Cora. I'll figure it out."

We stopped at the door of a small shop with an ugly sofa and chair in the window below a sign that said Sal's Slipcovers. The sofa and chair were upholstered in a light-colored brocade fabric with clear plastic covers.

This was what Jemma was doing? Plastic covers were supposed to protect furniture while allowing the fabric to show through. Some people went so far as to throw a sheet over their furniture to protect the plastic until company came. Even floors had plastic carpet runners.

In my opinion, what the covers did was make ugly furniture last forever. The plastic was stiff, tacky, and uncomfortable, with sharp spots on the seams that sliced your skin if you weren't careful. The plastic burned your legs and stuck to you in the summer, and in the winter it was brittle, cold, and slippery.

But the plastic fad was pretty much over now. I doubted anyone bought it anymore. It beat me why Sal thought this was the business to get into. Sure enough when we entered the shop the place was empty, and Jemma was reading a book behind the counter.

Jemma had bags under her eyes and was carrying more "baggage" in her butt. Although the mischievous look returned to her eyes when she saw us, her characteristic energy seemed to be missing. It made me sad. Jemma was just a little older than us, and, as far as I was concerned, *my* life was just beginning. Jemma looked like she was putting a good face on things to keep from giving up.

"There's nothing going on here," she said. "Let Sal handle things if anyone comes in. Let's go for a walk and then go eat."

We walked north on Cicero, passing storefronts and churches, until we got to the el station, turned east, and walked through old but quiet streets of brick bungalows that were more than fifty years old. Some had "Room for Rent" signs in the windows.

"How's newlywed life?" Jemma asked. "Getting enough?"

I felt my face turn red. I couldn't forget our former blunt conversations, but I was out of practice.

"We've got hand-me-down furniture. Our apartment is pretty nice. We have five rooms," I said, instead of answering her last question. "Cisco's full name may be Arturo Valentino Tozzi, but I can't serve him Italian food every night. I've had a few failures, like when I put two tablespoons of buggy paprika in beef stew. It was the first time I used paprika. I didn't know it wasn't supposed to be spongy."

Between their guffaws, Linda asked, "But did he like it?"

"He did, actually, until I noticed the little bug legs and made him stop eating it."

Jemma told us she had cousins, aunts, and uncles nearby, and they helped out. The neighborhood wasn't fancy, but it was safe and affordable. Her parents still lived in Oak Lawn, since their home had been untouched by the tornado.

"Sal wanted to use the insurance money to start a business. He said that's why he came to America. The money wasn't enough, of course, but he got more somewhere," she said.

"What do you and the kids think?" I asked. I wondered if any of Jemma's children had started school yet. Valerie and Pumpkin should have, I calculated, but Sally, or Little Sal, who we used to call Pudge, would be too young.

"Oh, men make these decisions," she said. "I didn't have much say."

"Maybe not," I said, "but you must have some feelings."

"It's okay." She looked resigned, but not unhappy. "The kids will make new friends. The schools are okay, and it's nice to have relatives nearby. The business…well, it's not making a ton of money, but it keeps me occupied, and you know I like to be busy." She laughed, seeming her old self.

"So, I saw the store, but where do you live?"

"Our apartment is upstairs from the business. It's pretty big: living room, dining room, big kitchen, two bedrooms, an enclosed porch."

It sounded nice. "Where was Sal when we left?"

"There's another room and a workshop in the back, behind the store. Sal hangs out there most of the time, even when we're closed. It's not that we get many orders or that his work is all that good, but he has a lot of friends coming in and out. Tell the truth, I don't know what he does back there all day. I'm persona non grata, haven't been back there for months, but I yell to him if I need him and he comes up front."

No wonder she was dejected. As outgoing as Jemma was, she must be lonely.

She told us a little about the business, how her part was to go to customers' homes to measure furniture and then deliver and install the orders.

"I even drive a truck, but you wouldn't want to be on the same street with me," she laughed.

We arrived at a small, red-brick building with a recessed doorway and a large window, the bottom half covered with simple white curtains. Inside were six square tables covered with red-and-white-checked tablecloths and white cloth napkins. Mid-afternoon, the place was empty of customers. A man came from the back and greeted Jemma with a smile.

"Let me see if there's an open table," he said, laughing and waving an arm around the deserted restaurant. We sat and he brought glasses of water with ice and lemon. He must have guessed we'd be sitting for a while.

"I gotta tell you this story," Jemma said lowering her voice. "The phone company gave us our business number, see? Turns out it used to belong to some guy, probably an enforcer, for the Mob. So we're getting his calls, right?"

"Uh, oh," Linda said.

"So Sal, he's a wise guy, right? Not a Mob kind of wiseguy, just a regular wise guy." She snickered. "And he thinks it's fun to play along, so he does. He pretends the guy they're looking for stepped out, and he'll give him the message. But of course, there's no guy to give the message to, but the jamoke that's calling doesn't know that. He's talking Italian, he sounds the part, and he hams it up."

I'm grinning now, knowing this had to be going somewhere.

"So one night I'm closing up and this big black car pulls up, double-parks on the street, and two big hefty guys get out and the driver stays put. They walk in and ask for Joey the Hammer. I know nothing of course and I look blank and shake my head. They go in the back and they drag Sal out. One guy is holding Sal's arms behind his back and the other guy is waving his fist and yelling in his face, demanding to know where Joey is and didn't Sal give him their messages."

"What did you do? Weren't you afraid?" I asked.

"What could I do? I let Sal handle it. He's excited, he's talking Italian, and he tells them about the phone number and having a little fun. And he's trying to laugh, and they're not buying it, until he tells them to check with Mickey. And they look at each other and they calm down. Finally the goons let him go. One of them says they should rough him up because he's too stupid to know this kind of business is no place for jokes, but because of Mickey they'll let him alone—this time."

It was a funny story, but it sounded dangerous. The more Jemma told us about her current life, the more I sensed there was something wrong.

If I dug further, the day could turn sour. There wasn't likely to be anything I could do anyway. What had always gotten us through was not thinking about bad times, but finding humor in our lives.

"I've been meaning to ask, Jemma," I said, starting the ball rolling, "do you still have that one long hair on your nipple?"

We carried on late into the evening, cutting loose like the old days. When Kathleen got there we fell into our old habit of teasing her, which she took with good nature. She didn't have a lot to add to the conversation, just laughed with us and looked stern when we got too loud and other customers glared at us. By the end of the night I had a generally better opinion of her.

Linda hadn't changed a bit. She still made outrageous comments and still only looked at the funny side of life. Yet, I wondered how funny her affair with Carlo was and how and when it would end, as it surely would.

Jemma kept up with us, but I couldn't shake the feeling that she was worried and unhappy, maybe even frightened. If it was Sal or something else, I had no way to know.

I had a college education, a job, a husband. My life with Linda and Jemma was in the past. Although they would always be important and fond memories, I was leaving these old friends to the new lives they had chosen and for the new life I had chosen. I hoped for the best for them.

It was many years before I saw Jemma again.

# Chapter 20
## 1979

Kathleen, who was living in Arizona, came to Chicago for her niece's wedding. She called Linda, who then invited me to join them for lunch at her house.

Cisco and I had two sons. We lived in a suburb southwest of Chicago, a starter home in a community of little boxes all the same. I worked evenings part-time in a nearby medical office.

Linda was married then too, but had no children. She lived in the western suburbs and still worked in downtown Chicago. Even though we lived barely an hour apart, we seldom talked and I'd never been to her home.

I got to Linda's house early because I wanted to see her more than I did Kathleen. We sipped coffee, falling easily into the mirthful patter of our youth.

"Where's Tony today?" I asked. I liked Linda's husband, Tony.

"I sent him to his sister's. I think we'll be too much for him." Linda never told me what happened between her and Carlo, and I didn't ask. Obviously the relationship had ended somehow.

When the doorbell rang an hour later it felt like an interruption.

"Did you get lost?" Linda greeted Kathleen at the door. I stood behind her.

"Lost! You haven't heard the worst of it," Kathleen said. She turned and beckoned to someone in a gray car in the driveway.

Jemma emerged from the car. Laughing uncontrollably, she staggered up the walk as if she were drunk.

Surprised to see my friend, I grinned, warmth filling my chest.

"Get in here, Jemma!" Kathleen said, biting her cheeks, her words a poor attempt at sternness. "Let's pour some wine before you tell them what you did." She held up a bottle and waved it.

Soon we were all seated at the kitchen table, smiling at each other fondly, observing changes. We had all gained twenty pounds or so. Jemma had a few gray patches, but the other three of us still had the mousy hair we had when we were teens.

Jemma dissolved into giggles again, and Kathleen shook her head, struggling to contain her mirth.

"All the houses on this block look alike," Jemma began, dashing tears from her cheeks with her arm.

"Oh no, you went to the wrong house?" Linda said. "Why is that so funny?"

"Worse than that—"

"Wait until you hear," Kathleen interrupted, putting her hand over her eyes.

"You didn't know I was coming. We wanted to surprise you."

"Yes…"

"So we went to the door, which was open, and the screen door wasn't locked. So I pushed it open, went in, did this little dance across the room, threw my arms out, and announced, 'We're here!'"

Shaking her head with a crooked grin, Kathleen said, "And I'm standing outside the door, and I'm looking at this man lying on the couch watching TV."

Jemma could barely talk again. "And he got up on one elbow…and said, 'Well…that's good. But who the hell are you?'"

Linda guffawed, spraying wine through her nose.

We all roared. We never needed a kick start to get rolling, but we had one nonetheless.

So the afternoon went on into the evening, our conversation as outrageous as if there had been no years between. No person, no topic was off limits. Some of that day comes back like it just happened last week.

"Last month was my mother's birthday," Linda said. Linda's mother suffered from Alzheimer's. "After she opened her presents we put them back in their boxes and gave them to her again. We kept doing that for almost an hour. She loved getting so many presents."

I felt ashamed for laughing, but Linda's cackle was contagious. What was the harm? It made Linda's mother happy. Wasn't it better to laugh than let it make you crazy?

I enjoyed being with my friends, but as the afternoon wore on I noticed that now and then Jemma seemed distracted. When I caught her eye, she'd grin and chip in a funny comment. A number of times she glanced around nervously. When a robin flew past the patio door, Jemma startled and said, "What's that?"

Kathleen put her hand on Jemma's arm and a look passed between them. "I'm such a birdbrain," Jemma said, laughing. "Don't know why I'm so jittery—guess I'm just excited to see you all again."

Jemma told us she and Sal had divorced. Kathleen had moved to Phoenix for health reasons and worked as a typist at an insurance company, sharing an apartment with Jemma. I remembered that Kathleen had liked to have someone to boss around when she lived with Linda.

Jemma told us she got her GED before her divorce and then got a degree as a laboratory technician. I was proud of her. It must have been hard to be wife and mother, run a business, and get a degree. I shouldn't have been surprised, since she had always been keenly interested in our schoolwork. Sal used to mock her attempts at education in front of us. He wouldn't have understood her desire to improve herself. Was that why they divorced?

"How are your kids?" I asked. Valerie should be out of high school by now, the others a little younger—what were their names? Oh yes, Pumpkin, but her real name? And the boy? Pudge?

"Oh, they're fine. They're still in Oak Lawn with my family. They didn't want to leave their friends."

I struggled to understand. How could she leave her children? Her reason seemed a poor excuse to me. Shouldn't they be with their father, Sal, instead of with her family? Why didn't she want to talk about them?

Then she changed the subject. "What's been going on in Chicago?"

"Chicago has a woman mayor now, Jane Byrne," I told them.

"We heard that. So Old Man Daley's gone after all those terms. How's that going?" Jemma said.

"Some people like Jane, others don't. She's making the city look good, putting on festivals and fireworks. People like that. She's strong-minded, which ruffles some feathers. She changes her mind a lot. Some people say that's what to expect from a woman."

"Ah, ah, ah...," Linda said, waving a finger in the air.

"I understand the Mob isn't too happy with her," I added. "Word is the Mob helped her get elected to control their interests. But the first thing she did in office was declare a cleanup of organized crime—supposedly the worst in the world."

Jemma went pale. Her jaw quivered. She excused herself and went to the bathroom.

I'd always been nervous about possible ties between Jemma's family and the Mob, while Jemma had seemed to casually accept this part of life. Strange that she would be uncomfortable now. Or, was I seeing things that weren't there?

Kathleen answered my unspoken questions.

"Jemma's older brother, one of the twins, was shot and killed by a gangbanger at Cabrini-Green," she whispered. "It hit Jemma hard and, to top it off, she couldn't return for the funeral."

That's right, Jemma's brother, one of the twins, was a Chicago policeman. But Kathleen had said it was a gang shooting... Why would talking about the Mob make her think of her brother?

"And don't ask any more about Sal or her children," Kathleen said. "She doesn't like to talk about them."

I changed the subject when Jemma returned. "What about when we had that séance at your house?" I said.

Jemma poured an inch of wine into her empty glass, picked it up, frowned and set it down again. She reached for a handful of potato chips instead.

"Well, that was doomed from the start. When we finally got the kids to bed, turned out the lights, and lit the candles, you were giggling so hard, Linda. What spirit is going to appear with you giggling like that?" said Jemma.

"I tried to stop, but I couldn't unless Linda did," I said. "And then when we finally got quiet that big sauce pot fell off the drain board and hit the floor with a crash."

"I wet my pants," said Linda.

"I still think a spirit pushed it," said Jemma, wiggling the fingers of both hands in the air.

"It was probably pissed at us 'cause it had something to tell us and we couldn't be serious," said Linda.

"It could have been that ghost you told us about, Jemma, the one you used to see when you lived on the farm, the one on the horse," I said.

"I don't think so," Jemma said. The smile left her face. She dropped her gaze and hugged herself.

Once again I seemed to have said the wrong thing. Jemma didn't want to talk about her kids, her brother, Sal, or the Mob. Now she didn't want to talk about the farm or the ghost. We used to joke about all this stuff.

With what seemed like an effort, Jemma grinned, jabbed an elbow into Kathleen's side, and said, "I bet they'd like to hear about my blind baseball team."

I had never heard of such a thing.

Linda got up from her chair, closed her eyes, and staggered around the room with her arms in the air, calling, "I got it! I got it!" Then she jerked her head as if struck and crashed into a wall.

Damn! I was ashamed for laughing, but Linda was so silly.

"How does that work?" I asked, trying to be serious.

"The ball has a beeper in it, and the pitcher has to call out 'ready' and then 'pitch' when he releases the ball, so the batter knows it's coming," Jemma explained.

"But…how does the pitcher know where to throw the ball?"

"The pitcher is sighted, and he has to try to hit the bat. If he doesn't put it in the right place, it's a ball." Jemma spoke slowly, as if to a child, but I still didn't get it.

I rolled my eyes. "Okay…I'm not sure that makes sense, but… Where does the ball go if it *doesn't* hit the bat?"

"The catcher gets it."

"How does he do that?"

"He's sighted too."

"So everyone can see except the batter?"

"The batter and the fielders are blind. If they can see at all they have to wear masks."

I just blinked. I wanted to keep it going. It was good to see Jemma relax at last. With every question from me and answer from Jemma, Linda got more hysterical. My rowdy friends had always thought I was gullible. I finally caught on and snickered.

"I got it. You're kidding, right? This is one of your jokes. There's no such thing."

Jemma was laughing too, but she *did* coach a blind baseball team, as it turned out, and was serious about her devotion to her players.

"What does the batter do when he hits the ball?" I asked, not convinced I wasn't still the butt of the joke.

"He runs to base."

"How does he know where to run?"

"The base beeps too. It's a different beep than the ball."

Linda fell to her hands and knees, feeling along the floor, going, "I know it's here somewhere."

"The bases are soft towers, almost four feet tall. You can't miss them."

"Unless you're blind!" Linda said, and hooted.

"And then he goes on to the next base?"

"No. There are only three bases: home plate, first base, and third base. He has to touch either first or third before the fielder catches the ball."

"Which one? First or third?"

"Whichever one is beeping—you never know."

"Crazy. You *are* putting me on, aren't you?"

"No—I'm not!"

"So let me see if I get this. He hits the ball and the crowd goes wild—"

"No, if the crowd tips off the fielder there's a penalty. The batter wouldn't hear the base beeping and the fielders wouldn't hear the spotters or the ball beeping so they could find it."

I had a visual. "So the crowd's all sitting there with hands over their mouths to keep from making any noise, and these blind men, some wearing blindfolds, are scrambling around the field taking directions from spotters so they can find the ball. Is that it?"

"No, the spotters can't tell them where the ball is, only which fielder is closest and should field the ball."

"Damn!" I said, shaking my head. "So that guy gets down on the ground and chases the beep, feeling around until he finds the ball. This game has got to be a lot of fun, especially for ignorant people that laugh at people falling down and getting hurt."

"People like us, you mean," Linda said.

By this time we had all had plenty of wine. Was that an excuse for our scandalous behavior? I felt guilty about participating, but knew we didn't mean to be cruel, only to find humor in life's challenges.

Despite our goofy remarks, we were impressed by Jemma's dedication to her team. Knowing Jemma, she would joke rudely with her players, same as she would with sighted people. Hating to be reminded they were different, they would love her for that.

I felt a warm spot in my chest and moisture in my eyes as I looked at my smiling friends.

I didn't understand why Jemma had chosen to leave her former life, but she seemed to be happy now and whatever had worried her earlier was forgotten. My fondest memory of her was in that moment, her eyes sparkling, her head thrown back, laughing with abandon.

I never saw Jemma again.

# Part IV

# Chapter 21
## March 2015

All Cora saw were toppled dead trees, thick tangles of branches, and decomposing leaves. Only a few colorful buds were swelling on trees and shrubs. Occasional patches of bluebells, violets, trilliums, and wild ginger studded the forest floor.

"It was right where we're standing! I know it!" Billy said. "I don't believe this!" He spun around, went back to the trail, stared down the way they had come, and returned. No building was here at the top of the bluff—certainly not a clubhouse. The clearing wasn't even big enough.

"Maybe it's a little farther. I'll find it." Billy waded into the brush and disappeared but Cora and Cisco stayed where they were. After a few minutes, his voice carried through the woods. "It *was* here! Here are the ravines I saw when I walked around the building. Right here is where I picked up the golf club head."

Cora had been relieved when Cisco decided to accompany her and Billy to the site of the abandoned golf clubhouse. He preferred to let people handle their own personal problems. If Billy had a problem, let Billy solve it. However, Billy's story was intriguing, and Cisco did love golf. He couldn't drive past a golf course without slowing down to take a look. He said he'd always wanted to see if there was anything left of the course.

Cora had no such reservations. "How can I say no? What if I said no and something bad happened? I'd feel responsible! And you're more of a soft touch than you admit," she'd told him when they first discussed it.

Now she fed Cisco's interest while they waited for Billy to return. "Remember the story about Al Capone shooting himself in the leg out here?"

"A gun hidden in his bag went off when he pulled a club out? You think that's true?"

"The story came from his caddy." She winked.

"Remind me why they closed the course," he said.

"They moved the Manhattan Project right next to it. The University of Chicago had doubts about safety, so they relocated the reactor and built a secret lab here in the woods." She waved an arm in the general direction of the old laboratory site.

He chuckled. "Right. How could I forget that? We found where they buried the nuclear waste about a half mile from here, but never the golf course," he said. "Maybe Billy discovered something, but that's hard to believe."

"It's odd that both Valerie and Billy mentioned the place, though. Wouldn't it be funny if both problems were connected?" Cora said.

"What did you think of Billy's story?" Cisco said, examining the edges of the woods from where he stood.

"It's not believable, is it? I found St. James and the old Argonne site on Google Maps but otherwise only bike trails and wilderness. No clubhouse, no farm." She poked around a bluebell with the toe of her boot.

"Rogers says there's nothing here," Cisco said.

She stiffened. "Officer Rogers? When did you see him?"

"Bumped into him at the bowling alley last night. He's had a promotion, by the way. He's a detective now."

"Why would you talk to him about this?" Cora asked, frowning. Cisco didn't share personal discussions.

"I asked him if he knew of any buildings out here. And who had jurisdiction, in case we find something."

"And?"

"He said kids party out here at night during the summer and have to be chased away. The Cook County Forest Preserves police patrol the area."

She raised an eyebrow. "Really? Not local, county, or state police?"

"Not unless FPD police can't handle it."

"Huh. Didn't realize forest preserves had their own police. But we're not expecting trouble, are we?"

Cisco shrugged.

She wiped her face on the sleeve of her jacket. "How's Rogers doing? We haven't seen him since last fall."

"He said he only comes around when the wolves are out."

Cora laughed. "He would say that."

"We're a puzzle to him. He doesn't believe a ghost guards you. Speaking of which, it seems like your wolf-friend hasn't been around lately."

"Nope. Maybe she's gone for good."

"Or maybe you just haven't needed her." He shot her an inquiring look. "You don't think this business with Billy…?"

She shook her head. "Let's not go there, okay?"

"So you don't believe Billy?"

"I think he's telling the truth as he sees it, but he's mistaken. I don't know what happened. The mystical power thing—that has to be his imagination. He's struggling with a lot of things. That messes with your mind. It'll go away when he gets his head straight." Cora shook her head. "But I feel bad for him."

"Did he show you the golf club head he mentioned?"

"No."

Cisco turned, his attention caught by something to his right. "How…? I thought…"

"What?" she asked, seeing a puzzled look on Cisco's face.

"Billy went to the left, but I heard rustling on the right. Could he be coming back a different way?"

Cora's ears tingled. She peered into the woods and listened carefully. "I don't hear anything, and I don't see him."

There was no sign of the clubhouse, and practical-minded Cisco was jumping at imaginary sounds. Cora was more than a little creeped out. Whatever sun had penetrated the bare branches earlier had disappeared behind a cloud, and she shivered as the air grew chill. She looked around nervously, imagining creatures lurking and motion out of the corners of her eyes, and she was startled by the crack of a branch and the rustle of some small creature through dead leaves.

She tossed off her jitters and touched Cisco's arm. She might not have the courage to speak plainly to Billy if Cisco wasn't here. What would she say when Billy tried to explain and didn't make sense?

But Billy had described the place so well….

Soon Billy appeared from the same direction he had gone.

"That sound you heard couldn't have been Billy," Cora whispered.

"Right. I wonder how much of what Billy told us is true."

Billy avoided their eyes now. He waved an arm randomly. "It's got to be here somewhere, behind all this…" He winced and pulled a few burrs from his sleeve.

"There was a golf course somewhere out here once, but it closed in the forties," Cora said. "Maybe you heard about it, and later you had a dream that seemed so real, like…"

Cisco cast a warning look at Cora.

She nodded and put a hand beside her mouth. "Not now," she mouthed. Let Billy form his own conclusions before she muddied the waters with her personal experiences.

"Look at this," Cisco said. He stooped down and picked up a piece of brownish-red terra-cotta poking through the leaves. "Didn't you say the old clubhouse had a red-tile roof?"

Billy took the object and turned it over in his hands. "Yes, a red roof, and I saw tiles like this too. But the whole building was here, just days ago!" He shook his head from side to side and hurled the roof tile into the woods. "I can't explain it, but the building was here! It was real!"

His eyes wild, Billy headed back to the trail. "The farm," he said, "let's go to the farm. See if that farmer is home. I don't know how I could have confused the location, but maybe he can help us."

They followed Billy to where he thought the farm was.

"Look," Cisco said, pointing to the sides of the trail, "fragments of a limestone wall. Might have lined the entrance to the golf course."

Where Billy stopped, the area was overgrown with dense shrubs, trees, and grasses, indistinguishable from everything else off the trail. No house, no barn, no clearing—certainly no farmer or horses. If there had ever been anything here, how could it have disappeared so completely in a few days?

They searched both sides of the trail and eventually found the remnants of a foundation on the left and on the right a large concrete-block-lined hole that could have been a basement at one time.

The sun had come back out, but a coldness settled around Cora's feet and worked its way upward. She had a distinct feeling someone was watching them. She checked to see if Cisco felt it, but he was looking at Billy. This place was as eerie as the first one.

She wondered if this was the same place Valerie's mother had lived.

Did what Billy saw have anything to do with his other experiences? Were Billy and Valerie channeling something between them? But they'd only met once....

Billy sank down on a large rock and put his head in his hands.

Cora put a hand on his shoulder.

He looked up. "It must be me, Cora. Something's wrong with me. I can't explain any of this. I must be having hallucinations."

The look on his face was something between fright, desperation, and bewilderment. He wasn't playacting. He was in pain.

Everything she knew about Billy was sad. His best friend ended up with Billy's childhood sweetheart, his friends were successful but he couldn't do anything right, and, when he did muster enough courage to better himself, his efforts ended in disaster. Now once again circumstances, or something inside him, prevented him from being the man he wanted to be. Yet he was a really sweet guy. It wasn't fair.

Cora caught Cisco's eye. "You see?" she mouthed. Cisco must understand now why she couldn't ignore Billy's cry for help.

"Did you really pick things up when you were out here before?" Cora asked to distract Billy from his funk.

Billy reached into his pocket and pulled out an L-shaped piece of metal.

"The man called it a Sabbath stick," he said.

Before their eyes, the object began to glow in his hand and then lost shape, melting and draping over his palm like a watch in a Salvador Dali painting. He stared in fascination.

Cora jumped back, her hand clasped to her mouth. Unable to pull her gaze away from the metal in Billy's hand, she squeaked, "Cisco!"

Cisco was already focused on the bizarre sight.

Billy's body tensed and then vibrated. He rose a few inches above the rock. The vibration ceased and he hovered there, motionless, his face expressionless, his eyes vacant.

Cisco said, "Damn it, Cora! Call your friends off! Don't let this stuff start up again."

But Cora was shaking her head. "It's Billy!" she said.

Without taking his eyes off Billy, Cisco also shook his head. "How the hell are you doing that?"

# Chapter 22

"Thought I was done with that girl. She better not start any shit with me. She don't treat me right, I'm done!"

Frannie jammed her foot on the gas pedal, pushing her 2010 sangria-red Mercury Milan above the 40 MPH speed limit, hands gripping the wheel at ten o'clock and two o'clock. Pausing in the left-turn lane, trouncing on the accelerator again when the intersection cleared, turning sharply onto Cora's street. Squealing brakes as the car came to a halt.

She turned the engine off, and her urgency suddenly vanished. She folded her arms across her chest and chewed her upper lip, staring at the gray car liner above her head, remembering the last time she had seen Valerie, more than two years ago. They had been at Cora's house that day, too, for a book group discussion. Frannie rarely shared private problems with her white friends, but that day she had yielded to an emotional moment and shared a personal tragedy. Valerie had made callous and derogatory comments relentlessly until Frannie dissolved in tears. Leaping to Frannie's defense, Cora asked Valerie to leave, starting a chain of events that changed the lives of all three women.

Now the three of them were about to meet again. Cora had asked Frannie to do this woman a favor. Curious, Frannie agreed to hear Valerie out. She smelled a mystery. She loved solving mysteries, and she hated being left out. She heaved a sigh, stuck her chin out, and marched to the front door.

Cora greeted her in the open doorway. Frannie said, unsmiling, "She here?"

Cora gestured toward the kitchen. Frannie peeled off a gray-and-black-striped fleece cardigan that further padded her already spectacularly sized bosom, dropped her sweater on a living room chair, and followed Cora.

When Frannie entered the kitchen, Valerie turned in Frannie's direction. Frannie hesitated, staring at Valerie across the oval wooden table. Physically the woman had changed little except for wearing dark glasses. What was that on her face, though? Hope? Fear? Hard to tell. Huh! She didn't expect that.

She moved forward. "Valerie…?" she said. Wary.

"Frannie," Valerie replied. Stiff-backed in her chair.

Frannie took a seat across the table from Valerie without speaking.

"Thank you for coming," Valerie said. "There's no reason you should want to help me, but I appreciate it."

Frannie blinked, pushed her stiff, graying hair behind her ears and then rested both hands on the table and sniffed. "I had some free time," she said, her voice noncommittal. Since retirement she was bored out of her mind. And, Cora seemed to fall into unusual, if not downright dangerous, situations. She was willing to deal with Valerie if Cora had something exciting going.

Valerie smiled. "Good."

Frannie threw Cora a questioning look, expecting help. After all, Cora was the go-between. Cora only pointed a forefinger at Frannie. Seemed she expected the women to work it out without her.

Frannie sniffed again and cleared her throat. "I see you're getting along pretty good. Cora said you had a dog. Where's he at?"

"I left *her* home today. Sometimes it's simpler to use a cane, especially in familiar places."

A teakettle began to whistle. Cora took mugs from an upper cabinet. Frannie watched without a word. Valerie played with her fingernails, as she had done the first time she and Cora talked. Boiling water hissed as she filled the cold teapot.

"Despite what you probably think, I was real sorry when I heard about your accident," Frannie said.

"Thank you." Valerie lifted her head and raised an eyebrow. "Cora explained what you two think happened. I'm not sure I believe it."

"Really. You should, seeing what that ghost did to you." Crap! Should she have said that?

Valerie didn't appear to notice. "I'd convinced myself I imagined the wolf, like the doctors said, and did this to myself." She pointed at her dark glasses. "I've never believed in ghosts—human or animal."

"Hang around us, you'll start believing it," Frannie said.

Cora placed steaming cups of tea on the table. Frannie wrinkled her brow and eyed the empty coffeemaker. She wasn't too fond of tea. Cora shrugged her shoulders and sat down.

"So what's going on? Why are we all here?" Frannie said.

Valerie turned toward Cora.

"I didn't tell her details, Valerie. Just that you needed some research done quickly," Cora said.

Valerie's last words two years ago played in Frannie's head, "You'll regret this!" She was unable to keep her simmering anger in check any longer.

"Seriously, do you even know how bad you treated me, Valerie?" she burst out.

Valerie flushed and put a hand to her mouth. Then she faced Frannie, her jaw set.

"Yes. Guilty. I was a bitch. I think you'll agree I paid a pretty big price for it. I'm trying to change."

Huh. Valerie wasn't defensive like Frannie thought she'd be. Seems like Frannie was the one being rude now.

Valerie heaved a sigh. "I appreciate your willingness to help. But I'm not going to beg you. Nor do I want to have to rehash old problems every time we talk." Her voice was soft but her words firm. "So let's get this over with and move on. Is there anything else you want to say, or would you prefer to bow out now?"

There wasn't a whole lot of warmth in Valerie's voice, but she didn't sound demeaning or superior, just making her feelings clear. Just like Frannie. If that kept up, Frannie could handle it. But she had her own feelings to make clear.

"I'm not some no-account fool and I don't want to be treated like one. I got opinions and feelings and deserve respect. Don't want to be feeling like you're putting me down, passing judgment on me, or thinking about the color of my skin, like you did before. We equals or we done."

Valerie paused, considering. "Fair enough. I think differently now I've had a taste of being a minority myself."

Frannie considered. Seemed like honesty was better than denial. She wiggled in her chair before saying, "That the case, what's this all about? Like I said, I got some time on my hands at the moment."

Frannie recognized a look of relief on Cora's face.

Cora cleared her throat. "I'll explain, if that's okay with you Valerie?" With Cora's tendency to control conversations, she'd probably been chomping at the bit to jump in.

Valerie nodded and leaned back in her chair. She seemed relieved to let Cora do the talking.

"Father McGrath has been helping Valerie through some emotional issues. She wants to go back to work, but she's always relied completely on herself. As a blind person, as you pointed out in *your* way, Frannie, she'll need to play better with others."

Frannie watched Valerie for reactions. She was rubbing her hands, her eyes closed, her head nodding. Accepting Cora's explanation.

Frannie found herself empathizing. "Two years ago, never thought the three of us be sitting here. I never had the feeling you valued me or my abilities, Valerie. What you got to say about that?"

"I got a cold shoulder from you, too, remember. Think I liked that?" Valerie sighed. "Now I *have* to treat people better. I won't always get it right, but I don't have a lot of choices."

Frannie burst out laughing. "We out in the open now! I like this humble-pie Valerie so far. Don't you worry, it don't take none of your strengths away, girl. You're stronger when you admit to faults, seems to me."

Valerie blinked, as if the idea was new to her. She turned her head in Frannie's direction with raised eyebrows.

"But why me?" Frannie said. "We been like oil and water!"

Cora opened her mouth, but before she could speak the doorbell rang. "That must be Billy," she said. "Good timing. I won't have to go through all this twice." She got up and left the room.

"Billy?" Frannie asked. "You know Billy?" Frannie had been part of Cora's writing team last year and was present when Billy had been injured. But how did Valerie know him?

"He came here last time I talked to Cora. She thinks he has information we can use."

"O...kay...," Frannie said, raising an eyebrow.

When Cora and Billy entered the kitchen, he took the remaining chair with only a nod at Frannie. He glanced quickly at Valerie and lowered his eyes.

Valerie turned away, as if she wanted to hide her expression.

Oh fine! What's up with these two now? wondered Frannie.

Cora brushed her hand through her hair. "Frannie, you and Billy might both be wondering why he's here. It's because Valerie hasn't seen her mother since she was a child, and Billy stumbled on something that may help us find her."

Frannie and Billy exchanged a blank look.

Cora explained the disappearance of Valerie's mother, the murder of her Uncle Angelo, and the traumas that interfered with Valerie's recovery. Frannie asked questions, but Billy only listened, shifting his position uneasily and looking around the room.

"When I heard the name Jemma DiMaso I suddenly realized the mother Valerie was talking about wasn't just *like* an old friend of mine, she was the *same* person, and I remembered Valerie as a baby," Cora said.

"No shit!" Frannie said.

Billy blinked, expressionless.

Frannie slammed her hand on the table. "Then you know where she is!"

Cora shook her head. "I wish I did. I haven't seen her for close to forty years. She never said why she left and never gave an address. We have to pick up her trail in Arizona somewhere, the only info we have."

"Yes. And now the time frame's been moved up…," Valerie trailed off.

Cora said. "Molly, Valerie's daughter, will be here in three months. They can't stay at her brother's house, where Valerie's living now."

"Huh. And you think finding her mother will help?" Frannie was doubtful.

Cora touched Valerie's hand. "We think it's important."

"I get it," Frannie said. "You want my research skills, my computer skills. What we got to do here is find this Jemma DiMaso, find out who really killed Uncle Angelo, and get Valerie a job and an apartment before Molly gets here, all in three months?"

"That's it," Cora said.

"Piece of cake!" Frannie said, shaking her head. *Impossible* in that time frame, but she and Cora had worked miracles before.

"I want to help," Billy broke his silence, his voice and face earnest. Cora and Frannie stared at him.

Valerie turned in Billy's direction, her eyebrows raised. "You don't have to do that," she said.

"I know I don't have to." He thrust his jaw forward. "I want to, though."

If Billy was in, Frannie wasn't about to sit back and be left out. "Let him if he wants, Valerie. Maybe he got time on his hands too," she said.

All four chuckled nervously.

"You got my answer, Valerie," Frannie said. "I didn't tell you, but I'm bored silly sitting around with nothing to do, just checking the news, looking things up for the heck of it. I want a purpose." She looked at Cora. "We're not writing no books, though. I draw the line at that. I had enough of that book writing stuff. Started out fun but not too much fun there at the end." She shook her head, alluding to a disaster that occurred just before their book was published.

"What can I do?" Billy asked.

"Here's the thing, Billy," Cora began, "Valerie's mother used to live at that farm we went to."

Billy blinked again. "Her mother? The missing woman?"

"I never went there myself," Valerie said. "But Mamma lived there when she was young."

"By the abandoned golf club, next to the lab where the Manhattan Project research was done, like the man on horseback told you," Cora said. "Jemma and her family must have lived in the course manager's house after the club was closed."

Billy opened his mouth, then closed it, and said nothing.

"Mamma told us she loved growing up there with her brothers and sister. She had a horse and rode in the woods."

"Billy's been out there?" Frannie asked.

"Is the farm still there?" Valerie was excited.

Cora's gaze met Billy's. "Not exactly. Tell us about the place, Billy."

Billy shifted in his chair, pushed his hair away from his face, rubbed his nose. "The first time I went there I found a deserted clubhouse and walked around in it. On my way back I found a farm, and I talked to a man on a horse. I thought he lived there."

"But then we went back together, with Cisco…," Cora prompted.

"When I went back with Cora and Cisco we couldn't find it, neither place. I was sure I knew where to go—I'm pretty good in the woods. But we couldn't find a thing. And then Cora said—"

Frannie saw Cora's leg press against Billy's. He glanced at Cora and stopped talking. Oh, oh. Must be something Cora didn't want her or Valerie to know.

"Maybe he dreamed it, like déjà vu or something. But the experience was odd, and it's the same place Jemma lived. I thought he should tell us about it," Cora said.

"What did the man look like?" Valerie asked.

"He was in his sixties with thick dark hair, slicked back. He was wearing a white button-down shirt, the sleeves rolled up, unusual for a man on a horse. He whistled a tune and spoke with an accent. He said, '*Calma, Bambina.*'"

"That's Italian," Valerie said. "It means 'calm down, baby girl.' What did the horse look like?"

"Big, slender but powerful, dark-brown, jumpy. A beautiful mare."

"Do you think you dreamed it? That sounds pretty detailed," Frannie said.

"I didn't think so at the time. But it did seem off, kind of unreal."

"Cora? Excuse me! Tell me there's no supernatural stuff going on here," Frannie said. She might have to back out if Cora was dragging her back into the world of ghosts.

Cora rolled her eyes. "Why would you think that?"

"Because I know you too well. Weird shit follows you, girl."

"You don't have to go *out* there. But we don't know what could turn up. We have to consider all possibilities."

Cora dropped her face into her hands and rubbed. When she lifted her head her eyes were still closed. "Okay, sorry. I learned my lesson. Everything has to be out in the open if we're going to trust each other. Billy, tell them why you came to see me in the first place."

A flicker of panic passed across Billy's face. She knew Billy was painfully shy. Then he swallowed and began to speak haltingly, relaying the events that led to his suspicion that he was experiencing supernatural phenomena.

Valerie frowned. She seemed disappointed instead of surprised. Frannie wondered if she expected something different from Billy.

"So what we got going on here?" Frannie asked. "Is one of your ghosts inside Billy, Cora? Can't you get rid of it?"

"Just suspicions, Frannie. No proof," Cora said.

"Damn! Guess I got to dig out all those paranormal notes I made two years ago, before something bad happens again," Frannie said.

"You still have them?" Cora asked. "Really? Can you review them considering what Billy just said? It would save time."

"In case you can't tell what the sounds you're hearing are, Valerie, that would be me grumbling. But I'll do it," Frannie said.

She wondered, though, if Billy was upset about all the attention Valerie was getting instead of him and his problems. Cora hadn't said anything about helping Billy too. But were his problems related?

"I think I should go back to the farm, Cora, after what Valerie told us," Billy said. "I'll look for clues—I don't know what. But if there's any connection, we'll never know if we don't look. I'll be confronting my own situation at the same time."

Frannie looked at Billy in surprise, impressed by what amounted to a speech.

"Would you mind going back? Won't you be afraid?" Cora said.

"I never felt threatened, Cora. Just weird."

Cora seemed skeptical. Billy seemed determined. Valerie seemed impressed. Frannie grinned.

"We need to plan." Cora got up and took a notebook and mechanical pencil from a table in the adjacent family room.

"Oh Lord," Frannie said. "She's bringing out her tools—the notebook and pencil. She's getting serious now, about to put us to work already and we only just agreed to do this thing. You guys ever worked with Cora before? You're in for it."

"Molly's going to be here in only three months," Valerie reminded them, her lower lip trembling.

Cora laid her hand over Valerie's. "We're going to get right to it. I don't want this to take forever either." She picked up her pencil again. "Let's decide what each of us is going to do right now, and leave here today with a prioritized work list. You too, Billy."

"See what I mean?" Frannie said, making a show of throwing her arms in the air. "Mark my words, next thing she be doing is making columns and lists on that page."

Cora grinned and drew a line down the page in front of her, dividing it into two columns. "Right. Let's brainstorm. Everything we know about Jemma and Angelo goes in the left column and what we need to know in the right. Then we'll list places to start looking for each missing piece of information and who's going to do that research."

Frannie grinned. Are you kidding? Not one mystery, but three: a missing woman, a murdered man, and Billy's spooky stuff—well, she'd put that last thing out of her mind. Had her full attention now. The day was looking up.

Frannie noticed that Valerie seemed lost. It was her problems they were discussing. She wondered if, like herself, Valerie hated being left out.

Just then, Cora put her hand on Valerie's arm again. "Do you have a smartphone you can use?"

Valerie grinned and brightened. "I do. I can make calls and do internet research on my laptop too. It has voice-over."

"Put your hand up in the air," Cora said.

Valerie did and Cora gave her a high five. Valerie grinned.

"Can you record our work sessions and dictate your thoughts and findings to share with us?"

"Absolutely. I may be slow, but pile it on," Valerie said.

"And this is important… Any time we can't agree, Valerie makes the decision. Got it?" Cora said.

Huh. We'll see about that, Frannie thought.

# Chapter 23

"I thought we'd never finish," Valerie said, shaking her head.

"Can we get Cora's list done in three days?" Billy said.

The truck hit a deep pothole and Valerie jumped. "Couldn't avoid that one, sorry."

They arrived at Valerie's house. "Let me get the door," Billy said, coming around the truck. "You said your brother and sister-in-law aren't home?"

"They're visiting friends."

"Let me get you inside." She took his arm and then waited as he opened the front door for her. "Be sure to lock the door behind me." He didn't move away while she closed the door.

What a courteous man, Valerie noted as she turned the deadbolt. She removed her sweater and hung it in the hall closet. Protected—it felt rather nice, a feeling she hadn't often experienced. Her smile faded. What did she think about this man, though?

It seemed Billy was sincere in his desire to help, to the point of setting aside his own issues in favor of her more immediate ones. But when the discussion turned to disappearing farms, ghosts, and supernatural powers, she had second thoughts. Valerie prided herself on quickly dealing with facts. The unknown, the vague, and the immeasurable weren't worth consideration.

How disappointing. Was he the quiet, serious man with strong ethics, kind intentions, and a hint of the mysterious that first impressed her? Was his air of mystery deepened by tonight's disclosures? Or did he reveal himself as a crackpot?

Still…whenever Billy talked, his concern for her seemed real. A man with vastly different sides. For some reason, she couldn't get him out of her mind.

Maybe she shouldn't care that Billy thought there was something supernatural going on. Surely facts would prove his suspicions wrong.

Stop it! Why was she thinking about this man when such important things were going on?

Lost in thought, she climbed the stairs. At the end of the second-floor hallway, she felt for the door frame to confirm her location, puzzled to find the door to her room closed. She always left it open when she wasn't in the room. Counting steps was intuitive now, but even small differences in her stride could, on occasion, like when she was tired or angry, get her to the doorway sooner or later than expected. Her toes contracted involuntarily. Toes, she reminded herself, making a wry face, were invented to help people find things in the dark, invariably painfully. Her toes had paid the price often enough. She supposed Sally or Grace must have gone into her room, although they usually remembered to leave the door open.

She turned the knob and hesitated before entering, listening alertly. All she heard was Corky, always excited when Valerie returned, anxious to get out of her crate. But tonight her whining had an edge to it, as if she was upset. When released, she rubbed against Valerie's legs, whimpering and trembling.

"I'm here, silly goose, calm down," Valerie said, chuckling. She stooped and rubbed the dog's neck affectionately with both hands. "That's enough now."

Corky followed Valerie into the bathroom, nails clicking against the tile floor. Leaving the door open, Valerie used the toilet, removed her clothes, and wrapped herself in the fluffy robe that hung from a hook behind the bathroom door. She waited for the water to run hot in the sink and adjusted the temperature. She reached for her facial cleanser, but in its place was hair spray. She frowned, rubbing her hands over the dots that identified the contents of the container and feeling the container's shape. Why was hair spray where the cleanser was kept? Everything on the counter had an exact position so she could find it easily. After rounding up all the containers, she identified, sorted, and returned each to its correct place. Was Grace so anxious to get her out of the house that she was trying to annoy her? She wouldn't go that far, surely.

Pick your battles. Keep the peace a little longer and your life will be your own, she thought.

Returning to the bedroom, she detected a faint scent. Ever so slight, sweet, a little musty, smoky—a manly scent? Maybe something she brought in with her from Billy's car—but she didn't recognize it. Must be imagination... She didn't smell it now.

She felt under her pillow for her sleep pants and T-shirt, but they weren't there. It was time to wash them—did she put them in the laundry basket that morning? She couldn't remember. She found a new set of sleepwear in her dresser, put it on, and slid between the soft, cool sheets, shivering.

A distant whoosh made her flinch. She listened carefully, relieved after a moment to realize the furnace had just turned on.

Must be nerves. She was keyed up from everything that'd been going on.

She lay awake waiting for the bed to warm. She burrowed her face into the pillow and then, turning onto her back, pulled the comforter against her neck.

Corky entered her crate, making rustling sounds as she turned in circles before dropping down with a contented sigh. Corky depended on Valerie for everything and that could be a burden, but the dog's love for her was unconditional. Corky was work, but she repaid her in emotional support.

She giggled. Billy had asked if she had named Corky after Cora. He couldn't know about the conflict between the two women.

"We had a neighbor named Corky when I was a kid," she had told him. "She used to use cork from bottle caps and wear the caps on her blouse like jewelry, so we called her Corky. I remembered that and thought the name fit. Goldens are the same color as cork."

"Corks in bottle caps? Huh?"

She had laughed. "Yes, before your time. Cork lined the inside of bottle caps, but you could peel it out. Then you could put the cork liner inside your blouse and the cork over it outside and push them together with the cloth between. They looked like jewelry. Corky wore dozens on her clothes. I never questioned why people called her Corky instead of Cappy, but they did."

"Huh," he had said again. Reminded her of Frannie, who was always saying, "Huh."

Now Valerie flopped onto her stomach, trying to find a comfortable spot for her forehead. She wondered why Billy as well as Cora and Frannie, women she had treated badly in the past, were putting themselves out to help her. Surprisingly, she was starting to care about them too. Knowing they had her back made her feel…well…more confident, less fearful.

How different from the first time she ventured out alone as a blind woman.

The experience returned vividly to mind. She had planned to get a few items from a grocery store. The store was unfamiliar, but offered assistance for the blind. She and Sally had practiced, running through the physical layout until she had it memorized.

Grace drove her, staying in the car with her cell phone in case Valerie had to call. With Corky at her side, Valerie walked to the door, felt a railing, and passed through a set of automatic doors. Rows of carts, according to plan, were just inside. Valerie waited for another shopper to approach, asked to be guided to the customer service counter, and requested an assistant. The assistant took a cart and guided her through the store, explaining labels and sizes and handing each item to Valerie to place in her cart. All went well. Valerie completed her short list of bananas, eggs, milk, pork chops, chicken soup, wheat bread, and peanut butter.

She asked to be left alone at the checkout counter—part of the test. She stood in line, removing each item as she checked it off in her head, placing the item on the belt, feeling in her purse for her credit card. Her confidence was growing as she neared completion of the task.

"What the hell is taking so long? Some people might be in a hurry," an angry male voice grumbled under his breath. "Dogs aren't supposed to be in here. What if that animal pisses on the floor and I slip and fall in it?"

Valerie froze, stunned and embarrassed.

"I can't *see* you, but I *can* hear you," Valerie had said.

"What are you blind or something?" the man went on.

"Yes, actually," she said.

"Yeah, right. I can wear dark glasses if I want to bring my dog in here too. Why don't you have someone shop for you instead of holding up other people?"

She had been warned about people like this, handicap-phobes. She wanted to lash back, but then she realized that two years ago she would have been impatient like him. Now she was the one holding up the line.

Her payment completed, she replaced her credit card in her wallet and moved to the side of her cart in the narrow aisle to check her bags, as her therapist had drilled into her. She misjudged the position of the back wheel, tripped, and sprawled on the floor between counters. Three people ran to help her, squeezing between cart, counters, and customers while behind her she heard, "Oh, for Christ's sake! What's next, lady? Didn't I warn you about that dog?"

She had been unhurt, but the experience had shattered her confidence. It had taken months to muster the guts to attempt the outside world unaccompanied again.

The memory still brought heat to her face. She flopped over in bed yet again. She'd been let down over and over since she was a kid. Could she trust anyone? Even Cora had withheld information from her—although her confession and apology had seemed genuine.

She felt a surge of optimism. After working out a plan together, she was beginning to believe they would actually find her mother. Her future—everything—would be better once she talked to Mamma.

She breathed a sigh of satisfaction and then sat up straight. Molly! She'd forgotten to call Molly! She wanted to know how she was getting along with Aster's parents and to talk about plans for coming back to Illinois. It was too late now—she'd have to call tomorrow.

Damn! She had forgotten to charge her phone. She'd need it in the morning. She got out of bed and felt for the charger, eventually finding it at the rear of the bedside tabletop instead of at the front where she could reach it easily.

Grace must be awfully angry to go to all this trouble. Maybe she was wrong to keep Sally in the dark about what she was doing.

For a moment it occurred to her that someone else may have been in her room. Nah, that's crazy. It was just the result of a long, emotional day.

# Chapter 24

Frannie rolled onto her side, pulled the sheets up to her chin, and snuggled into her pillow. A small noise from another room, a dish settling on the drain board or some such thing. The sound triggered a memory of other cozy mornings shortly after her marriage. Simon would rise early and put the kitchen in order while she stayed in bed, knowing she liked to dress and run out of the house at the last minute. She'd pretend she was still sleeping, wrapped in soft, warm bedding, listening to him move around—he was never very quiet about it. She felt secure and loved. Lord, she missed him, even now, twenty years after he passed.

She spent a few minutes thinking about the memories Cora had shared about Jemma. It struck her odd that Jemma had managed a baseball team for the blind, and here Frannie was now committed to helping Jemma's blind daughter all these years later.

She opened one eye a crack. Weak light came through the curtainless bedroom window. She liked it that way. An early riser now too, daylight woke her around six o'clock. She weighed her comfort against her excitement to start the day. Leap out of bed, girl. You got a shit-ton of work ahead. All right, so leap's a little strong. Ooze maybe more like it.

Shivering, she pulled on a worn, but comfortable, pink sweatshirt and pants, her lucky research outfit, a talisman to guarantee success. She'd never wear the baggy old rags in public, though. She took her blood pressure pill, but skipped grooming. Why bother? She would be at her computer the whole day.

She shuffled to the kitchen in fuzzy slippers, started the coffeemaker, and waited for her new laptop to boot up. A serious pain in the ass, converting and sorting the files from her old dying computer and getting accustomed to the new keyboard, operating system, and updated versions of Microsoft Office and Firefox. But the speed, uncluttered desktop, and portability of a laptop would come in handy.

Her workspace was a blond-wood, dining-room table with two leaves, a relic of the fifties inherited from her mother. Stacks of papers and books filled the tabletop, her seventeen-inch laptop on the end near the kitchen, its screen and keyboard almost as big as the desktop computer she was used to.

Beyond her dining table, light streamed through three large windows that overlooked the blank, brick wall of the next building, separated from her second-story flat by the width of a narrow gangway. Not what one would call a view, but that's how it was done in the 1930s, when the two-flat she inherited from her mother was built.

She poured coffee into her black-and-white mug, its cartoon face part-bunny and part-Batman, another good-luck research ritual. She added extra cream and two sugars. Plopping onto her work chair, she set the cup far to the right of her laptop. Reaching was safer than drenching another keyboard. She wiggled the fingers of both hands in the air and grinned. All right people! Time to make this a thing!

A plan of sorts was in her head. In front of her was a list of names.

– *Jemma DiMaso (nee Vitale): left Valerie in 1974, last-known address somewhere near Phoenix, Arizona*
– *Angelo Nicholas Vitale: killed at Cabrini-Green in 1975, details questionable*
– *Aniello (Nello) Vitale: location unknown*
– *Barbaro (Bobby) Vitale: location unknown*
– *Salvatore DiMaso Sr.: died of heart disease 1986*
– *Salvatore DiMaso Jr. (Sally): living in Lemont with his wife (Grace) and Valerie*
– *Paula DiMaso: last-known location somewhere in Arizona*
– *Linda Kuchar Ricci: living in Kentucky, in contact with Cora*
– *Kathleen Sweeney: last-known address somewhere near Phoenix, Arizona*

She picked up a pencil and jotted notes as thoughts came to her.

– *Per Cora, Jemma's family has questionable mob ties. Anything happen in or about 1974 the family could have been involved in?*
– *Arizona: Three people on list lived there. Coincidence? A reason? Did Paula have contact with Jemma and/or Kathleen?*
– *Old farm and golf course in forest preserves: what happened there? Jemma lived there late 1950s, her family until early 1960s. Buildings long gone —or not, per Billy. Research old golf course and farm.*
– *Billy: review paranormal phenomenon notes. Who, what, might Billy have seen?*

Crossing the room, she went to a five-drawer, lateral, metal file cabinet she got from a previous employer. She pulled open the third drawer, her research drawer. What had she called the folder? "Ghosts"? "Angel"? "Cora research"? She flipped through file tab after file tab, until she found a thick folder labeled, no duh, "Paranormal research." She cleared a space on the table; she'd read the file later, maybe tonight in front of the TV. Right now she wanted to get online and stay there as long as her back held out. Why was she cursed with all her boobage? Pulled her spine out of whack! She didn't need that today!

A doubt entered her mind. Why was she even doing this? She barely knew Billy and had never liked Valerie. What if her new laptop got a virus while online? Who was gonna pay for that? Those thoughts were followed immediately by others: a murder, a missing person, hella craziness in the forests. Her nemesis…curiosity. She wasn't about to let Cora have all the fun, and then when Billy stepped in! Really… Don't kid yourself girl. You thrive on this stuff.

She sighed. She'd start by doing a search for each name. Nine names. Each was likely to bring up multiple leads to follow. Angelo first, no-brainer. In addition to his name, she had his date of death some forty years ago. The killing of a Chicago cop would have been major news. She'd confirm the events, consider the information from Valerie's perspective, see if other information cropped up over time, and go where her intuition led her.

She launched Firefox, opened Google, and typed "Angelo Vitale Chicago 1975." As expected, many pages of results came up. She scanned the preview text for each reference on the first page. Most of the items were the correct person and pertinent to her search. Thank you, lucky sweats and cup.

The first link she clicked was less than two years old, an article in the *Chicago Tribune*. Three cop killers sentenced in 1976 were seeking parole. The men had been convicted of killing Angelo and another policeman Jim Carlson in 1975, using sniper rifles from an upper floor of Cabrini-Green, an inner-city, high-rise apartment complex. The men had been sentenced to 100 to 199 years in prison.

The facts were similar to what Valerie told them, except Valerie didn't mention another policeman had been killed along with Angelo and that there was more than a single sniper. But Valerie didn't believe the sniper story at all.

The second story was a 2005 interview with Jim Carlson's niece. Two Chicago streets had been renamed Honorary Officer Angelo Vitale Memorial Way and Honorary Sergeant James Carlson Memorial Way. Angelo's wife, Rosa Vitale, was mentioned in the article, but no reference was made to a sister, niece, or any other family member.

Next was a memorial website titled, Officer Down Memorial Page. A comment was written six years ago by Barbaro Vitale Jr., the son of Angelo's brother Barbaro.

"Huh. That family just keeps using the same names over and over again," Frannie mumbled, "No creativity."

"My father was a policeman stationed at Cabrini-Green too, just like his older brother," Barbaro Jr. said. "Dad was there days before Uncle Angelo was killed. My uncle was a great man. My father always said there was something more going on that day. It would have turned out different if the killings had been investigated right."

So Angelo's own brother was a witness and doubted the accounts too. What's up with that? Next to Barbaro's name on her list she jotted, "Where is Barbaro? Why is his son commenting on his behalf? See Angelo's memorial page."

On the same site, a couple of years after Barbaro Jr.'s comment, was a comment by Junior's mother, Rosa Vitale. So Angelo and Barbaro both married women named Rosa. Shut up! "My husband, Barbaro Vitale, was also in the 'Walk and Talk' community-relations program with the children in Cabrini-Green. Not everyone knows the story of his brother's previous confrontation on that fatal day except me, my husband, and our son."

With growing excitement, Frannie sent the documents to her printer and then realized the printer hadn't been installed on her laptop yet. Instead, she copied article after article into a document folder named "Angelo Vitale."

She included many pages of *Chicago Tribune* headlines: "Snipers Slay Two Policemen"; "Rifle Fire at Cabrini"; "Hundreds of Cops Join Battle"; "Police Dragnet Yields 100 Suspects in Cop Killing." Photos showed people running, police in action hiding behind police cars and aiming rifles at the upper floors of high-rises, a figure carrying a bloody body to a police car, and a car seat covered in blood. "Combat Alley," the place was called. The program was misnamed the "Walkie-Talkie" unit instead of the "Walk and Talk" unit. Angelo was characterized as happy-go-lucky, a hard worker, a dedicated man who thrived on the good he was doing in the community. Just before he was shot he had coffee with friends and strode off happily saying, "See you later."

Legacy.com had Angelo's obituary and a guest book started in 2010, with the following entry: "I lived near the Vitale family when I was growing up, and often went to their house. Angelo's mother was a great cook and the house always, always smelled 'Italian.' " The entry was signed by Bridget Sweeney. Frannie added Bridget to her list of names. She might be a relative of Kathleen.

Findagrave.com revealed Angelo was buried at St. Joseph Cemetery in River Grove, Illinois. Date of birth July 19, 1937. Date of death July 17, 1975. Age 37. What a waste. Angelo was even younger than Simon was when he passed, leaving Rosa Vitale, like Frannie, with a son to raise alone.

In 1981, stories ran about Chicago mayor Jane Byrne. The mayor had moved into Cabrini-Green, reportedly to see the violence for herself, hoping her presence would calm things down. One columnist called it a publicity stunt orchestrated by the feisty lady. "You go, Mayor Lady," Frannie said. "We could use more like you."

On recently created sites, information and financial help was sought to clear the convicted cop killers. The evidence was said to show the fatal shots came from the ground, not from snipers in the upper apartments, indicating the men had been falsely convicted. Alibi witnesses now placed the convicted men elsewhere at the time of the killing, saying they were reluctant to come forward at the time of the trial due to fear of reprisals. Conviction had been based on the word of members of a rival gang, who were themselves suspects in the killing; charges against them had been dropped in exchange for their testimony. These witnesses later recanted, claiming police and the state's attorney threatened them and coerced their false statements. The police and state's attorneys all denied that. A reference was made to former police commander Jon Burge, convicted of obtaining false confessions in a major Chicago police-crime investigation.

"What else is new?" Frannie mumbled. "This all been happening for years. Maybe Valerie's right. But then who *did* do it?"

A conflict occurred to her. If Angelo was living in Chicago with his wife and son, how was he so involved with Valerie's care in Oak Lawn? And where were the wife and son now? She made a note to ask Valerie.

Frannie put her hands on her back and stretched her aching muscles. She was also getting a serious butt cramp. She'd get some food, then start working her way through the other names on the list.

She stood at the open refrigerator, examining the shelves for anything lunch-worthy. Leftovers were gone. She didn't feel like eggs. The contents of the fruit bin were discolored and growing furry stuff. She regularly bought healthy fruit but rarely went so far as to eat it.

In her walk-in pantry she found a box of Kellogg's Special K Cinnamon Pecan cereal. This, now, was healthy food—if you didn't read the label too carefully. She poured a large portion into a blue Tupperware mixing bowl, added milk until it covered the cereal, and then stood over the drain board of her sink spooning it into her mouth and thinking about her next steps.

Jemma. Get right at it; see if she could find Jemma directly. Of course if it was easy, someone would have found her already. But then not everybody had Frannie's knack for spotting details and tracing them to answers.

She had already discovered that the publicized facts about Angelo were suspect, so it was worthwhile to verify other facts. She'd start with the obvious—search the web for Jemma's name and places she'd been known to live, add some dates, see what turned up.

She put her empty bowl in the sink, and from her file cabinet she pulled out a folder titled "Research Tools." Inside was a list of free people-finding websites. She'd run through the list quickly, and then go back to the better sites to search deeper.

"Ancestry is probably best, but first I'll run the free stuff," she muttered, hoping to strike it lucky. She would use exact information about Jemma and then try alternate spellings and dates at another session.

Zabasearch.com found Jemma DiMaso in Illinois and four other states, but all the women were born twenty years or more earlier. She clicked the "View Full Profile" button on the Illinois result, but she had to pay for that information, so she exited and crossed off Zabasearch from her list.

Next she entered "Jemma Vitale DiMaso Oak Lawn Illinois" in the Google search field. She read the preview texts, opening only those that seemed a strong match. The Oak Lawn Library website yielded a high school yearbook from 1959, with Jemma's photo among the freshmen. Subsequent years did not list Jemma, but Jemma had gone to Italy, married, and had babies. Frannie took a screenshot of Jemma's photo.

Spokeo.com listed a Jemma DiMaso who was the right age and living in a suburb of Phoenix. Names of numerous relatives were listed, but none were names Valerie had mentioned. Frannie wrote down the names and moved on.

She clicked on a Joseph DiMaso because the stated address was within a block of where Jemma had lived in Oak Lawn. After reviewing the sketchy information, Frannie thought Joseph was probably related to Jemma's husband. She jotted down the address and all names associated with that listing, in case she wanted to track down other relatives later.

Another site brought up Jemma DiMaso, age forty-five. Despite the age discrepancy, the address was the same as Jemma's Oak Lawn home. That house had been leveled by a tornado though. The house rebuilt and a woman with the same name living in it? Shut up! Frannie wrote down the name, age, and address. She'd search later for a phone number and check the Cook County Assessor's website to verify the owner. Surely this was another confusing, same-naming situation.

Having finished the most likely results, she went to Facebook. Friend search brought up five Jemma DiMasos, but none of the ages or photos matched.

Pipl.com found the same person she had found on Spokeo.com, but the names of relatives were different and included Paula. Frannie jotted down more names.

ZoomInfo turned out to be subscription-based and dealt with business data. She scratched it off her list.

She never entered the PeekYou.com website because typing the URL in the search screen brought up multiple keywords: peekyou opt out, peekyou removal, peekyou customer service, peekyou delete. Frannie didn't want to start a chain of pop-ups. The FamilyTreeNow search was a similar experience. "Who came up with this free list? Why you messin' with me?" she grumbled. She marked off both sites.

LinkedIn was a free site, but she'd have to register and deal with pesky emails it would generate. Vitalrec.com seemed promising at first, but her queries took her to other websites and links that gave error codes. She scratched Vitalrec.com.

She tried ssdeathindex.gov. Despite the .gov domain extension, clicks brought her to genealogy subscription sites like Ancestry and Family Tree. Frannie had now been full circle.

Stretching her back again, she finally clicked on an Ancestry link. She would use the free search and see if the limited info was of any use. She entered exact information, Jemma DiMaso, date of birth 1944, Oak Lawn, Illinois. The search did not bring up any matches. She tried Arizona. Nothing. She expanded the fields, using "sounds like" for the first name and +/- 2 years for the date of birth. This time two pages of results came up with various spellings and dates.

Her gaze froze near the bottom of the first result page. A sudden empty feeling invaded her chest, and something like a fist hit the pit of her stomach. She brought up details, hoping for an error, but there was no mistake. She stared at the screen, covering her mouth with both hands, and then sent the page to her printer, forgetting it wasn't installed yet. She ran through the set-up, taking deep breaths while she waited. Why was she so emotional? Calm yourself, girl.

Frannie finally picked up the printed document and, her eyes stinging, reached for her cell phone.

# Chapter 25

In her kitchen at seven o'clock in the morning, Cora wondered if Frannie had found any interesting information yet. Frannie would be excited by a new mystery and would want to get an early start. Cisco, another early riser, had already cleaned the kitchen mess from the previous evening. On the sofa in front of the television in the family room, he was tuned to a news program. Newspapers were strewn about, the front section on his lap, his Kindle DS on top of it. He would be reading a news article on the screen. A normal morning in the Tozzi household.

"Thanks for your help yesterday," Cora said.

"No problem," Cisco said, without looking up. He gave a snort. She saw he was about to start reading something to her and she interrupted him.

"Are you going anywhere this morning, hon?"

He looked at her over the top of his glasses. "You want me out of the house, don't you?"

"No, of course not," she said. "Well…I do have a lot of planning to do, and I'll need some private time."

"You want me out of the house," he said again.

Cora gave him a lopsided grin. "I could just lock myself in the office…."

He took a deep breath. "I need some things for the yard. Menards has a sale."

She went over and dropped a kiss on the top of his bald head. "Thank you."

It was hard for her to concentrate when he was underfoot. She felt like she should be helping him or devoting time to his interests instead of her own. But she wanted to get her commitment to Valerie over and done, and she made the most progress when Cisco was busy with some project that didn't involve her.

After he left the house, she sat on a blue secretarial chair at her desk in the upstairs bedroom they had converted to an office. She picked up her notes from the previous night, staring at cryptic scribbles. Neat to begin with, then as ideas flew and she tried to get it all down, the words became a jumble. She'd rewrite the notes while she could still remember. There were a lot—eighteen pages to be exact. She counted them so she could give herself a pat on the back when she was done.

Over an hour later, she moved on to star the tasks that needed immediate attention and those that could be completed quickly, subconsciously sorting information into logical patterns. That done, with a sense of accomplishment, she turned to more time-consuming matters.

Make appointments.

She called a co-volunteer at the Lemont Historical Society. Vicki could meet her at two o'clock that afternoon to help her search property records for Jemma's farm and the golf course. Cora would also review area maps and files about Mount Forest Island history.

She sent an e-mail to a reference librarian at Lemont Library. From past experience she knew librarians used better search criteria and advanced sites that would narrow the results, turn up more pertinent data, and save time. She wanted articles on mob activity in the southwest suburbs of Chicago, the Manhattan Project, Argonne Laboratories, and, on a whim, horse racing activities from the 1950s through the 1980s.

She called Linda again. Linda might know where Kathleen was, and Kathleen might know where Jemma was. Since they talked so seldom, she felt obligated to listen to Linda's small talk. Her mind wandered while Linda rambled on in great detail about her brother's prostate and a petty argument she'd had with a friend Cora didn't know. Cora bit her tongue and tapped a toe. What did Linda look like now? Had she lost weight? Was her hair still long? She wondered again if Frannie was having any success. And what was taking Cisco so long? She had had enough alone time and wished he was home.

Finally, a break in the one-sided conversation.

"Do you know how to get in touch with Kathleen?" Cora asked.

"I get Christmas cards from her now and then with a Chicago address, but she doesn't write anything in them," Linda said.

"Do you have the address?"

"I can look," Linda said. "I save cards for a year ot two. Hope I didn't get rid of it already."

Yes! Her patience had been rewarded.

"Can you look now? I'd like to try to reach her today."

"Really? It's that important? For your friend you said, right? What's going on?"

"We're really trying to reach Jemma. My friend is Jemma's daughter."

"No shit! Pumpkin or Valerie?"

"Valerie."

"The quiet, serious one. Kathleen might know where Jemma is, since they lived together in Arizona. Okay, I'll look. It could take a while. I'll call back when I find it, all right?"

She'd have to be content with that. She heard the garage door opening. Cisco was back. She made lunch for him, put a sandwich together for herself, and brought it back to her office. She checked the clock. Almost time to meet Vicki at the historical society, half the day gone.

Her cell phone rang. It was Frannie.

~ ~ ~

When Valerie opened the door, Cora thought she looked as if she hadn't slept well. She wasn't wearing her dark glasses in her home, and her anxiety was clearly visible.

"It's not good news, is it?" Valerie sounded frightened.

Cora entered the house, balancing her purse and two Starbucks cups. She didn't feel all that well either. Her stomach felt hollow, rumbled, and sent a bitter taste into her mouth. She swallowed and forced a smile to her lips, despite knowing it was pointless to Valerie.

"I brought some tea for you," she said, attempting to keep her voice even. "Can we sit in your kitchen?"

"Sure. Thanks." Equally direct. Something important was up.

Cora followed Valerie and waited for her to sit at the table. She put a cup in front of Valerie, dropped her purse next to a chair, and sat opposite her, reaching out to cover the hand Valerie was resting on the tabletop.

"There's no easy way to say this, Valerie. Frannie called me right before I called you. She found Jemma's death record."

Valerie's breath caught, and her face drained of color. She pulled her hand away. It fluttered in front of her face and then she held it to her chest.

"Valerie, I can't tell you how sorry I am," Cora said.

Jemma was so much a part of Cora's life at one time. Despite the years between, she couldn't believe Jemma was gone and that she couldn't track her down and laugh with her one more time. Fighting to control her own tears now, she hoped Valerie realized she was grieving too. How must Valerie feel? Oh, God. She felt so sorry for this poor woman and everything that kept coming down on her.

Valerie blinked rapidly, her lower lip quivering. "Maybe Frannie made a mistake?"

"She hoped it was a mistake, so she checked. How many Jemma DiMasos living in the Phoenix area with the same birth date as your mother can there be?"

Valerie's eyes filled with tears around her ocular implants. Cora watched without a word as they overflowed and ran down Valerie's cheeks, making shimmering silver paths that hesitated at her chin and then fell onto the table, leaving dark wet spots on the pale blue tablecloth. Valerie lifted a trembling hand a number of times as if to prevent Cora from talking.

"Frannie's not trying to get back at me, is she?" Valerie asked at last, her voice sounding thin and hollow. The question surprised Cora. She thought the two women had resolved their difficulties.

"No, of course not!" Cora said. "She was very upset. She didn't expect it and didn't know how to tell you. She was crying on the phone herself." Same as Cora had.

"Of course, I'm just…I'm in shock." Valerie nodded, stopped, nodded again. "Of course Frannie wouldn't…I never thought… When did it happen? How did she die? Where was she?"

"Frannie didn't look any further after she found the death listing. All she knows is her last-known residence was Chandler, Arizona. She died in 1991."

"I wasn't even married then. Oh! Why didn't I ever think she could be dead?" Valerie groaned, leaned her elbows on the table in front of her, and buried her face in her hands. She didn't sob, but between harsh breaths and choking noises she asked, "Does it matter anymore?"

"What do you mean?"

"What difference does it make now how she died? I shouldn't have waited so long. I can't ask her questions—like why she left—or make up with her. It's too late and I have to live without… Is her death *my* fault, because I didn't look for her until now? Is it Cora?"

Cora and Frannie had talked about whether there was any point in continuing to investigate Jemma's life. Anything they found out now would be opinion or guesswork, which could be worse than no answers at all. Frannie wanted to explore further before telling Valerie, but Cora refused. She wouldn't jeopardize Valerie's trust again by keeping secrets. It had to be Valerie's decision.

How to answer Valerie now? She asked another question instead. "She's been dead more than twenty-five years, Valerie. Would it have made a difference if you found her before she died?"

"Her death changes everything! I needed her! What do I do now?" Valerie lifted her head, her face contorted, whether from panic or grief Cora couldn't tell.

Once again Cora didn't answer right away. She had expected this question, though, and rehearsed her response while driving to Valerie's house.

"In your heart I'm sure you thought that when you found Jemma she would answer your questions. But did you expect her to magically come to your rescue and solve your problems too?"

"Yes, and the questions were *important*. So important we thought I couldn't handle my future without the answers. Now there's no one who…"

"There could be answers, or we could find out nothing. What's the most important question to you? To know where she went? Why she left?"

"I want to know…," Valerie sobbed. "I want to know why she didn't love me," she whispered.

Cora lost it herself then.

"We don't know that, Valerie," Cora said.

"Oh, *I* know that. I *lived* it." She sounded bitter.

"Oh, Valerie. Don't dwell on that now."

"What am I supposed to dwell on? Oh, you know, this was *so* important last night, but now she's dead and I should just put it all in the past?

If I have to, I'll find a way. But give me some time, okay? Give me that, Cora, please. Just…give me some time to digest this."

Cora went to the bathroom and came back with a box of tissues. She blotted her eyes and then placed the box in front of Valerie, who pulled out a handful of tissues and wiped her face and chin.

"Would you like me to stay or leave?"

"I think I need to be alone right now." Valerie slapped her hand against her leg. Corky came into the kitchen, went to Valerie's side, and rested her head against Valerie's knee.

"I'll call you tomorrow, okay?" Cora asked.

Valerie nodded, her hand moving over the dog's head as Cora left.

# Chapter 26

Valerie shivered in the cold breeze coming through a two-inch opening of the bedroom window next to her easy chair, but she left it open. She understood now why people cut themselves; physical pain overpowers emotional pain too intense to be borne.

Why hadn't she suspected Mamma could be dead? Maybe Mamma wouldn't have visited her, but surely the family would have heard something during all those missing years.

Perhaps she had kept Mamma alive in her mind because of all that was unsettled between them. As long as Jemma was alive, there was a chance Valerie could find her, face her, and make her explain. Always a chance she was mistaken in her conviction that Jemma didn't love her.

When Valerie was only in fourth grade, Mamma had made her responsible for getting Paula, Sally, and herself to school and home. One afternoon, Sally, a spoiled little boy back then, bit a girl in his class and was kept after school. When Sally didn't come out with the other kids, Valerie went back into the school to look for him, leaving Paula to watch outside. Instead, Paula left with some school friends, resulting in a neighborhood search for Paula. She was found unharmed.

"You're so *stupid!*" Jemma had accused Valerie. "Why can't you do the simplest thing? I can't run the business if I can't count on you."

Valerie had tried to explain. "But Mamma, I couldn't—"

"Just shut up, Valerie. You're always letting me down. I can't forgive you this time!" Jemma had said. The scene was just as clear today, the pain as sharp, the humiliation as crushing.

If her mother loved her, could she have said anything like that?

Her cheeks were dry now, but Valerie's eyelids burned. She felt as if she were watching herself from outside her body, as if nothing was real and she was only a witness.

Sally and Grace would be home from work soon. They didn't even know she was looking for Mamma or that her future plans depended on finding her and that she had no idea what to do now. Would Sally even care that his mother was dead? He was eleven when Mamma left, and he refused to talk about her to this day.

She'd tell them, but she needed a little time first.

Paula lost somewhere, Sally so remote, everyone else dead—no wonder Valerie had decided long ago to depend solely on herself. According to Father McGrath, her lifetime of self-dependency was based on misbelief. "People who care about us give us confidence," he had said. That's why he'd advised her to make friends and come to terms with past hurts.

Cora seemed to be behind her now, but Valerie wasn't sure she'd gotten over the sense of betrayal she felt when Cora kept important facts from her. And what made Frannie change her mind? And Billy—shy, distant, mysterious Billy—did she know him well enough to call him a friend?

These people were now waiting for her to tell them what to do. Did she have a right to depend on any of them? Unfamiliar territory, this friendship business.

She could no longer count on Mamma, but she still had to find a new place to live, a way to support Molly and herself. Her savings and insurance were running out.

What had she expected from a reunion with her mother? That all would be forgiven between them? They'd move in together and Mamma would take care of her and Molly? Maybe she was so upset because that was no longer an option.

What to do, what to do! Should she give up? Was she, in fact, useless to the world…to her daughter…to herself? A moan escaped her lips, waking Corky, who got up and put her chin in Valerie's lap.

Valerie stroked the animal's head with both hands. "Thank God for you, baby," she said. "You're a lot of bother sometimes, but you'll never call me stupid. You love me, no matter what I do."

Corky pulled away, shook herself, and laid down at Valerie's feet again. Their contact had cleared Valerie's head.

What was the point in knowing any more about Mamma if she could never talk to her? They could investigate Mamma's life later if she changed her mind. But she still wanted to know the true circumstances of Angelo's murder. She'd let Mamma's death sink in and distract herself by looking for Angelo's real killer.

She went through both sides of the family again. She never knew much about her father's family, except that most of them were still in Sicily. She probably couldn't find Uncle Nello, but maybe she could locate Uncle Barbaro or Angelo's wife, Rosa. Or Luisa, the daughter of Jemma's cousin Luisa. They had once been close. She'd never know if she didn't try.

She might call Father McGrath, too. Looking for Mamma had been his idea. He might have some advice now that had turned into a dead end.

The cliché jarred her and she barked a harsh laugh. Dead end, for real. What a sick joke. How could she have such thoughts? Was she feeling bitterness or grief? She'd never asked herself if *she* loved Mamma.

She dropped her face into her hands and rubbed, exhausted. She'd nap before Sally and Grace came home. She slipped off her shoes and slid them beneath her chair, moved to her bed where she curled onto her side, and pushed her face into her pillow. Her tears came freely.

A long forgotten image came into her mind: a family gathering, Mamma at the stove stirring a pot with a long wooden spoon, her head thrown back, shouting with laughter.

She drifted into sleep, asking: *Did I love my mother? If I didn't, why does my chest hurt so much?*

*What happened to us, Mamma?*

# Chapter 27

Frannie didn't agree. Valerie was afraid now that they couldn't get answers directly from Jemma, they'd uncover only meaningless guesswork that would make matters worse. Valerie and Cora had told Frannie to stop research regarding Jemma, but Frannie was sure there was more to know. And she wasn't about to wait around for Valerie to give her a go-ahead. She could decide what to reveal *after* she knew the story.

Like a hound after a fox, once she was on the hunt she didn't want to be called off. She couldn't rest until she found answers. After all, in her opinion, what she was doing was in Valerie's best interests. Valerie would come around sooner or later. What was the harm in staying ahead of her?

All right, so she started off in a snit with Valerie, but she cooled down. When she heard what they wanted her to do—well, she just loved solving mysteries. And the girl really did seem like a different person than the one she used to know. So okay, she'd give it her best shot. But then, for some reason, finding Jemma's death listing hit her like a truck. She instantly saw Valerie for who she really was, a desperate person badly in need of help. Frannie knew what that felt like. And she was the one who found something that hurt the poor girl very badly. She was not only sympathetic, but she also felt responsible. The Frannie she played in public might seem hard and heartless, but underneath, the part she didn't show, was a soft spot for people in trouble.

Besides, who was better than magic-finger Frannie to find out what really happened?

In front of her computer again, she waved her fingers in the air to prepare. She wanted to find out why Jemma left, how she lived her life, why she never contacted her family, why she died, who was with her at the time. Was she still living with Kathleen when she died? And why was Jemma's other daughter, Paula, in Arizona? Did she spend time with Jemma and Kathleen?

Frannie was on the chase!

Now she had the date of Jemma's death, it was easy to get the names of local newspapers and search for Jemma's obituary. She found the same obit in both the *Arizona Republic* and the *Chandler Independent*. The obituary read:

**DiMaso, Jemma Rosa**

*Jemma Rosa DiMaso, nee Vitale, age 46, of Chandler, Arizona, formerly of Chicago, Illinois, and Oak Lawn, Illinois. Wife of the late Salvatore DiMaso. Loving mother of Valerie DiMaso, Paula DiMaso, and Salvatore DiMaso Jr. Sister of Lucia Vitale (deceased), Angelo (Rosa) Vitale (deceased), Aniello Vitale, and Barbaro (Rosa) Vitale. Aunt of Barbaro Vitale Jr. Beloved friend of many. She worked as a laboratory technician at Banner Desert Medical Center, Mesa, Arizona, for many years and was a devoted volunteer for Southwest Slammers baseball team. Visitation to be held at Legacy Funeral Home on Tuesday, August 27, 1991, from noon until 9:00 P.M. (For information, call 480-555-3207.) Funeral Mass at St. Mary's Catholic Church on Friday, August 30, 1991, at 10 A.M., 230 W. Houston St., Chandler, AZ 85225. Private family burial ceremony. Memorials can be sent to the American Breast Cancer Foundation or Susan G. Komen for the Cure.*

She must have died from breast cancer. So Rosa was Jemma's middle name, and Barbaro and Angelo had both married women named Rosa. Salvatore and Barbaro had both named their sons after themselves. No wonder Salvatore Jr. was called Sally with all the name confusion in that family.

Frannie called the funeral parlor, which fortunately was still in business. She asked to speak to the funeral director. He was out, so a secretary took her call. Frannie crossed her fingers and knocked on her wooden table. Here's where clean living, good luck, and a bit of skill came in. Had to weasel the information out of the secretary.

"I'm with St. Joseph's Hospital near Chicago," Frannie fibbed. "We have a patient here, Valerie DiMaso. Her mother's funeral services were handled by your establishment. We need to reach some family members and hoped there might be some information in your file, like who paid the funeral expenses. The deceased's name was Jemma DiMaso."

"We don't usually give out that information…," the secretary began.

"The information could affect our patient's chances for recovery. Surely you want to help."

"Well…I can have the director call you back when he returns."

"It could be dangerous to wait. Do you know how to find the file?"

"Well, yes, I'm actually the person who handles the files, but…uh…"

Frannie heard a loud sigh.

"What was the date of death?"

Yes! She banged her fist softly on the table. Got her! "She died in 1991."

The secretary groaned. "1991! Those records are in the basement. I'll have to go down there, search through boxes… Really, can't this wait?"

"No, I wouldn't be calling if it could. I'm sure you can find it, if you do the filing…"

"All right." Another loud sigh. "Give me your number. I'll call you back."

"Can I wait on the line? I'm not always at my desk."

"It might be a while."

"That's okay. It's important, so I'll wait."

Frannie wasn't as patient as she tried to sound, but she was afraid the funeral director would return and override the secretary's decision. She stomped, heavy-footed, from one end of her flat to the other until her downstairs tenant banged on the ceiling.

"All right, all right!" she yelled.

It only took the secretary about ten minutes, although it seemed longer.

"The bills were paid by a Paula DiMaso, the deceased's daughter. Funeral arrangements usually cost more than people are prepared for, but this was a modest plan. Few people were expected to attend, and the body was sent to Illinois for burial after the funeral Mass."

"Where in Illinois?"

"The cemetery was St. Joseph Cemetery in River Grove, Illinois."

Huh. Same place Angelo was buried. "Do you have an address and phone number for Paula DiMaso?"

Frannie wrote down the information, grinning widely.

"This is strange though… I've never seen this before…," the secretary said.

"Yes?" Frannie breathed.

"There's a note here in red. Looks like someone was to be refused admission to the visitation or funeral Mass if she showed up. It says the daughter was very insistent and was going to take her mother elsewhere if we wouldn't agree to police the situation."

Frannie held her breath. "What was the person's name?"

"Her name was Kathleen Sweeney."

# Chapter 28

Billy hurried up the Palos Woods trail after his shift at OfficeMax. Why had he opened his mouth and promised to come out here again? What the hell did he expect to accomplish? The visit might tell him more about what was happening to *him*, but his friends were expecting him to come back with information that would help answer Valerie's questions, not his.

With dusk approaching, he hurried to the clubhouse first. Only last year's debris, dry and brown, still covered the remote wilderness. Buds, but no new leaves. He pushed his way past stiff branches, brushed away dry leaves with his boots, looking for reasons to explain the building's disappearance. He found only more pieces of red roof tiles like Cisco found.

Disappointed, he headed toward the old farm. As he neared the place, he heard a jingle and a soft whinny. Horseback riders sometimes strayed onto bike paths from nearby bridle trails, and he stopped and glanced around uneasily. The path ahead curved and branches hid the distance. He heard the same occasional sounds when he walked on.

Soon, off trail on his left, beyond slender tree trunks, he saw the gray pole barn and then the lane and the red farmhouse. He slowed and felt for the flashlight he might need soon—for light or weapon. He was ready. He picked up his pace.

Shielding his eyes from the glare of the setting sun that reflected off the windshield of the shiny, black vintage Cadillac, he entered the yard. There was the same man he had met before, seated on a top porch step, knees bent, black riding boots resting on the second step, watching Billy approach. The man wore the same clothes, black pants and white shirt, and still did not wear a jacket.

Billy had come here hoping to find this man, but now his palms grew moist and a line of cold sweat trickled down his temple. Was this man only in his imagination or was he real? Had he wandered into some time warp, alternate reality, or something else entirely? The man couldn't be real—or could he? And where were the buildings when Billy came here with Cora and Cisco?

Seeming relaxed, the man didn't speak, only whistled and watched Billy approach. Waiting for Billy to make the first move.

"I've come back. I hope you don't mind," Billy said.

The man only gestured at a lower stair. Billy sat, fidgeted, and looked across at the barn. What now? A chilly breeze blew through his hair, and he shivered.

After a long moment, Billy said, "I don't see your horse. Didn't you go riding today?"

"She's in the barn," the man said.

"She's a pretty fancy horse for trail riding."

"She's retired now."

"Retired? From what? She looked pretty healthy to me."

"No more racing for her."

"She was a racehorse?"

The man nodded.

"That's what you do with old racehorses, ride them? Why out here?"

"Dolly Val, she's special, not just any horse, even any racehorse. None like her."

His second question hadn't been answered, but Billy didn't press the point.

"Why's that?"

"There's more than winning," the man said.

Billy knit his brows.

"Like breeding, you mean? But if she's too old…"

The man's face grew red and he threw an arm into the air. Billy flinched.

"Winning, breeding, dat's only part of the game. And she's not *old*, she's retired."

It seemed pointless to inquire further. Billy glanced toward the trail, saw that a mist was starting to gather, further reducing visibility. Perhaps he should leave. Curiosity won out.

"I'm Billy Nokoy," he said, holding out his hand. "Who are you?"

The man stared at Billy's hand but didn't take it.

"Jimmy to most people. Al called me Vincenzo."

"That's Italian, right?" *Who was Al?*

He snorted. "Yes, Italian. Not Siciliano."

Something clicked. Horseracing, profits, Sicilians…the Mob? Illegal activities? This man had hinted at danger the first time they met. At the time Billy hadn't sensed danger. But today… He shivered again.

"When I was here before, you warned me about picking up anything at the clubhouse. Why?" Billy said.

The man narrowed his eyes.

"Best you don't get involved."

"You said something to me then, when you turned to put your horse in the barn. In Italian, I guess."

"You mean '*Uarda la ciunca!*"

"That was it. What does that mean?"

The man's gaze was penetrating, his eyes seeming to be lit from within. Billy couldn't look away.

He narrowed his eyes to slits. "Means be careful, you might get hurt."

Billy finally managed to pull his eyes away and gave his head a shake.

"What might hurt me?"

Jimmy stood up, waved both arms angrily, stepped up on the porch, and slammed his fist against the porch rail. "Why you think I'm still here?" he roared.

Billy slid away. He felt an intense need to urinate.

"I don't know…why you're here at all."

"He took the things I loved! Destroyed them! Ruined me, ruined my reputation! My own *il socio* I trusted!"

Who was he talking about? Billy eased toward the far edge of the step, ready to jump up and run. He said, "Who did?"

Jimmy was no longer listening. He paced the porch, waving his arms even more violently, giving vent to rage. Although his steps were heavy, eerily they made no sound. The back of Billy's neck grew cold.

"I told him, 'Forget the ponies, you don't know the business.' But no, he's greedy, had to go where he don't belong. When I was gone, he take control a the business, kill my *tesoro*, my Dolly Val, ruin everything, him and his crazy brother."

He stomped down the steps as Billy leaped to his feet and backed away. He passed Billy and started across the yard.

"Wait, don't go yet," Billy called, remembering Valerie. "Did you know a family named Vitale? They lived here too."

Jimmy stopped and turned.

"Vitale? My stable man?"

"No. A girl. Jemma."

"Jemma? A sweetheart. He ruin her too, Mickey and his crazy brother."

"You knew Jemma?"

"Later. They think I was gone, but I couldn't leave, you see."

He turned away again and Billy called, "Stop" once more. But Jimmy didn't stop this time, leaving Billy looking after him and wondering what the hell the man was talking about. This was the second time he mentioned being gone. Gone where?

Jimmy appeared to fade into the trees. Probably a trick of the dim light.

# Chapter 29

Frannie was ready to impress her friends. Let's get this show going! They had postponed serious discussion until after dinner. Cora had surprised them with lasagna she made using the recipe Jemma had taught her.

"That smells like Mamma's gravy," Valerie sniffed as she entered the house. "If I wasn't convinced you knew Mamma before, I am now. She taught me to cook Italian too. It's harder now. I miss that." Valerie appeared solemn, as expected, but determined.

After dinner they all moved to the living room, where a plate of Italian pastries Cora purchased on Taylor Street rested on a traditional cherry cocktail table, along with bottles of wine and a pot of coffee.

Frannie sat on a sofa, a well-used, large purple tote bag on the floor at her feet, a stack of manila folders on each side of her and another in her lap.

Frannie thought both Cisco and Billy, seated across the room, seemed uncomfortable. Cora appeared organized and businesslike as usual, elbows on her chair, pencil in one hand and clipboard in the other. The clipboard was filled with the blank sides of previously printed sheets. Just like Cora not to let anything go to waste. You'd think she was hard up.

While Cora told Billy about Jemma's death, Frannie worried about giving away that she was still investigating Jemma, despite Valerie's request *not* to.

"So, Frannie," Cora said, "what have you found out?"

Looking at Billy, Frannie said, "Let me start with the spooky stuff. I think a psychokinetic ability called SLI might be what's going on here."

Everyone looked blank. "It stands for 'street light interference,'" she explained. "Lights go off and on, electrical and mechanical equipment, like computers and watches, go haywire or burn out. Just like what you told us, Billy. People with this ability are called 'SLIders,' the *S*, *L*, and *I* in capitals. They can affect things without touching them. Strong emotion can bring it on."

"Really?" Cisco said. "How did you find this?"

"I sent a Facebook message to Ursula Bielski, a ghost expert in Chicago who wrote *Haunted Bachelors Grove* and other books. She named it and gave me some references. Do you want the list, Billy?"

"I do," Billy said, leaning forward, his eyes wide. "Can I control this thing?"

She pressed her lips together and shook her head. "I can't tell you that. There are only a few articles. Most paranormal activities, from what I read, are unpredictable."

"Why didn't this happen before Billy came to Lemont?" Cora asked.

"My guess, from the research we did a couple of years ago, is because of a nearby energy source," she said.

"Is there more energy around here? Why?" Valerie asked.

"There's Argonne," Cora said immediately.

"Yes!" Cisco said. "The nuclear waste from the Manhattan Project is buried right next to the golf course and farm!"

"But that's not near the island where the first episode happened," Billy said.

"No," Frannie said. "But this whole area is on top of limestone and full of quarries. Studies show limestone increases paranormal activity. It has to do with electromagnetic fields, imprinting, and other technical explanations I only skimmed. You get the idea."

"Thanks for finding this and the list," Billy said. His usually immobile face looked relieved. She nodded at him and then glanced at Valerie.

When Frannie called Cora to tell her about Jemma's death, she was so upset she didn't mention what she knew about Angelo. She now told everyone what she discovered and recent developments that threw doubt on the guilt of the convicted killers.

"Didn't you ever read this stuff, Valerie?" she asked.

"Nonna kept it from me when it happened. Later it was a painful memory," Valerie said.

"I understand. But one thing confused me. Didn't Angelo have to live in Chicago to be a Chicago cop? And he had a wife and kid. But you said he was with you in Oak Lawn."

"I may have exaggerated a little." Valerie turned away for a moment. "Like I said, he was upset about a lot of things and spent more of his time at Nonna's house than at home. I don't know if he was having trouble with his wife or trying to protect his family, but something wasn't right."

That was interesting. "Did you ever ask his wife's opinions?"

Valerie lowered her head and shook it, a blush coloring her cheeks. "She didn't want anything to do with us, after. She thought our family was too close to the wrong kind of people."

That made sense. Frannie went on. "When I searched other family members, I couldn't find Aniello—only his birth record." She took an unnecessary look at her notes and paused. She had to be careful not to mention Paula. "Jemma's kid brother, Barbaro, was another story. I'm sorry to say he's passed too, Valerie." She watched Valerie's face.

Valerie remained expressionless. "I barely knew him," she said at last. "He was years younger than Mamma and rarely showed up at family doings. Neither Sally nor I have had anything to do with our relatives for years. How did he die and when?"

"He died over ten years ago," Frannie said. "The death certificate says coronary artery disease. He was fifty-five."

"Heart disease seems to be a curse in Sicilian families—part genetic, part diet and lifestyle," said Cisco.

Frannie remembered that Cisco was Sicilian. His father and three of his uncles had died from heart disease, and Cisco had multiple cardiac stents.

Frannie flipped pages in her lap, looking for a specific note.

"That's why his wife and son wrote in Angelo's memorial book on Barbaro's behalf," she said. "Seems he was a patrolman with the Chicago Police Department same time as Angelo, but he was let go in 1990 for failure to pass a drug test."

"And you know this based on…?" Cora asked.

"An article in the *Chicago Tribune* later that year. Here it is." She read from the page. "Barbaro was arrested in Orland Park for drug dealing. Indicted for participating in a drug ring. He drove to Florida to pick up cocaine that came from Colombia to bring it to Chicago. When they searched his house in Burbank, near Oak Lawn, they found…," she ran her finger along the printout, "seventy-five guns, including an AR-15 machine gun, and more than one thousand rounds of ammunition." She looked up. "He was one of the dealers involved when the drugs were distributed."

"Whoa," said Cora. "Was he convicted?"

"He was. He got ten years, served eight. I suspect the review boards were miffed because he was dealing while he was still on the Chicago police payroll, selling cocaine in bars in the west and southwest suburbs. If a bar owner objected he was told 'enforcers,'" she made air quotes, "would break his windows or his legs. Coming from a policeman, the owner had nowhere to turn."

"What does any of this have to do with Angelo?" Valerie interrupted.

Frannie, carried away by the attention she was getting, remembered this wasn't her own dog and pony show but the lives of others. The information was having its effect on Valerie, sitting with her hands in tight fists, her lips pressed together. How would Frannie have felt if *her* family was involved with drugs?

"Good question," she said, in a softer voice. "There *is* an implication here. Nine people were picked up in that raid, and every name sounded Italian to me. The U.S. attorney wouldn't confirm or deny a link to the Chicago Mob, but he did say the investigation was conducted by…," she read from her notes again, "'the Organized Crime Drug Enforcement Task Force. DEA agents confirmed that the ringleader was known to report to two suburban mob chieftains.'" She looked up. "Draw your own conclusions."

Cora, Cisco, and Billy exchanged glances and then looked at Valerie, who now had her arms crossed over her chest.

"Are you telling me Uncle Angelo dealt drugs for the Mob?" she asked.

"No, no, I'm not saying that at all! I'm saying maybe Angelo *knew* something and because he was on the police force the Mob had to silence him, *that's* what I'm saying." Angelo could very well have been in deep, but Valerie didn't need to know that now.

"Maybe Angelo knew mob secrets because *other* members of the family *were* involved," Cora guessed. "Remember the suspicions I had when I knew Jemma?"

Valerie was shaking her head continuously. "I never had any idea. It was just my family, you know, and I was pretty young. They never talked about anything like that."

Cora reached out and put her hand over Valerie's. "Remember we were afraid we might turn up things you don't really want to know? First about your mother, and now your uncle—do you want us to stop?"

Valerie blinked, her chin in the air. She swallowed with difficulty. Her facial expression changed from panic to determination.

"I don't want to stop." Her voice was soft but decisive.

Everyone eyed each other.

Cora cleared her throat and said, "Did you find anything else, Frannie?"

"Some little things, unimportant, but interesting. You told us about Jane Byrne moving into Cabrini-Green to take a stand against the gangs. That really happened."

She flipped through pages again and found and held up a screen print. "I ran across another Vitale: Theodore Vitale. Seems he was picked up and questioned in a murder investigation in 1959. That would have been while Jemma was in Sicily. The bodies of three young boys were found in the forest preserves in 1955, and then in 1956 the bodies of two teenage sisters were found in the forest preserves near Willow Springs."

Frannie took a sip of wine but found it difficult to balance glass, cannoli, and her paperwork, and she placed the glass back on the table. "He was with the boys the day they disappeared…and later with the sisters. He worked at stables near both forest preserves where the bodies were found. He also managed a horse-breeding farm in Tinley Park owned by a mob boss from Chicago Heights. The mob boss, Jimmy Emery, was banned from horse racing in 1954 for illegal betting and fixing races. Vitale, his right-hand man, was guilty by association. They didn't find any evidence to keep Vitale, but I thought the name and connection worth mentioning."

Valerie seemed thoughtful. "Great-Uncle Ted. Nonno's brother. I forgot him. He lived on the farm too. I never met him, but Angelo talked about him. He did have something to do with horses." She exhaled at length and sank back into her armchair. "So now my family is in the Mob, one uncle is a drug pusher and another a child molester and murderer who worked for a mob boss. This is unreal. I never felt my Italian ancestry was a big part of my life."

"Sometimes your heritage has more impact on your life than you realize," Cora commented.

Watching Billy out of the corner of her eye, Frannie noted that at the mention of Jimmy Emery he had stiffened and leaned forward. Then he folded his arms across his chest and studied the floor.

She flipped through more notes. "Let's see…the guy Billy met at that farm called that metal piece a Sabbath stick. In the early days of golf, men were forbidden to play on Sundays. So they disguised a golf club as a walking stick, using the club head as a handle. They're worth about $500 today on eBay.

"One last little thing," Frannie said, as she started to gather her folders. "I found a nice little story in the *Southtown Economist* about Jemma. In 1958, when she was fourteen, she found some sort of rare jellyfish and handed it over to a naturalist. It was a freshwater jellyfish about an inch long that looked like a layer of Vaseline. The naturalist said it hadn't been seen in Illinois for over a hundred years. Not important, just a cool story."

When Frannie finished, Billy lifted his head and cleared his throat.

"I think that mob boss is the man I met at the farm. But he must be…" He stopped, raising his eyebrows in surprise. "That fits," he mumbled.

He cleared his throat again, seeming uncomfortable with the sudden silence in the room and all the eyes on him.

"I went to the farm, like I said I would, day before yesterday," he began. "I couldn't find the clubhouse, but I did see the farm and the man I met before."

Frannie reached for her wine, spilling some on the table. After Cisco mopped up the spill, Billy explained the encounter.

"I figured from what he said that he was involved in horse racing and there was something illegal going on, both on the farm and at the clubhouse. He said his name was Jimmy, but that 'Al' called him Vincenzo. He confirmed what he said the first time, that the place was dangerous. He went on a rant about someone named Mickey. He said they both knew Jemma, and Mickey and his brother had ruined both Jimmy and Jemma, but he didn't say how."

"Wait, wait, wait!" Frannie said. "When? Dude ought to be dead by now."

"Right, I think he is dead. He kept talking about being 'gone,' and… yeah, well, you all think I'm crazy enough already, so what I'm gonna say now's gonna reinforce that. But I swear the experiences out there weren't in my head."

He turned toward Cora with a question in his eyes.

"We can't explain what happened when we went out there either," Cora said, shaking her head. She caught Cisco's eye, remembering previous ghost encounters that had nothing to do with Billy.

"I've been talking to a ghost, unless I wandered into some kind of time warp," Billy went on. "How else is he gonna be here today, gone tomorrow, and the whole damn farm with him? I swear when he walked away from me this time he just got more and more transparent until he was completely gone. I tried to explain it by the light and the mist, but now I think I was right."

Cisco clamped his jaw and grimaced.

"Not again," Frannie said, shooting an angry look at Cora. This was what she'd been afraid of.

"I don't believe in ghosts," Valerie said. "There must be another explanation."

Frannie read her friends' faces. Cora seemed excited, Cisco resigned, Valerie doubtful, Billy defensive. Her own face probably mirrored Cisco's, with a bit of irritation thrown in.

She made a pretense of reluctance, letting out a long breath. "You think we can get this ghost on our team, Billy? An informant against the Mob? They can't hurt him no more, he's already dead."

When the chuckles died down, Cisco said, "An interesting concept, though."

"Odd thing," Frannie said, "those murdered boys were found in Robinson's Woods, one of the most haunted spots around. Now we're smack in another haunted woods. And you got to know too, spirits have no sense of time. It's going to be confusing trying to figure out anything this guy says."

Cisco looked at Billy. "You thought he was referring to mob operations?"

"Definitely," Billy said. "I tried to figure it out yesterday, reading online about illegal horse racing in the late fifties, but I didn't get anywhere. Now that Frannie's found some names, maybe I can narrow it down and identify Mickey too."

"How about Uncle Teddy?" Valerie reminded him. "We know he was there and could have been involved. I wonder if he's still alive."

Cora scratched away with her pencil. Cisco passed the plate of pastries. Billy held up a forefinger to indicate he'd like another beer and Cisco left to get it, coming back with a bottle for himself, too.

When everyone was resettled, Cora asked for attention. "It's getting late, but there's one important thing I have to tell you before we decide what each of us is going to do now."

"Yeah, we just waiting for you to tell us what to do," Frannie said, and everyone laughed.

Cora didn't laugh, but she smiled good-naturedly. "Linda called me this morning with Kathleen's address. Kathleen's living in a senior housing complex west of Chicago. I checked her Facebook page. I couldn't tell much, just some pictures with family or friends and games she plays online."

Oh, oh. Might have been better if Frannie had said what she knew, but now she'd look even worse if she let on she hadn't told them about Paula and Kathleen.

But Cora was saying, "Here's the question. I can call her or go out to visit her? We decided not to track Jemma any further, but now we have an opportunity."

Cora turned to Valerie. "It's your decision, Valerie."

"I don't know, Cora. Will she talk to you?" Valerie said.

"I have no reason to think she'd refuse."

"Any reason she wouldn't want to talk about Jemma?" Valerie said.

"None I can think of," Cora said.

Frannie could think of a reason though—the animosity between Kathleen and Paula that she wasn't supposed to know about. She shuffled her papers, bounced her leg, and looked at the floor. Keep your mouth shut, girl.

Valerie dropped her chin and took a few calming breaths. "Okay," she said at last. "It's the first real chance to know anything about her. Go for it. How can things get any worse?"

"That's the spirit!" Frannie said. But don't be too sure about that.

Before Valerie left, Cora and Frannie surrounded her. "Are you okay?"

Valerie turned down one side of her mouth. "No. Tonight was more bad news, but there's some satisfaction knowing my instincts about Uncle Angelo have been right all these years. I'm holding up. I get jumpy and notice too much, hyperaware, I suppose you'd say, if you want to avoid the 'paranoid' word. The other night I even imagined someone had been in my room." She laughed.

"Why?" Frannie asked.

Valerie told them about things being out of place. She laughed again. "My sleep pants and T-shirt haven't turned up yet. It was probably Grace —accidental, I'm sure. Just me getting a little crazy."

"Be careful anyway," Frannie said. "All this nasty stuff may have happened a long time ago, but me and Cora, we know shit has a way of cropping up when we start digging into the past."

Valerie chuckled. "You didn't tell me that part, Cora."

Frannie saw Billy watching them, a look of concern on his face. "Billy, when you gonna go talk to that ghost-guy again?"

# Chapter 30

"Not a blessed thing on Facebook!" Frannie said, pounding away at her keyboard, finally having time to look for Paula.

She switched to Google and entered Paula's last known address in Arizona. An hour later, a break finally came when she stumbled on a 1993 real estate sale showing Paula DiMaso as the listing agent. The agency was no longer in business, but Paula was listed on the Arizona Department of Real Estate's website.

Paula got an Illinois real estate agent license in 1984. In 1990, she was licensed in Arizona and worked in Phoenix until 1995.

Huh. Arrived a year before Jemma died, stayed four years after she passed.

Paula then went from agency to agency at increasingly frequent intervals, landing in Las Vegas in 2001, where she remained until 2007. She came back to Illinois in 2007 and worked until 2012, when her work history stopped abruptly in Joliet, Illinois.

"Girl sure moves around a lot," Frannie mumbled, jotting down places and dates.

An article in a 2011 *Joliet Herald News* described a complaint filed with the state against Paula DiMaso for unethical behavior. "The woman shouldn't be working with the public," Melanie Lauder accused. "She seemed fine at first, but when I caught her misrepresenting details she swore at me, called me names, and waved her arms at me. It was bizarre. I felt threatened and couldn't sleep for nights afterward."

Frannie called the Re/Max agency mentioned. The office manager remembered Paula but was reluctant to discuss her employment or whereabouts. Her tone implied it had not been a good work experience. After Frannie explained that she was trying to locate Paula on behalf of her blind sister, the woman named an assisted living community in Joliet.

She dialed the facility's number and asked to be connected to Paula DiMaso. She wondered if Paula was an employee or a resident.

"Who are you?" Paula said.

"Frannie Berkowitz. A friend of your sister, Valerie DiMaso," Frannie explained.

"I don't talk to my family," Paula said. "Haven't for years. Don't want to now."

"Your sister is having a tough time. She's blind now. She could use your help."

"Ha! That's a good one. I can't do for myself without help."

"You have *information* that might help her."

"Sorry. Call someone else," Paula said. The line went dead.

Damn! She wasn't about to take that. After crushing Valerie by revealing her mother's death, she felt driven to make it up to her by finding some positive information the gal needed. So far all she was doing was making things worse.

Frannie slipped her cell phone into her pocket, but it rang almost immediately. Was Paula having second thoughts, using the recent call feature on her phone?

No, it was Cora. "Thought I'd keep you up-to-date. I reached Kathleen. I'm seeing her Monday afternoon," Cora said. "Anything happening on your end?"

Frannie made a rapid decision. She couldn't very well say she'd been looking for Paula after Valerie said she didn't want her to. Kathleen would probably tell Cora about Paula anyway. Should she stop what she'd been doing? They need never know she'd found Paula. Yet, due to the conflict between Paula and Kathleen, the two women would probably tell different stories. She'd gotten this far; she couldn't pass up the opportunity to be the one to fix things. She didn't even know if she could get Paula to talk, but if she *was* successful, she'd deal with how to tell the others afterward.

"Oh, just pretty much spinning my wheels," Frannie said. "I already took the family investigation as far as I could go. You're meeting Kathleen, and Valerie's looking for Ted Vitale. With Billy doing the supernatural and Mob stuff, there's not much left for me to do."

"Don't sound so disappointed. I bet your mind's working overtime in other nooks and crannies," Cora laughed.

"It could happen," she admitted, rolling her eyes at the ceiling.

~ ~ ~

That afternoon, Frannie pulled up in front of Joliet Manor, an institutional-appearing, five-story, red-brick building that looked as if it had been built in the 1950s on the government's dime. It sat in the middle of a blacktopped parking lot with minimal and poorly maintained landscaping. Only a few older-model cars were in the lot. Benches near the door were empty. She wondered if the apartments were similarly uninspiring. When her turn came, she hoped to find a livelier place.

As she approached the entrance, glass doors slid apart, opening into a vestibule blocked by another set of locked glass doors. Frannie peered into the lobby. A heavyset, black woman with short, dyed-blonde hair wearing a yellow, floral-pattern dress sat behind a desk. The woman looked up, saw her, and pointed to a button at the side of the doors below a sign that read: "Ring for Entry."

Really. She rolled her eyes and pressed the button.

"Yes?" The voice came over a speaker in the vestibule.

"I'm here to see Paula DiMaso," Frannie said.

The woman frowned and knit her eyebrows. "She expectin' you?"

"No. I was in the neighborhood. Thought I'd take a chance," Frannie fibbed.

A buzzer sounded, unlocking the door. Easy so far. Frannie entered.

"Hey girl! You got to sign here to go in," the woman called, sliding an open book across her desk. She chuckled. "I'm going out on a limb letting you in. But Paula, she never has no visitors, and we was just talking about how she needed some attention. And here you come, like an answer to a prayer." She paused and narrowed her eyes. "You a friend?"

"Not exactly. I know her sister. Promised I'd come visit. Can you tell me how to get to her room?"

"She ain't in her room. In the office down the hall there, last door on the right." The woman pointed down a carpeted hallway with a couple of dated cabinets, landscape paintings, and multiple doors along the walls. "She's the only one in there. Paula does some paperwork half a day. Helps pay for her room."

The secretary or whatever she was frowned again. "Hope she takes kindly to you. She don't always. No point tellin' her I let you in, though—maybe say you's here visiting someone else and looked her up."

Frannie smiled, nodded her agreement, and started down the hall. Okay, Paula's employed. Can't be too nutty. Maybe that woman at the desk let her in because she thinks of Paula as staff—but if Paula's a resident, she must have some level of incapacity.

She lingered near Paula's open office door, studying the occupant before entering. The woman looked fiftyish. She was taller than Valerie, stocky, her dark, graying hair poorly cut and styled. She looked up at Frannie and then back at her computer screen a number of times. When Frannie didn't go away, Paula glared at her.

Frannie entered the office and sat in a straight-backed chair, the only empty one in the small room.

"Make yourself at home," Paula said in a sarcastic tone. "Who are you and what do you want?"

"Like I said on the phone, Frannie Berkowitz, a friend of your sister. I'm not what you expected, am I?"

"You. How'd you get in here?"

"Never mind that." When expecting hostility, best to be direct. "I came here to talk about your mother. You were with her when she died, I understand."

Paula blinked. She looked at the work on her desk, running a shaking finger over a page next to her computer. When she looked up again she was slightly flushed but appeared less irritated. Did her mother carry more weight than the mention of Valerie? Was she feeling guilty? Angry? Threatened? Was she hiding a secret?

"My mother?" she said, with a defensive edge. "Did you know her?"

"Here's the thing. Valerie's looking for information about her mother—your mother. All she knows is she left Chicago and went to Arizona when you were both in your early teens, and she died in 1991, probably from cancer. I found out you were with her when she died. So you know more than we do."

Paula snorted. "Valerie and Sally, too, they never looked for me or for Mamma either. Let her find out on her own. I hope you didn't come here with any crazy ideas about getting us back together."

Frannie leaned toward Paula. "That's not why I'm here. Valerie *can't* find out on her own, Paula. I told you, she's blind. She maybe could eventually get things done on her own, but there's circumstances. She needs to know right away, so I'm helping her out."

But, she didn't need to know Frannie was there without Valerie's knowledge.

Paula's face lost some of its anger. She hit a few keys on the keyboard, pushed it out of the way, and leaned back in her chair. A good sign. Frannie studied Paula, recognizing the same high-and-mighty expression she'd often seen on Valerie's face.

"If you know all that, you must have a good idea why I had to get away from my family."

"Uh huh," Frannie said, nodding and assuming a sympathetic demeanor.

Paula's gaze wandered around the room vaguely. Was she even following the conversation?

Then she said, "Mamma left, Papá was always off on some business or other, Nonna's place was a zoo, Valerie bossed me around, and Sally played cruel pranks. The only good person was Uncle Angelo, and he got himself killed."

Okay. She was with it, but something wasn't right. "That's pretty much what Valerie said. It wasn't so great for her either."

Paula looked away again. Was she ashamed?

"I grew up wanting to escape and to never look back."

"I can understand that. How'd you get out?" Frannie made a show of studying her nails, but kept checking Paula's expression.

"I moved in with a friend from high school who had an apartment in the city. I store-clerked until that got old, then checked out real estate. It seemed a good fit."

Sales a good fit? She doubted Paula's social skills had been any better than Valerie's.

"How did you find your mother?"

Paula sighed and slouched in her chair, looking past Frannie. "I didn't. Real estate was hot in Phoenix at the time…," she smirked, "no pun intended. So I thought it was a good opportunity and moved there. I had a vomiting spell one day and went to the hospital emergency room. Who comes to take my blood but Mamma!"

"That must have been a surprise."

"Later I realized Mamma must have known. My name would have been on the order. If she didn't want to meet me she could have had someone else take my blood, but she didn't."

"And you continued to see each other?"

"We had dinner, and she asked me if I remembered Kathleen." She stopped. She seemed to be wrestling with her expression, the same angry or fearful or guilty expression she had earlier. Clearly the thought of Kathleen was disturbing and she was hiding something.

"Who was Kathleen?" Frannie said, playing dumb. She crossed her legs and pretended to relax.

"Mamma was friends with her back when I was a kid. Turns out after she moved to Arizona, Mamma and Kathleen shared an apartment and later a home."

"Did Jemma tell you why she left?"

She shook her head. "She wouldn't talk about it. She said she didn't want to leave, but she had no choice."

"Why?"

"She didn't say why. Later, I guessed."

Frannie raised an eyebrow.

Paula stared back. "I don't want to talk about that."

Better not to press and annoy her...she'd stop talking. "Okay. So you kept seeing Jemma and Kathleen?"

"Yeah, Mamma started bringing her along to dinner. And we went to one of those beep baseball games for the blind Mamma was involved with. Do you know what beep baseball is?"

Frannie nodded. She had looked up the Southwest Slammers mentioned in Jemma's obituary and read about blind baseball.

"Most people don't." She gave Frannie a quizzical look. "Did you say Valerie is blind now?"

Frannie nodded again. "Had an accident a couple of years ago."

"How strange. Mamma so devoted to the blind, never knowing her own daughter..."

"Yes, it is. Did you resent Kathleen?"

Paula stiffened. "Why would you say that?"

"I don't know. A notion. Forget it. Why didn't you tell your sister and brother you found Jemma? Didn't you think they'd want to know?"

"After all I did to leave them *out* of my life? I hadn't talked to them in years and I didn't know how to explain Mamma's new life. Had my own problems…and then trying to figure out how I felt about Mamma myself. Didn't want to bother making peace after all those years."

Problems? It was hard to believe Paula would prefer life alone to the support of her family, but Valerie said Paula had been moody and troubled even as a kid. Had this turned into a mental disorder in later life?

Valerie had created a friendless life too. It could be for the same reasons.

Frannie grinned. "Could be you're more like your mama than you want to admit."

Paula turned dark red and stood up, slamming a fist on the desk. "Don't say that! You *don't* know me! I'm *nothing* like Mamma!"

"Okay, sorry," Frannie said, holding up both hands. "I thought it was a compliment."

Paula sat back down, pulled a tissue from her pocket, and wiped her nose.

When she seemed calm again, Frannie asked, "And then Jemma got sick?"

"She'd had a mastectomy years ago, and her cancer recurred. But she didn't tell me until the last couple of months when she got really bad."

"It must have been hard to let go of her just when you got to know her again."

Paula's eyes filled with tears and she looked away.

"I'm sorry, Paula. These memories must be painful. You loved your mother, didn't you?"

When she turned back, her face was contorted, her eyes filled with fury. "I hated her! Trying to make up with me, using me to try to reach Valerie and Sally at the end, and all the time, even her last days…"

Frannie held her breath.

"She was a lesbian! My mother and Kathleen were living as lesbians all those years! Mamma left us for a woman lover!"

# Chapter 31

"I didn't expect you to buy me lunch, Kathleen. How nice!" Cora said, seating herself.

Tables for four filled the large dining area. The institutional-green carpet was faded and worn, and the dark wood chairs were scratched and scraped, but with new blue-and-yellow, brightly striped fabric. Yellow plastic tablecloths covered the tables, and vases with assorted plastic flowers were at their centers. They were trying.

"Food here's only passable, but Monday's always good," Kathleen said. "They use up leftovers from the week and the kitchen's pretty creative. Today is chicken potpie, a chef special, so I wasn't embarrassed to invite you. I get one free guest a month." She chuckled.

They studied each other. "I've gained some weight," Cora said. "When did we last see each other? About 1980?"

"No, 1979. We came to Chicago for my niece's wedding, the same year Jemma and I bought our house in Chandler."

Kathleen always had a memory for details. She'd gained weight too. Her shoulder-length hair was as bushy and out of control as Cora remembered, but was now a dull gray. A shorter style would be more becoming, but Kathleen had never spent much effort on her appearance. A few upper teeth were missing, which she didn't try to hide. She wore navy-blue knit pants and her long-sleeved, blue-plaid blouse pulled at the buttons. Matronly.

As they examined each other, Cora wondered what Kathleen thought about *her* appearance.

"How long have you lived here?" Cora asked.

"At Peaceful Village? Or back in Chicago?"

"Both."

"I've lived at Peaceful eight years now. Moved back to Chicago in 2000. New millennium, new lifestyle. We lived near Phoenix before that, you know. Something was missing after Jemma died. I moved around, tried Florida for a while. I felt empty. I finally decided, since I still had family here… As you get older, especially if you live alone, family starts to be more important."

"So you moved back?" Cora leaned forward, chewing a thumbnail.

"Yeah. Worked awhile, managed a business office for a shipping company. I was good at it, but I got tired and I've had health problems. It was time to retire. With social security, retirement, and savings, this was what I could afford. But I *could* afford it. It's decent here. Never regretted my decision."

"How do you spend your time?"

She laughed. "You could call me a senior activist. I head a committee of like-minded seniors who get together to be sure the place stays on its toes. We bring problems to their attention and suggest ways to fix things."

Cora remembered how bossy Kathleen had been. The role she found for herself seemed a perfect fit.

"And you?" Kathleen asked.

Cora filled her in on her own life with Cisco, her two sons and three grandchildren, her career, retirement, and post-retirement activities. They reminisced about the sixties and gossiped about Linda. A server arrived and set a tray of food in front of each of them.

The farmhouse soup was excellent. The salad, described as greens with pears and pecans, sounded interesting but it came on a warm plate, the lettuce wilted, and the pears and pecans sparse. It was accompanied by a corn muffin.

Cora tasted the potpie and raised her eyebrows in approval. The crust was flaky, the richly flavored chunks of chicken tender, and the vegetables were roasted, not stewed. "This is amazing," she said.

Returning to their conversation, Cora chuckled. "Mysteries keep falling in my lap, it seems." She told Kathleen censored versions of her experiences at St. James at Sag Bridge and of publishing a book about an American Indian woman.

A kitchen worker picked up their trays and asked if the women would like dessert. "Get the lemon cake," Kathleen advised. "For me, a banana. Seniors value a great bakery, but if I indulged every day I'd be even bigger than I am now."

After lunch, they moved to a lounge area near the front door and sank into comfortable sofas facing each other.

"Sounds like you've had some adventures, but you didn't look me up after all these years for no reason, Cora," Kathleen said, peering into Cora's eyes. "What's up?"

Cora chuckled, and Kathleen raised her eyebrows.

"I'm laughing because my friend Frannie is home dying to be here to pick your brain. She's working with me and ran out of things to do." Cora gave Kathleen a crooked smile. "We want to know about Jemma."

Kathleen stiffened.

That was interesting. Why did she seem suddenly reluctant?

"Why's that?" Kathleen asked.

"As it happens, one of our friends is Jemma's daughter. She never understood why Jemma disappeared from her life. We thought you'd know."

Kathleen's face reddened and she pushed her shoulders back into the sofa. "I don't want any part of helping Paula," she said.

Okay. What was that about? "No, no," Cora said. "Not Paula. Valerie."

Kathleen relaxed, her blush fading. "Valerie? I haven't seen or heard of Valerie or the boy, since Jemma left them. Why didn't she come see me herself? Why'd you come instead?"

She omitted Paula. Did that mean she *had* heard from Paula? What wasn't she saying?

"You and I were old friends. We thought it'd be easier for you to talk to me than someone you only knew as a child."

Kathleen's face expressed suspicion. "Why does she want to know after all these years? She never tried to contact me before."

Cora described Valerie's blindness and her desire to raise her daughter. "She's always wondered why Jemma left. She's been seeing a counselor who thinks clearing up some traumas in her past may give her enough confidence to live independently." She paused and closed her eyes for a moment.

"I'm afraid if Frannie and I don't help give her this chance, Valerie will fail. The poor woman's been through enough."

Kathleen's expression softened and her eyes grew bright. "I wish I could help, Cora, but I really don't have answers for you. Jemma wouldn't even tell me why she left, only that she wished there was some other way. She hated leaving her kids—her husband not so much—but she said leaving would be better for them."

"Was it Sal? Did he beat her?"

"He slapped her around a little, but she gave it back at him. No, she could control Sal, and she'd never have left the kids with him and her family if he was the problem. Something in Chicago frightened her. That's why she'd never go back, even when Angelo died. That one trip we made together when we saw you, she was a wreck the whole time. Just hid out in our hotel room."

"Did that 'something,'" Cora made air quotes, "frighten her until she died? That was over fifteen years later."

"I couldn't understand either. I kept suggesting she get in touch with her kids. First she said she couldn't, and years later she'd always say she wanted to, but they were better without her and it would only complicate things. She always had excuses: they must hate her, and it would hurt them more if she returned rather than if she stayed out of their lives. Whatever frightened her, I didn't know if it was still there, but she just wouldn't take a chance."

"It left Valerie thinking her mother didn't love her, you know."

Kathleen looked sad and shook her head.

"Oh, Jemma loved her all right. Whenever we talked about her kids, Valerie was the one she talked about most. She had a real soft spot for that girl. She'd try to hide it, but I caught her with tears in her eyes. She was so proud of her. Mother and daughter, they were a lot alike. She always said they probably battled as much as they did *because* they were so much alike. She missed Valerie terribly, more than the other two, although she loved them as well. I'm not sure how much she loved Paula at the end though."

Another negative comment about Paula. At the end?

"You mean you *met* Paula? Did Jemma see her before she died?"

Kathleen raised an eyebrow. "You didn't know? Didn't Paula tell her brother and sister? Well, I guess that's just like the bitch."

"What do you mean?"

Kathleen took a deep breath and stared at the ceiling. When she turned back her eyes were angry and her voice bitter. "Paula lived near Phoenix for a while. She and Jemma found each other and we spent some time together before Jemma died. The breast cancer had returned by then and had metastasized, but Jemma thought she had to patch things up with Paula before she told her she was terminally ill. Then Paula realized the nature of our relationship and couldn't handle it. She hated me, blamed me for everything, and did whatever she could to get Jemma away from me."

Their relationship? Oh! The clues fell into place. Her eyes widened, but she had to ask.

"What do you mean, your relationship? Was she jealous?"

It was Kathleen's turn to look surprised. She searched Cora's face. "You didn't know either? We loved each other, Cora. I mean, Jemma and I loved each other in every way."

Cora covered her mouth to stifle a gasp. She looked away, trying to tie the convoluted threads of Jemma's life together. How would Valerie react to still another shock?

Kathleen shook her head sadly.

"You disapprove too, Cora? You should see your face."

"I'm just surprised... I never thought..."

"But you disapprove?"

Cora lifted her head and met Kathleen's eyes. "It's not up to me to approve or disapprove. I just never had any gay friends."

"You *did* have gay friends—me and Jemma. We're the same people you knew."

She couldn't see any way to explain. "Please, Kathleen. I'm not being judgmental. I don't want to get into personal opinions or gay rights. I just want to understand Jemma's life insofar as it affected Valerie."

"And you're not curious yourself?" Kathleen gave her a half smile.

"Well, okay, that too. But let's just go back to talking about when Jemma was dying, all right? You're implying it was bad enough that the woman you loved was dying, but Paula made things worse. What did she do?"

"She acted like a lunatic. She'd make a scene, screaming at Jemma, accusing her of leaving her family for weird sex, and worse. She'd rant, call on the phone, and reduce Jemma to tears. She made Jemma feel guilty. Jemma tried to tell her that wasn't how it happened. She had left for other reasons, and we got together after we ran into each other over a year later. Paula wouldn't believe Jemma. I was hurt and angry. I wasn't about to explain, and she wouldn't have listened to me any more than she listened to Jemma."

Kathleen might have felt a need to confide in someone—or she wanted Cora to understand. She crossed her arms over her chest and spoke softly.

"I knew for a long time I was homosexual and I had a crush on Jemma for years, but she had a husband and children and never guessed. I was as devastated as anyone when she disappeared. One day I stopped at her mother's house to say hello. Jemma had sent a card for Valerie's birthday, and Nonna had put the envelope in the trash, probably so the kids wouldn't see it. But I saw it, and the postmark was Phoenix. My doctor had advised a healthier climate, so I decided to try Phoenix too."

She paused and cleared her throat.

"Jemma had gotten her GED in Chicago and talked about working in a hospital, maybe a laboratory, some day. So when I got to Phoenix I checked hospitals for medical techs. Eventually I found her. When she first saw me, she panicked. But then she was glad to see me—to see anyone probably."

"She was so outgoing and fun-loving. She must have missed her friends terribly," Cora said.

"We moved in together because it made sense. We both needed a friend, and neither of us was likely to end up with another partner. We could live better together than we could live separately, and so we did. Eventually we fell into a physical relationship. The physical part meant a lot to me, and Jemma loved me, even if in a different way."

Memories of Jemma in her kitchen singing "Walk like a man," in a deep voice, her refusal to wear makeup, her somewhat masculine facial features… Kathleen wanting to "mother" her friends. Indications had been there. Yet Cora would probably never fully understand.

Kathleen was still talking. "We had a good life, Cora. We worked hard and we played hard and we made friends. We attended church, went to plays and concerts, entertained. And there was the beep baseball team. It wasn't popular for gay women to be 'out' at that time, so only our closest friends knew."

"I remember us talking about the baseball team. But your life must have been stressful."

Kathleen gave a half grin. "Relationships like ours are always stressful at times—it goes with the territory. But there were pluses too."

"But then Paula came, and she couldn't understand."

"Never even tried. She was wrapped up in her own feelings. She thought we were disgusting." Kathleen sneered, wrinkling her nose.

"So when Jemma's cancer got worse…?"

"Paula got worse. But Paula was family, I wasn't. That meant everything in 1991. When Jemma went into the hospital and then later into hospice, Paula took control. I'd go to the hospital and be told visitors were restricted to family. Jemma tried to tell the nursing staff, but Paula told the nurses I'd make trouble. I couldn't afford to miss too much work, but Paula stayed all day, complaining to Jemma about me much of the time. She blew up when I tried to visit, so I stayed away so Jemma didn't have to see the fights. Then when she died I was banned from the funeral home. I knew there would be another scene if I went to the services. I didn't want Jemma's memory tarnished, so I stayed home." Tears were flowing down Kathleen's cheeks.

"I'm so sorry, Kathleen. I had no idea," Cora's voice broke. She never imagined… Gay couples were more accepted now, but she and her friends grew up joking about these things, never thinking people they knew were lesbians—especially those they were close to.

Cora wiped her own eyes with the back of her hand and took a staggered breath. Did she really want to know this much about her friends? The sadness was getting painful. She wished this search was over and she and Cisco could just go on their planned trip. But she owed it to Valerie to ask a few remaining questions.

"Why do you think Paula didn't contact her sister and brother and let them know Jemma was dying?"

"I have no idea. That was between them. Maybe Jemma asked her not to. Maybe Paula didn't want anything to do with her sister and brother.

Maybe she didn't want them to know the nature of our relationship or to share her mother with them. Who knows? Maybe she is gay herself and doesn't want to admit it. I thought she'd tell them later though."

"But she didn't. Valerie and Sally have had no contact with Paula. We don't even know where she is."

"Doesn't surprise me."

"Tell me one other thing, Kathleen. Did Jemma ever talk to you about living on a farm when she was a kid?"

"Oh, God, yes! She loved that farm. She talked about it a lot toward the end. That part of her life she was truly happy. I always thought there was something she wasn't telling me though."

"Something that happened there? Or why she went to Sicily?"

"She didn't tell me any of that. I don't know any more than we did when we all hung out together—that Jemma and her mother didn't get along, she was sent to Sicily to learn a lesson of some sort, and then she came home a couple of years later with a husband, child, and another one due any day."

"Didn't you want to know more?"

She smiled and shook her head. "Jemma told you what she wanted to. Didn't you ever get the feeling that whole family had secrets?"

"I did. Did you ever think she or her family had connections to the Chicago Mob?"

Kathleen laughed. "Of course. I'd be surprised if they didn't. But Jemma didn't talk about that either."

# Chapter 32

If he could locate information the others missed, he'd prove he wasn't a loser.

Sitting with his back to the wall in a rear corner of Starbucks during his lunch hour, Billy booted up his new Lenovo laptop. He'd had his eye on this model. When it went on sale, he used his OfficeMax employee discount to purchase it. He'd still have to use the library or other public places for internet access, since his apartment didn't have Wi-Fi, but now he could copy information directly to his hard drive and have it available wherever he was.

Oddly, electronics at OfficeMax only went berserk occasionally when he was near them, but the effects were unpredictable. His employers had not noticed yet that he was the cause. He held his breath now, but the laptop gave him no trouble today. Go figure.

Using the URLs Frannie had given him, he read about "street light interference," or SLI, and then followed other information trails. Frannie had been wrong when she said there was little information on the matter; it would take hours to read it all. What *was* true was that the information was guesswork, with very little documentation.

One popular theory, described by Michael Persinger, was called "tectonic strain theory." Billy found what he read impossible to understand without a background in multiple scientific subjects like geophysics and neuromuscular physics. He shook his head.

From what he could gather, energy fields such as geomagnetic forces had effects on parapsychological phenomenon. Certain people seemed to be more sensitive to these fields, resulting in events like ghost and poltergeist activity, telepathy, ESP, telekinesis, clairvoyance, time travel, parallel universes, and more. Both spontaneous and experimental experiences were reported, but research was still preliminary.

He wasn't about to be a guinea pig. Growing impatient with scientific details, he checked some definitions. Clairvoyance was not fortune-telling but was referred to as "the ability to observe objects beyond ordinary perception." Examples described affecting objects without touching them and seeing things that couldn't be seen by others. He snorted. He'd certainly been there!

A geomagnetic field was "an ever-changing layer of energy that covers the earth's natural outer shell, with the ability to affect human activity in myriad ways."

He called it a day when he found himself baffled by "quantitative electroencephalographic measurements, sensed presence of 'sentient beings,' temporal lobes, and left hemisphere awareness of the right hemisphere equivalent to the left hemispheric sense of self." He shook his head over the mumbo jumbo.

Lunchtime was half over already, but he had a sense of accomplishment, reassured by the fact that he wasn't the only person with this phenomenon. His concern about managing it, however, was not in the *least* reassuring. But he was now convinced his curious incidents were real—he wasn't going crazy.

Could everything be explained by a single phenomenon, though? The "SLIders" theories gave possible explanations for his paranormal experiences, but they didn't explain how he could converse with a ghost. How much of what had happened at the farm was reality versus false impressions, he still had to figure out.

One website discussed types of hauntings, and he added the site to his favorites to return to later.

A large, white-haired man entered the coffee shop and sat near the door without approaching the service counter. His unusual size, powerful build, and regal appearance made him noticeable, despite his outdated trench coat. He looked vaguely familiar, but Billy couldn't place him. The man caught Billy's eye, and then turned away quickly.

With about thirty minutes left, Billy began his search for Jimmy Emery.

Now that he had a name, he could Google it. The top result was the name of a real estate broker, but the second cited a book *The Boys in Chicago Heights* that told of a meeting between Al Capone at the home of one of Chicago Heights' most notorious gangsters, Jim Emery.

Billy clicked the link and a photo from the prohibition era came up. He was shocked to recognize not only his ghost but also Al Capone among a group of nine men posing on a lawn. The caption identified the man stretched out near Capone as Jimmy Emery. Also in the picture was Jimmy's daughter, identified as Al Capone's goddaughter.

The photo was taken at Jimmy Emery's home in Chicago Heights, about thirty-five miles south of the Chicago Loop. The town was known for bootlegging and illegal gambling. The reason for the meeting wasn't certain, but the subsequent murders of seven members of a rival gang was mentioned.

There was no longer any doubt who the ghost was. Billy logged onto the Lemont Library website and reserved a copy of *The Boys in Chicago Heights*. Returning to the Google result list, he clicked on Myalcaponemuseum.com. Here he found more information about the photo and Emery. From what he read, the photo was taken in the fall of 1928 and recorded a major conclave of the "muscle" of the Chicago Outfit at that time.

The previous boss of Chicago Heights, Dominic Roberto, had fled to Italy, rather than face liquor charges. That left Jimmy Emery, Roberto's lieutenant, the logical successor. This move had to be confirmed by Capone and the key mob leaders, who would then install Emery as boss of Chicago Heights.

Billy looked up for a moment to find the large man near the door staring at him. The man probably thought Billy looked familiar too and was trying to figure out why. Billy checked the time and returned to his article.

The story suggested the meeting had a secondary purpose: it speculated that the Outfit had brought a gang of bank robbers and executioners from St. Louis, led by Fred "Killer" Burke, to carry out what became known as the St. Valentine's Day Massacre in 1929. Chicago Heights was a convenient stopping point between St. Louis and Chicago. Capone himself had once used Emery's home to hide out, so it was logical to think that Burke's squad of killers hid there until they were needed. The guns used had never been recovered. It was rumored they had been buried many years later in a forest preserve.

A forest preserve… But that's 1929—Jemma didn't move to the farm until the late 1950s, thirty years later. What was Emery's attachment to her farm and why was his ghost haunting it?

Soon he found a clue: "Emery was the de facto boss of the southern suburbs for the Chicago Mob until his death in 1957. He was said to be the top member of the Chicago Outfit at thoroughbred racetracks. He was banned in 1954 because his horses had a habit of finishing last when favored and first when rated as long shots."

Further reading revealed that Emery had operated a horse-breeding operation in Tinley Park in the 1950s. Billy pulled up MapQuest. Tinley Park was about six miles from where he'd met Emery, the area between sparsely populated and mostly forested even today.

Billy's skin tingled. Emery died the year before Jemma moved to the farm. Had he moved operations there after being banned? Frannie said ghosts had no sense of time, so the ghost probably wouldn't be able to sort out past from present. Mobsters, illegal horse racing—no wonder the ghost of Emery had warned him away. Was secret Mob activity going on when Jemma lived there? Emery had clearly wielded a lot of power in organized crime and would have been considered dangerous. Was his ghost dangerous too?

And who was Mickey?

Billy tried to recall exactly what Emery said: "…My own *il socio* I trusted …took control of the business…the ponies…greedy Mickey and his crazy brother…he ruined her too."

Billy had been reading about bosses, underbosses, lieutenants, leaders, bodyguards, execution teams, members—Mickey could be anywhere in the mix. Maybe he wasn't important enough to be found in the history of organized crime. There was no mention of anyone named Mickey in the articles about Emery. Even Emery's material was scant.

Emery's ghost seemed to know something about Jemma they didn't know. Could it be a clue to Valerie's mysteries?

Billy shut his laptop. Time to go back to work. He'd go to the library after work and pick up the book he had reserved. Maybe there'd be more in the book.

He'd accomplished a lot in a little time and it felt good. With a confidence he hadn't had in years, he stood to leave. The man near the door met his eye with a penetrating glare that caused Billy a moment of alarm. The man suddenly looked formidable…powerful despite his years, and his angry expression made Billy's neck tingle. But the man only stuck his hands in his pockets and walked briskly out of Starbucks.

It suddenly struck Billy where he'd seen the man. When Billy drove Valerie home after the meeting at Cora's, he had noticed a light-colored, older-model sedan parked about a half block from Cora's house. It was the only other vehicle on the quiet suburban street, where residents parked in garages or driveways. Assuming the car belonged to a visitor, Billy pulled away, but as he did so the car's lights came on. It struck him odd that both vehicles were leaving at the same time.

Coincidence or his SLI phenomenon again? When he arrived at Valerie's home and was helping her out of his truck, he thought the same car passed. It drove on, but circled the block and came back more slowly. Someone could have been looking for an address, or maybe it wasn't even the same car. Was he overly jumpy, thinking of Valerie's notion of someone in her room? He had stared as the car passed her house the second time, trying to see the driver. Through the car window he saw a large, thickset man with a full head of white hair. As the car passed under a streetlight he was able to read and memorize the license plate number. He wrote the number down later and then put the matter out of his mind.

Was this the same man he'd seen in the car? Billy ran to the parking lot. The man was not in sight, nor any car that matched the description of the light-colored sedan.

As he stood in front of the restaurant, another memory struck him: a large white-haired man behaving suspiciously in the library the first time Billy had seen Valerie.

Was someone following Valerie…and now him, too?

Telling the women might upset them and they had enough worries. Surely he was blowing things out of proportion.

But if not, it was important to protect Valerie.

Maybe he should tell Cisco. Cisco said he had a friend with the Lemont police department. Maybe his friend could check the plates, find out who owned the car, tell them if there was any cause for alarm. It couldn't hurt.

He'd call Cisco tonight. While he was at it, he remembered he'd finally opened that film container he found at the clubhouse. He'd been afraid to open it sooner, thinking he might expose undeveloped film, being unfamiliar with pre-digital photography. When he learned there was little risk, he opened it to find the canister didn't contain film after all. Maybe Cisco could help him figure out what it was he'd found inside.

# Chapter 33

On edge, Valerie didn't want to admit that the pressures of the last few weeks were getting to her. She wondered what Cora, Frannie, and Billy were doing. She was tired of sitting around while others took action on *her* problems. She had to contribute.

She wasted the morning pacing the house, unable to focus. She jumped when the dishwasher kicked into another cycle. She'd been jumping a lot since Frannie suggested she be careful. What if it wasn't Grace in her room after all? Who else would be in her room? A burglar? Had they stirred up something dangerous by digging into the past? No, that was crazy. Stress was making her paranoid.

But Frannie *had* revealed connections to the Mob. Didn't that make anything possible? She had to be sure it was safe before Molly came here.

Molly! She hadn't talked to her in days. Today was a teachers' off day, Molly had told her. She'd call right now.

"Mom!" Molly whined. "Aster's mom won't bring me to Shannon's house."

"Her mom has things to do at home with Aster's father being sick. I'm sorry honey, but she can't take you everywhere you want to go."

"But it's so boring here! I finished all my homework and all I can do is play games on my phone."

"You like to play games. Doesn't Aster's mom give you more game time than Aster and your dad did?"

"I suppose. But I have more fun with my friends."

"It's just temporary, honey. You'll be here with me soon. Aren't you looking forward to that?"

"I still won't see my friends."

Valerie's stomach churned. Molly was having a rough time too.

"It'll be fine, honey. I'll make it fine, I promise. It'll be just you and me."

But after she ended the call she wondered exactly how she was going to keep that promise with no place to live and little remaining savings. And now she couldn't even be sure she was safe herself.

She had to stop dwelling on nonsense and fix her life.

She picked up the phone again and started calling relatives she hadn't heard from in years. What she *could* do, she hoped, was find out if Uncle Teddy was still alive and if so, arrange to talk to him.

She remembered him as thin, red-faced, and with ears that stuck out. Mamma had a picture of him in an old album; he was sitting on a picnic bench in a flowered shirt, wearing a big white hat, a cigar between his lips, and playing a ukulele. He looked like he'd be fun, and as a kid she wanted to know him better. But Mamma said he drank too much.

A series of calls finally led to Luisa, the daughter of Jemma's cousin Luisa. Valerie had once been close to her. She was—what did they call it? First cousin once removed? Luisa called other relatives, and finally in the afternoon she called back with the information that Ted was alive, living in a nursing home in Westchester, Illinois. He was over ninety years old and both his health and mental status were declining. Valerie called the home to arrange a visit.

She was feeling better. Successful detective work was inspiring—the joy of discovery. She began to understand why Cora and Frannie thrived on this sort of thing.

But then the doorbell rang and it was Cora on her front stoop.

Oh, oh. This couldn't be good.

"What bad news did Kathleen tell you, Cora," she said.

"What makes you think it's bad news?"

"You always call before you come. This time you just rang the doorbell."

"Well, I don't know if it's good or bad news," Cora said, moving past Valerie into the living room. "Depends on how you view it."

They went into the kitchen, where Valerie filled cups with teabags and water, using a finger to tell when the cups were full, then heating them in the microwave. She smiled nervously. "Tea isn't at its best when nuked, but I don't run the risk of burning myself."

She listened without interruption while Cora told her about Jemma and Kathleen's lives, describing where they lived and worked and the interests they shared.

"It sounded like they had a good life." Cora stopped.

"But did she tell you why Mamma left us?" Valerie asked.

She heard Cora's deep breath and then, "Kathleen said your mother loved and missed her kids, especially you. She didn't want to leave Chicago, but she told Kathleen she had no choice. She missed you all the time. She was proud of you."

Valerie wanted to believe what Cora said. But could she?

Then Cora told her that in the months Jemma was fighting breast cancer, Paula had shown up and the ugliness started.

"You mean Paula actually saw her all those years ago, and never told me or Sally?"

"It appears that way. Do you have any idea why she wouldn't tell you?"

"Other than she doesn't want anything to do with us and she's a selfish bitch, no. But you'd think, when Mamma died... Well, I guess that's Paula. Why should I expect anything else from her?"

Valerie sensed Cora was holding back again.

But Cora wasn't finished. And then she *was* finished. And she hadn't held anything back. For a moment Valerie thought it might have been better if she had.

How did she feel about her mother having a lesbian relationship? About her self-involved sister who made her mother's final days miserable out of anger and spite? What would she have done if she were the one to discover the situation? Another shock, another slap in the face from fate. Take that, Valerie. How do you like them apples?

Valerie considered herself open-minded, but this was her mother. She couldn't stop the picture forming in her mind of Mamma in the arms of another woman, a woman Valerie barely knew. Well, at least get the picture right.

"What does Kathleen look like now?" she asked.

When she thought she could visualize Kathleen from Cora's description, Valerie considered how the picture fit the mother she remembered.

"Kathleen said Mamma left us for a different reason, but she didn't know what? And they got together later? Did you think she was saying that because she thought that's what I'd want to hear?"

"I didn't think so. It could be, but I thought she was telling the truth."

Valerie sat with her chin in her hands, breathing deeply.

"There's good news here, Valerie," Cora said. "Your mama *did* love you, and she was reasonably happy."

"But she stayed away, never tried to contact us…"

"Because she had to…"

"For reasons we still don't know… And she did it while in the arms of a woman, and her life with my father and us was a lie." Valerie couldn't control the bitter edge to her voice.

"Valerie, I feel so bad about shocking you again. Maybe Jemma made the best life she could after she was forced to leave."

"You want me to feel sorry for her? And for my only sister, who could have gotten us all back together before Mamma died, but didn't? I'm in no mood to be that generous right now, Cora."

"But they may have had reasons, too. Reasons you don't know but might understand if you did know."

She couldn't think straight—too much information. No, not enough information. How could she process all of this—and get back in control of her life?

She had another question. "Is Mamma buried in Arizona?"

"Kathleen said Paula brought her body back to Illinois, but I didn't get the name of the cemetery."

Valerie closed her eyes and stuck her chin in the air. "I want to know where she's buried and where my damn sister is."

Cora didn't respond. Valerie lowered her chin and raised an eyebrow. "You don't agree?"

Cora heaved a sigh. "Unfortunately, I do agree. We're in so deep now, we need to know all of it."

"Including why Mamma went to Sicily and came home with me and Papá."

"Yes, if we can find your Uncle Nello. Everyone else who was there at the time is dead."

"Not Uncle Teddy. I found him," Valerie said with pride in her voice.

"Okay," Cora said. "I'll call Frannie tonight to have her find out where Jemma's buried and start her looking for Paula. Is Teddy nearby? Do you think you and I can see him tomorrow?"

# Chapter 34

The next afternoon, a nurse's aide at the senior home seemed pleased to welcome Valerie and Cora. "Mr. Vitale is looking forward to talking to you," she said. "As you must guess, with no children and most of his family gone, only distant nieces and nephews visit and even that's rare. He had some falling-out with his family years ago, he told me."

The aide's chatty, even bubbly, Valerie thought.

"Tell me what to expect," she said to the aide. "I'm an RN, so you can get as technical as you like."

"Well, HIPAA you know, but if I don't get into medical details...," the aide said. "He's been here about four years, ever since he couldn't take care of himself anymore. He had some money and then we got him financed through the state. He spends most of the day in a wheelchair, legs weak and he needs help to stand. Mind is...well, it depends on the day. Most of the time he's like most men his age, remembers what he wants to and mostly wants to remember the old days. Pretty cognizant, but forgetful. Not sure you can depend on what he says. Likes to have an audience and tell tales about old times with the Mob, if you can believe that." She chuckled.

Valerie felt for Cora's arm. "He knows we're here? Is he ready to see us?"

"Oh yes. He got a glint in his eye when I told him who you were."

"Does he remember me?"

"Not really, but he says he remembers your mother. He's in the solarium. Let's head that way."

Valerie felt the warm sunlight before they entered the room. She stopped, reached a hand for the door frame, and whispered to Cora, "Describe him to me so I can picture him while we're talking."

Cora squeezed Valerie's arm softly and spoke in a low voice.

"The room is all windows with a tile floor and cushioned outdoor furniture, yellow and green. He's in a wheelchair in the corner looking out at the garden. An oxygen tank is nearby, but he doesn't have the tube in his nose. He's sitting so it's hard to tell, but I'd say he's about six feet tall, very thin, and weak looking. His skin is pale. He just realized we're here and now he's watching us. He's bald on top, the rest of his hair thin and white, with gray stubble on his chin. He's wearing glasses with large outdated frames, and he has big ears with hair sticking out and bushy white eyebrows. His hands are holding the arms of the wheelchair and they look huge. He seems relaxed and alert. He's grinning, a wry sort of grin. I'd say he's planning to mess with us and looking forward to it. Is that enough?"

"What's he wearing?"

"A blue checked flannel shirt, dark gray sweatpants, and black orthopedic-looking shoes."

"Let's go meet him."

After they introduced themselves and sat, Ted spoke first. "Nancy Nurse didn't tell me you was blind. Took some effort to get here, then. Must be important."

"Important to me, yes," Valerie said.

"So you're Jemma's little girl, are you?" His chuckle sounded good-natured.

"That's right."

"I remember your mama real well. She was very…what's the word? Precocious. Liked to fish. Liked to read. Smart as a whip. Gutsy and persistent. Very curious, noticed everything, asked a lot of questions. Things that could get her in trouble."

Valerie jumped to a conclusion, reflecting her inner fears. "Was that dangerous?"

"Could a been. Might a been." He paused. "So now, like your mama, you come askin' me questions. Lookin' to get in trouble too?" He was teasing, but she sensed warmth and maybe even affection. She gathered he had fond memories of her mother.

"I hope not. Mamma ran off in 1974, left us kids and Papá. We never saw her again. I'm trying to find out why she left." She tried to smile, but felt like it didn't come off well.

"Why don't you ask her?"

"Can't. She died in 1991," Cora said.

"Oh. I'm sorry to hear that. I was fond a that girl," he said, sounding sincere. "What do you know already?"

He seemed hesitant. Was he protecting family secrets?

Valerie felt he was treating her like a child and had an impulse to shock him.

"We know she was living with a woman in a lesbian relationship when she died."

"Damn! I find that hard to believe. Don't seem like her," he said. She heard rustling sounds and assumed he was shifting uncomfortably in his wheelchair. She hoped he'd take her more seriously now.

"I think that too. Mamma's lover didn't know why she left either, said she wouldn't talk about it."

"Why would you think I'd know anything about that? I don't. Last I saw Jemma, not long after she came back from Sicily, you weren't even in school yet."

Valerie hesitated, rubbed her nose. "There was some stuff going on we thought you might know about."

"Stuff going on? Like what?"

"Something strange was happening at that farm when you and Mamma lived there. We connected a mob boss, Jimmy Emery, to the area, and we think the family might have been involved with the Mob."

"You think that, huh?" The room was silent, except for Ted's deep breaths. When he spoke again his voice was softer and had lost the teasing edge. "Surprised you know about Jimmy and all that. Suppose it doesn't make any difference now. Everybody's dead and gone."

*Unless Billy's really seeing a ghost,* Valerie thought, but she only said, "Guess that's true."

"I arranged for the family to live on that farm, you know," he said, sounding proud. "My wife and I lived there for a while too. Times were hard back then. Free rent was worth some inconvenience."

"You worked for Jimmy Emery, didn't you? We found your name connected to his."

"When I got picked up for killing kids, you mean?" he snorted, his tone sharp. "I had nothing to do with that sad business. I may have done other things, but I'm no child abuser or murderer. Just happened to be in the wrong place. Don't like talking about that."

Would he admit it if he had been guilty? He didn't seem capable of murdering children, but she had heard they never do. How would she know? She'd never known a child killer.

"We didn't come about that," Cora said. "Valerie just wants to know about her mother."

He went on in a calmer tone, slowly as if reading a book he had once loved and then forgotten. "In those days, Jimmy got himself real involved in horse racing. Neglected other aspects of his business, stuff I had nothin' to do with, but I figured out what was going on. I just ran his farm for him out in Tinley Park. Cared for the horses, handled the breeding, some a the business end. Then he got himself in trouble with the racing commission, got banned from the track, and the boys started comin' after him at the same time for not runnin' other things right. He loved those horses, 'specially one, and he was afraid he'd lose them."

"Is that how the forest preserves farm came in?" Cora asked.

"I had friends with the forest preserves, found out they were lookin' for someone to stay at the farm and keep an eye on things. I convinced Jimmy it was a good place to hide out. We sold the Tinley Park place and most a the horses, moved a few to the forest preserves. After Jimmy died, his partner sold off the rest."

"And then Jemma and your family moved in?"

"That's right. Stayed until…let's see. I think it was 1962 or so, sometime after the police picked me up and it hit the papers. Jemma's mama, your nonna, she was always warnin' Jemma about wanderin' in the woods, because a what happened to those poor boys and girls, so when they questioned me about those crimes, she got suspicious about me too. Then, I was boozing pretty good. My wife left me, and the family told me to get lost. I was mad, but I suppose I got what I deserved. My brother stayed another year or so and then moved to Oak Lawn. I didn't see much a them after that—just holiday get-togethers, family picnics."

"Jemma wasn't around in 1962?" Cora said.

"You're right, she wasn't. She was in Sicily when all that happened."

Valerie released a long breath. So far all Ted had done was confirm their guesswork.

"Why did Mamma go to Sicily? She was just out of grade school, right?"

"What did she tell you?" He sounded cautious again.

"That she and Nonna didn't get along and it was sort of a punishment to straighten her out. I always thought there was more to the story."

"Maybe I shouldn't say if your mama wanted it that way."

When she felt Cora squeeze her arm again, Valerie pulled away and said, "I want to know. I have to know. It's time for secrets to come out."

He cleared his throat and Valerie heard him fidgeting. "Well, I sure hope you really want to know and can deal with what you find out." He paused again and then took a deep breath.

Valerie straightened her spine.

"I told you earlier your mama was precocious. It was more than just being smart." His voice softened and Valerie guessed he was visualizing her mother as a teenager.

She pictured Jemma in her mind, too, as a young girl with long dark hair, grooming her horse in the sun—a picture she had never envisioned before. She started to follow Uncle Teddy's words with mental images.

"Jemma had the body and the sex appeal of someone closer to twenty than fourteen. She had a boyfriend, but she never told the family about him. And she got herself pregnant, the summer before she started high school. He was older, in his early to mid-twenties. He should have known better, but that's the kind a guy he was. Smooth talker, handsome, the morals of an alley cat and twice as dumb."

"So Jemma got pregnant and the family sent her to Sicily to have the baby?" Cora said.

Valerie just listened, letting Cora and Ted talk it out.

"They were real upset, but they weren't going to send her away. That was Mickey's doing."

"Mickey?" Cora said.

"Mickey Romano, Jimmy's partner. Jimmy was gone by then. Mickey took over the business and before a year was out sold all the horses except Dolly Val. Out a loyalty to Jimmy, I made her part a the deal to keep my mouth shut. I renamed her Baby and Jemma used to ride her. I told Jemma the horse came with the farm. Afterward, Mickey used the old clubhouse to hide things like gambling equipment when the gang got wind of a raid."

Wouldn't Billy love to be talking with someone who knew Emery when he was alive? Maybe that could be arranged. But at the moment, Ted sounded like he was enjoying himself.

"Mickey was a funny kinda guy. He had this irritating habit of snifflin' all the time, screwin' up his whole face. He was a small guy, and Jimmy used to say he had something he called a Napoleon complex. It galled Mickey that he was so short, especially since his dumb kid brother was tall and hefty. Mickey seemed friendly, but underneath he was always schemin'. That attitude was bound to cause trouble with the higher-ups."

"But what did Mickey have to do with Jemma going to Sicily?" Cora said.

"Mickey's kid brother, Petey, is the guy that got Jemma pregnant. Mickey was real pissed about the whole thing and wanted it covered up. Jemma's mama and papa wanted Petey to marry Jemma. Petey went to his brother to get him out of another jam. Petey was all charm, no brains, and Mickey was always fixing situations Petey got himself into. Another guy in the outfit had sent his daughter to Sicily when she got pregnant—that's where Mickey got the idea. He convinced my brother or made an offer he couldn't refuse—I don't know the details—and off Jemma went. Came back a couple a years later with a husband and baby."

"What happened to the baby she was pregnant with?" Valerie said.

Valerie felt a huge warm, dry hand cover her own and squeeze it gently. "That was you, Valerie," Ted said. "Thought you'd catch on to that."

She should have. She must have tried to deny the obvious. She moved her hand in Uncle Teddy's for a moment, withdrew it, placed her hand over his, and stroked it before placing her hand in her lap.

"So Petey's my father. Not Sal. No wonder Papá and I weren't close."

She drew her head back and breathed deeply. A mother she never understood, and now her father wasn't her father either, but some man she'd never met. Who was she?

"Did he love my mother?" Valerie asked.

"Who knows? He could have. From what I saw, mostly Petey loved Petey. He was nothin' like his brother: big and strong, smooth talker, but not too bright. A dreamer, with crazy ideas, impractical get-rich schemes.

Dependable as shit, not showin' up for jobs. He got in so much trouble with the boys, Mickey had to arrange protection, and then he got Petey a job as a janitor and handyman at this little one-room school Jemma went to. That's where he met her I suppose.

"Last I heard he'd gotten into show business, playing his guitar and singing. Mickey got him booked to some second-class joint in Vegas. Don't know what happened after that."

So the man she had called Papá, who had been good to her despite other failings, wasn't her father. And her real father was the no-good brother of a mobster and apparently couldn't do anything right on either side of the law. She had asked the question. She didn't know what she expected, but it wasn't this.

"Salvatore knew of course, but he needed a wife to get to the States. This arrangement was common in the old country. But raisin' someone else's kid, part of the deal would of been that he be a good husband and father," Ted said.

What about Papá? Was he involved with the Mob too? Implication after implication flashed through her mind, but first she had to find out everything Ted knew. She'd try to make sense of it later.

"Did the whole family know about Mickey's business and the Mob hiding things at the clubhouse?" she asked.

"Your grandfather, Nonno, did. So did the twins, Nello and Angelo. Mickey would call me, usually at night, and I'd wake my brother and the boys to help unload or load. Then the boys hung out around the place durin' the day to chase off anyone who might come by so long as the stuff was still in the clubhouse. My brother's only involvement was to do favors now and then. He had a trucking business and the equipment to move stuff. Likely he had no choice. You don't say no to certain people."

"My uncle Angelo?"

"The boys—well, Nello wanted to move up in the organization, wanted to look good, you know? Angelo, he just followed orders. He knew what was goin' on and kept his mouth shut, far as I know."

"We haven't been able to find Nello, and Angelo was killed in 1975. You knew that right? Anything more you know about his death?" Cora asked.

"Haven't thought about Angelo's death in years. You could try lookin' for Nello out west, in Vegas or Reno. If things got hot here, that's where lots a the boys went. I always assumed Nello disappeared out there somewhere. Angelo, of course, he went straight as far as I know. Got himself shot in a Chicago gang thing. It was all over the papers."

"I never believed what was reported," Valerie said. "I thought something was up before it happened. He was jumpy, like he was being followed. The sniper story was just too convenient."

"She might be right," Cora said. "We're finding the published story is suspicious. Do you have any ideas, like mob activity or something we may not have thought of?"

"As I said, I always thought Angelo wanted to avoid organized crime. That's why he became a policeman. But the Mob may have had other ideas. It's no secret they got men they could trust into useful positions inside the police force. I wouldn't of thought Angelo would be one a their guys, but who can say? That was after I became persona non grata with the family. It was more than ten years later he was killed."

All this information, and yet Valerie still didn't have answers to her most important questions: why did her mother leave her, who killed Angelo, and for what reason? Was she going to have to accept the fact she would never know? And now she had a missing father too, one she'd never known about. Her life just kept getting crazier.

"One last thing," Cora said. "Jemma used to see and hear strange things at that farm, thought it might have been haunted. Did you see anything like that?"

He laughed. "You got to be kiddin'. Jemma used to tell me that too, and her kid brother Barbaro, like lots a boys, talked about monsters. It was probably just the traffic when Mickey's guys were around. Although I have to admit some nights I was too soused to notice anything subtle, you know? It'd have to hit me over the head."

He laughed again. "Maybe Jimmy was hauntin' the place. All his dreams ended there."

# Part V

# Chapter 35

After too many exhausting and emotional days, Cora slept until eight A.M., nuked a package of date and walnut instant oatmeal, poured a cup of coffee, and then engaged in a burst of activity. She cleaned the kitchen, took ten minutes to "patrol" the gardens, straightened the bedroom and bath, and put away office clutter.

She found Cisco in the garage, getting the lawnmower ready for spring.

"I have to get a grip," she announced. "I'll be buried in the office. With the door shut."

He rolled his eyes. "I won't bother you. Think I don't know what a shut door means?"

"Yes. But I want you to know I won't be available for a while."

"I think I can mow the grass without needing to consult you." He peered over his glasses at her.

"Maybe." She grinned. He didn't. She sighed. He didn't always get her jokes.

"The Valerie business getting to you?" he asked.

"Yeah. We're taking too long…close to a month. Time to get it over with."

"Can't argue with that. Well, let me know if you need anything done before you go upstairs. I might go out for a bit, pick up some gas for the mower. Be back before lunch."

"Which means you might decide to get lost. Fine, but be sure you take your phone."

After Cisco left, Cora picked up her cold, untouched cup of coffee. She removed the coffee cup Cisco had reheated in the microwave, which was cold again, reheated hers, and climbed the stairs to her office. In a chair where she could look out the window, she sipped, remembering one of her favorite cartoons. It showed a cave man and cave woman facing each other with clubs raised. The caption said, "Can we talk about this after they invent coffee?"

Lists would help her sort her jumbled thoughts. She grabbed a notepad and propped her heels on a stool, biting on a thumbnail. After a moment she wrote at the top of a page: What We Know.

When she finished, she rearranged the list into chronological order.

– *The farm in the Palos Forest Preserves had previously been used as a horse-breeding operation owned by mob boss Jimmy Emery in the mid-1950s. Uncle Teddy was Emery's farm manager.*
– *After Emery's death, Jemma lived on the farm in the late 1950s with her parents, siblings, and Teddy.*
– *Emery's partner Mickey Romano used the clubhouse to hide gambling equipment.*
– *Mickey's brother Petey got Jemma pregnant, and she was sent to Sicily in 1959 to have the baby, then moved to Oak Lawn in 1962 with a husband and two children.*
– *Valerie is Petey's daughter.*
– *In 1974 Jemma left Chicago suddenly and without explanation, whereabouts unknown. Kathleen found Jemma in Arizona.*
– *In 1990 Paula, Valerie's sister, found Jemma and made her life miserable out of anger over her mother's lesbian relationship.*
– *Jemma died of breast cancer in 1991.*

Cora put her head in her hands and rubbed her eyes.

The most important question, why Jemma had left her family, remained unanswered. Their efforts had only deepened the mystery and caused Valerie more pain. Since she could no longer work things out with her mother as she'd hoped, Valerie was left to guess about Jemma's true feelings and reason for leaving. The obvious reason—she left for a lover—was denied by Kathleen. Another possibility, organized crime, might be worth pursuing. Were all the people involved dead? What about Mickey Romano? Or Valerie's father, Petey Romano?

She picked up her pencil and made a similar list regarding Angelo.

- *In the late 1950s Angelo had participated in hiding gambling equipment for Mickey.*
- *Supposedly he turned honest, became a Chicago cop, and was killed at Cabrini-Green in 1975.*
- *Family members were involved with the Chicago Mob and recent evidence suggested that Angelo's killers had been falsely convicted.*

It was starting to look like Angelo was working inside the Chicago Police Department as a tool for the Mob and might have been the target of a mob hit. That would be devastating to Valerie. Was he killed because he knew too much? Or was he a loyal cop and his death a random shooting after all?

Other developments clouded the issue. Was Billy actually talking to the ghost of Jimmy Emery? Was Teddy really innocent of the murders of those children? What did those things have to do with Jemma hiding out in Arizona or Angelo's death?

Not to forget Billy's ghostly encounters, street light interference, and the nuclear waste buried nearby… Other than scant scientific findings, they had little but speculation about Billy's problems.

She couldn't shake the suspicion someone had broken into Valerie's room. Was their investigation putting them in danger now? Cora's prior ventures into mysteries of the past had resulted in present-day threats and supernatural encounters. She didn't want to believe it was happening again, but how could she not after what she and Cisco had witnessed when Billy took them to the farm? Cora shuddered.

After reviewing her lists and notes, she started a to-do list. They needed to know more about Emery and the Romano brothers, especially their whereabouts. See what Emery, the Romanos, and Angelo and Nello were doing in the seventies. And, in case Valerie's house was broken into, maybe Cisco would be willing to talk to Rogers at the police department.

Intuition told her all the answers had to do with the farm, including Jemma's disappearance, Angelo's murder, and possibly the present threat.

~~~

Cisco pushed the mower around their backyard lost in thought.

At Cora's last get-together, he had spent his time watching while everyone talked. He caught Frannie gazing into space. That wasn't like her. When Frannie was sharing freely she was excited and direct, even blunt. Instead she chose her words carefully, giving him the impression she was being evasive.

Valerie seemed to be fighting her emotions, normal enough under the circumstances. But considering her lifetime of self-dependency, her facial expressions made him think she was suspicious of her friends and wanted to pull back into a shell. Her words, though, didn't reveal distrust.

He turned off the mower, moved a hose out of the way, and then started circling the yard again.

In his opinion, Cora's little task force wasn't being honest with each other. He foresaw trouble. The group verged on being pissed-off in a major way.

Cora, at least, was completely forthcoming, to the point of overselling—a backlash from when she had kept information from Valerie, as well as her obsession with truthfulness. She would be angry with him when he revealed the discussion he had with Billy last night. Frannie and Valerie probably would be too.

He had promised Billy he wouldn't tell the women about the possible threat and the plan to talk to the police. It would only upset them, probably needlessly. Cisco felt uncomfortable about not telling Cora, but surely it would come to nothing when he talked to Rogers.

It wasn't up to him to tell Billy what he knew from Valerie's great-uncle Teddy, so he didn't. That was up to Cora or Valerie. When it came to hiding information, Cisco and Billy weren't any better than the rest.

Cora had promised Cisco he didn't have to get involved. Well, it was too late for that now. He couldn't very well let Cora run around the woods alone, especially if it was dangerous. He had to protect her. He shook his head but grinned. He wanted to resent being dragged in against his will, but had to admit he was interested at this point and wanted to see Valerie succeed.

Finished with the yard, he hosed off the mower and returned it to the garage.

Now that Rogers was a detective instead of a patrol officer, he wouldn't be scheduled on patrol, but could be out on a call. Cisco took a chance on catching Rogers at the station and got lucky.

Rogers, tall, slender, with short brown hair, and a look of authority, stepped from a back office and held his hand out.

"Seen any wolves lately?" Rogers said.

"Nope. Just hear coyotes barking and yelling at night is about all," Cisco said, shaking the offered hand.

"They're getting peskier and peskier, aren't they?"

"Seems so. Listen, I wonder if you would do me a favor."

"If I can." Rogers seemed hesitant. When Cisco remained silent, Rogers looked around. "Do we need privacy?"

Cisco looked uncertain. "Come on," Rogers said, leading the way to a conference room across from the front desk and closing the door. "What's up?" he said, as they took seats at the end of a long wooden table surrounded by a dozen chairs.

"Some friends of ours think they're being followed, maybe stalked. I got a plate number and description of the car. I wondered if you could check it out. See if the guy's dangerous at all?"

"Why don't your friends file a report?"

"The guy hasn't done anything; they just keep seeing him. His appearance is a bit menacing too. Billy ran into him at Starbucks and got a close look at him before he bolted."

"Billy—that's the guy who found the strange stuff in the forest preserves that you asked me about before?"

"The same."

"Do you believe him?"

"About this? Yeah."

"Anything more going on out in the woods?"

"Well, since you asked…" Cisco gave Rogers an edited version of what they'd discovered without mentioning the supernatural developments.

"You think the Chicago Outfit may have been using the place into the sixties? Interesting. But why are you involved with that?" Rogers asked.

"Cora's friend brought it up. Her mother grew up there. Lived in the house the golf course supervisor used when the course was open." He chuckled. "You know how Cora is when she finds an interesting historical fact. You try to stop her, I can't."

Rogers leveled his gaze on Cisco as if he expected more. Cisco added, "Cora and I went out there. There's nothing there anymore, except the foundation of the farmhouse and some tiles from the clubhouse roof."

"Really? That's kind of cool. No wolves though?" Rogers laughed. Cisco joined him, although the wolf wisecracks were getting old.

"Look," Rogers said. "I got to get back to my desk, but I can get a name from the plates and a CQH pretty easy. If it indicates anything out of state I'll need a CQR1, and that takes a little longer. If the guy's got a record I can't divulge that information, but I can let you know if his record's clean. Might wander over to that clubhouse area myself. You got me curious. I'll call you later. What's a good number?"

Cisco was smiling when he left. Now he'd see if the library could give him the name of an Italian tutor. Tutors often met their students at the library, and he hoped someone would translate the single-page letter Billy found rolled up in the film canister he picked up at the clubhouse. Billy thought it was written in Italian and that Cisco spoke the language, but Cisco never had. He was sure the letter would turn out to be unimportant, but because it was written in Italian he felt compelled to confirm its uselessness.

~~~

Rogers had heard of weird incidents in the forest preserves reported over the years, particularly the area Cisco mentioned. Lights in the depth of the woods, sounds like large trucks or parties going on, the whinny of a horse in the quiet night, had all been described.

He sought out Officer Joe O'Connor at his desk.

"Hey, Joe. Didn't you tell me you had a strange call out in the woods near Saganashkee Slough some years ago?"

O'Connor, a short man with a beer belly and male-pattern baldness, was nearing retirement. He rubbed his chin. "Oh, that, yeah," he said. "Me and Kurt. Hard to forget."

"Remind me what happened, would ya?"

"Sure. Few years ago, a summer night, we responded to a call. When we investigated we saw through the trees a large area all lit up. The light didn't bounce around like a flashlight or lantern, just stayed stationary like a building. We knew there was no building out there. It was a clear night, and loud party sounds carried down to 107th Street. Seemed to be coming from northwest of the eastern parking area for Saganashkee Slough, across the road up on the hill, where the light was. We called for backup and then started up there, shielding our flashlights, thinking it was kids partying, just wanting to lay eyes on the situation before we spooked them and chased them off, you know?"

He leaned back in his chair and glanced away, as if visualizing the night. "When we got close, everything just shut off—no lights, no sounds, quiet as the dead. It was eerie as hell. Creeped me out, and Kurt too. The backup guys thought it was pretty funny, but I swear something was out there. Reported it to the forest preserves police. They investigated but didn't find anything out there, no trampled grass or anything, just the trail cutting through like always. Weirdest thing we ever encountered, Kurt and I. Why do you want to know?"

"Friend's been asking. Wanted to know what I knew, and I just remembered what you said is all. Nothing important."

Next Rogers checked the registration of the license plate number Cisco had given him. The owner of the car was Peter Romano. Further investigation showed the guy had minor arrests over the years for petty brawls and drug possession and had been questioned on a number of occasions for connections to a minor mob figure. Romano had been living in Vegas from the 1960s until a couple of years ago. A few minor convictions in Nevada, a Peeping Tom charge, but no jail time. A photo from ten years ago showed a large, powerful-looking man with a slick look about him. Romano would be old now, late seventies.

He put out a BOLO for Romano's car. It was found later that afternoon parked in front of Main Inn, a bar in the historic district of Lemont. Rogers went to talk to the man. After studying the car on the street, he entered the place. A large, muscular man was tending bar. Rogers introduced himself and asked the man's name.

"Pete Romano."

"Do you own that tan Ford Taurus parked out front?" Rogers asked.

"I do." Romano narrowed his eyes. "It's parked legal, isn't it?"

"It is. But that car has been seen following some people here in town. You know anything about that?"

The man's gaze shifted briefly and then he stared into Rogers's eyes.

"It's a small town. Must be a coincidence. I'm sure not following anyone."

"Did you loan it to anyone? Who else uses it?"

"Only me." Romano picked up a towel and wiped the bar.

"Well, I'm glad to hear it," Rogers said. "But we have to check these things. I'll let the department know you seem to check out, but don't be surprised if you get stopped a time or two in the next few days."

Anger flashed in Romano's eyes, but he remained polite. "I've heard police in these small suburbs are a pain in the tuchus, but I've got nothing to hide. If they stop me, I'll say so."

"Do yourself a favor and try to avoid suspicious behavior," Rogers said, and then walked out.

He notified the department to keep an eye on Romano. Although the last report was years ago and there was no record of violent behavior, the man did have some connection to the Mob, and his powerful appearance was threatening. Rogers wouldn't have wanted to meet him alone in the dark, despite his age.

Rogers was skeptical about mob activity in the forest, but this was Cisco and Cora telling him. Nothing that involved Cisco and Cora had ever turned out to make sense—or to be without warrant. They made his life interesting though. He'd been fascinated by Lemont's quirky history even before he met the wacky but likable couple with their weird experiences. They were starting to seem like friends and what Cisco had told him was intriguing.

He hated loose ends. It was late afternoon and the forest preserves weren't Lemont jurisdiction. Nonetheless, after stopping to grab a sandwich, he drove to Palos Woods and parked the squad car on the road near the trail where strange things were supposed to have happened.

The path was blocked by a chain that prevented four-wheel vehicles from entering, although motorcycles and small ATVs might be able to get by. He stepped over the chain and headed uphill.

The top of the hill where Joe O'Connor had described his experience with the disappearing lights and sounds was the same place Cisco said a golf clubhouse had once stood, which could have been a site of mob activity in the fifties and sixties. Rogers had heard rumors about the former golf course and Al Capone, but he had never been there. Today, as expected, there was nothing but bare trees and brush.

He shook his head and headed the other direction, where Cisco said a farm and maintenance facility for the golf course had been. This information was new to him. He never would have known he was in the right place except Cisco had described the pole barn's foundation. But if the foliage had been leafed out he doubted he could have found it even with directions. Beyond the foundation was a depression filled with shrubs, dead leaves, and some early green ground cover poking through.

On his right was a big tree, its size unusual in this forest where only a few large trees remained, since the area was reforested farmland. Curious, using Cisco's landmarks, he searched for the farmhouse foundation. He pushed through knee-deep brush and slender trees, concentrating on his footing and looking for a large hole lined with concrete blocks, fearful of falling into the old basement.

As he passed the tree, he sensed a presence just before he heard the sound of something whizzing through the air. A large object struck the side of his head, knocking him to the ground. Dazed, he shook his head to clear it and rolled, his arms raised to protect his head. He heard heavy footsteps running away, but he could not get up quickly enough to see his attacker.

# Chapter 36

"So you decided, all on your own, to invite everyone here? And you don't have time to explain before they get here? Is that what you're saying?" Cora wanted to swing at something, but clenched her fists instead.

"Your little group is on the verge of being at each other's throats." Cisco flung the words at her. "You're too busy chasing details to see what's happening."

"But *you* know best, right? You didn't think you should consult me? Or even let me know what's going on?"

"You just got home, and it's done. It *had* to be done."

"I have a phone, you know. You could've called. Did you ever think of that?"

"You're too pissed now to give me credit, but I *was* trying to call you. You didn't answer, and I was busy meeting someone at the library. Where were you anyway?"

Cora pulled her phone from her pocket. There was a missed call from Cisco. She remembered silencing the phone when she was at the Sagawau Environmental Learning Center's library. She jammed the phone back in her pocket. Cisco rolled his eyes toward the ceiling.

The doorbell rang, putting an end to their argument but not to Cora's anger. She'd act civil in front of her friends, but this wasn't over—not by a long shot. How dare he take control without telling her? She supposed he thought he was doing the right thing, but this was *her* project.

"Now I'm about to be blindsided and made to look a fool in front of my friends, thank you very much," she said as she stomped toward the door, feeling some satisfaction from getting in the last word.

As she walked back into the kitchen followed by Billy and Valerie, Cora was surprised to find that Cisco had pizza keeping warm in the oven and tableware, wine, and beer set out on the kitchen island.

Frannie arrived last. When everyone had filled paper plates, poured beverages, and taken seats at the kitchen table, Cora met Cisco's eyes. Stony faced, he shrugged his shoulders, deferring to her.

"Cisco thought it was best if we all got together as soon as possible," Cora began. "And I guess he's right." She looked at him out of the corner of her eye again. He nodded.

Maybe it *was* a good thing they were meeting now. The sooner everyone was on the same page the better. Truth be told, she was tired. Maybe she did have to let someone else take over now and then.

"I for one feel we're not making meaningful progress. We're getting facts, but they don't resolve anything, and we're getting stressed out. I know I am. Are we making matters worse instead of better? I'm afraid we'll spin our wheels forever unless we do something to bring closure to this quest we're on. I know I said I don't believe in closure, but I can't find a better word right now."

Cora pushed her empty plate to the center of the table and straightened the notes in front of her before sweeping her gaze over her friends.

"I summarized our findings earlier today," she went on. "I'll make copies for you, but I just got home." She reviewed her opinions about the facts and remaining questions.

"I can't prove it, but I think everything—Jemma's life, why she left, Angelo's death…and maybe even someone breaking into your room, Valerie—all trace back to when Jemma lived on the farm." She saw Cisco glance at Billy, who gave a little shake of his head. She wondered what that was about. Had they been cooking something up?

"So I went to Sagawau Education Center this afternoon looking for clues. I wanted to see if the forest preserves library had better records than the historical society had on the old golf course. Sagawau is near the former farm. I was able to confirm the dates the course was built and when it closed and that the buildings were not demolished until the sixties. There's no suggestion of mob activity, but there are reports of vandalism, partying, and permits being issued to a ham radio club that used the clubhouse each summer during the fifties.

"The town of Sag Bridge, which is now part of Lemont, had a one-room schoolhouse. That was probably the school Jemma attended." She stopped and took a sip of wine. "Sagawau itself is interesting," Cora ran her finger down a page in her notebook. "The only canyon in Cook County is on the property. Its walls are a rare form of limestone. In 1936 the Chicago Young Women's Christian Association operated a summer camp for girls there. They built cabins and a pier for rowboats and they allowed swimming in the quarries on the property.

"The camp closed in 1951, before Jemma arrived, but she would have known the place. The property was fenced, but there was no other security. While Jemma was living on the farm, the Forest Preserves District of Cook County purchased the Sagawau property and in the summers ran a facility for training teachers. The place was vacant between sessions, which was most of the time."

She looked up and caught Frannie and Billy exchanging glances. Frannie shrugged.

She continued. "The original farmhouse and a new learning center are there now, along with hiking trails and cross-country skiing in the winter. But in the fifties and sixties it would have lured young people like Jemma, who would have wanted to explore the place."

"Why do we need to know this, Cora?" Frannie said.

Cora sighed. "I guess you don't. I was trying to understand Jemma's world back then. But I have another lead. The director recommended a Facebook page, Exploring Mount Forest. The author spends a lot of time at Sagawau doing research and providing trail information. He's explored the golf course site, photographed remnants, even made a map of the course based on his findings. It's all on Facebook. I sent him a message and hope to talk to him."

Cora saw expressions of approval. She doodled a star in front of her note about the Facebook page.

Valerie was wearing her old aloof expression. Cora suspected she was nervous about telling Frannie and Billy what Uncle Teddy revealed. Cora had already told Cisco.

When Cora was finished, Valerie smoothed her hair and began talking in a flat voice, gradually relaxing as she continued. She told them about why Jemma went to Sicily and about her father. Billy's jaw dropped, followed immediately by a sympathetic expression. He leaned toward Valerie, sliding his hand across the table but stopping just short of touching her. Frannie, on the other hand, avoided Cora's gaze. What was going on with her? Was Cisco right about the group starting to self-destruct?

"Now that you gave me names, Mickey and Petey Romano, maybe I can find them online," Billy said, withdrawing his hand and tucking it into his armpit.

In the silence that followed, Frannie coughed, rubbed her hands together, and then said, "I want to come clean. I knew you guys didn't want me to dig any further into Jemma's life, but I just couldn't let things sit like that. Then you all found out the relationship between Jemma and Kathleen. Well, I was ashamed to tell you I already knew. I found Paula, Valerie. I talked to your sister. She's living at a senior place in Joliet, not far from here."

Valerie jerked backward, as if slapped. Cora wondered if she was upset with Frannie or Paula. Maybe both.

"Go on," Valerie said through gritted teeth.

"Like you told us, Valerie, your sister's no easy gal to talk to. Hostile, kind of irrational." Frannie explained how she found Paula and got her to talk. She didn't paint Paula in a very kind light. "I thought she maybe had a soft spot when she started to cry about Jemma's death, but then she said she was disgusted with Jemma being the way she was, you know? Said she hated her for leaving them to take a woman as a lover. Seems to me she was more sorry for herself than for Jemma."

"Paula never married, right?" Cisco asked.

"Don't think so. I always found her using the same name. Made her easier to track. I know she's alone now."

"Maybe she's bitter because she's struggling with her own gender identity," Cisco suggested.

"That didn't occur…" Frannie blinked and fell silent.

"Did she ask about us, Frannie?" Valerie said, her voice softer after Frannie's account of the meeting. She seemed more sad than angry now.

"No. When I told her you was blind, she did say how that was strange because Jemma was devoted to a blind baseball team."

"I remember that!" Cora said.

"And she said Mamma never told her why she left us?" Valerie asked in the same small voice.

"She said Jemma told her she didn't want to leave but had no choice." She paused. "Of course, Paula made up her mind that Jemma left you all for a secret lesbian relationship. But how reliable is Paula?"

Billy, the only one who didn't know about Jemma and Kathleen's life in Arizona, sat in wide-eyed silence.

"Well, there's nothing new. We got all this from Kathleen," Valerie said. The others were quiet. She sighed. "And now I know my sister's still a crazy bitch. Thanks for finally telling me, Frannie. It clears up something I was wondering about, why you seemed so gung ho one minute, than close-mouthed the next. Something had to be up."

"There's nothing else, Valerie, I swear. That's all of it. Once I hid it, I didn't know how to let it out," Frannie said.

"What about the rest of you?" Valerie asked. "Anyone else have secrets to put on the table?"

Frannie seemed relieved. Valerie did seem to be more tolerant than she had been in the past. Had Cora been too hard on Cisco earlier?

Billy cleared his throat and shuffled his feet. Cisco stared in Billy's direction. Before either man could speak, the doorbell rang.

"I'll get it," Cisco jumped up and left the room like he was escaping. What was up?

"Good thing that doorbell works, Cora. It's been getting a lot of use lately," Frannie muttered.

Cisco's voice came from the living room. "Rogers! What happened to you?"

"That place you told me about, could be something *is* wrong out there," a deep voice replied.

"Hi Cora," Jeff Rogers said as he entered the kitchen with Cisco. "You haven't lost your talent for finding trouble, I see. These must be the friends Cisco told me about. Am I interrupting?"

Cora was surprised to see a large red lump on the right side of Rogers's forehead. His right eye was almost swollen shut.

"What happened to you? That looks painful!" she said.

"Wish I could say it was in the line of duty," Rogers smirked. "It's more of a curiosity and the cat thing."

The group exchanged looks. Cisco pulled a chair from the dining room. "Have a seat Rogers. You have incredible timing. We were just getting to you."

Cora had always found Rogers's combination of wry humor and air of authority amusing, but why was he here…and looking freshly beaten up? Cisco and Billy were making eye contact. They must have planned something that involved Rogers. Cisco could have told her but didn't. Her earlier anger, tempered during tonight's discussion, flared.

"Billy called me yesterday," Cisco said. "He noticed a car following Valerie, and then he thought the same guy followed him to Starbucks. He didn't want to upset all of you needlessly, so he gave me the plate number and I asked Rogers to check it."

He turned to Rogers. "I assume you're here because you have some information? Is the guy dangerous? That's not where that bruise came from, is it?"

"Don't know if the bruise is related or not. I went to check out that old farm you told me about. I didn't see a thing, other than someone mustn't have wanted me to be there. The perp hit me from behind and ran off. I recommend you stay away from that place."

Cora kept looking back and forth between Cisco and Billy, distracted by her thoughts. Why didn't Cisco tell her about talking to Billy and Rogers?

"Did you check the plates?" Cisco asked.

"I did. Guy has no significant record, just some minor stuff and questioning on a mob-related case in Vegas some years back. Nothing came of it, no convictions, but some minor-player mob ties seem likely. Born in Chicago, but spent most of his life out west. Just came back to Illinois a couple of years ago and no trouble here."

Cisco set a beer in front of Rogers. Rogers hesitated, shrugged, picked it up, and took a gulp.

"I paid the guy a visit at Main Inn where he works. He seemed okay, although he's a big brute of a guy and irritates easy. I came to see if any of you know him."

"What's his name?" Cisco asked.

"Peter Romano," said Rogers.

Valerie's hand flew to her mouth, but not before "my father!" escaped from her lips.

# Chapter 37

"Things turned out all right, I suppose. You would have told me about what you, Billy, and Rogers were up to if there had been time, wouldn't you?" Cora leaned back on their family room sofa, tucked her legs under her, and folded her arms across her chest. She needed Cisco's reassurance before he turned the television on.

Cisco met her gaze from his recliner. "I thought it would turn out to be nothing. Billy didn't want to alarm you without reason."

"There *was* reason to be alarmed though. Do you think Petey hit Rogers?"

"He could have. Billy and Rogers both thought Petey was pretty fit for an old guy. Never entered my mind he'd be Valerie's father. But if it was him, why would he be out in the woods? And why would he hit Rogers?"

Cora reached for an afghan and draped it over her legs.

"Do you need me to turn the heat up?"

"No, I'm fine. Do you agree everything's related to Jemma and our investigations? I can't imagine how anyone knows what we're doing, but it looks like someone doesn't want us out there."

"Could be just coincidence, but it's suspicious. I wonder how dangerous he is...."

Cisco reached for the remote control.

"Wait, before you do that...Rogers said Petey was a Peeping Tom? I can't remember the last time I heard that term."

"Probably not popular with news reporters these days."

"Good thing Billy waited until Rogers left to fill us in about Emery. Can you imagine the look on Rogers's face if he knew we were chasing ghosts again?" Cora snickered.

"Yeah, Rogers might bow out. I hope we don't need him, but I'd like to have that option."

Cora adjusted her position and relaxed, convinced that Cisco was telling her everything.

"I loved that picture Billy brought of Capone and his buddies. Only Billy has seen Emery's ghost face-to-face. Now I know what he looks like." She grinned and pumped a fist in the air. "Yes! Al Capone, Valentine's Day Massacre, illegal horse racing, and Emery—an important, albeit *dead*, crime boss! Isn't this fun? But what do you think about that 'message in a bottle' paper Billy found?"

"I got lucky there. An Italian language tutor happened to be in the library when I called, so I ran right over. Like I told everyone, the paper Billy found in the canister was handwritten by a veterinarian. It said there was no way the mare he examined could ever carry a foal because of severe endometriosis."

"The letter was addressed to Jimmy Emery? The horse wasn't named and there was no date?"

"I got the impression some confidentiality was involved. But the date would have to be before Emery died, before 1957."

"Right. And then someone rolled it up into a film canister." She shook her head. "Why would anyone do that?"

Cisco shrugged his shoulders. "That's how Billy found it."

"Does it have anything to do with our case?"

He looked over his glasses at her. "We're on a case, huh?" He shrugged again. "Who knows? But now that we have full names for Mickey and Petey Romano maybe we can fill in some blanks."

Cora got up and sat next to Cisco, taking his hand in hers and resting her head on his shoulder. "I hate it when we fight. Are we okay now?"

"I was doing my best Cora. I wasn't trying to invade your territory." He squeezed her hand.

"I know. It's just hard for me to give up control."

"Tell me something I don't know," he said, but his voice was soft.

"I know you're trying to help because you love me."

"Sometimes," he said with a grin.

She grinned back and kissed the side of his neck. "Do you think the group got back on track? Are we all trusting each other again?"

"I think it's better. Certainly Frannie is. It's hard to tell what's in Billy's head; he's so quiet. Valerie—for a moment there I thought she was actually ashamed of her suspicions after Frannie fessed up to finding Paula. We can't expect Valerie to change all her stripes in an instant, can we?"

"I suppose not," Cora said. "She's really trying, though, I think."

"Yes."

"What about going forward? Did we cover everything?"

"I doubt *everything*. Like you suggested, Frannie and Billy will continue internet research, Rogers and I will try to track down Petey and comb the woods, and Billy can connect with Emery's ghost if need be." Cisco pointed the remote at the television and pushed the on button.

Cora placed a hand on his arm. "And new information will be passed to me, and I'll jump in as needed or with new ideas. I just hope we can end this and soon."

"Right," Cisco said, his attention fixed on the channel guide.

~~~

Piles of paid and unpaid bill statements were scattered over Cora's desk when the landline interrupted her work the next morning. She glanced at the time on her computer screen. Almost 10:30 A.M. She sighed. What the hell. She was almost done.

She picked up the phone and leaned back. It was Frannie.

"You won't believe this!" Frannie said, between laughs. "Guess what Petey was doing all that time out in Vegas?"

"I don't know—entertainment of some sort, Teddy said."

"He was—get this—an Elvis impersonator!" Cora couldn't help but catch the merriment in Frannie's giggles.

"Apparently he's quite the ladies' man," Frannie said, containing her amusement at last. "He was married a couple of times, but both marriages were short-lived. One woman filed a suit against him for unwelcome sexual advances. It was dismissed. I watched some of his old YouTube clips—not a bad singer, by the way, but not my taste. Can't deny he's good-looking. Nothing recent, though. He seems to have dropped out of sight the last few years. There are older pictures of him hugging middle-aged women, more than a few. Seems just like what Teddy told you, making a living off charming the ladies."

"Once a snake, always a snake," Cora said.

"Now Paula, there's nothing to laugh about *her* situation. Remember I told you her career went downhill after Jemma died? I found a short item in a Phoenix paper. Appears she attempted suicide some time before she left Arizona and moved to Vegas. Of course, the paper didn't say that, only said a neighbor found her unconscious with an empty pill bottle, which doesn't need to be spelled out. But here's what I think… I think this gal was carrying a load of guilt about the way she treated her mama, adding to Jemma's misery during her fatal illness and all. According to Valerie, Paula never was what you'd call stable, even as a kid. I think that nasty business when Jemma died and other disappointments ate away at her leaving the gal a tortured woman to this day—why she's ended up where she's at. That's what I think."

"I wonder if Jemma realized Paula's mental status." Cora gazed out her window, rubbing her chin, watching a FedEx truck turn onto her block.

"Well, I only know Jemma through you all. But if I was that gal's mama, and I knew my daughter wasn't right in the head, I'd want to help her. No matter what she did to me. That sounds more like the Jemma you knew than the one Valerie remembers, though. Could also be why neither one of them ever told Valerie and Sally they met up again. And then Jemma got cancer and died."

When the call ended, Cora was still wondering if Frannie's opinions about Paula were right. The phone rang again. This time it was Billy. He had spent the morning online and had new information about hauntings. He wanted Cora's advice before he visited Emery again.

"There are two kinds of hauntings, intelligent and residual," Billy told her. "With residual haunting, it's like an old film playing over and over. They call it an imprint: an experience imprints itself on the atmosphere of the place where the event happened and captures its energy."

Cora guessed Billy was probably reading from his computer screen.

"The energy stays there but changes form and can discharge or play itself at any time. A psychic impression. Sometimes it's visual, or it could be sounds, smells, whatever."

"And that might be why the clubhouse, the farm buildings, and Emery all appear to you?" Cora said.

"Right. Trauma, emotion, and high energy from nearby sources make places more likely for this kind of haunting and make the replays stronger."

"So you think because of the crimes, the nearby quarries, and the buried nuclear waste, your experience is residual haunting."

"Exactly. Like a giant battery."

"So what's the problem?"

"With residual haunting, ghosts typically just repeat themselves. They don't react to living people."

"I see. So what's the other type?"

"Intelligent haunting. This kind of ghost interacts with living people in a way that seems intelligent. The ghosts are people who once lived and are trapped in our world or another realm and travel between realms. They act human, their personality usually the same as how the person was in life. They want attention from living people and will do whatever it takes to get that attention. They may want assistance to pass over, or they may have an uncompleted task they badly want finished. They may or may not know they're dead."

"So an intelligent ghost can communicate directly with you."

"Right."

"And that's what's been happening, right?"

"It is."

"Again, what's the problem?"

Billy exhaled loudly. "The problem is that we're looking for information we want from the ghost, but Emery is obsessed with what *he* wants and we don't know what that is. We'd be better off if we knew that before I went out to see him again. I mean, why does he communicate with me but not show himself to you and Cisco? Does he want help to travel between realms, to move on, or is it something he left undone?"

"Your experience has the characteristics of both kinds of haunting, doesn't it?"

"Yeah. If I understand right."

"Hmm. It might be better if you learn more about Emery before you go out there again. Now you've got me wondering if Valerie should go with you. She's the most emotionally involved and linked because her mother lived there. Emery knew Jemma, even though she didn't move there until after he died. How can that be?"

She paused and started putting stamps on envelopes while thinking.

"Maybe he's been hanging around as a ghost ever since he died," she said. "Maybe he was there as a ghost when Jemma lived there. Who says you're the first person he communicated with? I remember Jemma talking about strange things she saw and heard there. Maybe he appeared to her. There could be common ground between Emery and Valerie."

Billy seemed doubtful. "How can Valerie go out there? Would she go, do you think? I mean, would she be able to walk the trail? Besides, she keeps saying she doesn't believe in ghosts."

His concern was clear in his strained voice.

"Why don't you ask her?" Cora suggested.

Before they hung up, Cora told Billy about Petey's career as an Elvis impersonator. If Billy found the information amusing, he didn't let on. His only comment was, "I wonder what Valerie will think?" When Cora asked him if he found out anything new about the Romano brothers, he said he wanted to get his thoughts clear about Emery before he switched gears. He'd call back later.

The call had reminded Cora of her encounters with Angel at St. James a couple of years ago. Was some sort of channeling happening between Billy and Emery? Despite having had direct experience with the spirit world, she preferred her life free of ghosts. This time it was Billy's experience, not hers. Just because something *can* happen doesn't mean that's what *was* happening. Yet she couldn't help but wonder what Valerie's reaction would be if she met the spirit of Jimmy Emery.

～～～

By lunchtime Cora had a neat pile of envelopes ready to mail and was reviewing the notes she'd gathered about Valerie.

She had just viewed two YouTube clips of Petey's performances. He was attractive and suave. Something smarmy about him though. A sham designed to charm Elvis addicts. His performance was reasonably good, but he didn't blow her away. Over-staged and kind of hokey.

"Information Central," she said, picking up the phone yet again. This time the caller was Cisco. "Petey's flown the coop, we think." Cisco had gone to see Rogers.

"You think he's gone but you're not sure, or you're sure he's gone and think it's because he knows we're on to him?"

"Both. Rogers and I went to Main Inn so I could get a look at the guy. Rogers wanted to question him again, see if he acted guilty, like he might if Petey was the guy that hit him. Since Rogers had talked to him only a short time before, he would be suspicious if they both turned up in the same place. Petey might have panicked and knocked Rogers down to avoid being seen. But a different bartender was there. Pissed because he had to come in at the last minute when Petey didn't show."

"Petey's starting to look more involved, isn't he?"

"Yeah. So we drove to his apartment, and he didn't answer. We rang the supervisor. He and Petey were pretty friendly. He hadn't seen him since yesterday. He wouldn't let us in the apartment, but at Rogers's insistence, he went in himself. Petey wasn't there, but the place looked untouched."

"So Petey spent the night somewhere else?"

"Yeah. According to the super, Petey has pretty regular habits, so he was surprised. Did you 'detectives' find anything new?"

"I'll fill you in when you get home. I'm glad you're staying on Petey though. We'd really like to talk to him, but we need to know what he's up to first."

"I couldn't agree more."

"Are you coming home?"

"Not yet. I'm gonna get some personal stuff done. Text me if you need me."

Petey's disappearance was disturbing. Jemma, her parents, and siblings were either dead or couldn't be found; Jemma's husband was dead. Emery was dead. They had almost exhausted all print, online, and interview options and were at a dead end, with Petey the only remaining living person to ask, unless his brother Mickey could be found.

Petey's sudden disappearance was not only frustrating it also made her uneasy. Assuming they were able to find Petey and depending on what kind of guy he turned out to be, did Valerie want to meet him? How could Valerie consider bringing her daughter Molly here if Petey, or someone else, turned out to be dangerous?

~ ~ ~

Frannie called again later as Cora was standing in front of the refrigerator trying to decide between pancakes leftover from breakfast or a remnant of liver sausage hard around the edges.

"Hang on. I'll be right with you," she said. Balancing the phone against her ear, Cora grabbed the pancakes, put them on a plate with syrup, and placed the plate in the microwave.

"How much do you trust that Ted guy?" Frannie asked.

"I liked him. Why?"

"Do you remember those murders of the kids back in the fifties, the ones that were dumped in the forest preserves?"

"The Grimes sisters and the Peterson-Schuessler boys? Had me scared to death at the time. I know Ted was questioned. But there was no evidence against him and he denied it when we talked to him."

"What's he gonna do, admit it? It's just there was always this suspicion the two cases were related, and the guy who was convicted for the boys' murders was a stable worker. Took forty years to catch him. The stables weren't far from your farm either. Just seems like too many coincidences to me."

Cora had a momentary chill, but tossed it off. "I don't want to think that, Frannie."

Frannie sighed. "Well, I said my piece. I'm not finding anything more about Petey, and only a little on his brother. Mickey took over Emery's operation locally, but articles about him are slim to none. He couldn't have been very successful or important to the Mob. But I ran across another guy that was important, Jimmy Catuara."

Cora groaned.

"What?" Frannie said.

"Don't we have enough mobsters already without bringing in a new one? My head is spinning. Can't we focus on the ones we already know?"

"No. We can't. I got the feeling this is important."

"Okay." Cora let out an exasperated breath. "Go on." She pulled her food from the microwave, grabbed a notepad and pen, put the phone on speaker, and sat at the kitchen table.

"After Emery died, Catuara moved to Oak Lawn and became a major Mob figure in the southwest suburbs."

"Oak Lawn? He operated out of Oak Lawn? Where I lived, and where Jemma raised her kids?"

"Yeah, that's right. Catuara was a real mean guy, and he'd been in the business a long time. Jimmy the Bomber they called him, because he made his name blowing up taxicabs during the twenties and thirties in what they called the Taxi Wars. He was imprisoned in Joliet for that until

1942. Later Catuara had been Emery's main enforcer; so after Emery died, Jimmy the Bomber started running his own crew on the southwest side and suburbs—gambling, loan sharking, extortion, the usual stuff. I figure he'd just been waiting to make his own move."

"Let me think," Cora said through a mouthful of pancakes. "This was when Jemma lived on the farm, right?" He could have been giving the orders about hiding gambling equipment at the clubhouse and still been in control when Jemma disappeared and Angelo was killed.

"Right. Now get this. His cover…he was masquerading as a *furniture salesman!*"

"I don't get it."

"Didn't Jemma and her husband have some sort of furniture business when they moved to Chicago? Where'd they get the money?"

"Yeah, but—"

"Let me finish. So, Catuara, he didn't get along with just about anyone. He started the whole chop shop racket back in the sixties, and it got big. The rest of the Outfit wanted in on the action, which led to twenty murders in the Chop Shop Wars. By the late seventies, the big bosses sat on him to tone down the infighting. He refused to back off and got himself shot, gangland style."

"When was that?"

"On July 28, 1978."

"Three years after Angelo."

"Right."

"Hmm. So what's all this mean?"

"Well, I don't know, Cora. But we're looking for a bad guy with ties to what was going on mob-wise from the fifties through the seventies. Capone's the most famous, but did you know the highest number of arrests for gambling were from 1957 through 1966? The Bomber was the baddest of the bad during those years, seems to me. He was in the right places at the right times and he was mean and powerful."

Cora's mind was racing. "Do you think Petey would have known this guy?"

"Catuara ran Emery's former operation in Mickey's territory. Mickey had to have either worked for him or against him, and most certainly would have known him. We have to assume the same goes for Petey, at whatever level he was involved. What do you think?"

What she thought was that she would call Billy.

# Chapter 38

Petey Romano groaned, rubbed his stiff neck, and stretched his painful back. A sliver of light penetrated a slender gap in his "roof," a tarp that kept field mice and larger predators out of his "bunker." A cold night on a foam pad, no matter how comfortable the sporting goods salesman promised, was not as easy as when he had been younger.

When the stiffness in his muscles eased, he pushed the tarp aside and climbed out to face the dawn. His hideout was off trail, near the edge of a pond. Using a firewood lighter, he ignited the wood he had laid in a small fire pit the previous evening. He huddled beside the flames, his sleeping bag across his shoulders. As he stared at the glistening surface of the water listening to chickadees, robins, and sparrows, he mulled over the events that had driven him into the woods.

The idea had come to him in the late fifties. Walking along the canal, he had stumbled across a cold campfire next to a half sheet of plywood on the ground. Curious, he had lifted an edge of the plywood to reveal a deep hole. Inside were a sleeping bag, a backpack, a small shovel, an ax, a flashlight, a frying pan, and more. Someone, probably a vagrant, had dug a shelter and was living there. He had found the discovery amusing.

In those days, Petey had enjoyed roaming the woods near the one-room schoolhouse where Mickey had gotten him a job as a handyman. Although he had a dim view of the job, one positive was his daily contact with three cute seventh and eighth grade girls. His wink soon had them giggling.

His much-older brother Mickey ordered Petey where to go and what to do. Mickey thought he was careless and had harebrained ideas. The brothers shared street smarts, good looks, and charm, but their resemblance stopped there. Mickey was short and skinny like Sinatra. Petey thought Mickey was jealous of his tall, muscular build and the fact that he started having sex at the age of twelve.

Petey's favorite spot was a small pond near the vacated Argonne Laboratory, about a mile from the school. That's where he dug his own shelter beside the pond, similar to the one near the canal, just to see what it was like. Curled up underground, he could escape Mickey's nagging and convince himself his dreams, which Mickey called stupid, would come true. Before long, his hole in the woods became a refuge and a place to entertain girls.

"A secret bunker? No kidding? What's a bunker?" they'd say when he asked if they wanted to see it. Secrets turned them on, and, as intended, the dark, close space led to other pleasures.

Somehow he'd never taken Jemma to his bunker, although she'd been special. She made him laugh, but she never laughed at his dreams, only shared her own. He visualized her now, snuggling and giggling on that old blanket under the tree she was so fond of. Jemma: smart as a whip, but also naive and impressionable. She was crazy about him. He tested her loyalty now and then with silly requests. He could have married Jemma, if he hadn't valued his freedom more.

She had had one wacky idea, a suspicion that the farm where she lived was haunted. A friendly spirit, she had said, who appeared whistling a tune. He never believed that crap. The sights and sounds were probably the boys doing nighttime jobs for Mickey or Jimmy the Bomber. He used to razz her. "Maybe it's Emery, the guy used to live there before you. He was real attached to the place, probably because of that horse he was so in love with," he told her. Emery had reason to be pissed off enough at him and Mickey to hang around as a ghost. Maybe it wasn't a crazy idea after all.

Then Mickey asked him to hide the letter, and he had Jemma help him, to prove his influence over her. He jammed the letter in a film canister to protect it from the elements, and Jemma said she knew just the place. She took him to a canyon on the other side of the valley, where they got through the fence and hid the container behind a rock in the canyon wall.

But then Jemma got pregnant. Petey was sorry to lose Jemma, sorry to let her down, but what could he do? He wasn't ready for a family. And wouldn't you know it, that's when Mickey decided he wanted the damn letter back. When he went to get it, it was gone and Jemma was gone too, sent to Sicily suddenly without a word to anyone. She must have removed the letter before she went. Sicily was Mickey's doing too, to protect Petey, so he claimed. Mickey got him out of a marriage, but then Petey was in trouble for losing the letter.

"Why did I ever trust the damn thing to you? Like everyone keeps sayin', my kid brother's an idiot! You got something missing—when you gonna grow up, stop acting like a brat?" he had said, pinching Petey's cheek cruelly. "Why did I even *keep* the damn thing, instead of destroying it to begin with? Stupid, stupid!"

After the outburst, Mickey calmed down saying gone was gone, and maybe that was a relief after all. But Petey'd better hope and pray the damn thing never turned up.

Then Mickey had sent Petey to Vegas. "You've got yourself in too many fixes. The boss is fit to be tied. I don't get you out of here, someone will put a hit out on you or, worse yet, on me for covering for you. What the fuck were you thinkin', screwing the daughter of a family we depend on? You knock her up, cause an uproar, make me save your ass again. Whadda you want from me? I've had enough a your shit. Go play your guitar out in Vegas, away from my operation. Behave yourself and you'll be safe and outta our hair. Get outta here and don't come back."

A shiver stopped his memories—the fire was burning down. Petey shrugged the sleeping bag off his shoulders, got up, and added some wood. When the branches and coals were burning well, he sat back down and returned to his thoughts.

He had never struck it big in Vegas, but he lived well enough. He had fans, women who were into entertainers. And sexy showgirls, who dressed provocatively and didn't always close their curtains. That was on them, but he was the one got caught "peeping." What was the big deal? So he was curious by nature. How was he supposed to control that? Vegas wasn't a bad place, as it turned out, but still, he'd rather have been home.

Then a couple of years ago the greedy bitch he'd been living with took him to the cleaners—okay, it was her money, but they had agreed to share it, hadn't they? She was pretty stupid if she really thought he intended to marry her. The thing was, he hadn't been too smart either, forgetting about the fact that her brother was a lawyer. They stacked the deck against him and the court took her side.

He'd had to start over before, but he'd been younger then. No one was interested in an Elvis impersonator in his seventies, and he didn't relish the idea of establishing a new act so late in life. He didn't seem to have many options.

He began to long for the place of his youth. Mickey, Catuara, and the boys were all either dead or whereabouts unknown. He could be happy if he moved back and all his problems would go away.

His career as a performer over, alone in the world, he arrived in Lemont early last summer, convinced that whatever future he had left would be there. He found work as a bartender to supplement his meager savings and retirement income and got a roomy apartment in town. He spent the next months, summer and fall, walking for long hours in the forest preserves, remembering his youth and remembering the farm where Jemma had lived.

Before he died, Mickey had told him Jemma returned from Sicily with a husband and Petey's daughter, who was named Valerie. They had moved to Oak Lawn, where Jimmy the Bomber lived. He had begun to wonder if he could find the daughter he never knew, Jemma's little girl. He had no other children that he knew of, would have thought he'd been shooting blanks if it weren't for knocking up Jemma.

Weren't children supposed to take care of their parents when they reached old age? It was time he got to know his daughter. Maybe he could make things up to her, finally do something worthwhile with his life. Maybe even do some good in the eyes of God. He couldn't remember the last time he'd been to Mass. He'd put that on his to-do list. Go to that old church in the woods he used to attend off and on.

He sought out places of his fond memories: the school he once maintained and the woods where the Outfit hid their crimes in a crumbling clubhouse. It didn't take long to discover that everything he remembered was gone, the buildings demolished, their former sites overgrown and unrecognizable. Signs now marked where the old Argonne buildings had once been and where the reactor was buried, and he found the pond where he used to bring his girls.

Out walking the woods one day last fall, Petey yearned for the sense of peace he once got in his hole in the ground. Why not recapture it? He went to Walmart and purchased a folding shovel and a camouflage tarp; on the far side of the pond, unseen from trails, he dug a hole five feet by seven feet and five feet deep. It would have been hard work for most men his age, but Petey took pride in staying strong and fit. He covered his "shelter" with the tarp, anchored it with stakes, and spread dry leaves and twigs over it. Then he crawled inside. Immediately the old feelings of peace returned. He would have to make some improvements: a pad of some kind, a sleeping bag, a flashlight, and a plastic tarp to line the inside walls. Maybe a heater…

Then after a leisurely walk around the edges of the pond, he made the discovery that would change his life at long last. Long ago he and Jemma had laughed about it. But now he realized the discovery would bring him fame and fortune. He had started the first steps and had only to let it play out. He would be wealthy beyond his dreams, secure for the rest of his days. This time he knew he was right!

Next, he would set out to find his daughter. But first, he'd find Jemma.

After some difficulty, he discovered that she had died long ago. Sad, but she'd been out of his life forever. Where, then, might his daughter be?

A name…what was it? He knew her as Jemma Vitale, but her married name? Yes! DiMaso. Jemma had married a distant cousin in Sicily, one of the DiMaso boys looking for a ticket to the States. Mickey had taken the guy under his wing, introduced him around, got him work. Must have been something in it for Mickey, of course. So, Valerie DiMaso. Where is she now?

She would be…what? He calculated her approximate birth date and age. At the Oak Lawn Library, with a librarian's help, he learned that the Vitales and DiMasos left Oak Lawn in the sixties. The DiMasos' home was destroyed in a tornado in 1967.

"That was probably why they moved," the librarian said. Jemma had moved to Chicago.

"We don't need an address, though," the librarian said. "With her name, we can check state birth, marriage, and license records." They found Valerie's married name, Pawlik. Searching the name Valerie Pawlik brought up a nursing license and an article about an accident that left her blind.

His daughter was blind. That was unexpected. But the more he thought about it, the more he saw Valerie's blindness as an opportunity to get close to her. He'd be her savior, the father she never had.

The article mentioned a brother, Salvatore DiMaso Jr. Petey found an address for him right here in Lemont. He would visit the brother and ask where Valerie was.

The next day he parked on the street in a modest subdivision near a newer-style, white-brick and gray-sided, two-story home. As he sat in his car rehearsing an opening line to tell the brother, a car pulled into the driveway. A petite woman with short, dark hair, dark glasses, and a golden retriever guide dog got out of the car. She followed the dog to the front door after the car drove away.

His daughter! Valerie! His scalp tingled, and he dropped out of sight instinctively, laughing at himself when he realized she wouldn't be able to see him.

He had only expected to question the brother. Was he ready to meet her? He could approach her any time, now he knew where she was. He drove home to think things over.

What if she was angry and refused to let him in? Or would she be happy to finally know him? Did she know that Sal DiMaso was not her real father? Should he try to befriend her without letting her know the truth?

He didn't know how to approach her, how to tell her he was her father. He procrastinated all winter, but often drove by her home just to see her again. Whenever she left the house, he followed, learning where she went. He admired her courage, going out alone by cab or on foot, guide dog at her side...or sometimes only with a cane.

In bed at night, he imagined Valerie was sitting next to him. He would read to her, talk to her about his days in Vegas, tell her stories about her mother. She would laugh, touch his face, kiss him lightly on the cheek. His daughter! How she loved him! One day she'd take care of him and she'd stay by his side throughout his old age. The two of them would mean everything to each other.

With that scene in his mind, he'd fall asleep smiling.

Sitting by his campfire now, Petey's legs were starting to cramp. He got up, stretched, and walked to the side of the pond, his gaze directed at the woods on the far side. It was peaceful out here, but for some reason his thoughts were restless.

Many times during the winter he had followed Valerie. A few weeks ago, she had taken a cab to a house on the other side of town and then went back there a number of times. Other people joined her.

What were they doing? He had to know. And so one day after dark, Petey went to Valerie's house. No one was home, and he found an unlocked kitchen window, squeezed through it, and located Valerie's room on the second floor. The dog in the cage fussed the whole damn time, and he was relieved no one was home to hear.

His daughter's room! He fingered her personal items in the bathroom, around the bed, in drawers, and on her bedside table. He sniffed her bath gel, sprayed her perfume into the air, inhaled the smells of the products she surrounded herself with, visualizing himself once again sitting by her side. He made an effort to carefully replace the items he touched so she would never know anyone had been in the room. But then he undid that effort when he found her sleepwear under her pillow and could not resist taking it with him when he left, to remember her scent. But he found nothing to explain where she went or what she was doing.

The next night, she went again to the house on the other side of town. Who were these people? He was Valerie's savior, not some gaggle of random do-gooders. They had no right to interfere.

One day she left the do-gooders' house in a car driven by a scrawny young man with dark looks and hair down to his shoulders. Who was this guy and what did he want with Petey's daughter? The puny creep was clearly much younger than her, so he couldn't be a boyfriend. Puzzling. He followed the car to Valerie's home. But the man noticed him, so Petey took off.

He decided to start following the creep, too, one day trailing him to the parking area at Saganashkee Slough. He took the same path Petey used to go to his shelter! What was he doing in Petey's woods? Did it threaten Petey's secrets? He'd better find out.

Puny creep followed the path uphill toward the former clubhouse. Staying well behind, Petey could see the guy wandering around and poking at the ground with his foot. Then he turned around, heading toward the area of the farmhouse where Jemma used to live. He seemed to know where he was going.

The man took a seat on a fallen log. He appeared to be talking to someone or thinking aloud. From behind a large tree, Petey saw him suddenly jump up and spring back. He seemed agitated. What the hell was the idiot doing? He seemed to be calling to someone, raising an arm, shouting, "Wait!"

After the guy left, Petey remained behind the tree in the dim light, thinking the man had a screw loose and wondering what his relationship to Valerie was.

A few days later Petey was no closer to knowing when he followed the man to Starbucks. He got a good look and formed an opinion—a loser. He saw an OfficeMax name tag on the man's shirt when he got up to leave: Billy Nokoy, Sales Consultant. What kind of name was Nokoy?

What about the old couple who lived in the house Valerie visited? Why was she going there? Someone told that cop that Petey was following Valerie, either the loser or the old guy. The old couple was a pain in his ass too.

After the cop came to Main Inn, Petey went back to the farm to look for clues as to why the Billy creep went there. And what the fuck? The cop shows up there too! He shouldn't have hit him, but he panicked. What if the cop found him out here when he had just left him? How would he explain? It'd look like he was following the cop too. He couldn't be seen, couldn't let anyone suspect something important was out there.

The cop said Petey was being watched. It seemed smart to disappear for a while. He had to hide and protect his discovery. He had to be sure no one stole it from him before he reaped the rewards—the fortune that would carry him flush through his remaining days.

Fortunately, he had just the place ready and waiting: his "hidey hole." There he could keep an eye on things....

# Chapter 39

After Sally and Grace left for work, Valerie dressed and went down to the kitchen.

Her stomach was in knots. She only wanted a cup of tea, but the bitter taste prompted her to push the cup away with a grimace. Corky slipped under the table and put her head on Valerie's knee.

"You always know when I need you, baby," she said, rubbing Corky's head.

This dependency on others to solve her personal problems...she didn't like it! She felt like she was reverting to form.

She paced from the kitchen to the front door, Corky dancing along behind until she realized they weren't going out. Valerie heard the soft padding on carpet change to clicking when Corky entered the kitchen, and then the soft plop and sigh as she lay down. Good girl. She would be under the table, knowing not to lie in places Valerie might trip on her.

Cora had updated her on the phone last night. Afterward she tossed and turned through the night. A lifelong doer, all she was *doing* was approving what others did. She itched to be part of the action.

Damn it! Time was ticking away, minute after minute. She was no closer to finding a place to live or a way to support herself and Molly. Why had she wasted time trying to find Jemma? She should be calling social organizations and employment agencies. She had to get her head together.

She picked up her cell phone and turned it back on. She listened to a voicemail from Jean Hillebrand, an old acquaintance and the head of nursing at the hospital where she had last worked.

"Hi Valerie. It's been a long time since we talked. Can you give me a call when you're free?" was all the message said. Another sympathy call? Valerie was in no mood to chat with a woman she had respected but not been close to. She'd call back another time.

She considered calling Father McGrath for encouragement and then decided he'd only urge her to be patient and let others help. She'd tried that and it wasn't enough. This friend business was all fine and good, but she wanted her life back in her own hands.

When clues had started turning up, she was lulled into believing she could finally come to terms with the past. Now, despite many discoveries, the past still haunted her and she felt only disappointment. No, disappointment and *fear*—fear of the answers, the future, and now potential physical danger.

Everything about her whole damn family was a lie. Nothing she had believed was true.

When Cora told her Jemma had died, she resigned herself to being an orphan. Then a father she had never known had turned up. Possibly a criminal, certainly a louse, but blood of her blood and alive, for whatever good that was. Valerie wasn't sure she wanted to know him, but she did want to know *about* him. Why did he show up now, after so many years?

Sal DiMaso, the man she had thought was her father, she had loved him, despite his shortcomings. Dead now for many years from a heart attack. Cora asked where he got the money to start a business. Was he fronting for the Mob? Perhaps a mob boss drove Jemma from Chicago.

Only her brother and sister remained, Sally and Paula…

Paula lived not far away now. Valerie could easily reach out to her, but didn't Valerie have enough problems of her own? Why force herself on Paula, even if Paula could put her hurt and anger aside. A big "if" that was!

And who was her mother, really? According to Cora, Kathleen, and Uncle Teddy, not the person Valerie remembered. She'd never seen Jemma's fun-loving side and that hurt even more than her mother walking out without a word of explanation. But what could explain leaving her children?

It dawned on Valerie that she had left her own daughter, and the reasons *were* beyond her control. It had nothing to do with her love for Molly and everything to do with her personal sacrifice to give Molly a better life. Had Mamma had a good reason too?

That epiphany halted her. Maybe she would feel better with some food in her stomach. She made toast with a smear of peanut butter, sat at the table, and returned to her thoughts.

Was Petey dangerous? Would he hurt his daughter? His granddaughter? Was her "new" father still involved with organized crime?

And who killed Angelo? She had wanted to know, but really, what did it matter? It was beginning to look like Angelo had been killed by the Mob instead of a sniper. But Frannie's discoveries suggested Angelo wasn't the pure and innocent man she had believed he was.

As if this wasn't enough, her friends were chasing, of all things, the ghost of a mobster and spending their time in haunted forests, somewhere she'd never been and had no way to get to.

Crap! Just crap! The whole damn thing, crap!

Maybe Father McGrath had been wrong from the beginning. Oh, she saw the value of friends now, but they were only part of the equation. She couldn't leave things in their hands, and she wasn't doing enough herself.

She needed the old self-reliance she had before her accident. How could she get back control of her life?

Valerie's cell phone rang, interrupting her thoughts.

"What?" she answered.

"Uh…did I get you at a bad time?" Billy said after a pause.

Valerie took a deep breath. "No, Billy. Sorry. I'm just in a funk. Maybe it's a good thing you interrupted me. What's up?"

"Uh…I know this is impossible, but Cora and I were talking, and she thought…uh, we thought… Well, there are reasons we think…it would help if you…uh…went with me to the farm. Would you think about—"

"Let me make this easy for you, Billy. Yes."

~~~

After lunch, Rogers stopped at the Main Inn to question Oscar Baptista. He knew Oscar was one of those harmless drunks thought of fondly by bar patrons, like the place's mascot. Oscar practically lived at the bar and would get progressively more soused as the day wore on, but before the bar opened, he cleaned the place.

Perhaps Oscar knew where Petey was.

Rogers banged on the dark-stained, double-entrance door and then peered through the window. "Lemont police," he announced, "let me in."

An emaciated man of about fifty with a few thin strands of hair plastered over his scalp opened the door, his eyes wide and fearful. "I'm s'posed to be here," Oscar said, in a thick Spanish accent. "Cleaning. The owner, he pay me." He leaned a mop handle against a wall, wiped his hands on his worn, sagging jeans, and tried a tentative grin. *"Dinero* for *cerveza."*

Rogers smiled, walked around a pool table, and sat on a stool with his back to the bar. "I just want to talk to you, Oscar. Don't you know me?"

The man nodded, but his expression remained blank. Rogers tried to remember if he had ever talked to Oscar when he was sober.

"Sit down," Rogers said. Oscar pulled a stool away from the bar and sat next to him.

"Petey Romano seems to have gone missing. Do you have any idea where he might be?"

"Don't know anything about him, man. Only I see him when he working."

"Do you know who he hangs with or where I might look for him?"

Oscar shook his head. "No, man. Only he works here." He lowered his head and stared at the floor.

"What are you not telling me?" Rogers asked.

"Nothing, man. Just…"

"Yes?"

"Most people here be nice to me. Petey not so good. No *problema,* but he treat me like no account, you know? Like I a dirty person."

Perhaps that's all it was. It was consistent with what Rogers knew of Petey.

"Okay, then tell me what you *do* know about him. Does he have any friends?"

"No, man. Just customers. I never see him come in or leave with anyone. Only do his job." Oscar rubbed his fist over his mouth. "He like the ladies."

"What makes you say that?"

Oscar shrugged. "He different person with ladies, more attention, more talking and laughing, more touching, hands and hugs. He make men laugh, but he flirt the ladies."

"Did he ever leave with any of the ladies?"

"No, man. I no see."

Looked like a wasted trip. Rogers tried one more question. "Did you ever see him do anything unusual? Or talk with anyone unusual? Something that may not have been legal?"

Oscar shook his head. "No, man. Nothing like that." His eyes widened before he shifted them again.

"What?"

"Just...not a bad man or illegal. But one day he all excited. Customers want drinks and he wave them away, tell them he get to them when he can, but he and a man talk quiet. I no hear what they say."

"When was that?"

"Long time, I think after summer."

"Do you know who the man was?"

"I see him before but he no here much. He was dark skin, no black or Spanish. He was young man, long hair, in tail." Oscar mimicked pulling his hair back behind his neck. "He no have accent. Someone say he scientist, smart man from *laboratorio* across the river."

Argonne National Laboratory. That was interesting. Why would Petey be having a private conversation with a scientist?

"That's all you saw, just them talking?"

Oscar rubbed his forehead, thinking. He looked up. "Petey go outside. Come back with little plastic bag. I think from his car. He give it to the man. The man take bag when he leave."

"You have no idea what was in it?"

Oscar shook his head. "Only it look heavy, like a jar. But the man come back, a month maybe. I think before Thanksgiving."

"And?"

Oscar frowned and shook his head again. "Nothing. They talk only. Petey he excited, ignore customers again, ignore man too. Only walk around behind the bar. Sometime he smile and laugh. Sometime he only looking at the wall. The man leave, Petey say 'I'll call you.' That's all I know."

Back at the station, Rogers pushed papers around his desk without accomplishing anything. What the hell was Petey's connection to Argonne? Was it only coincidence the clubhouse and farm Cisco and Cora were investigating were adjacent to the old Argonne Laboratory—the lab's location during the Manhattan Project before it was relocated across the river? And why did the man come to Lemont and begin stalking Valerie and Billy? Something wasn't right.

Rogers's gut told him Petey was the guy who had struck him in the woods.

He opened Google Maps, zoomed in where the old clubhouse and farm had been, and changed to satellite view. He examined the area closely, measuring the distances between the clubhouse, the farm, and the old Argonne site A. He looked for trails that connected the areas, copied and printed a view showing the existing trails, and placed Xs where he estimated the clubhouse, farmhouse, and Argonne site had been.

He identified three ways to approach the Argonne site, one from a forest preserve parking lot along Archer Avenue, one from a closed access road farther southwest on Archer, and the third from the same path he had used on his previous visit. The approaches were all through isolated woods and about equally distant from the Argonne site. He'd use the same route he'd taken before to get a better feel for the relationship between the areas.

He realized he'd already decided to return to the woods. No time like the present.

Joe O'Connor was at his desk.

"I'm going out for an hour or so. Call me if something comes up."

O'Connor frowned and looked at his watch. "What's up? You're off in a couple of hours."

"I'm not sure. Probably nothing. Just following a hunch."

O'Connor knitted his eyebrows. "Anything to do with that situation in the woods you asked me about?"

"Not that, but nearby. Guy says something's not right. I'm sure he's wrong but I told him I'd take a look."

"That's FPD jurisdiction."

"Yeah, but it involves Lemont residents."

A question was on O'Connor's face, but Rogers said nothing more.

He changed into jeans, black Nikes, and a lightweight gray insulated jacket and strode out of the station.

He parked the squad car on the side of the road across from Saganashkee Slough and started hiking up the same overgrown road he'd taken before.

Lingering at the old clubhouse site, he scraped the ground with his shoe, hoping to find some of the roof tiles Cisco mentioned. No luck.

Consulting the Google Map, Rogers climbed to the top of the hill, turned right, went northeast, then curved north, and descended into a ravine filled with dry vegetation.

A tall, healthy-looking man met him coming down the ravine from the opposite side. He wore a dark-red hoodie, his head wrapped in a bright orange bandana, the scarf ends below the knot falling behind his neck. He carried a gray backpack and a walking stick. He looked like he spent a lot of time in the woods and was comfortable there.

"Nice day," Rogers said.

"Yes. It won't be long before the bushes leaf out and put an end to my hikes, though." The man spoke slowly and softly.

"Why's that?"

"I get an awful rash from one of the plants that grows out here. But you can see a lot more before the leaves hide everything, so there's benefits."

"Didn't think of that. You spend a lot of time out here, do you?"

He shrugged. "A hobby. You find interesting stuff off trail if you know how to look. Just getting some exercise today?"

"I'm looking for the old Argonne site."

"Ah. Most people follow the trail from Red Gate Woods." He lifted an eyebrow, but Rogers chose not to explain why he was walking in the woods. "From here, though," he went on when Rogers remained silent, "stay on this trail and keep bearing either north or east whenever it branches. You'll come to some signs. You're not a smoker, are you?"

"No. Why?"

"Look around you. It's been really dry this year. The Forest Preserves people have been asking everyone to be really careful."

"Thanks. I won't be smoking," Rogers said, quickly dismissing the thought. "Say, you ever have any bad encounters out here?"

"With fires or with people?"

"People."

"Odd characters now and then, but nobody dangerous. Why?"

"Couple of days ago near here, someone hit me from behind. Knocked me down and ran off." Rogers pointed to the swollen blue-and-purple discoloration on his temple.

"Really? I've never had anything like that happen, and I'm out here quite a bit."

"Let me know if you run across anything." Rogers pulled a card from his pocket and handed it to the man. He saw the man's eyes widen, but he made no comment about the Lemont Police logo on the card.

"Thanks. I will." He started away and then turned back. "If you're interested in this area, you might want to check out my Facebook page. It's called Exploring Mount Forest."

"Thanks. I may do that."

Fat chance. Rogers considered social sites a necessary evil and avoided them when he could.

He climbed the ravine and, as the man had said, the trail led north and then veered east, up and down hills in the rugged glacial terrain. It was obvious why these trails were popular with mountain bikers. Once he thought he heard someone whistling a tune in the distance, but it was probably a bird or a breeze whispering through the trees.

Before long he came to a cross trail where a sign marked the location he sought.

*You Are Now Entering SITE A*

*Looking for a remote location to conduct top-secret nuclear experiments, the U.S. Army Corp of Engineers built the Site A research facility on land leased from the Cook County Forest Preserves in Red Gate Woods.*

*In addition to research labs and reactor control rooms, the complex included a guardhouse, dog shelter, library, cafeteria, dormitory, and recreational spaces. The scientists who lived and worked there throughout World War II maintained a strict code of silence, as their discoveries were critical for the success of the U.S. military's atomic program.*

*After extensive cleanup, the site is safe for public recreation.*

So damn safe, right. Rogers felt his hair standing on end.

Shaking off the feeling, he looked around, remembering what happened the last time he was in these woods. He wasn't about to be taken by surprise again. Alert for any sound, he heard only silence. There was no breeze to rustle the bare branches, and for the moment no birds or small forest creatures could be heard calling or scrambling through dry leaves on the ground. The stillness was just as disquieting. He couldn't shake the feeling someone was watching him.

Must be his mind was playing tricks, but he touched his gun and his radio.

If Petey had any connection to this place, there was no indication at the clubhouse area or on the way here. He'd walk the perimeter of the lab, with no idea what to look for—just something that shouldn't be there.

The hiker he met earlier said go east. That was the direction the trail continued, so that's the way he went. Despite denser brush here, he could see at least fifty feet through the branches should anyone be lying in wait for him. All remained eerily quiet. His footsteps seemed loud and hollow on the earthen trail. Every now and then he spun and checked all directions.

He came to a pond, a pretty little thing, reflecting the blue sky, the afternoon sun casting silvery threads across the surface. It was surrounded by a wide grassy area, the grass melting into thickets and scrub trees that edged the woods. Rogers had always been drawn to bodies of water. The trail ahead was empty and uninteresting. On impulse he decided to circle the pond.

As soon as he stepped off the trail he remembered the rash the hiker mentioned. He avoided wooded areas and kept to thick grass and clumps of dead leaves. He had gone more than half way around the pond and reached a curve in the shore that hid the trail from sight. He saw some burnt branches, looking suspiciously as if someone had tried to hide the evidence of a campfire. As he moved closer, the ground gave way beneath his feet and Rogers was swallowed into the earth.

# Chapter 40

Squinting in the bright morning sunlight reflecting off Saganashkee Slough, Cora watched Valerie climb from Billy's dark-blue truck. Valerie waited while Billy locked the truck, then, cane in hand, rested her left hand lightly on Billy's arm. Billy stared for a moment at the other cars in the lot, then turned his attention back to Valerie.

Cora and Cisco followed Billy and Valerie up the same trail they hiked before. Valerie swung her cane from side to side; the uneven surface seemed to pose her no more difficulty than it would to a sighted person. Cora caught Cisco's eye and nodded at Valerie, then stumbled, even with a trekking pole in each hand. Cisco grabbed her arm to prevent her fall.

She chuckled. "Valerie does better with no eyes than I do with two reasonably good ones," she whispered.

"Wonder why she didn't bring the dog," Cisco whispered back.

"Corky would have been more of a distraction than a help out here," Valerie called over her shoulder.

Cora laughed again. "You weren't supposed to hear that."

As the woods closed around them, Cora lost sense of the outside world. Her mind was on potential outcomes. Would today's excursion reveal more bad news or, worse yet, accomplish nothing?

Their footfalls made soft hollow sounds on the spongy, newly thawed surface, punctuated by the occasional tick of Valerie's cane or Cora's poles striking stone in the hushed atmosphere.

"Good thing Frannie didn't come. With her fear of ghosts, this silence would be driving her batty," Cora whispered.

"Why are we whispering?" Valerie asked.

"Situation just seems to call for it," Cora said. "Don't you feel it?"

"I guess." Valerie sounded doubtful.

They came around a curve where their path ended ahead at a cross trail going west toward the clubhouse site or east to the farm. Billy stopped abruptly and touched Valerie's shoulder. He turned to Cisco and Cora with a finger to his lips and gestured toward a man walking hurriedly some distance ahead. Cora saw the man glance over his shoulder before taking the clubhouse branch and vanishing. He gave no sign of having seen them and hadn't looked directly at them.

Billy was clearly alarmed. "That's Petey!" he whispered. "That must have been his car in the lot after all. What's he doing out here?"

Cora raised her eyebrows at Cisco, surprised by the size and vigor of the man she had only been told about.

Valerie's face flushed. "Don't let him know we're here! I'm not ready!"

"Letting him know we're here should be the last thing on our minds. Remember, he could be the man who attacked Rogers," Cisco said.

"How do we know he didn't see us? He doesn't know who we are, right?" Cora said.

"He's been following us," Billy pointed out.

"Why the hell is he going toward the old clubhouse?" Cisco said, echoing Billy's question.

"He's not just out for a walk. He's carrying stuff—a blanket or something and a white paper bag, like from a fast-food place. As if he's going on a picnic," Billy said.

They looked at each other. "Do we want to come back tomorrow?" Billy asked.

"No!" Valerie said. "I'm not sure I'd have the courage to do this again."

"He's not going to the farm. He went the other way," Cisco pointed out.

Cora reached for Cisco's arm. "We have an opportunity here."

"An opportunity?" Billy raised his eyebrows.

Cisco rubbed his forehead, dragged his hand down his face, and sighed. "She'll want to follow Petey and spy on him. Why not just call Rogers?"

Cora shrugged her shoulders. "Go ahead. You got his cell number. Call him."

Cisco pressed the number into his iPhone. "It's going to voicemail," he said, then after a pause, "Rogers, it's Cisco. We found Petey. Call me."

"He's up to something. He'll get away," Cora said, looking from face to face.

"Cora, sometimes you have more guts than sense," Cisco said. "The man could be dangerous."

"All the more reason to find out what he's up to, so we can protect ourselves." She squared her shoulders, tapping the toe of her brown, leather hiking boot

Billy glanced at Valerie. "Uh, well…I don't think we want to drag Valerie into that."

"No, no," Cora said. "You two should go on to the farm. Cisco and I will follow Petey. If he's spotted us he'll be watching for four people, not two. Whatever happens at the farm, just head back to the parking lot. We'll join you there. We have phones."

Her suggestion was met with silence. She pointed at the brown leather jackets and dark khaki pants she and Cisco both wore.

"We're dressed almost like camouflage, if you put that cap in your pocket." She poked Cisco's red baseball cap. "He's never seen me or Cisco. We're just an old couple taking a hike. We'll keep our distance and just see where he's going so we can tell Rogers when he calls back."

She was anxious to be off after Petey. At last! They were closing in on the person who probably had the final pieces of information they sought. The end could be in sight!

Cisco frowned, shook his head, and then forcefully exhaled. He looked over the top of his glasses at Cora. "No. I'll follow Petey. You stay with Billy and Valerie and I'll catch up with you after I know where he's going."

Cora shook her head. "No way. You're not going alone. We look less suspicious as a couple. Besides, only Billy and Valerie have ties to Emery. He might not show if we're there, like the last time we tried to meet him."

"Cora…," Cisco said.

She stuck her chin in the air. "No. I'm going with you."

~~~

Billy had been worried even before he spotted Petey. Petey wasn't here only by chance. Let Cora and Cisco take care of Petey while he and Valerie went the opposite direction. He had his own problems.

Valerie still insisted there were other explanations for Billy's experiences, such as hallucinations, and she said she was tired of hearing about everything secondhand and wanted to be part of the action. She wanted to be somewhere that had been important to her mother. That put Billy in the role of protector.

But what exactly would he do in the event Emery showed? What made him think the spirit would answer his questions or do him any favors? Emery said what Emery wanted to say; there was no give and take here.

How would Billy get Emery to put mother and daughter in contact? The ghost's motivation for keeping an earthly attachment was sheer guesswork; he had no bargaining chip. Should he mention Mickey's name or Catuara's to provoke a response? What was even possible in Emery's world?

But would Emery's ghost show up?

He could do this. He had to.

"You're awfully quiet," Valerie said, keeping up with him easily as he steered her around obstacles, putting distance between them, Cora, Cisco, and Petey.

"I'm always quiet," Billy replied.

"You're having second thoughts about bringing me out here, aren't you? Well, don't."

"That's not it." He couldn't let her sense his doubts. "I'm just trying to be sure we make the most of any opportunity."

"What could happen? I fall down, and you help me up. Your ghost shows up or he doesn't. I feel some vibes or I don't. All pretty harmless, isn't it?"

"I guess so," he said. But *he* had had the experiences, which put a slant on his hopes and fears she wouldn't understand.

Why did Emery hate Mickey? Did he know anything about Jemma's disappearance or Angelo's death? The ghost had known things he shouldn't, things that happened *after* Emery's death, like Jemma's presence at the farm, which didn't occur until a year later. Billy pictured Emery, surroundings visible through his filmy body, hanging in the air, observing what happened in these woods. He shook his head and grumbled at the image.

"What?" Valerie asked.

"Nothing," Billy said. "Just crazy thoughts."

His gaze scanned the woods for the buildings he should see by now, but he saw only stark and barren trees. As they neared the site, a sense of the unreal possessed him: the silence total except for their soft footfalls, the occasional tick of Valerie's cane seeming muted as if from a distance. The atmosphere seemed to glow and flicker where the day's bright sun penetrated, branches looking sharp in a way that was unnatural. The air was filled with the moldy scent of thawing earth and vegetation.

He stumbled over a moss-covered foundation stone and realized the barn foundation was on his left. He narrowly missed pulling Valerie down with him. She dropped her cane and clutched his arm with both hands. Her face was stiff and pale. Behind her dark glasses he could see her eyelids were closed.

He picked up her cane, needing to pry her fingers open to place it in her hand. She seemed almost unaware of his presence. "Are you okay?"

Her hand on his arm moved slightly. "Yessss." The word sounded like a hiss.

She moved a hand to her jaw and opened her eyes and blinked, appearing dazed. "Billy? Are you here?"

"I'm here."

"I'm so tired Billy. I can't take another step."

She weaved from side to side, appearing about to crumple. Billy wrapped an arm around her waist and glanced about frantically. He saw landmarks—the giant cottonwood tree near a stony pit that could mark the farmhouse ruins and near the cottonwood a large fallen tree. He guided, almost dragged, Valerie there and settled her, supporting her back and head against a large branch. She closed her eyes and went still.

He pulled at his hair with both hands. How could she fall asleep out here? What was wrong with her? Her breathing was slow but seemed normal. He felt her wrist: her pulse was strong. He shook her gently and called her name. She didn't respond. She was either deeply asleep or in some kind of trance.

Near panic, he looked up to find Emery standing beside him. The pole barn, the farmhouse, the old Buick, all had materialized once again. What was different was that Valerie lay on the ground near the old giant tree.

"Don't worry," Emery said, "your friend is fine. But she cannot be here."

"You did this to her?" Billy said angrily.

"She's fine. She *will* be fine when I leave." Emery waved his arm at Valerie and laughed, seeming unconcerned. "Call it fairy dust."

"But...I brought her here to meet you."

"No, I cannot do that. But why did you *really* bring her here?"

"I thought you would answer some of Valerie's questions, if you met her."

The penetrating stare, the one that had frightened Billy the last time, returned to Emery's eyes. Again, Billy found he could not look away.

"Why should I do that? Who is this Valerie? I don't know her."

"You knew her mother, Jemma."

"The girl Jemma, the one who used to ride Dolly Val?"

Billy sought release from the gaze boring into him. He forced his eyes closed. Think! Emery must be referring to Jemma's horse, Baby—Emery's Dolly Val, like Ted said.

When Billy opened his eyes, Emery was no longer at his side, but instead seated on the porch steps. Valerie still appeared as if she were only sleeping peacefully. He touched her shoulder. She drew her eyebrows together, smiled, and murmured, "Valerie?"

It made no sense. Why would she call her own name? He pulled her jacket collar snugly around her neck and stepped back, torn between his concern for her and the need to accomplish what they had come here for—to find out what Emery knew about Jemma and Angelo. He could think of nothing to do for her now.

Without moving his gaze from Valerie, he moved to the porch, and sat on the step below Emery. The intense stare had gone, and the ghost seemed distant. Man and ghost sat for all the world as if they were having a normal man-to-man conversation.

"Jemma is dead. I thought you could contact her for Valerie."

Emery barked a laugh. "How am I supposed to do that?" His voice was deep and hollow with a faint echo. His *S* sounds were prolonged. Billy shivered. He tossed off thoughts of evil.

Billy clenched his fists and spoke through gritted teeth. "How should I know? Channeling or something? You're the ghost here. I can't tell you how to contact another spirit. I just know we need you to do it."

Emery seemed surprised. "I'm a ghost? Really? So that's why things make no sense…thingsss make no sssenssse."

Billy remembered reading that ghosts can be confused and not understand their state. He tried a different question.

"Listen. You said Mickey Romano and his brother ruined Jemma. How did they do that?"

The mention of the Romano brothers turned Emery's face red and contorted. He waved his arms angrily. "Both brothers no good. The crazy kid brother, he got Jemma pregnant. Mickey sent her to Sicily. She never come back here. The family moved, but Mickey stayed."

"She did come back, with a baby, a couple of years later, but she lived somewhere else. That baby is Valerie," Billy said.

Calmer, the ghost stared into the distance, as if he were thinking. Not only had Emery been dead at the time, but also much of the story didn't happen in these woods. Billy didn't know how Emery could know the answers, but he had to try.

"Years later, when Valerie was still young, Jemma left her family. She said she was forced to leave. We want to know why," Billy said.

"Why should I know?" Emery asked.

"We hope you know."

Emery said nothing for a long while, only stared into the distance. Sitting so close to the ghost, Billy felt cold radiating from him. He shivered again and pulled his hands inside his jacket sleeves.

"Mickey always trouble," Emery said at last, bitterness clear in his tone and expression. "I never shoulda had nothing to do with him. He ignored the rules, always to impress the bosses, act like a big man, boasts…lies."

He fixed his angry gaze at Billy for a moment, then waved his arm again, looked away, and went on. "Mickey takes my farm; then Jimmy Catuara, he takes over the territory, becomes the guy Mickey had to please. But Mickey tells one too many lies, makes one too many bad deals, lies about my Dolly, and Catuara he finally gets suspicious. Catuara puts pressure on Mickey, then Mickey he puts pressure on everyone else. He can't take responsibility for screwups; all the time makes somebody else the fall guy. That's the kind of guy Mickey was. A greedy bastard."

"And Petey?"

"Petey, not a bad man, just a stupid man. Always in trouble and Mickey have to save his ass. Then he kill my Dolly. For that, he have to pay."

Emery jumped up and paced near the stairs. As before, his steps made no sound, but energy seemed to radiate from him; air currents swirled about him. He stopped in front of Billy and waved a finger as a sudden wind struck Billy in the face.

"He pay!" Billy jumped back and winced.

Emery resumed pacing. "Then Jemma leaves; Mickey sends Petey for Dolly Val. Petey takes her outta her stall, she high-strung all the time, he don't know how to handle her. He leaves the gate open, she runs off. She runs to the road, gets hit by truck. I watch her scream until they find a gun to put her out of pain. You wonder why I never rest? I never forgive that *buttagots*."

Billy caught his breath. Revenge for the death of his prize horse. So that was Emery's motivation for remaining earthbound.

Emery captured Billy's eyes with his gaze again. "I make you deal. I get Jemma, you make Petey pay."

Billy wasn't about to promise, feeling like he would be making a deal with the devil. Instead he said, "Why did Mickey care about the horse? She wasn't racing anymore, right?"

The ghost seemed too angry to answer, but Billy remembered what Emery said the second time they met: "Horses are valuable in other ways."

Emery sat down, stared, pointed his finger at Billy, and said, "We have deal."

Although Emery never moved his gaze from Billy, bare twigs began to become visible through Emery and then through the farmhouse. Billy found himself suddenly on the ground; the steps he had been sitting on were gone.

He got to his feet and brushed dry leaves from his jeans. Suddenly Emery returned in front of him, fully materialized again. "You must go!" he said, waving his arm toward the west, wind once again circling around him. "Wake the woman, and go to your friends. Rescue them before it is too late. It is your opportunity to keep your promise to me. My part is done."

"What? Where are my friends? What's wrong?" Billy asked, his heart racing.

"Past the clubhouse, the pond near the lab. Take the woman there. Hurry!" The last word rang like an echo as Emery faded again before Billy's eyes and the breeze disappeared.

"Wait!" he called. "What about Jemma?"

Billy spun in a circle, searching the barren woods, listening for any sound, but all was still and silent in the crisp, brilliant air.

# Chapter 41

Cisco rushed Cora past the former clubhouse site, following a bike path uphill and across a deep ravine. Petey was getting too far ahead.

"He moves pretty good for such a big man. Have to worry more about keeping up than staying far enough behind," he said in low tones.

"His blue jacket is easy to spot. It would be harder if these branches were leafed out," Cora whispered. She waved at the surrounding bare twigs. "He keeps turning around. I don't think he's seen us, though. He isn't walking any faster."

"Shit—he just dropped out of sight! Probably gone down into another ravine. No wonder bikers love this place," Cisco said.

He increased his pace. "Come on. We're going to lose him," he said, whispering despite doubting their voices could be heard at this distance.

A strong breeze came out of the southwest, whooshing through the dry branches and chilling his bald head. Cisco wished for his red baseball cap, crumpled and hidden in his pocket.

"I'm trying, I'm trying," Cora said through gritted teeth, her breath labored. "You know I'm not good with hills."

"You're the one who was so hell-bent on doing this."

"Yeah, I know. Just give me a minute." She rested both hands on her thighs and took a few deep breaths before starting uphill again.

"We don't have a minute. The trail could fork any time."

Cisco was more sympathetic than he let on, though. Cora was reasonably fit, but she had injured both knees years ago. She could walk forever on level ground with her trekking poles, but hills were a challenge.

He caught a familiar spot of blue moving up ahead on his right. When they topped a rise, the trail ahead was empty.

He let Cora catch up.

"Aren't we getting close to where the lab used to be? Where the reactor is buried?" he asked.

Cora reached his side, switched both poles into one hand, and leaned on them. "We should be. I've explored the area on Google Maps. It's different on foot, but near here," she said between labored breaths.

"I saw his blue jacket on the right. He's either taken a fork or gone off trail."

"Just give me another minute to catch my breath. You go ahead. He's got to stop sooner or later and I'll find you. Remember, stay back, so you can just see him."

Cisco rolled his eyes. "You think I don't know by now we're trying not to be seen?" He turned and strode away rapidly, launching into the marching cadence he had learned many years ago in army basic training.

He instantly regretted his sharp words. His reward—read punishment—for humoring her was that, once again, he got stuck with taking the lead. But she'd do her part without complaint.

He followed the patch of blue, bobbing ahead at two o'clock. When he looked for Cora, there she was, poles digging, gamely trudging up another hill. His "quarry" far ahead, his wife far behind, Cisco felt like the ham in a ham sandwich.

At the top of the next hill was a clearing with signs about Argonne Laboratory. He must have just walked through where the buildings once stood. All that remained was a wilderness of grasses and scrub trees.

"Blue Jacket" had gone into woods on the east side of the former lab and was again lost to sight. Cisco hurried that direction, slowed by the need to stay quiet. He reminded himself that Petey could be the guy who had struck Rogers. What if Petey was lying in wait? Maybe he should go back and tell Cora to forget it.

He thought he heard a whistled tune in the distance. Someone was enjoying himself out here.

The woods thinned on his right. He saw Petey clearly now, walking around the far side of a pond. Cisco went off trail, ducked into the woods that surrounded the pond, and picked his way as silently as he could after the man, moving from tree to tree, placing his feet carefully, trying not to move any branches.

Petey kept looking about furtively. More than halfway around the pond, he stopped and set the items he was carrying on the ground.

Cisco ducked behind a cluster of tree trunks. He heard voices, sharp and angry, but could not distinguish words. Petey waved his arms wildly. It looked as if he was yelling at someone on the ground. What the hell?

Thinking Petey's actions strange, Cisco was willing to bet he wasn't up to anything good. He couldn't see the trail from here, and Cora would never know he went off trail. They'd be separated. Petey seemed to have reached his destination.

Cisco cautiously reversed his route. He'd bring Cora back and they'd keep an eye on Petey until Rogers returned his call. He pulled out his cell phone and put it on vibrate.

~ ~ ~

Cora was also puzzled by Petey's behavior. She elbowed Cisco from a secluded spot behind thin-trunked trees that grew closely together.

"He acts like he's talking to someone, but I can't see anyone. Think he's talking to Emery?" she whispered, frowning.

"Strange idea, but why not?"

She shrugged her shoulders.

Petey stopped waving his arms, picked up what appeared to be a gray blanket, shook it out, and threw it down. It disappeared.

"Where did it go? Too bad you didn't bring the binoculars," she said.

"Shit," Cisco said. "Forgot I had them." He reached under his jacket and pulled a small set of binoculars from a case hanging from his belt, raised them, and adjusted the focus.

"What's he doing?" Cora said.

"Damned if I know. Can't see anything on the ground, just leaves. It's like he threw it in a hole or something."

"Let me see!" Cora reached for the binoculars and readjusted them. "He's just sitting there now. His mouth is moving...he's talking." She handed the binoculars back to Cisco, her eyebrows raised.

Petey glanced around again before getting up.

"He's dropping down—there must be a hole there—he's out of sight,"

Cisco said. "Wait! He threw something out—looks like a rope. He's reaching for the bag he brought and taking out two white paper cups...it looks like food from McDonald's or someplace." He lowered the binoculars and replaced his glasses.

"A picnic out here by a hole in the ground?" Cora said. "Talking to himself or to a ghost? This is really weird."

"Bringing food and a blanket to bury in the ground?" Cisco rubbed the back of his neck.

"Shh! He's pulling himself up...and now he's waving his arms again. He looks furious," Cora said.

Petey took a few steps, returned, paced, put his head in his hands, and groaned. Then he pulled some metallic objects from his pocket and dropped into the hole again. After a short time he came back out and fussed with something on the ground. He paced again; his angry voice a persistent distant rumble. Then he raised both arms and yelled, "Fuck!" And he started stomping in their direction."

"Drop down!" Cisco whispered. He sank down and pulled Cora close.

The hairs of Cora's neck stood on end. She pressed herself against the ground, heart pounding. Footsteps approached, rapid, hollow thuds on the freshly thawed ground, rustling through dry grass and leaves and getting closer. She held her breath. He must be almost upon them. She squeezed her eyes shut and tensed, could almost feel the blow she expected from behind. But the sounds passed and then diminished.

Cisco lifted his head cautiously. "He's leaving. He isn't checking around anymore, just storming off, like he's in a hurry."

Cora shook her head, bewildered. "This makes no sense...."

"He's out of sight. Coast is clear—shit!" Cisco said.

"What?"

"How are we going to get out of here? We have to go the same way he just went. We could run into him if he decides to come back. Damn! Why doesn't Rogers call?"

Cora froze. "Let's just think this through...."

"Wish we knew what was in that hole."

Cora lowered her eyes and pressed a forefinger against her lips. "He's gone. We could find out."

Her eyes met Cisco's. He stood up.

"Let me go. You stay here in hiding."

"You're not leaving me out! Besides, I'm the one with the closest thing to a weapon," Cora said, standing up and swinging her trekking poles.

~~~

"Oh…my…God!" Cora said, incredulous.

She and Cisco stared into a large pit between the edge of the pond and surrounding savanna-like woods. The pit had been cleverly concealed with a tarp and leaves.

Muffled sounds came from under the tarp, more urgent than threatening. Cora's pulse raced as Cisco pulled an edge of the tarp away, revealing a dim space beneath. Rogers, on his side curled into a ball, a gag in his mouth, squinted in the sudden light. A gray sleeping bag was thrown over him. His face filled with relief at the sight of Cisco.

Cisco slid into the hole and removed the gag from Rogers's mouth.

"Thank God!" Rogers said. "Get me out of here!"

When Cisco pulled the sleeping bag off Rogers, Cora saw handcuffs around Rogers's hands and feet, the two sets of cuffs joined by a short chain.

"Are you hurt?" she asked.

"Damn right I'm hurt! Cracked my head when I fell in and landed on some kind of heater—knocked me out. My ankle hurts like hell. I think it's broke. The damn handcuffs are digging into it."

"He didn't kill you," Cisco observed.

"God only knows why not. He could have, easily, especially before I regained consciousness."

"I wonder why he didn't." Cisco said.

"I don't think he wants to kill me, more like he can't figure out what to do. I seem to present a danger to him for some reason. He's got a screw loose. He babbles and acts like he's the victim instead of me. Keeps saying I'll find his secret."

Cisco scratched his head. "How can we get you out of these cuffs? Couldn't you have called the station for help?"

"When I woke up, everything was gone—my gun, my phone, my radio. I was cuffed and tied. I was freezing—my head and ankle hurt like hell. He was sitting in here just staring at me. First thing he said was, 'Well, you're alive, but what am I going to do with you?' He sounded like he really didn't know."

"Was that today?"

"Late yesterday."

"And you've been here ever since?"

"He stayed here guarding me all night." Rogers snorted. "I couldn't tackle him, tied up and injured like I was, and he's a big guy. I tried to stay awake, but with two blows to my head I kept drifting off. Whenever I woke up he was moving around and mumbling. Even if I had a plan, which I didn't, there was never a chance to escape."

"Why would he trap you?" Cora asked from the pit edge.

"I don't think he did. I just fell into this hole he was using for some other purpose, God only knows what."

"He just happened to have handcuffs?"

"He used my cuffs and rope yesterday. Went out this morning and came back a short time ago with another sleeping bag, food, and cuffs." Rogers shook his head and then winced. "Ouch! Seems he can't make up his mind whether to keep me and make me comfortable or get rid of me."

"Give me your cell phone, Cisco. I'll call 911," Cora said. She reached over the edge of the pit to take the phone from Cisco's hand and stepped aside to enter the number. She heard pounding behind her and turned.

Petey ran straight at them, brandishing a thick branch in both hands. He would be on them in seconds.

"Cisco! He's back!" Cora yelled.

She looked around wildly for a way to escape.

Cisco pulled himself out of the pit and grabbed Cora's hand and started pulling her toward the woods.

"Wait," she said. Stooping to pick up her trekking poles, she ran with him.

It was no contest. Cora's running days were behind her. Cisco got to the woods. Cora saw him searching frantically for a weapon.

Cora, white-faced, confronted Petey, pointing the sharp end of a pole at him with a shaking hand.

Petey stopped, hands on his hips, looming over her and laughing. "You're not going to use that."

Cora eased away and said, "Try me."

Petey stepped in quickly and snatched the pole and swung it, knocking her second pole out of her other hand. Flinging both poles away, he grabbed Cora's arm. She tried to wrench herself free, then jerked back her leg and kicked him in the shin. He grunted and then tightened his grip. He pulled her face close to his and snarled, "Try that again, I'll hurt you."

Cora stopped struggling. Then Petey yelled over his shoulder toward Cisco, standing in the woods, "And you. You're not going to run off and leave your old lady, are you? Get over here."

When Cisco didn't move, Petey wrapped an arm around Cora, pulled what was probably Rogers's gun from under his jacket, and waved it clumsily in the air. "I said, get over here."

Petey was right. Cisco wouldn't leave her to get help, not knowing how long it would take or what might happen to her. And she had his cell phone. She stifled a sob, not sure if she wished Cisco had gotten away or if she was relieved they were still together.

Cisco approached slowly. Cora knew he'd be looking for a way to take Petey down. The guy outweighed Cisco by at least eighty pounds. *Please! Don't try anything!* she prayed.

"Quit stalling," Petey said. "Down on the ground."

As Cisco lowered himself, Petey drew Cora to him with a sneer and growled into her ear. "You. Get that rope over there and tie his hands behind his back, and then pull it down and tie his feet." He pushed her away roughly. "If you don't know how to do it, I'll tell you. Make it good and tight. I'm going to check when you're done, so don't try anything—it won't work. And give me that cell phone." He grabbed the phone from her and stuck it in an inside jacket pocket.

Sitting on the grass, Cisco glared, his face red, chest heaving, fists shaking. Fighting dizziness and with sweating hands, Cora fumbled with the rope.

A calm voice came from the pit—Rogers, momentarily forgotten.

"Petey? You didn't know what to do with one prisoner. What are you going to do with three?"

# Chapter 42

The experience was disorienting, like a dream that would all be over when she woke.

At least Cora's ankles were free. And her hands were tied in front, unlike Cisco and Rogers who sat on either side of her, their ankles cuffed and hands tied behind their backs. Petey must think he could catch Cora easily if she tried to run—or he could simply take out Rogers's gun again.

The three sat on a log at the edge of the woods that surrounded the pond, Petey on another log ten feet away, facing them. He sat stiffly, his jacket unzipped, arms across his chest, with an angry glare probably meant to inspire fear. Cora thought he was desperate, a more dangerous mental state.

Cora's gaze traveled from the shimmering pond to Petey to the pit on his left. The sun was bright, the breeze mild. It was pleasantly warm, the surface of the pond glistening peacefully, the contrast mocking the dire circumstances of Petey and his prisoners.

Thank God, Rogers had defused the situation. With difficulty, he had convinced Petey to give them a chance to help him out of his dilemma. Petey had paced between the logs, shaking his head, his expression changing from anger to fright to confusion. Eventually he agreed to Rogers's suggestion.

Now Petey probably wanted to be anywhere except where he was. Cora's instincts told her they weren't dealing with an evil person, just a man who was greedy and perhaps stupid, reacting to being caught in a bad place. That didn't mean emotions couldn't ignite in aggression at any moment.

Meanwhile they had bought some time—anything was better than fury and panic. Her heart rate had gone from a gallop to a canter.

"All right, who's gonna start?" Petey growled, staring from one to the other.

"You might tell us what this hole is doing here," Rogers said.

Unexpectedly, the man's face turned red. "It brought back memories… when I was a kid."

A youthful sanctuary? Really!

"So you didn't dig it to trap me?" Rogers asked.

"Ha! You just fell in, you lummox," Petey barked.

"Convenient. But why don't you tell us why you're keeping us here and why you were stalking Valerie and Billy?" Rogers said.

Petey shook his head. "I wasn't stalking them. I just…"

Rogers had told them Petey had been picked up for being a Peeping Tom. A pattern of spying on people…

"You were watching them then. Because Valerie's your daughter?" Rogers said.

Petey blinked. "You know that?"

"Yeah. We know that." Rogers met Petey's eyes.

"I got no one else anymore. I thought…maybe… I wanted family." He leaned a little forward and looked from face to face as if seeking understanding. "I didn't know how to… Then some guy started driving her to *their* house." He pointed at Cora. "They were up to something. I wanted to know what." He stiffened and folded his arms across his chest self-righteously.

Rogers nodded his head. "Sure. You had to watch over your daughter."

Cora admired Rogers's skill as impromptu hostage negotiator, but Petey's forehead was starting to glisten with beads of sweat and he tugged at his hair. If she distracted him, though, she might get into his head, gain his trust, stall for time, and get answers to Valerie's past, all at once. After all, Ted had said Petey wasn't very smart. Surely she was more than a match for him—if she was careful.

And there were three of them against one not-very-bright man.

She glanced at Cisco. His silence and clenched jaw told her he was trying to control his anger. As the most able-bodied person at the moment, he would be feeling responsible for the outcome. She caught his eye and gave a small nod. Would he realize what she was doing?

"You saw us following you, didn't you, Petey?" she said. "You only pretended to leave so you could come back and catch us. Pretty smart."

He smirked. Yes! Her compliment hit home as she intended.

"We were just trying to fill in some blanks for Valerie," she explained. "I bet you could help us with that."

Petey narrowed his eyes and looked at Cora with suspicion. "How did you find me?"

"Ted Vitale, Valerie's uncle, told us you were her father," Cora said.

"Ted—yeah, I remember him. Emery's stable man."

"Obviously you lived out here when Jemma did," she said. "There was some secret about the place, wasn't there? Something to do with the Chicago Outfit, or Jimmy Emery?"

Petey raised his eyebrows, his eyes wide. "You know about Emery? You guys have been busy." He rubbed his mouth with his hand. Eventually he said, "They're all dead now. No harm telling you."

He leaned back, wrapping his hands around a raised knee. A change came over his face. He seemed to actually welcome talking about the past, but she couldn't let her guard down.

"Mickey worked for Jimmy Catuara, and Catuara worked for Emery," Petey began. "That was the chain of command."

At mention of Catuara, she glanced at Cisco, who nodded. Frannie had been right. Cisco realized what Cora was doing and would play along. She hoped Rogers would too. She was afraid he'd want to take the lead.

"Back then this place was ideal for the Outfit. It was still secluded because they hadn't done a cleanup of the old lab yet." Petey made eye contact with her. "You know about the lab?"

"We do," Cora said.

"Okay. So we hid gambling machines and bookie records in the clubhouse when a bust was going down. We'd just haul stuff in, and after things cooled down we'd send it back with only a little downtime."

"We figured something like that. What did Jemma and her family have to do with it?"

"Her father had trucks and two muscled kids to help load and unload."

"Jemma's father was part of it?"

"We didn't give him no choice. Nello, though, he took to the business. Wanted to be a made man."

"What about Angelo?"

"He went along."

She'd drop that line of inquiry for the moment. "So, Ted said you got Jemma pregnant and she got sent to Sicily to find a husband. What did you do then?"

He lowered his eyes and bit his lower lip. She watched his face—this could take any direction.

"Mickey sent me to Vegas. Set me up at the Frontier."

"You were an Elvis impersonator?"

Petey's chin jutted up defiantly. "Eventually, yeah. It paid the bills and attracted women. It wasn't a bad life."

Cora felt Rogers's leg bump hers and glanced his way. He pressed his lips together and rolled his eyes. She felt like giggling but controlled it. Cisco didn't seem to be finding anything humorous. She reminded herself that Petey was wired and unstable.

"You sound hurt. Why did Mickey send you to Vegas?" she asked.

"Mickey was always mad at me for some damn thing. He wanted to take over after Emery kicked, but he had to report to Catuara, who wasn't a guy to mess with. Catuara was blowing up stuff for Capone when he wasn't much more than a kid. Mickey said I made him look bad in Catuara's eyes." Petey fidgeted—his gaze roaming and his legs moving. She couldn't allow him time to think.

"Doesn't seem fair he'd take it out on you. Was it because of you getting Jemma pregnant?"

"That and other stuff. When I lost the letter it was the last straw."

Cora felt Rogers's thigh nudge hers. Signaling her to keep going.

"What letter?"

"From the vet." Petey gave a sigh and seemed to visibly relax again.

"Emery got in trouble with the racing commission, so Ted moved some stock out to the pole barn, afraid the horses would be confiscated. After Emery died, Catuara wanted a toy, like Emery had. He told Mickey to get him a foal by Dolly Val, so Mickey sells him one. For big money."

Rogers cleared his throat. "It didn't turn out well?"

Petey shook his head. "Nope. Dolly Val was sterile. That letter we hid was from some vet the Mob used. He said there was no way that mare could carry a foal. But Mickey, he had to make points with the boss, so he substituted another colt. Told Catuara it was Dolly Val's last foal, he was lucky to get it and that's why it cost so much. Catuara was a happy camper until the colt turned out to be a bust."

"And the evidence of the scam was in that letter."

"Right. Before the scam went down, Mickey told me to hide the letter and not let him know where, so he couldn't get it if Catuara caught on. So me and Jemma hid it in some canyon. Then Mickey had second thoughts and told me to destroy it, but when I went back I couldn't find it." Petey shrugged his shoulders. "I told him what's the big deal, the letter was gone, just what he wanted. He said I'd better hope it never turned up. I think he was pissed with himself for not destroying it to begin with."

"But the letter did turn up," Cisco said.

Petey turned to Cisco, eyebrows raised. "What?"

"It was stuffed in a film canister Billy found at the site of the golf clubhouse."

Petey shook his head. "That letter could of got Mickey killed if it turned up while Catuara was still kicking. Catuara would never stand for being made a fool of, no matter how long after he was scammed."

"So Catuara never found out?" Cora asked.

"No. But Mickey had to manipulate things."

Rogers's thigh pressed Cora's again. "Meaning?" Rogers said.

"In that business, you got to do what you got to do. Everything died down until the mid-seventies; Catuara got involved in more important matters and forgot about it."

"But Mickey did something?" Rogers said.

"Like I told you, they're all gone now. And I had nothing to do with it."

"To do with?" Rogers persisted.

Petey shifted, feeling in his pockets. Cora hoped he wasn't reaching for Rogers's gun, and she stiffened. But it was a false alarm. Petey only heaved a long sigh, his shoulders slumped. Cora guessed the man would jump at any excuse to avoid dealing with the situation they were in.

"Mickey was paranoid…all the time paranoid. But around the mid-seventies, Catuara got pissed at Mickey for something and started looking for evidence Mickey scammed him about the colt. Me, Angelo, Nello, and Ted knew the truth. And Jemma knew about hiding the letter and that Baby didn't have a foal, because she'd been riding the mare."

Cora was confused. "Baby? I thought we were talking about Dolly Val."

"One and the same," Petey said, circling a forefinger in the air. "When the family moved to the farm Ted told her the horse came with the farm and her name was Baby. I didn't tell her no different."

So Ted knew all of this, and had held back parts of the story when Cora and Valerie talked to him. Or, perhaps, his memory had been faulty after all.

"So what did Mickey do?" Rogers asked.

"Nello was working for Mickey by then, so Mickey knew he was loyal. Ted had disappeared in some alcoholic la-la land somewhere I suppose. Jemma was living in the city; she and her husband were running that business Mickey fronted for Sal to launder money or do other favors. Sal was related some kind of way."

Cora elbowed Cisco. "I suspected something like that, remember? Way back when I visited Jemma in Chicago?"

Cisco rolled his eyes, still playing along.

"I repeat," Rogers said, "what did Mickey do?"

"Sal knew nothing, but Mickey couldn't be sure about Jemma, who could expose Mickey's rip-off to Catuara. Mickey had to get her out of the way. I don't know what he threatened her with, but she disappeared."

Cora shook her head. "I'm glad I didn't know your brother. I see why Emery said he ruined Jemma."

"Emery? What do you mean, 'he said'? Emery's dead."

Cora waved her hand dismissively. "You're right, he's dead. Forget it. What happened to Angelo?"

The sun went behind a cloud and a stiff breeze from the southwest hit them. Cora shivered in the sudden cold.

"At first Mickey trusted Angelo. He thought a Chicago cop was an asset for the Mob. But Angelo was loyal to the police, although he never betrayed the Mob in any way—just kept his mouth shut. But after Jemma disappeared, Angelo suspected Mickey and confronted him. I shouldn't need to tell you how that went down."

"Angelo threatened him, didn't he?" Rogers asked.

"Told him he'd better get Jemma back or he'd tell what he knew to Catuara and to the CPD."

"That wasn't very smart on Angelo's part. Mickey ordered a hit, didn't he?"

"He had no choice. You always 'know a guy' in Mickey's business, and with Angelo assigned to the gang projects, it was easy to have him followed and taken care of when the circumstances was right."

"Wait a minute," Cisco said. "If you didn't have anything to do with this, how do you know about it? Weren't you in Vegas in the mid-seventies, when all this happened?"

"Came back in 1984 for Mamma's funeral. Mickey and I visited the old haunts and talked. I mentioned Jemma, wondered where she was, and he told me what happened. Never saw him again—he died not long after that."

Petey's eyes were shining. Cora was willing to bet it was because he was feeling sorry for himself.

"All right, why did you come back here, then?" Rogers asked. "Why didn't you stay in Vegas?"

"I told you. There's nothing there for me anymore. And I wanted to find my daughter."

Rogers leaned forward, his voice soft. "Why are you holding us prisoner, Romano? How can we possibly pose a problem so important you'd take this risk?"

Petey rocked back and forth in his seat and his expression hardened. It seemed he didn't trust Rogers. "You came out here looking for me—you must have an idea. You think I'm going to spell it out for you? That'd be pretty stupid, wouldn't it?"

"Not as stupid as taking three prisoners—one of them an officer of the law—and then not knowing what to do with them."

Petey leaned forward, his legs wide apart, jabbing a finger at Rogers.

"You know, I've had enough. You told me you'd find a way out of this situation. You're all playing me. This is a fucking waste of time!"

He pounded a fist against the log, then jumped up and started pacing between the pond and where they sat. His hand went into his pocket again, and Cora thought, *Gun!*

She jerked backward and exchanged frantic glances with Cisco and Rogers, wracking her brain for something to calm down Petey. Were they all going to die right here?

It was Rogers who spoke. "We were just getting to that, Romano. Sit back down and we'll get right to it. We can't think straight with you stomping around like that. We'll all brainstorm this now that we understand you better. There has to be a rational way out of this and four minds are better than one."

Despite the rock in her stomach and shaky limbs, Rogers's words impressed Cora. She tried to control her rapid breathing and pounding heart.

"Don't tell us your secret," Rogers continued. "We don't need to know that. But first, it's getting cold. No reason we should all suffer. Why don't you build a fire—start with that branch you were carrying before. There's plenty of tinder about to get it started." Rogers grinned pleasantly. "I'd do it, if you untied me."

Petey sneered. "Fat chance!" He kicked debris from the ground into a pile directly in front of his captives. Cora was sure he was intentionally raining dust and other debris on them to demonstrate his control over them. She covered her face with her arms to keep the dust from her eyes.

He lifted the thick branch and brandished it over his head. Before he could throw it on the pile, Cora heard a hissing sound accompanied by a loud roar and a green flash. Petey dropped the branch and went windmilling forward, thrown into the air to land stunned, twitching, and unconscious on the ground at their feet.

Simultaneously the dry grass behind them burst into flame.

# Chapter 43

*You must go!* the rematerialized Emery had said. *Wake the woman, and go to your friends. Rescue them before it is too late. It is your opportunity to keep your promise to me. My part is done.*

*What? Where are my friends? What's wrong?* Billy had asked.

*Past the clubhouse, the pond near the lab. Take the woman there. Hurry!*

The ghost's words replayed in Billy's head as he and Valerie rushed along the path they had taken earlier. Jimmy Emery's ghost had never lied to him. If Emery said Billy's friends were in danger, it must be true.

Emery's words implied that Petey was the cause and that Billy was the one who had to rescue them. And bring Valerie. The reason was unknown, but in any case there was no time to take her to safety.

He'd tried to reach Cisco on his cell phone, but Cisco hadn't picked up.

So Billy had rushed to Valerie's side. "Valerie," he said, touching her cheek. She turned her face toward him with a smile but didn't speak. He shook her arm gently. She startled awake; her eyelids behind the dark lenses flew open. "Billy?"

"Yes, it's Billy. You're safe, but we have to go, quickly. Cora and Cisco are in trouble." He didn't want to alarm her, but he couldn't keep the fear and urgency out of his voice.

Valerie struggled to a sitting position groggily and placed a hand on her forehead. "Where are we? I don't want to…let me go back to sleep… I wasn't done—"

"You can't. We might be too late. We have to go right now. Hurry."

She held her head in both hands and rubbed her temples, then felt around for something. Billy handed her hat to her and she put it back on.

"How do you know? Did Cisco call you?"

"No, Emery told me."

Completely awake now, her face froze. "Emery told you. He appeared? He told you to rescue Cora and Cisco?" She shook her head. "Come on, Billy. You expect me to believe that?"

"I trust him, Valerie. You just have to come with me, now. We can talk on the way."

"Do I *have* to go with you?"

"I'm going. Do you want me to leave you here?"

She frowned and started to push herself up. "Where's my cane?"

He took her hand, helped her up, and handed her cane to her.

He couldn't blame her—waking her with crazy-sounding instructions from a ghost she didn't believe he saw. But he had to give her credit. Once they started back down the trail she did her best to hurry. But it was still much slower with her in tow than if he could trot back alone.

"Just let me know when I have to avoid something," she said. "I'm going to be trusting you instead of my cane." She tucked the cane under her left arm, her right hand below his elbow.

"Can't you just call for help?" she asked.

"I tried. Cisco didn't pick up. Who else would I call? And tell them what? That we're out in the Palos Woods and our friends are following a suspicious man? Or maybe that a ghost told me they need rescuing? I'd call Rogers, but Cisco couldn't reach him earlier. Maybe he's called back by now."

"Okay then, tell me again why we have to go?"

"Because Emery said I'm the one who has to save them."

"And you believe him"

"I *do* believe him. Yes."

Valerie's breathing was labored and she stopped talking. He slowed his pace a little, realizing she was concentrating on every step, placing each foot carefully. It had to take considerable effort. She wasn't about to let her blindness defeat her.

He had doubts, though—not about what Emery said, but about his ability to carry out what he had to do.

First, he had to find Cora and Cisco. Emery's directions were vague:

by the pond near the lab, past the clubhouse. The lab had to be the old Argonne site, less than a quarter mile northeast of the clubhouse. He'd go where the clubhouse had been, then follow bike trails north or east. Once he got to the lab area he'd look for a pond. Hopefully, he'd find it in time.

And when he got there? What sort of danger did he face? From Petey or some other situation his friends had run into… He had to protect Valerie too. Billy wasn't a physical match for Petey. There could be weapons involved, and he had none. He'd have to figure it out when he got there.

When they came to the place where Billy and Valerie had separated from Cora and Cisco, they started up a gradual incline. The trail widened with moss-covered flagstones here and there on both sides. The stones must be remnants of what once lined the entrance to the golf course. He watched for a weapon along the trail. A rock? Too heavy to carry. A short piece of rusted rebar? That could do. He picked it up and tucked it into his belt.

*It is your opportunity to keep your promise to me. My part is done,* Emery had said. What the hell did that mean?

*I make you deal. I get Jemma, you make Petey pay.* That must be the promise. But what had Emery already done? There had been no contact with Jemma, no answers revealed about her life. Yet Emery expected Billy to punish Petey in some way.

Billy's stomach was in knots.

Valerie's hand tightened on his arm as they stepped over a mass of roots crossing the trail. He wanted to put his hand over hers and squeeze it to reassure her, but he chickened out. Would he be able to keep her safe during whatever crisis they were racing into? He felt guilty for dragging his vulnerable friend into trouble, but intuition told him she had to be a part of everything that happened from now on.

"This is where I saw the clubhouse," he told her, quickening his pace, "where I picked up the film canister."

"Or where you imagined the clubhouse when you found the film canister," she said.

He slowed a little. "We're about halfway. After we swing right, we cross a ravine, then uphill again. Are you doing okay?"

"I'm fine," she said. "Let's get this over with."

"It's wide open here, but the ground is a bit rocky."

"Thanks. I'll need to concentrate then."

Her lips moved silently and rhythmically as they proceeded.

Rushing up and down hills and ravines, they took branches and intersecting trails to the north or east, moving as rapidly as they could across the uneven terrain. Over their soft footfalls, echoing eerily on the earthen trail, Billy thought he heard Emery's voice. "Hurry," the voice said, a distant rumble. He stopped.

"Did you hear something?" he asked Valerie.

"Like what?"

"A voice. Somebody…"

"No. Nothing like that. Maybe an airplane."

They went on and came to a treeless area near the top of a hill.

"There's a clearing here and some signs." They approached a waist-high information sign. "We're in luck. Here's a map of the old Argonne site—it shows a pond nearby. It must be where Emery wants us to go." Valerie rested both hands on the sign, panting, while Billy studied the map.

"The pond is just east. Stay here. I want to read that other sign."

He was back shortly. "Great. That one shows the current trails. The pond is still there, just to the right. It's close."

Valerie tucked her cane back under her arm and straightened.

"It's so close, we'd better stop talking," Billy said. "Walk as quietly as you can."

They continued for a distance without speaking. The trail was strangely silent, increasing their awareness of the slightest sound and the musty scent of awakening vegetation, magnifying the soft thuds and whispers of their feet. Soon they came to a pond on their right.

"Here's the pond," Billy whispered in her ear. "I don't see them. Maybe they went around it to the other side."

Valerie nodded. "If they're here…"

"The pond is surrounded by deep grass and then woods. Can't tell if there's marsh or rocks under the grass, so we'll stick to the woods."

After circling the pond a short distance, he saw people on its far side. It must be Petey, Cora, and Cisco. No, there were four people, three sitting on a log and another large man across from them. That must be Petey.

"I see them," he whispered. "But there are four people. They look like they're just talking. I'm going to leave you here and get closer. I want to know what's going on before I approach them."

Nearby was a cluster of trees where Valerie wouldn't be seen. After settling her on a fallen log, he said, "Stay still and quiet until I get back." She nodded her head and squeezed his arm.

His soundless footsteps were careful and slow to avoid rustling leaves or snapping twigs. He stayed out of sight, creeping from tree to tree as his Potawatomi father had taught him long ago when hunting in the north woods.

Nearing the group, he recognized Petey sitting alone on a log. Across from him on another fallen tree were Cora and Cisco, and the third person was Rogers. They were leg to leg, hands behind their backs, feet close together. They seemed uncomfortable, rigid. Prisoners, he realized. No wonder Cisco and Rogers hadn't called back.

He sneaked closer, dropping to the ground, crawling on hands and knees, until he reached a sheltered spot about thirty yards away. He could hear the drone of voices now, but the conversation was unintelligible until Petey began to wave his arms and yell. Even at a distance Billy could feel the tension. He made out, "…I've had enough…a fucking waste of time!"

Petey slammed his fist on the log he was sitting on and then jumped up and stomped wildly in front of his captives.

Cora jerked backward, leaning behind Cisco. Cisco and Rogers leaned forward and said something, but Petey didn't appear to be listening. He moved toward them and started kicking dry grass, twigs, and dirt at his prisoners.

Cora, between the two men, winced and pulled up her arms to cover her face. Her wrists were tied.

Billy stood up and stepped out of cover. Unseeing, his back to Billy, Petey picked up a heavy branch from the ground and swung it over his head, advancing. He was going to attack!

Billy's anxiety reached the boiling point. He was transported to another time and place, another body of water, this time a river, another person dear to him in danger. Billy had been injured on the ground that time, but he was still able to gather the power to save her. He knew now Nick had been right in his impression of last year's tragedy.

As if no longer in control of his actions, both Billy's arms swung upward, pointed toward Petey, and from his fingers flew something that looked at first like lightning but went on and on—a vibrating, pulsing thing, a flashing, flickering bolt, greenish in color. It ran from Billy's hands to Petey's back, like a force that connected the two of them for a moment. It threw Petey into the air and dropped him in an unmoving heap at the feet of his captives. The force continued, hissing and roaring now, a flashing ball of green light, into the dry grass beyond, which burst into flame.

# Chapter 44

For a moment, Cora was too stunned to move. Then a fiery twig popped loudly. Everyone sprang into action.

Cora, Cisco, and Rogers leapt to their feet. Rogers leaned over Petey. Cisco hobbled forward. "Jesus, Billy! Am I glad to see you!"

Cora turned toward the fire behind them. Fifty feet away was a carpet of flame, crackling and rumbling, devouring dry grass and leaves. Smoke filled her nose. Already tendrils of flame were creeping up nearby tree trunks and igniting dry vines that wound around them, and sparks could be seen rising off smoldering dead trees. She thought the fire would soon be out of control.

They had to get away and get help. She turned to Cisco, who was staring at Billy.

Billy slowly dropped his arms and shook his head violently, as if trying to wake himself. He took a step, paused, and took another step. His eyes met Cisco's for a moment. Then he ran to the unconscious man on the ground.

"Is he…what did I…oh, my God! It just happened!" he said. He grabbed Petey's shoulder, attempting to roll him on his back.

Rogers said, "Get the handcuff key. In his pants pockets. He had a knife too."

Rogers's tone seemed to calm Billy. Hands shaking, he emptied Petey's pockets onto the ground.

"There—the single key, the knife, and the phones," Rogers said. He turned and exposed his tied wrists. "First the knife."

Billy, with fumbling fingers, sliced the rope binding Rogers's wrists.

Rogers took the key and unlocked the cuffs on his ankles. "Now give me my gun."

Cora felt as if she were watching the scene instead of living it.

After freeing Cisco and Cora, Rogers dropped beside Petey. Cora knelt next to Rogers. "We can't leave Petey here to burn, no matter what he's done," she said, glancing at the fire over her shoulder.

Billy moved from foot to foot, staring and rubbing his hands together.

Cisco's eyes widened as he caught sight of the fire. "I think we'd better get out of here."

Cora felt Petey's chest. "His chest is moving. He's breathing."

Rogers placed two fingers on Petey's neck. "He has a pulse. It's fast, but it's strong. Maybe he banged his head when he landed."

"He's not dead then," Billy said. He clutched his chest. "Are you sure? Is he...is it because...did I...? Oh, God!"

One look at his trembling chin told Cora the idea of injuring Petey was awful to Billy. She had only seen the green flash and Petey landing near her feet. If Billy caused this, was it purposeful or accidental? Or perhaps it had nothing to do with Billy and everything to do with Emery.

Rogers placed cuffs on Petey's wrists and patted him down. "No sign of my radio. Cisco, grab one of those phones so I can call the station."

"The fire...," Cisco said again, pointing at the blaze. "It's getting close..."

Rogers looked around. "It's turning into a wildfire. We've got to take Romano with us. Give me some help here."

Cisco and Billy grabbed Petey by the shoulders and dragged him closer to the water's edge, away from the immediate area of the fire.

Rogers tried to follow them. "Ahh!" he yelped, almost falling. He caught himself and hopped after them on his left leg.

Cora started to pick up some of Petey's cash that was blowing across the ground and then stopped, feeling foolish. She picked up one of her trekking poles, used it to hook a sleeping bag from the pit, and started beating at the burning grass.

Cisco grabbed her arm. "Stop! If that bag catches fire you'll get burned."

She couldn't stop. Billy jumped into the pit, grabbed the other sleeping bag, and started flailing at the fire beside Cora. The odor of burning grass and leaves gave her a sick feeling in her stomach, but fortunately the smoke was drifting away now instead of toward them.

With two of them beating at the flames, they were able to prevent further spread, but they made no headway on the main part of the blaze.

Cisco took the phones, grabbed his, and used his thumbprint to waken it. "Shit, piss," he said. "It's not working. Must have broken in the fall or gotten fried or something." He tried another phone. "Same thing," he said. He slammed the phone to the ground in frustration.

"That one was mine," said Rogers, watching it land. "The last one must be Romano's."

Cisco was poking at the phone randomly. A chirp sounded. "Thank God, this one's working, if I can just…I need an ID."

"Try his thumb," Rogers said. Cisco bent down and pressed the unconscious man's right thumb against the home button and then his left thumb.

"Nothing," he said.

"Try 911. It should work even if it's locked," Rogers said.

Cisco did. "Nothing. Damn. Don't you carry a radio or something?" Cisco asked.

"He must have taken it away this morning."

"Goddamn it! What now?"

"This isn't working," Billy called, flailing furiously at the flames. "It's spreading!"

Billy dropped the sleeping bag and tried his cell phone. He couldn't get reception either.

"They worked before," Cisco said.

"It's erratic out here. We're deeper in the woods," Rogers said.

Cora had a sudden thought. "Where's Valerie?" she said.

"Valerie!" Billy said. "Oh my God!" He dropped the sleeping bag and ran off in the direction from which he'd arrived.

"Billy!" Cora yelled after him. "We need you! What the hell!"

Rogers had a panicked look on his face. She went cold. Their situation must be dire if Rogers was losing it.

A large, heavy man, unconscious on the ground; Rogers unable to walk on a broken ankle; Billy run off to God knows where… Only she and Cisco to get help before the fire reached the two injured men. Leaving them behind was not an option.

She remembered her trekking poles, retrieved both of them, and gave them to Rogers. "Can you manage on these until we get clear of the blaze?" she said.

Rogers looked relieved and calmer, but still doubtful. "I'll try. What direction is the wind?"

Cora stared into the woods. The fire's intensity seemed to be increasing as it spread. She felt her legs heating up and imagined her shoes and pants about to ignite. They would be forced into the water soon.

"The grass fire is spreading in all directions. The smoke—and the main fire, I think—is moving away from us, deeper into the woods." She looked around to get her bearings. "Northeast."

"Bad for the woods, good for us," Rogers said. "We're going the other way, south and then east. We can go back the way we came. We won't have to outrun the fire, using the trail we already know."

They exchanged glances.

"I'll do my best with these poles," Rogers said. "But you two are going to have to drag this guy. Get that tarp and pull him on it."

Cisco retrieved the tarp. They rolled Petey onto the makeshift sled.

Rogers checked the cuffs on Petey's wrists. "Better safe than sorry," Rogers said. "He could wake up or he could be faking it."

"Why not put his arms inside the jacket instead of the sleeves? Like a cocoon?" Cora suggested.

"Good idea," Rogers said, fastening the cuffs in front of Petey, then zipping the jacket over his arms. "Let's go."

Cora didn't expect an easy task, and it wasn't. The tarp slid well over the grasses, but still required a lot of exertion to pull the heavy man. She put her all into the effort and watched Cisco closely. "Don't push yourself too hard," she said, her own chest heaving.

"I'm fine, Cora."

"You're sure?" She couldn't get his four cardiac stents out of her mind.

"I told you, I'm fine," he said through gritted teeth. Was he angry or exerting himself too much? She tried to take an even bigger share of the weight.

What would happen when they reached the dirt and gravel trail? And when they had to go up those hills? *Oh God, please send us help before we get to a hill. Tell me what I can promise you, God. I'm too busy to figure it out at the moment, but whatever it is, I'll do it.*

Rogers maneuvered on Cora's poles with difficulty. She had been on crutches after a knee injury and knew it was the handgrips that took the body's weight. Trekking poles, held at the top, wouldn't take enough weight off Rogers's ankle. He winced with every step, but he managed to keep up with them.

When they got far enough from the fire, they could stay put and send Cisco for help. If only Billy hadn't left.

As they rounded the pond, the scent of smoke faded. Feeling encouraged, Cora took a deep breath. Then she saw Billy running toward them.

"She's waiting for us on the trail," he said, panting.

"Valerie?" Cora said, realizing that's where Billy had gone.

"Yeah."

"Wondered where the hell you went," Cisco said.

"Shh, Cisco," Cora said. "We're all here now."

They changed positions. Billy and Cisco pulled Petey. Rogers leaned on Cora's shoulder, her arm around his waist, with both poles in his free hand. This worked better, but it was still ten minutes until they joined Valerie.

"Petey—my father—how is…?" Valerie said.

"He's not conscious, but his pulse is strong," Cora said. "We have to get out of here and get help."

Valerie pressed her lips together and nodded.

They changed positions again. Cora supported Rogers on her left with Valerie holding her right arm. Billy and Cisco continued to pull Petey.

"The rough surface is tearing the shit out of this cheap tarp," Cisco said before long. "It'll be nothing but shreds pretty soon."

"Let's get as far as we can," Cora said. "Then one of you two can go for help."

As she finished saying this, a gust of wind struck them. "Damn!" said Rogers.

"What's the matter?" Valerie said.

"The wind. It's shifted and gusting, coming from the northwest now," Rogers said.

Billy and Cisco looked alarmed. Cora soon realized why.

"What?" Valerie said again. "What's that sound? It's not rain, is it? I don't feel rain."

Now Cora heard it too. It did sound like rain, but with sizzles and crackles, accompanied by an underlying rumble.

And then she smelled smoke again.

~~~

"If only it were rain," Cora said. "The wind is blowing the fire right at us now. It's behind us. There isn't a worse place we could be."

"She's right," Rogers said. "We can't go back, and we can't stop. We have to run in front of it and pray it doesn't catch us."

At that moment Petey coughed and rolled off the tarp. He struggled into a sitting position but couldn't get any further. He wobbled from side to side.

"Romano? Can you hear me?" Rogers asked.

Petey stared around blankly. He moved his mouth, but no sound came out.

"The right side of his face looks like it's drooping," Cora said.

"See if he can hold up his right arm," Valerie said.

Rogers removed Petey's jacket and cuffs. Cora and Valerie moved to Petey's side, and Cora lifted Petey's right arm. It fell back to his side when she let go.

"Petey, look at me," she said. He turned his head in her direction. "Do you know where you are?" she asked.

"Uhhh…," was all he said.

"He might have had a stroke," Valerie said

Valerie put her hand on his right foot and told him to push. He did. She repeated with the left foot and got the same result.

"He can move his legs," Valerie said. "See if you can get him up so you can support him instead of dragging him."

Billy and Cisco got Petey on his feet, supporting him with an arm around each side. They moved him forward—head hanging, arms dangling. It was easier than dragging him but not much. They started down the trail, Cora with Rogers and Valerie following Billy, Cisco, and Petey.

Cora glanced behind. She could see flames on the ground on both sides of the trail licking at dead trees, sparks floating upward, clouds of smoke rising. The wind had increased, and the sharp, acrid odor of burning leaves filled her nostrils. She coughed.

"Here's that gully we crossed," Billy said. "Once we're on the other side we're near the clubhouse site. Less than a half mile to 107th Street."

"Maybe the gully will stop the fire, like a windbreak," Rogers said.

They descended into the gully and struggled up the far side and then turned to watch hopefully. The fire slowed as it descended the slope, but the dry foliage that filled the ravine caught with a whoosh that raced uphill.

It was like videos Cora had seen of a flash flood, only it was fire instead of water that filled the ravine. They rushed from the edge of the gully and down the dirt trail, flames alarmingly close, heat blasting at their backs.

If only Cora could run ahead—but she could not leave the others to struggle on their own. She blessed the forest preserve staff that had improved the trail. The grasses that lined both sides reduced leaf litter and would prevent rapid spread across their path and through the woods. If worse came to worse, it would be like traveling through a tunnel—a pretty damn hot tunnel!

Just as she had that thought they were engulfed not by flames but by clouds of billowing smoke. Coughing and choking, she lost contact with Valerie and Rogers; her eyes burning and tearing, she was blinded, standing in confusion, sense of direction lost.

"Which way? I can't see the trail," Cora said, rubbing her burning eyes, taking a single step, and then doubting it. She tried to feel the wind, knowing it was blowing out of the northwest. But she felt only heat, confusion, and panic.

"I can't tell where the trail goes! Can anyone see it?" Cora asked. She fell into a fit of coughing. She heard coughs and panicked breaths all around her.

"Cisco!" she cried.

"I'm here," Cisco said in a choked voice.

Then she heard Valerie's voice.

"This way," Valerie said, pulling on Cora's arm. "Follow me."

Hearing the confidence in Valerie's voice, she grasped Valerie's hand and reached for Rogers.

Valerie said, "We've got to stay together. Make a chain. Cisco, put your hand on Rogers's shoulder. You and Billy bring up the rear with Petey."

Cora prayed that Valerie knew what she was doing.

She felt Valerie swaying from side to side and realized she was swinging her right arm and cane in front of her.

"We go to the right here," Valerie said. "Pull a piece of clothing over your nose and mouth. Do it now. Breathe slow and easy. Count with me. It will help you focus."

Cora heard the others arranging themselves. She coughed and wiped her eyes with the back of her hand, but they burned so badly she couldn't keep them open. She fumbled her jacket up over her nose, then reached for Valerie's hand and squeezed it before holding her arm out again.

Valerie took Cora's arm. "Let's go now. This hill is gradual, and there are no turns. There's a big tree root across the trail when we get to step forty-eight. Now, one, two…"

Cora was amazed. Valerie must have memorized every step, every curve and obstacle on the trail, on her way to find them with Billy. And the skills she had developed for emergency situations when she worked as a nurse hadn't been lost.

When they reached a count of 144, Valerie stopped. The roar of the flames sounded closer. Cora could feel the heat, and, despite covering her nose, it was getting harder to breathe. She heard coughing and gasping behind her. Was it Cisco?

"Let me confirm." Valerie swung her cane widely. "The trail should branch here." She stepped away. Cora dropped Rogers to keep a hand on Valerie's back as she went from side to side, measuring the width of the trail, searching for a curve on the left. She found it and selected a new direction. The group reformed their chain.

Completely disoriented, Cora hoped they weren't heading back into the fire. She was more than willing to let Valerie take the lead. In fact, anyone, so long as *she* didn't have to do it.

Another severe coughing spell behind her—Cora was pretty sure it wasn't Cisco. If it was Petey it might be even harder for Cisco and Billy to walk him out. She wished she could help, but there was no way. She had to just keep going and trust Cisco and Billy to deal with their situation.

"Smoke rises," Valerie yelled. "If you're having trouble breathing, try bending forward, head down."

It was even harder to walk that way. Cora called, "Cisco, are you and Billy still there?"

She was relieved when Cisco replied. "We're with you."

"What about Petey?"

"We got him."

"Okay, here we go," Valerie said. "There are more rocks on this part of the trail. Place your feet carefully or you'll trip or twist an ankle. We'll slow down a bit. Count with me to eighty-five this time. Let's go. One…"

The sounds, heat, and smoke worsened. When they got to the count of eighty-five Valerie stopped again. This time she held Cora's hand, moving in a circle, searching. Cora heard a dull click of cane against stone. "Found it!" Valerie said. She sounded relieved. "Hold on now. We're almost home free. This is the stone border of the old golf course entrance road. We only have to follow it downhill from here. Four hundred and thirty-two steps will get us to where the road divides, than another three hundred and nine and we reach 107th Street. We're in the homestretch. Ready?"

Was it only because they were near the end or was the heat and smoke starting to lessen? Maybe they would get out of this after all… Cora began to breathe easier, cough less, and she once again glimpsed the others through furiously blinking burning eyes and blurred vision. "I think we're getting ahead of it!" she said.

They didn't have to go the entire distance. Moments later she heard and then saw people on the trail ahead. Two firefighters rushed up to them.

"Man, are we glad to see you!" Rogers said, wiping his free hand over his teary eyes.

One fireman supported Rogers, while the other went to Petey. "We need paramedics here," the man said. He pulled a radio from his belt and spoke into it.

"Let's get the injured into the truck. Hurry up now," one of the firefighters said.

"Yeah," said the other. "The FPD guys are already out here with UTVs and wildland firefighting equipment. Archer Avenue and 107th Street are closed, but the fire's coming this way and we've got to get our truck out. Can't wait for the ambulances."

"How did you know to look for us?" Cora asked.

"Cars in the parking lot had to belong to someone." The man adjusted his helmet. "Who's going to move those cars before the fire gets to them?"

"You're not going to fight the fire?" Cisco said.

"The FPD guys are calling the shots. They're the experts, and they want us to stand by. They're getting it from the back. They've got two crews out there, approaching from Red Gate Woods and Wolf Road Woods. The crews are heading the fire this way, where 107th Street and Saganashkee Slough are natural breaks. That'll take care of it. What about those cars?"

Cora and Billy pulled their car keys out of their pockets. Rogers handed the squad car keys to Cisco.

"Guess Petey's heap will be sacrificed to the fire. Can't say I'm sorry about that," Cisco said.

# Chapter 45

That evening, Billy paced his lonely apartment, too keyed up to relax. He tried to watch television, but his mind kept wandering. He felt empty and a little fearful. Their investigations could be at an end and along with that any reason to hang around Cora, Cisco, and Valerie. He might soon be alone again.

And, after all, what had they accomplished? They had discovered no good news about Valerie's past, and as for Billy's "superpower," he had only demonstrated conclusively that he could not understand or control it.

At least he didn't kill the guy. That would have been hard to live with.

He put three slices of leftover pepperoni pizza into the microwave, but when it was heated he did no more than nibble the first slice while sitting on a stool at his kitchen counter. It was eight o'clock in the evening… not too late. He'd walk off his frustrations and pay his friends Nick and Dawn a visit. He put the remaining pizza back into the refrigerator and grabbed a zippered hoodie from the front closet.

"Come on in," Nick said. "Dawn's out for the evening—a good time for us to catch up. What's been going on?"

During the next hour over beers, Billy told Nick about his search for explanations; his experiences with the ghost of Emery, the clubhouse, and farm; Valerie's family; and the confrontation with Petey that resulted in the forest fire earlier that day. As he was nearing the end he saw Nick looking aside and biting his lower lip.

"You're skeptical and humoring me. I don't blame you," Billy said.

Nick sighed. "There are possible natural explanations, of course, like spontaneous combustion, electrical disturbance in a setting of unusual dryness, or glass litter catching the sun like a magnifying glass. Even paranormal causes have a scientific approach. We can work on it together. But you never found out what Petey was guarding by the pond?" Nick asked. He seemed to be hiding a grin.

Billy shook his head. "Nope. Never did. I know Argonne is a huge place, but I wondered if you had any idea who Petey might have talked to."

Nick slapped his palm on the arm of his chair and burst out laughing. "You're looking at him."

Amazed, Billy stared. "You? I only had to ask *you?* That's too easy!"

"How many scientists do you think there are at Argonne who are experts in freshwater biology and live in Lemont? I'm surprised you didn't come to me right away."

"So what was it? What did Petey find?"

"I knew as soon as I saw the jar that it was filled with jellyfish—freshwater jellyfish. An unknown species, in fact."

*That's right,* Billy remembered. *Frannie found a newspaper article about Jemma discovering jellyfish. Jemma must have told Petey, who remembered and found them last fall.*

"Why would he think jellyfish were worth a fortune?"

"I told him jellyfish, especially mutated varieties, can be a source of enzymes and toxins that could be valuable in medicine or in other ways, and I'd take some to the lab to find out. From then on he refused to tell me where he found them or to believe facts. He only saw dollar signs."

"How much could the discovery be worth?"

"That's what I tried to tell him. We're still running it through the lab, but even if the samples produce useful enzymes or toxins, now that we have some we're growing them in the lab. Harvesting them from that pond you described could make things easier, but the property is part of the Cook County Forest Preserves. Petey would have no rights to anything."

"Poor guy," Billy said, shaking his head and reaching for his beer. "Just like everyone said about him, he always had crazy ideas."

On the walk home from Nick's, slightly tipsy from the beers, Billy's thoughts turned to Valerie. He'd said nothing to her about seeing her again. Their backgrounds, interests, and ages were as far apart as two people could be. Yet, from the beginning he had felt drawn to her, and he sensed she felt the same.

When he had left her at her door he'd said only, "Well, see you."

And she'd said just, "Yes," with a little smile, and then she'd gone into the house.

And closed the door.

Should he ignore his ridiculous attraction to the woman or might she still want to hear from him? Cora had advised him some days ago when she suggested bringing Valerie to the farm, "Ask her." That was simple enough. He could do that.

As he strolled under a streetlamp, the light went out. That did it. It might be time to stop messing around on his own and contact a professional ghost-hunter. He'd think about that tomorrow.

~~~

Maybe Cora was coming down with something, or maybe she had to admit she wasn't as physically strong as she had believed. Whatever the reason, the previous day's events had taken a toll, and she had a bad night.

Exhausted when they arrived home, too tired even to eat, Cisco had fallen asleep in front of the television with a headache. Despite labored breathing and nausea, Cora called Frannie to tell her everything that happened. She then undressed and was in bed by nine o'clock, only to awaken with an upset stomach at two in the morning. She tossed and turned between three bouts of vomiting and coughing episodes, unable to clear her throat. At five she finally fell into a deep sleep from which she didn't wake until after 10:00 am.

Cisco, an early riser, would have been up for hours. She dressed and wandered downstairs where she found a note taped to a kitchen chair: "Be back by ten." It was after ten, but she was only mildly irritated. Cisco often misjudged how long he would be gone. The dreary morning matched Cora's mood and added to it: cloudy, dark, drizzly. She drifted into the living room and picked up a treasured keepsake—glazed pottery, a black panther designed by her uncle. She moved it to a credenza in the dining room. Did it look any better there? Not really. She took it back to the cocktail table and wandered into the den. A layer of dust covered the table next to her favorite reading chair. She brushed it with the sleeve of her sweater. Who cared? The sweater was going in the laundry tonight anyway.

She should be grateful they had survived, but she felt empty after the previous day's disasters. She couldn't think of any new avenues to investigate. Their search could be at an end.

She heard the garage door open and went into the kitchen, taking a seat at the table. Cisco walked in from the garage, took off his jacket, reached for a letter opener, joined her at the table, and began slitting open the day's mail.

His way of sorting mail had never made sense to her. When he finished it would be unfolded and spread over the entire table. She frowned. The movement caused a pain under her right jaw. Touching the area she found a small, tender, pea-sized lump.

"You okay? I tried not to disturb you this morning," Cisco said.

"Yeah. Didn't sleep well. And I guess I'll have to stop procrastinating and see the dentist." She probed her jaw and winced. "A tooth here's been giving me trouble—must have infected a gland."

She sighed. "I'm restless today. Not bored so much as let down. I don't know if anything we've done has helped Valerie."

She picked up the mail that needed handling and stacked it in a single pile.

"Where did you go?" Cora asked.

"I talked to Billy on the phone, then went over to get an update from Rogers."

"What did Rogers say?"

"Petey's in the hospital. He didn't have a stroke after all, just had the sense knocked out of him. Rogers said he had a 'blow to the brain,' but the swelling is going down, and he'll recover."

"And he'll go to jail then?"

"Probably," Cisco said. "Actually, Rogers was the only one who was hurt physically, and he fell in the hole on his own. Petey held us for a while, but we don't know any harm would have come to us. Rogers said he would probably be charged with unlawful restraint and assault for striking a law officer. If they go with minor charges, and Rogers thinks that's what will happen, he'll only get a couple of months or even a suspended sentence. If Rogers asks the state's attorney for leniency, Petey could even just get probation."

"Actually, I hope he does get a light sentence. I feel sorry for him, and I'd hate to think Valerie's father is such a bad guy. She's had it too tough already. So Rogers feels sorry for him too?"

"I guess so."

"And what did Billy have to say this morning?"

"You're going to like this. Turns out your mutual friend Nick is the guy Petey shared his 'treasure' with."

"No kidding! But of course! Why didn't I think of that? What was it?"

"Jellyfish," Cisco said with a grin.

Cora stared. "Jellyfish!"

Cisco went on to describe in detail what Billy had told him.

"Poor Petey," Cora said. "Seems he just couldn't do anything right. Doesn't it seem just like him to think something as crazy as jellyfish were worth a fortune? But how did Billy feel about what he did yesterday? Is he still going to try to meet up with Emery?"

"Emery did show up yesterday."

Her eyebrows raised. "Really? What happened?"

"Mostly just what Petey told us, about the Romano brothers, Catuara, and the scam with Emery's horse. Emery was pissed at Petey because the horse got killed while he was taking care of her. Then he told Billy we were in trouble and where to find us."

"How would he know that?"

"I wondered that too. How do you explain how he knew so much, and why he insisted Valerie be brought to Petey?"

"If his spirit was attached to that spot, maybe he could see what happened there. If you think about it, everything he told us happened there in the woods," Cora said. "Perhaps he thought Valerie could lead us out of the fire."

Cisco lifted an eyebrow. "A ghost that tells the future? Like talking to crows."

Cora wrinkled her forehead. "What's that mean?"

"An old Sicilian expression from my father. Means the information he had was from a supernatural source. Seems appropriate, doesn't it? What I *can* believe is that the horse meant a lot to him, and the way everything went down was a big insult. A mobster, especially a boss, would have felt dishonored. You don't scam a mob boss. It's just not done. The humiliation of ruining Dolly Val's reputation, the betrayal by people who worked under him, the horse carelessly gets killed—he wouldn't be able to rest until Dolly Val was vindicated," Cisco said.

"Do you think Emery caused the fire instead of Billy?"

Cisco shrugged his shoulders. "We'll never know. How did Frannie react when you told her last night?"

Cora laughed. "About as you'd expect from Frannie. Said she 'felt like chopped liver,' being left out of all the excitement. I had to remind her she had wanted no part of meeting up with Emery. Unlike Valerie, Frannie believes in ghosts but is scared to be around them. Said she was glad all the visits to senior housing were done with, as she was starting to feel we were practicing for our own futures. She called Billy 'Lightning Man,' and said it sounded like the Force was with him."

Cisco chuckled. "Sounds like Frannie." He coughed and then caught his breath. "Guess I got some smoke in my lungs too. Never thought we'd be in a forest fire. Never even heard about one around here, even though Lemont is surrounded by woods."

"I checked into that a couple of years ago, after wondering as I was driving down Archer through the woods and hearing about a California fire on the radio. Fires here are pretty easy to control. Trees that grow here don't burn easily. Even dead trees only smolder and burn out. Lightning only comes along with rain and that puts out or slows fires down. There are a few times when it's unusually dry, but forest preserve people do controlled burns and rely on natural barriers like roads and lakes."

Cisco got up, poured a cup of cold coffee, and placed it in the microwave. "Have you talked to Valerie?"

"Not yet, but I imagine she'd like to talk about now. I'll call her."

"Good idea. You should do that."

She trudged up to her office on the second floor. Instead of picking up the phone she turned on her computer and checked e-mails. One that caught her attention was from Sister Mary John, who Cora had met some months ago at the library. Sister John wanted Cora to help her write a history of their convent. It would be a big job, time-intensive and all-consuming. Did she want to tackle that? Of course, she'd only agree to help this time. A voice in her head said, "Right. It's never that simple."

She'd think about it before replying. She should call the dentist about that swollen gland, but she didn't do that either.

She spent a few minutes on Facebook and played a game of solitaire. She headed toward her bedroom to straighten her closet, but stopped, went back to the office, picked up her cell phone, and called Valerie.

"Oh hi, Cora." Valerie's voice was flat, unemotional.

"You sound like I feel," Cora said. "Like, what's it all mean, what's next?"

"That's about it."

Both women remained silent.

"I just wanted to see how you are today—if you need anything?" Cora said.

"I need a clear head. Think I could borrow yours?"

"Not that mine would be any better. Are you alone?"

"Yeah."

"Did you tell Sally anything yet?"

"Not yet. Just said I wanted to talk to him tonight."

"You want to talk things over with me first?"

"That might be a good idea." Valerie sounded relieved.

After another pause, Valerie said, "There are some things you don't know. About yesterday."

"Billy filled you in about what happened to Petey when he took you home, right?" Cora said.

"He did."

"Is it something Emery said or did?"

"No, not that. Something else."

"You were awesome yesterday, Valerie. We wouldn't have gotten out of the fire without you."

"Maybe. Can you come here?"

"Sure." Cora glanced out the window. The drizzle had stopped and the sky was beginning to lighten. "It's supposed to get warm soon. Can you stand to be outside? I'll pick you up and we'll go for a ride."

She rushed to her bedroom to change her dusty sweater, energized by the knowledge that Valerie had more to tell.

# Chapter 46

"It's like yesterday, a lonely spot in the Palos Woods, but without the fear and the fire," Cora said, chuckling.

"I don't know why you wanted to come here," Valerie said, her hand resting on Cora's elbow.

"I'm not sure either. It just felt right for some reason. I hoped you'd feel it too."

She looked around as they climbed the steps from the parking lot and then stepped into Our Lady of the Forest Grotto, a garden at St. James at Sag Bridge. Cora guided Valerie to a wooden bench facing the grotto. She rubbed her hand over the wood; despite the morning's drizzle, it was dry enough to sit. The two women settled themselves a little stiffly.

Cora sighed. Chilly, overcast, but at least there was no wind. Something about this place put her at peace. At her back was the cemetery and church where she had walked with Father McGrath to discuss Valerie's problems. It seemed long ago, but unbelievably was more like only three weeks.

In the car on the drive over, Cora had filled Valerie in on what Petey had revealed before the fire: Mickey scamming Catuara and forcing Jemma to leave home, the Mob "hit" placed on Angelo, and Petey's search for the daughter he'd never known. Cora could tell Valerie was in a pensive mood, but she had only nodded.

"Describe where we are, Cora," Valerie said now.

Cora redirected her gaze as she spoke. "We're facing a large grotto made of irregular, multicolored brown and tan stones. A statue of the Virgin Mary is in a niche in the center, with an angel on either side. We walked down a paver path between gardens. Later in the year the gardens will be full of blooming roses, perennials, and annuals. Today, near the grotto is a magnolia tree with a few open blooms, and there are a few crocuses, but mostly only dried foliage and branches with swollen buds. The parking lot is on our right down the hill we just came up. The rectory is on your left and the cemetery and church in back of us. Past the grotto is forest."

She paused and looked behind her. "To our left is the Sag Valley, and beyond the church grounds, less than a mile behind us, is where the golf course and Argonne were and where the fire was yesterday. There's only a faint odor of smoke here. The wind was blowing the other direction."

"I do smell smoke a little," Valerie said.

Valerie reached for Cora's hand and squeezed it. Her smile faded and she turned her face away. "I feel like some elemental change has happened, Cora, but I don't know what it is."

"I have the same feeling."

"Is this all there is? Am I missing something?"

"About yesterday? I meant what I said about how amazing you were. You saved us."

A corner of Valerie's mouth turned up in a pleased smile. "It's learned ability, plus emergency training from my nursing days."

"Yes, I realized that. I was never so glad to have someone else step up and take over."

When was the last time she stepped back and let another person take control? And felt good about it?

Cora pulled her hand away and slipped her hands into the pockets of her light jeans jacket. The sun broke through the clouds and a slight breeze lifted a few strands of hair from Cora's brow and rustled nearby branches. Their car was the only one in the lot. Birds chirped and called from the woods. Cora's heart rate slowed and her spirits lifted.

"Do you feel it, Valerie? We can talk here."

"That sounds good." Valerie seemed relieved.

Their conversation in the car, under most circumstances, would have been an information overload, but Cora knew Valerie had more to say. She prepared herself for an emotional unburdening.

"What else happened yesterday, Valerie?"

Valerie removed her glasses, slipped them into her purse, and folded her cane, placing it on the bench beside her. She opened the buttons of her navy peacoat and leaned against the back of the bench, appearing relaxed at last. "I don't know what I expected to happen, but it was pretty much nothing. Billy didn't tell you—maybe he thought I'd be embarrassed—but almost as soon as we got where we were going I fell asleep."

"Asleep? That's weird." Cora leaned back too, crossing her arms over her chest.

Valerie nodded vigorously. "Yes. It was. It didn't *feel* weird though. Peaceful, like something good was about to happen, that's how it felt. I was suddenly so tired, overcome with fatigue. I asked Billy to find a place where I could sit and as soon as I was off my feet I conked out."

"So you never met Emery or found out any more about your mother? You must be disappointed."

Valerie shook her head. "It doesn't make sense, but I'm not disappointed. I never expected anything from Emery, but in the car when Billy drove me home he said Emery appeared after I fell asleep."

Valerie may have a more detailed version than Cisco. "Really! Did Billy tell you what Emery said?"

Valerie frowned and shook her head. "I can tell you what *Billy* said, not what happened. I still don't believe in ghosts."

"'There are more things in heaven and earth, Horatio, than are dreamt of in your philosophy.' Is that how it goes?"

"I'm trying to keep an open mind, for Billy's sake. He's a gentle soul and he's been good to me, but I think these encounters are in his mind." A glance revealed Valerie was blushing.

"In his mind or not, Emery's never been wrong, though. We've verified much of what he told Billy."

"Yes, Billy said that too. He thinks his ghost is reliable." Valerie raised her chin to the breeze and paused.

The sun was directly overhead now. Cora reached for the sun hat she always carried, slipped it on, and, like Valerie had done, opened her jacket.

"Let's say for the sake of argument Emery was revealing the truth. Was there anything new?" she asked.

"The conversation was mostly about Mickey, Catuara, and the horse fraud. Do you know about that?"

"Yes, Petey told us."

"Billy thinks Emery haunted the farm, wanting revenge on Petey for letting his horse get hit by a truck. Emery promised to contact Jemma in the afterlife for me if Billy took revenge on Petey. That's what *Billy* said, remember."

"Petey told us Jemma knew about the fraud and Mickey threatened her. Did Emery say what the threat was?"

"No, but I have a good idea."

Cora knit her eyebrows. "Really? What? Why?"

"Because something happened to me while I was sleeping."

Cora twisted her body toward Valerie, their knees bumping. She left her knee against Valerie's.

"I guess it must have been a dream, but it felt so real—about Mamma. When I woke…you know how sometimes a dream is so vivid you feel it, and you feel it so much it stays with you, maybe makes something understandable or clears up a misconception. It can be so strong it changes how you view things? Did that ever happen to you, Cora?"

Cora realized her answer was important to Valerie. "I know what you mean, so I must have." She squinted into the sun and repositioned her hat while she searched her mind, then chuckled. "Once I dreamed about a guy who was really fat. He hugged me, and it felt soft and really good. When I woke up, fat people seemed likable to me, and I ended up being more tolerant of people I used to look down on. Is that the sort of thing you mean?"

Valerie chuckled. "I was referring more to beliefs, but you've got the idea."

"Do you want to talk about your dream?"

"I do. It changed the way I think, not only about my mother, but also about me and the way I relate to people. I want your take."

"Sure. You said it was about Jemma?"

"Yes. Actually, I felt like I *was* Jemma."

# Chapter 47

"It wasn't like any dream I've ever had. At first I didn't realize the person I saw wasn't me," Valerie said, facing Cora. "Then I didn't know who it was. It was like watching a movie, and then someone who looked like my mother turned to me and said, 'Valerie?' It was like I was watching her, and at the same time I *was* Mamma, seeing and feeling what she saw and felt."

Cora understood what Valerie was describing. "I've had that happen too," she said.

Valerie said, "I saw a dark-haired teenage girl. She was crying. I *felt* her sadness, and her anger. She went into a metal barn and came out even more upset. She walked for a long time, through woods, along a road, then woods again. She came to a chain-link fence and slipped through a break. She walked a bit longer and then climbed down into a canyon. She looked and looked, and then she took a little black canister from the canyon wall. She put it in her pocket and left, retracing her steps but then taking a different path. She came to a large, abandoned building with a red roof; she went in, up some stairs, and out onto a terrace. She put the canister behind a loose brick and replaced the brick. I guessed the building was the golf clubhouse and the film canister was the one Billy found."

"So you were watching Jemma hide Billy's canister?" Cora said.

"Yes. It was my mother when she lived on the farm, before she went to Sicily. I felt as if I was sharing something with Mamma; I couldn't tell what: her body or her dream or her memory. I had her thoughts and felt her emotions."

"What were they?"

Valerie turned toward the grotto. "She was thinking, *How could he leave me when I need him the most? I can't have this baby alone.* She wanted to hurt him. And she was scared. Scared to leave her family, to live in Sicily, to have a baby. She worried about the baby too."

The Jemma Cora had known was impulsive. Her immediate reaction to someone who hurt her would have been to lash out.

"She knew Petey's brother Mickey was worried about a big mob boss and suspected whatever was in the canister she and Petey had hid was dangerous to them. If she moved the canister, Petey wouldn't be able to find the letter, and Mickey would be furious with Petey."

Just like Petey had told them. Cora said, "You felt like you were in Jemma's head and understood her."

Valerie nodded and continued. "Just like in dreams, the time and place morphed into somewhere else. This time, Mamma was in a house I'd never seen, a large sunny room, white curtains blowing on open windows—an old building with stone floors. She was smiling and cradling a sleeping baby in her arms. I knew the baby was me."

Valerie paused and smiled. "I felt Mamma fill with warmth and pride, just like I felt when I first held Molly in my arms, like my heart kept stretching and stretching until it could burst. I'd never loved someone so intensely. Mamma felt just like that."

Cora remembered that feeling too, holding her own sons and later her grandchildren.

"A man came into the room. He was short, stocky, with thick, dark, curly hair—very handsome. He spoke Italian, but I understood, because I was Mamma. He said everything would be okay. He would care for my mother and me, and they would have more babies. He said she would learn to love him. He cuddled me, and Mamma smiled. She didn't love him, but she liked him. She was happy and believed everything would be as he promised. Her life might not be what she dreamed, but it would be good."

"Your dream represented how Jemma felt in Sicily," Cora said.

"No—it was more like a *memory* of Sicily than a dream." Valerie's eyes were dry, but she rubbed them for a moment and then went on.

"Another scene change. This time we were in a house with mismatched furniture. I was in a playpen in a kitchen, and Mamma had a huge belly. She was holding a baby girl to her breast, and the same man, who I now realize was Papá, walked into the kitchen. Two teenage girls sat at the kitchen table. Papá started to flirt with one of them."

Cora felt her face grow warm. She remembered that day. She had been the girl Sal flirted with.

"Mamma was angry, but she hid it. She thought Papá was acting rude and wanted other women. Then she felt sad. Maybe he acted that way because she wasn't able to love him as he hoped, and it was her fault. Or maybe he hoped to get rich in America, and instead he was digging sewers and loading trucks. He made good money, but that wasn't his desire. Although they weren't close, he treated her well and she felt bad about disappointing him. However, he was not Petey, and he was not charming or playful or exciting or fun like Petey. Petey had betrayed her, but she still thought about him.

"So my mother pretended she was happy. She was bold and witty like Petey, and everybody thought she was fun to be around. But her pretense was a sham: if Papá felt unsuccessful and unloved, so did Mamma. But not entirely… She had me to remember Petey, and I made her life worthwhile. Some day she would educate herself and be respected and truly happy."

Valerie turned toward Cora again. "That must be when we lived in Oak Lawn. I wish we'd never left there. But the tornado changed all that."

Valerie relaxed against the bench again, her hands resting on her thighs. "New scene again. My mother was in a shop in an old building. The floor was packed with sofas and chairs, with and without cushions; rolls of plastic and cloth; and tools. A short, angry man in a fancy suit stood over Mamma, who sat in a chair in back of the shop. He was yelling at her. 'I set up my wop cousin in business, and you're telling me you ain't got the money again? What kind of gratitude is that? You can't keep holding out on me, I'm telling ya.'

"Mamma was frightened, but gave vent to pent-up anger. She said, 'You're getting the better part of the deal. You promised Sal he'd make a fortune. He kisses your butt every time you come around, while money fills only *your* pockets and what's left barely puts thrift-shop clothes on our backs and cheap food on our table.'

"'Well that's the way it goes, babe,' the man said. 'It's up to you to make the business pay. I did my part, now you do yours.'

"'It's a crap business and you know it,' Mamma said. 'Nobody covers furniture no more—they buy new. You didn't do this for us, you did it so you could launder money in our back room or whatever the hell you and your boys are up to back there. We're never going to get ahead with you giving the orders, only get ourselves in trouble with the bosses or with the law. *If* we continue to keep our mouths shut.'

Angelo had warned Mamma just that week that a big mob boss was asking questions again about Mickey selling him a worthless colt years ago. Mickey wanted to be sure she would keep quiet about anything she knew. She knew Dolly Val, who she called Baby, was involved, and she felt sure the film, or whatever was in the canister she had hidden, was damning. That might be enough to scare Mickey.

"'So what's this? I can't depend on you to keep your mouth shut? Are you threatening me?' he demanded. He raised a hand as if to slap Mamma. She ducked and said, 'If the shoe fits.' And he said, 'What's that supposed to mean?' And my mother said, 'You know Sal and Angelo won't say a word because they're in too deep. But nobody's got nothing on me, and I'm not afraid of you. I don't *want* to tell nobody because I love Angelo and respect Sal, but I swear if you don't leave us alone I may be forced to tell someone about that horse. Someone 'higher up,' if you know what I mean.'"

Valerie gripped her thighs tightly, blinking rapidly.

"The man pulled Mamma off her chair and pinned her against the wall. He yelled in her face, spit flying at her. 'You will do no such thing, and I'll tell you why. That little girl you're so fond of, Petey's little brat…if you love that kid, here's what you're gonna do. You're gonna leave this town, without a word to anyone, and you're gonna disappear. And if you don't or if you ever come back here, you'll regret it, if you know what *I* mean.'

"Mamma was still angry but felt a chill. She wiped her face, straightened her back, and stuck her chin in the air. She said, 'Or you'll do what?' And the man said, 'Or I'll see that my brother gets custody of the kid and you and your family will never see her again.'

"My mother couldn't forget Petey, but knew he was irresponsible and couldn't be trusted to raise the daughter he'd never shown any interest in. She was frightened and her face crumbled. 'You couldn't,' she said. And he said, 'I can and I will. You can be sure I know the right palms to grease to make it happen.' And Mamma was cold all over now because she believed what he said. The man turned around. It was like he had a cape on that whipped around him as he stomped away from her, but he didn't have a cape, it just seemed like he did. A buzzer sounded loudly when he opened the door and stopped when he slammed it. Mamma walked to the chair, sat down, put her head in her hands, and moaned."

Valerie wiped tears off her cheeks with her sleeve, and when she placed her hands back in her lap they were shaking.

Cora didn't know what to say. What an incredible sacrifice that would have been, to know that if Jemma sought to see her loved ones Valerie would be taken away. She would have believed Mickey's threat, and she didn't want her daughter to be raised by mobsters. Somehow, despite it all, Cora knew Jemma had laughed and loved and made a new life.

She placed a hand on Valerie's arm. "It was a dream, Valerie."

But was it really a dream? What Valerie was describing was logical, real—not like dreams at all. It occurred to her that it was more like Emery fulfilling his part of the deal he made with Billy, having Jemma's spirit answer Valerie's questions while she slept.

Valerie's lower lip trembled and she continued in a soft voice, "There was one more sequence or memory, whatever. It was night, and a hot breeze blew through an open window where my mother was in bed with a woman beside her. Soft light from a distant streetlamp cast a few shadows and reflections on the walls. They used no covers. The woman was plain, a little overweight, with thick, bushy, mousy-colored hair."

Valerie rubbed her face with both hands. When she went on, her voice shook but gained strength as she continued. "Mamma was older this time. She wore a short sleep shirt, black with llamas on it, something a child would pick. Her face was haggard, her arms and legs incredibly thin, her skin sagging. Only wisps of white hair covered her head. Mamma was sweating and staring at the ceiling.

"'The air conditioner guy can't get here until Monday,' the other woman said.

"'We'll handle it,' Mamma said.

"'I don't know how you can be so patient.'

"'Do we have another choice?'

"The other woman swore and grumbled under her breath. They were quiet awhile and then the woman said, 'Do you want to talk about it?'

"Mamma smiled and said, 'You can always tell, can't you?'

"'Is it Paula?'

"'I never should have gone to the ER. I could have made an excuse, let someone else draw her blood. I hoped seeing her… I miss them so much, Kathleen.'

"I had figured out the woman was Kathleen," Valerie said.

Cora had realized the same thing.

"My mother went on. 'I thought Paula would talk about them, bring me a little piece of their lives, you know?'

"'She didn't. She only brought you bitterness and pain,' Kathleen said.

"'I never guessed she lost contact with them too.'

"'She wanted nothing to do with her family. I don't even know why she's here now.'

"'I'm her mother.'

"'And that entitles her to treat you like shit?'

"'I can't help but feel her mental problems are my fault, Kathleen. If I hadn't left…'

"'Which you had no choice about, you said.'

"'Yes, but, even before. I think she always knew it was Valerie I cared about, even though I tried to be a good mother to all of them. Maybe Paula would have turned out different if she thought I loved her as much as Valerie. It's terrible not to be able to help her now.'

"'What about Sally?'

"'Sally was independent from the day he was born. He never needed me, didn't need anyone, probably still doesn't. I could have placed food and drink in bowls on the floor like we did for our dog and he would have grown up just fine.'

"Mamma laughed and Kathleen giggled. They looked at each other and smiled. 'That felt good,' Jemma said. Then her face turned sad.

"'Valerie, though, she had Petey's charm and my brains and spirit. I was too hard on her, wasn't I, Kathleen? She was smart and strong, the person

I wanted to be. I pushed her because I wanted more for her than I had, but I was so proud of her. My biggest regret is that I never had a chance to tell her, never got to see her grow into the woman I knew she would be. Tell me she's successful and happy, Kathleen. Please tell me that.'

"Kathleen reached over and wiped a tear from below Mamma's eye. 'Valerie is successful and happy, Jemma. I'd bet my life on it.'

"'It won't be long now, Kathleen. I'm going to die without seeing her, aren't I?'

"'Shhh,' Kathleen said.

"Mamma shivered despite the heat in the room.

"'Don't you leave me, Kathleen. There's been too much leaving.'

"Mamma rolled on her side and rested her head on Kathleen's chest."

# Chapter 48

"Oh my God, Valerie. I don't know what to say." Cora's eyes burned with unshed tears.

Valerie's head drooped and she wrung her hands in her lap. Cora placed an arm around Valerie. After a long moment, Valerie reached a hand up to squeeze Cora's.

Cora gently pulled away, reached into her purse for a handkerchief, blew her nose, and wiped her eyes. A twinge of pain struck her jaw. Yes, she'd have to call the dentist first thing next morning.

She said, "Almost no one uses hankies anymore. But tissues are too irritating. I dug some handkerchiefs out of storage and put them back to use. Cloth is so much better."

"I'll have to remember that," Valerie said.

Cora smiled. Her comment had succeeded in breaking the tension.

"So you believe it too, Cora—that my dream, or whatever it was, tells the truth about my mother?"

"Absolutely. The woman you described is the Jemma I knew. I recognized some of the places and events, too."

"She was a very complex person. I had her wrong, didn't I?"

"Yes. She was tortured in many ways, but she had courage. Her life was awfully sad, Valerie. I can't imagine how you're feeling."

Valerie chewed thoughtfully on a thumbnail, her face calm. "Probably better than what you're thinking."

Cora raised her eyebrows. "Really?"

"Remember what I said before? About how real a dream can be and how it can change the way you view things?"

"Yes."

"When I woke, I didn't want to leave Mamma. For the first time in my life I understood her and forgave her—no, not *forgave* her. She never did anything that needed forgiving. The only thing she did, her whole life, was to live as well as she could under awful circumstances and love her children—love me." She choked on the last words.

"You think your subconscious mind took the facts we discovered, connected the dots, and put it all in a dream?"

"I don't know what happened. It was like I was there, but I wasn't there."

"Does it occur to you that it *wasn't* a dream?"

"What else could it be?"

"I'm not sure what I believe myself. The mind does funny things. Maybe you're right, and Billy's hallucinating. But think about what Billy said, that he made a deal with Emery. Billy would punish Petey in exchange for Emery putting you and Jemma together. Emery told Billy he had already done that. Billy didn't understand what Emery meant—you were sleeping then. If it was sleep… Maybe Emery made it happen."

"You mean Emery put me in some kind of trance and had my mother come to talk to me, like a vision from the supernatural world?"

"Yeah, well…keep an open mind."

Valerie wagged her head.

"And, did you ever hear of dream walkers?" Cora said.

"Sounds like a TV series. Some guy saves people based on his dreams."

Cora laughed. "Dream walking is more complex. A dream walker *shares* the dream of another person, can alter that dream, plant beliefs in the other dreamer's mind, and control their lives."

"You mean I was sharing my mother's dream and that's why I thought I was her in the dream?"

"If she was really desperate to reach you…maybe channeling through Billy?"

Valerie frowned. "How do you know this stuff?"

"Frannie and I did a lot of research when we were trying to find out if I was being haunted."

"So Jemma's watching me from the afterlife or Emery set it up, and she shared her dreams with me so I'd understand her?"

"If you buy into the concept of dream walking, or even the idea of life after death, is it so much of a stretch to think that either explanation is possible?"

"All I know is I believe, based on everything we've learned about my mother, that her life and her decisions were what I saw while I was sleeping. Emery, ghosts, and the supernatural don't have to have anything to do with it. Can't I just have a plain old regular dream that expresses my subconscious? Like the whole purpose of dreams to begin with?"

"There's also that," Cora said.

After a moment both women giggled and then slumped back into the bench, their legs stretched out side by side and crossed at the ankles.

"Regardless of how it happened, Cora, the importance is the effect on me. What really matters is I don't feel hurt, angry, or defensive anymore. We achieved what we set out to do, didn't we?"

"I guess. We're probably not going to discover any more."

"I keep wondering, though—why *did* Mamma stay away all those years after Mickey was out of the picture? Was it because of her relationship with Kathleen? Maybe my mother was afraid to tell us, and when Paula showed up she proved her right."

"We'll probably never know. We do know Angelo was the subject of a mob hit ordered by Mickey Romano. I wonder how the Mob managed to make the snipers take the fall."

Valerie nodded. "Angelo must have made a lot of noise about Mamma's disappearance. And he paid the 'ultimate price.'" She made air quotes.

She paused. "If he had to be killed, at least his death wasn't pointless and random. He tried to make things right for Mamma—for all of us, really."

"So he's a hero—even more than he was before."

"Yes. Sad, but true. And I love him and miss him more than ever."

They sat with their own thoughts for a time. Then Cora said, "Our goal was to remove obstacles from your past so you could live independently and take care of Molly. Do you think we've done it?"

Valerie took a long time to answer. "Whatever combination of digging, talking, or supernatural gobbledygooking just took place, I feel in my gut I know the real Jemma now. I believe what came to me while I slept was what she experienced. It's too fresh to know how much of a change that will make, but I can say that today I feel more positive than I have for a long while."

After a pause, Valerie confessed she was conflicted about getting to know Petey when at some time in the future the situation presented itself. It could make her life easier if there was someone around she could depend on. "He didn't mean to hurt anyone. Seems he had a lot of hard knocks his whole life."

Cora advised caution. "I wouldn't give him that much credit. You may be trying to rationalize your father's place in your life, but remember he was a Peeping Tom. Do you want Molly exposed to that?

"And what about Billy? I thought you two hit it off pretty well. Did he act like he wants to hang around?"

"Billy?" Valerie's cheeks turned red. "Why would a young man like Billy want to hang around a woman my age with all the baggage I carry, not to mention a teenage daughter?"

"Why don't you let him decide that? He might feel differently."

"I'd rather it be his idea. If he contacts me, we'll decide then."

Cora chuckled, drawing up a knee, crossing it over her leg, and holding it with both hands. "Frannie would say this 'new Valerie' is understanding and considerate. The 'old Valerie' wouldn't have felt empathy for Petey or Billy."

Valerie laughed with her. "Now I can't see, I have a lot of soft spots I never recognized when I could. I see a lot differently now."

"So you say you're ready. What's going to be your next step? Any ideas about being an independent woman?"

Valerie faced Cora with a self-conscious grin. "I think so. I didn't want to say anything, until I was sure. I don't know if I'm thrilled to death or scared to death, but I may have a job!"

"Oh, my God! Really! Tell me!"

"Jean, a woman I used to work for, left a voicemail for me a couple of days ago. I hadn't talked to her for over two years, since she left our hospital to accept an administrative nursing offer at an academic medical center. I didn't want to talk to her right away, but I called this morning. She said her hospital had a position she thought ideal for me, if I was ready to rejoin the work force."

Valerie described the position. "The tentative title is director of disability training. I would not only make decisions about how the hospital side adapts to include employees with disabilities but also develop programs for the nursing school in sensitivity training for treating people with disabilities. I'd have an assistant and any technical equipment I needed. She really wanted a person with a high-level disability for the position, but it's been difficult. Not many are qualified educators or nurses. She wanted to know if I was interested."

"And you said?"

"Of course I was interested! I'm going to interview next week, but Jean said the interview is a formality and that after all human resources steps are dealt with, the job is mine for the asking. They're even sending a car to pick me up for the interview and promised to arrange ongoing transportation."

"I wish you could see my face, Valerie. I'm so happy for you." Cora took both Valerie's hands in hers and pumped them up and down.

After a moment Cora said, "You know many of the answers we were chasing were actually chasing us. Petey had already found you and if we had only sat tight I bet he would have revealed most of your past. Even your job offer came with little effort on your part."

The sun moved behind a cloud and Valerie shivered, pulled her jacket together, wrapped her arms across her chest, and closed her eyes, deep in thought. Then she lifted her head and said in a firm voice, "Father McGrath was right. Knowing the truth about my mother and Angelo gives me a sense of release. I think I can learn to depend on others, and I feel better about myself, more confident."

She laughed. "I used to feel out of place around people, especially women. Look at the two of us now, sitting here sharing our most personal thoughts. It won't be easy, but I'm ready to start a new life."

"You're a fighter, Valerie. That hasn't changed."

"You and your friends—our friends—I'm comfortable around people now. I can accept and trust others, instead of thinking everyone's out to get me and trying to get them first."

"You're smiling, Valerie. Do you realize it?"

Her grin got bigger. "I am. I do. I like it."

They sat a moment shoulder to shoulder in silence, and Cora's thoughts turned inward. When Valerie had led them out of the fire, Cora had not only been relieved, but willing, even glad, to step aside and let someone else take over. She, like Valerie, had always believed her way was the only way. Something Cisco had been telling her.

"I'm starting to think you're not the only one who's had a change of view," she said.

Valerie knit her brows. "What do you mean?"

"I got angry at Cisco when he called everyone together the other night instead of letting me make that decision. It bothered me, not because my irritation was *unlike* me, but because it *was* like me. A me I'm starting not to like so much."

"Yes?"

"That night, every one of us confessed secret agendas. But each of us also contributed to solving your problems. If anyone didn't do his or her part, we wouldn't succeed."

"It takes a village, you mean?"

"No, each *individual* was vital to our success. It's different from acting as a group, do you see? Each person has to be free to act on his or her own."

Cora looked at her friend. Valerie was nodding her head.

"It doesn't have to be up to me to do it all, and I don't have to micromanage. Cisco was right—I need to trust others more and lighten my load. If they screw up, what's the big deal? I don't need to be the one to do it; there are other ways to get things done." She chuckled. "Maybe not as good as my way, but still perfectly acceptable."

"What changed your mind?"

"Yesterday, in the woods. Rogers was calm and competent, Cisco showed common sense and quiet strength, I used my wits to distract Petey, Billy tackled a dangerous situation, and you led us out of the fire. Frannie, who wasn't even there, gave us information we all needed when the time came."

"You might say, to strike when the fire was hot," Valerie said, giggling.

Cora giggled too and then turned thoughtful. "You know what I think true friendship is? It's not about strong people supporting a weaker person. It's honestly respecting what each person has to give and allowing them the freedom to act."

"Amen." Valerie raised her palm into the air and Cora slapped it in an enthusiastic high five.

The sun came out again. The two friends turned toward it and basked in the warmth, each pursuing her own thoughts and feeling no need to fill the silence.

~~~

# Afterword

*The Mystery at Mount Forest Island* is based on a real place with some historical figures and events. As in my previous novels, the story and the present-day characters, as well as some of the historical characters, come from my imagination. The background, the locations, and some of the figures and events of the past are real, but the story is pure fiction.

Some years ago I spoke at the Lemont Historical Society on the history of local golf courses. While doing research, I stumbled across one of the first courses in the area, the Palos Golf Course, owned and operated by the Forest Preserve District of Cook County (FPDCC). The course opened in 1921 and closed in the early 1940s, when property in Red Gate Woods was leased by the FPDCC for the purpose of creating a nuclear reactor (the Manhattan Project) under the direction of the University of Chicago. This led to creation of the atomic bomb. Because the property was adjacent to the golf course, the top-secret nature of the project mandated closure of the course.

Hearing about my talk, David Harris contacted me through the historical society, wanting to compare notes about the old golf course. Dave and his sister Sandy, who accompanied him when we met, told me about their days as children living in the Palos Woods in a farmhouse that was previously occupied by the caretaker of the Palos Golf Course. Dave and Sandy said that although the course had been abandoned, the clubhouse and farmhouse were not demolished until the early 1960s.

Research had placed the course in operation during Prohibition and documented Al Capone's passion for golf. Lemont anecdotal data claimed Al Capone had played the course and Ralph Capone operated a bottling company in Lemont during Prohibition. That information appeared credible to me, but other claims less so.

I knew from previous research Lake Michigan was once a much larger body of water held by a glacial moraine, its western shore lying about thirty miles farther west than it does today. Near the southwestern tip was an island that geologists called Mount Forest Island. When the waters broke through the moraine, the triangular elevation that was left is mostly forest preserve today and includes the former sites of the Palos Golf Course and the Manhattan Project, as well as the still-present St. James at Sag Bridge.

For a number of years I had been wanting to write a story about a courageous woman of Italian descent, outwardly a life-of-the-party sort, but underneath someone traumatized by an event that happened to her in eighth grade. The pieces clicked: the Chicago Mob, a woman struggling to provide a good life for herself and her family, and a setting that included a secret laboratory and abandoned clubhouse. The place also fit the paranormal component my readers enjoy. A plot began to form and so, *The Mystery at Mount Forest Island.*

The information that follows is based on extensive research. Some is documented fact. Some is filtered through the eyes of those that wrote the original material I read, and then filtered again by my belief in the material. The reader can make an independent conclusion.

– When the Lemont area was settled in the 1830s, what was initially forest and prairie was converted to farmland. In 1916 the Forest Preserve District of Cook County began buying up farmland to return the area to forest for permanent preservation and recreation. Due to the popularity of golf at the time, a course was built in Palos Woods, an area convenient to major roads and railroad transportation.

– Much of the forest preserves in Chicagoland is not ancient but man-made, including lakes and waterfalls. The Civilian Conservation Corps (ccc), with a camp at Lemont, was largely responsible for this work during the Great Depression of the 1930s.

– The history of the Palos Golf Course, the farmhouse property, and Argonne National Laboratory is accurately portrayed in the book. Descriptions came from interviews, research, and photographs.

- The Facebook page Exploring Mount Forest is a real page.
- Argonne National Laboratory operated the first nuclear reactors, CP-2 and CP-3, in Red Gate Woods for ten years. The reactors were shut down on May 15, 1954, and buried on site. The cleanup involved transferring high-level nuclear waste to Oak Ridge, Tennessee, for disposal. The remainder was buried forty feet deep, encased in concrete, in Red Gate Woods Forest Preserve, where a monument marks the burial site.
- The information that Al Capone's brother Ralph operated a bottling company in Lemont during Prohibition is anecdotal but believed to be true. It has been documented by a number of sources that he also ran the bottled water and soda market at the 1933 World Fair.
- In Lemont's early canal days tunnels were dug connecting buildings to underground rooms to store coal and merchandise from canal boats. It is likely these rooms were used during Prohibition.
- The Brown family of Lemont had a stone barn on their property, built in the 1830s, with gun slits for windows, in anticipation of attacks during the Blackhawk War (although the wars never came as far east as Lemont). According to family lore, mobsters used the barn during prohibition. The premise that Ralph Capone used this barn is not documented but is plausible.
- Jimmy Emery was a real person, but his appearance in the story is pure fiction. Emery was the de facto boss of the Chicago Outfit in the southern suburbs from approximately 1928 to his death in 1957. He was also a significant figure in thoroughbred horse racing, until he was banned from the sport due to illegal track activities. His horse Dolly Val had a habit of finishing last when favored and winning when she was a long shot. Emery kept a string of horses in Miami, and operated a horse-breeding farm reportedly in Tinley Park, some ten miles from the story's setting. He drove a 1930 V-12 Cadillac. He never lived on the Palos farm featured in the story, nor are there reports of him appearing as a ghost.
- The group photo Billy discovered that shows Emery and Al Capone in a group of men taken on the lawn at Emery's home in Chicago Heights is a real photo.
- The golf course, clubhouse, and farm buildings were real and were not demolished until the early 1960s.

– The guns used in the infamous St. Valentine's Day Massacre have never been found. It has long been rumored they are buried somewhere in the area's forest preserves, but it is no more likely they would be buried in Palos Woods than any other place. It is not known but is reasonably speculated that Jimmy Emery was involved in the planning of the killings, however. It is known that Al Capone was the godfather of Emery's daughter and that Emery's home in Chicago Heights, far south of Chicago, was used for meetings and likely as a hideout.

– Jimmy "The Bomber" Catuara was a hit man for the Mob from a young age. He earned his nickname by blowing up taxicabs in the '20s and '30s, and was jailed in the late '30s and early '40s for bombing activities. After his release, he became Emery's chief enforcer. In the 1960s he ran chop shops, a major mob activity that led to the Chop Shop Wars and many gangland deaths. He was short, thick, and bald-headed and had a violent streak. In the mid-1960s he lived in Oak Lawn, masquerading as a furniture salesman, and controlled mob operations on the South Side and in the southwest suburbs. Because he shorted mob bosses of their full share of profits and promoted violence and infighting, thereby drawing much unwanted attention, the Mob eventually replaced him. However, he refused to leave, and when it was rumored that he had turned informant he was found shot gangland style on July 28, 1978. There is no reference to Catuara having an interest in owning a race horse.

– St. James at Sag Bridge is a real place, and the claim that Marquette and Joliet stopped there is not documented but is commonly believed. The only priest assigned to the archdiocese in northern Illinois established the site as early as 1833, traveling there every three to four months to celebrate Mass in a log cabin. Completed in 1865, the church is the oldest continuously operating Catholic church in northern Illinois. Today it is still active and still charmingly surrounded by its cemetery and forest preserves. The area along Archer Avenue where the church is located has long been associated with reported ghostly sightings, perhaps the most famous being "Resurrection Mary."

– The bodies of a number of murdered children were found in the forest preserves around the time Jemma would have lived at the farm in Palos Woods. Kenneth Hansen, a horseman and stable hand, was convicted many years later of the murders of young Robert Peterson and the two Schuessler brothers. A possible link to the murders of the teen Grimes sisters was never proven. Uncle Ted, however, is a fictitious character and any resemblance to Hansen is coincidental.

– Sagawau Canyon, "the Gully," where Jemma and Petey hid the film cartridge, is a real place, and the only canyon in Cook County, Illinois. It is located not on Mount Forest Island, but at the foot of the adjacent Sag Valley. The limestone walls and quarries in the area, like Bachelor's Grove Cemetery in Rubio Woods, are rumored to increase paranormal activity, ghostly sightings, and other supernatural events that continue today.

– The tornado that struck Oak Lawn in 1967 was a real tragedy. The storm killed thirty-three people, including several children at the Oak Lawn Skating Rink, and injured about one thousand. The destroyed buildings included a high school, a grocery store and other businesses, and 152 homes. Losses came to $50 million, with an additional nine hundred homes damaged.

– Beep baseball is a real sport for the blind. Information can be found online.

– Cabrini-Green was an inner-city, high-rise housing development in Chicago and the site of much crime. Two policemen were shot there by snipers in the 1970s. The author has used some of the facts and changed names and circumstances to fit the story. There was no known connection of these killings to organized crime.

– Jemma's discovery of the two-headed snake and unknown variety of jellyfish was based on the actual experiences of David and Sandy Harris, who while living at the farm in Palos Woods in the 1950s discovered both curiosities. Freshwater jellyfish exist. Jellyfish toxins and enzymes are being found useful in industry and medicine.

– Jemma, her family, and Cora's friends are fictional. Mickey and Petey Romano, the two priests in the story, and all the present-day characters are fictional. Any resemblance to real persons or events is purely coincidental.

The author is responsible for any inadvertent errors that may have occurred in portraying historical people, events, or places.

# Acknowledgements

When I began writing I believed that if one person told me my story had touched their life, it would have made the work worthwhile. Instead of one, there have been many. I thank the readers who inspired me with their kind words about *The Mystery at Sag Bridge* and *The Mystery at Black Partridge Woods*.

With almost three years spent in writing about friendship, I truly value the astonishing number of people who honored me with their friendship and contributed their time, expertise, and support during the writing of *The Mystery at Mount Forest Island*.

I must begin my thanks with David and Sandra Harris, who actually lived at the farm in the Palos Woods and shared their stories that inspired my book's setting and made it come to life. Dave and his wife, MaryLou, entertained me in their home, where they and Sandy answered a never-ending list of questions and read early drafts.

For the memories I drew on to create Cora's younger years, I will never forget Betty, Dorothy, and Joann, who lived them with me.

For developing a real feel for present-day Mount Forest Island, I am indebted to Kevin Coyote, who writes the Exploring Mount Forest Facebook page, and who introduced me to today's Palos Woods, leading me to off-trail remnants of the former golf course, clubhouse, and farm. Our exploration gave the site both past and present perspective.

Many good-hearted people work for the Forest Preserve District of Cook County (FPDCC) and have been supportive of my work in more ways than I can mention. John McCabe, Director of Resource Management for the FPDCC, not only answered my questions about forest fires, staffing, and resource management, but was kind enough to read and comment on parts of the manuscript. Michael Konrath, Leslie DeCourcey, and Laura Brown gave generously of their time, answering question after question while I poked into every nook and cranny of a period farmhouse and Sagawau Canyon ("The Gully") at Sagawau Environmental Learning Center. General Superintendent Arnold Randall, Jim Carpenter, Joe Swano, Jim Chelsvig, and Stephen DeFalco welcomed me and encouraged my participation in FPDCC events and activities.

Shari Stahl and Christine Malec helped me understand what it was like to live as a blind woman, fielding many questions and correcting my errors.

I am grateful to the many authors of books, articles, and web sites about organized crime in the Chicago area that gave me a good feeling for what was happening south of Chicago in a variety of time periods. I am especially grateful to John Binder, noted organized crime authority and author of *Al Capone's Beer Wars*, for taking time to answer my questions. I hope that he will excuse any factual errors or alterations to enrich the story.

I'm grateful for the friendship and encouragement of Ursula Bielski of Chicago Hauntings, author of *Haunted Bachelors Grove* and many other books on Chicago ghost lore. Ursula is my go-to person for all things paranormal.

Commander Thad Mezyk of the Lemont Police Department helped me define the character Jeff Rogers, and kept me from going too far wrong in police matters.

As any writer will tell you, the opinions of those who read our early work are invaluable in helping us revise our manuscripts to completion. Thanks to my early readers, Clare Dempsey, Carolyn Jamieson, Dorothy Bogan, Gail Ahrens, Karen Kirk, Dave Harris, MaryLou Harris, Sandy Harris, Shari Stahl, Dorothy Stahl, Ed Sarna, Pam Holtman, Michael Cebula, and Jeremy Brown.

Comments and suggestions from my writers' groups, Room Seven Writers, Downers Grove Writers Workshop, and the Lemont Writers Group, have helped make my work richer. I must make special mention of Fred Meek, Luisa Buehler, Lee Williams, and Rod Brandon.

I am grateful for the friendship and support of the wonderful Augie and Traci Aleksy of Centuries and Sleuths Bookstore and Sue Roy of Smokey Row Antiques, as well as my friends and associates at the Lemont Area Historical Society and the Lemont Public Library District.

An outstanding medical team helped me fight the cancer that interrupted for a time the writing of this book, making its completion possible: Jennifer Earvolino, M.D.; Thomas Nielsen, M.D.; Neilayan Sen, M.D.; Mary Jo Fidler, M.D.; Robbie Stines, R.N.; and others too numerous to mention.

I am thankful for the fortunate circumstances that led to my continued happy association with Amika Press and their excellent team: publisher and editor Jay Amberg, designer Sarah Koz, copyeditor Ann Wambach, and editor John Manos. Once again, their encouragement, judgement, and advice have been spot on, helping me to produce novels I am proud of.

Most important of all, I am forever grateful for the support of my husband, Chris, my sons, daughters-in-law, grandsons and granddaughter. Writing takes much of my time from you, and your understanding makes it all possible. You are my life.

# Book Discussion Questions

1 The opening chapter with Al Capone presents him as a generous family man, burned out by his "business." Do you think this side of him existed?

2 Why did Emery remain on earth as a ghost? Did he appear to people other than Billy, like Jemma? What was important to the ghost? How was he able to know things that happened after Emery's death? Do you think he was satisfied with the outcome? Will he remain a ghost?

3 There were two forest fires in the story. Who started the first one? Did Billy start the second one? Do you think Emery was responsible for both of them? Or were they started by natural causes?

4 Do you have any personal knowledge of the Chicago Outfit? How might you feel if you found out your family, or someone you loved, was involved in organized crime?

5 Why was it so important to Valerie to find her mother? Do you believe, as Father McGrath did, that her misconceptions were standing in the way of her rehabilitation and her future?

6 Would it have changed their relationship if Cora had been honest with Valerie about everything she knew from the beginning?

7 Discuss Valerie's strengths and weaknesses. How did the search for her mother and uncle change her?

8  Why did the young Jemma fall for Petey?

9  Did you see the friendship between Jemma, Cora, Linda and Kathleen as typical or unusual? What did they see in each other? Why did they drift apart?

10  Compare the young Cora to the mature woman. Did her friendship with Jemma and Linda shape the woman she became in any way?

11  Did Jemma make the right decision about leaving her family? Why was she unable to return years later? Discuss your thoughts about her relationship with Kathleen.

12  Why was Paula so angry with her mother? Was it only because she disapproved of her life choices? Why was she unable to accept her mother for what she was?

13  What do you think will happen to Billy in the future? By the end of the story, does he still think of himself as a loser, or has he gained confidence?

14  Why does Frannie decide to get involved? Why does she feel as badly as she does for Valerie?

15  Does Cisco get involved only to protect and humor Cora? Is he kidding himself when he pretends to want nothing to do with helping her? Why is he important to the story?

16  Petey might seem more bumbling than terrifying as a villain, yet the characters see him as dangerous. Were they overestimating or underestimating his potential threat? Do you think Valerie will want to know him in the future? Would that be a good idea or a bad idea?

17  How many generations in Jemma's family were affected by the relationships between mother and daughter? Do you think Valerie is a good mother to Molly?

18  Do you think Angelo was more involved with the mob than Valerie wanted to think? Was he the person she thought he was?

19 How did you view the relationship between Billy and Valerie? Why would they be attracted to each other? What do you think their relationship might be in the future?

20 Did Cora resent or relish her involvement in the lives of others? Do you think her revelation at the end of the book about letting others take the lead will have any effect on her future behavior?

21 In the dedication, the author states that this story explores the value of friendship. Discuss.

# About the Author

Pat Camalliere is the author of the popular, five-star-rated *Cora Tozzi Historical Mystery Series*. She lives with her husband in Lemont, Illinois, a suburb of Chicago. She serves on the boards of the Lemont Historical Society and Lemont Public Library District and is a member of the Chicago Writers Association, Sisters in Crime, and Society of Midland Authors. She speaks locally on a variety of topics and writes a blog that features unique history stories. Visit her at patcamallierebooks.com.

~~~

If you enjoyed *The Mystery at Mount Forest Island*, please help other readers discover it. Tell your friends about the novel in person, over e-mail, or on social media. A brief review on Amazon and/or Goodreads would be very appreciated by the author.

Made in the USA
Monee, IL
05 March 2024